THE SCIENCE OFFICER OMNIBUS

VOLUME 1

BLAZE WARD

KRP

The Science Officer
Omnibus 1
Volumes 1-4

Blaze Ward
Copyright © 2017 Blaze Ward
All rights reserved
Published by Knotted Road Press
www.KnottedRoadPress.com

ISBN: 978-1-943663-49-1

Cover art:
Copyright © Philcold | Dreamstime.com - Exploring Far Planets Photo

Cover and interior design copyright © 2017 Knotted Road Press

Never miss a release!
If you'd like to be notified of new releases, sign up for my newsletter.

I only send out newsletters once a quarter, will never spam you, or use your email for nefarious purposes. You can also unsubscribe at any time.

http://www.blazeward.com/newsletter/

CONTENTS

THE GILDED CAGE

THE PLEASURE DOME

ALSO BY BLAZE WARD

THE SCIENCE OFFICER

PART ONE
BOOK ONE: PIRATES

PART ONE

JAVIER QUICKLY SCANNED the boards on his bridge console, on the off-chance that an asteroid was on an intercept course. The jump drives would require another hour to recharge after this latest hop, and the engines were off-line for now as the computer worked out a preliminary scan of the new system they were here to survey.

Space was really, really big. The odds of any two objects intersecting accidentally were extremely low. Like, lots of zeros behind the decimal low. But always followed by a one. Javier never forgot that. Eventually, your number would come up. Hopefully it would be old age that got you, though, instead of a jealous boyfriend.

The immediate area, out to around half a light-second, was clear. In the distance, a dim reddish-orange sun fought fitfully to warm the neighborhood. Just another boring star system on the far side of beyond. Another day, another *drachma*.

"Suvi. Mission log," Javier said, keying the computer system live with his voice. It wasn't really a she, and she wasn't really intelligent, but the AI was a pretty good facsimile of a person. And he had tweaked her programming over the years to get her just right.

The fleet hadn't bothered with a name for the little vessel. They never did with probe-cutters. Scouts like this one usually just had hull numbers. After Javier had bought her from the wrecker yard, he had named the vessel *Mielikki*, after the Finnish Goddess of the Forest. He had reprogrammed the AI to appear as a petite Anglo woman, an elfin blue-eyed blond, and named her Suvi. *Summer*. It was a nice contrast to his own dark hair and dark skin. Reminded him that the galaxy was a big place filled with all sorts of strange humans.

"Go ahead, Javier," Suvi replied crisply. She appeared on a side screen as if she was sitting in an office on an old warship, dressed in a uniform vaguely modeled on a fleet yeoman from a century ago, just before the Great Wars broke out. Javier was positive the AI hadn't originally been programmed with a sense of irony and humor, but, looking at her attire, she had developed one over time.

"Mission day 237, newly arrived and scanning. Tag this as part of Campeche Sector, system number seven," he said, bringing up a holographic star map of the neighborhood. "Sometime in the next two or four systems, we'll transition to Quintana Roo Sector, before we hit the edge of the local arm and enter a gulf. Please remind me."

"Will do, Javier," she replied, appearing to type something on a keyboard in front of her.

"Very good, Suvi. You have the deck. I'll be in back getting some food and checking the botany station." Javier unbuckled, rose from his chair, and made his way aft. He stretched his arms overhead and tugged his tunic back down into place after he scratched an itch by his kidney.

Behind him, the beaming elf took charge. "Roger that, Captain."

JAVIER PLUCKED a second berry from the bush as he carefully spit out the first seed into his hand. The berry was almost the size of a grape, but shockingly pink and very sweet. Javier smiled at what he'd been able to accomplish with a full research lab and several years of solitary patience. He might have invented another new species of fruit. One of these days, he needed to go visit some parish fair back home, just so he could win all the ribbons for fruits and vegetables. Maybe.

Around him, *Mielikki's* original cargo hold had been split into two pieces. The interesting half was now dedicated to botanical research, with a small arboretum, fruit and vegetable patches, a hydroponics rig with several species of fish, and a seed library better than many agricultural universities maintained.

Fleet Operations had laughed when he demanded real Ukrainian dirt from the homeworld, rich and black, but had shipped him out nearly fifty cubic meters of the stuff as part of his contract. On his side trips back to "known" space, admirals and legates were always quite happy to have fresh picked grapes, or blood oranges, or blue asparagus to serve with dinner.

For now, Javier pulled one of the small bags from his pocket, kept for just this purpose, and added the seed from his hand. He placed the sealed bag in a netting shelf nearby and pulled out a clear box for the berry. That went into a small refrigerator, until it could be scanned, cataloged, and planted in a fresh pot, to see which way grew better, naked seed or buried fruit. Ah, science.

A sound attracted Javier's attention. He glanced over as Athos, one of his chickens, emerged from the vegetable patch and cocked her head at him. She stared at him for a moment longer, decided there wasn't going to be any food, and went back to scratching in the dirt for anything interesting to eat.

Javier smiled and took a really deep breath. He sighed. Most of the planets he had visited didn't have air this clean and fresh, to say nothing of warships that kept amenities to a minimum, or sector stations that didn't even bother with that. Fresh water, clean air, and no people. This was paradise.

"Captain to the bridge," came the sudden interruption. Suvi's voice was poised and calm. "Emergency. All hands to battle stations."

FOURTEEN YEARS as a *Concord* Fleet officer had left its mark. Javier covered the distance to the command room almost before the echoes of her voice had faded.

Even before his butt hit the chair, he was assessing screens. "Suvi. Status report," he called as he brought his boards live and considered his options.

The probe-cutter boats had been armed when commissioned, but *Mielikki* had had most of that stripped when she was turned into a long-range scout. Sure, there was still a little twin-pulsar in a dorsal turret, but that was mainly useful against unexpected asteroids in tight quarters. Javier reached for the armaments console, and then stopped when he saw the image on the secondary screen.

"Crap," he said quietly. "Where did she come from?"

The hull displayed was a flat charcoal gray shark so dark as to almost be almost black. Even at a range Javier could call knife-fighting, the vessel was hard to see. The scanners, however, showed her just fine. Now.

"Working," came the response, even though the AI was much faster than that. "She appears to have been cloaked and nearby when we arrived. The vessel appears to be a…"

"She's an Osiris-class heavy corvette," he cut her off mid-word.

Javier knew the class. He still remembered many midshipman cruises at the *Concord* Academy on Bryce aboard the old *Bannockburn*, one of this one's sisters. He was out-gunned by orders of magnitude, and couldn't possibly run away from the fast vessel. And the jump engines wouldn't be online for another twenty minutes. He was right proper screwed.

"Suvi," he said, face twisted up in a sideways scowl, "have they hailed us?"

Her image showed fierce concentration. "Negative. No wait, stand by." She paused, a look of incredulous shock growing on her face. "Oh, my…"

The image on the screen was ancient, dating back to the distant past, when humans were confined to a single homeworld and ships floated on water instead of sky. A human skull, white on a black background, with crossed thigh bones behind.

Javier had just enough time to realize that the flag was black instead of red, and then the vessel opened fire.

DARKNESS.

Utter silence.

Something bumped him on the head.

Javier blinked.

The emergency backup lighting came on.

Javier was floating. The bump was the ceiling.

Crap. Grav plates were off.

Mielikki was dead in the water.

Of course. They were pirates. They had ionic pulsars. One overwhelming surge of static later, and every system on *Mielikki* was overloaded. It would take three hours to reset all the breaker boards and bring everything back on line at this point. He probably had three minutes. *Needs must, when the devil drives.*

Javier pushed off from the ceiling, moving through the air like a porpoise.

Emergency lifesuit first. Unarmored. Barely reinforced. Keep him alive if they blew the airlocks out.

Forty-seven seconds. Some skills never faded.

Computer next. He held the console with one hand and climbed underneath to access a panel. It wasn't the computer core. That was down in the bowels near the power systems. He just wanted his logs, and Suvi's personality files, intact.

Javier swapped the fifth chip from the left for a spare his fleet-trained paranoia kept taped close by. With Suvi tucked into his pocket, he smashed the blank replacement with a small hammer, as well as all the rest of the chips and boards. Standard procedure when about to be captured, although he was supposed to destroy the chip with data, not try to smuggle it past the enemy. Tough. He liked Suvi. Now, to hide her.

Javier checked the clock in his head. Two minutes gone.

He dove headlong down the main corridor to the veterinary station, which was a very fancy term for a chicken coop and examination table. He cracked a feed bucket open just enough to slide Suvi in and then latched it back down.

There was amazingly little debris floating around. Fourteen years active duty, four years Academy, and several years of private space flight will do that to you.

The chickens didn't mind zero gravity. Well, they minded, but they were chickens. Everything offended them. They didn't appear to be much bothered. Another couple of hours and they'd probably prefer to live in a place where their wings worked.

He might have to try that as an experiment someday. *The Effects of Minimal Gravity from Birth on Terran Chicken Breeds*. Javier snorted at the thought of a research journal article. Pirates first. Tenure later.

The whole ship rang like a bell.

Time's up.

Javier considered the personal sidearm he kept in his cabin. That would just get him killed quickly. Talking seemed to offer the only chance of getting out of this alive. Not much, but better than sure death.

He moved to the main corridor and set his radio to scanning for frequencies in use.

It didn't take long. They were on a default fleet channel.

"Greetings," he said. "Can we talk?"

Javier waited patiently. Everyone had gone silent as soon as he spoke. He let them talk on another channel for a few moments before he went looking for it.

"Hello," he said, interrupting a man and a woman talking.

"Who is this?" challenged the male voice. Gruff, hard, professional. It reminded him of one of his instructors from his Academy days.

"The guy on the ship," Javier replied, careful to keep his tone light and friendly. Never antagonize people with guns pointed at you. "Since you didn't blast me, you don't want me dead. I figured I'd try to make this a little easier, so you don't have to shoot me when you open the hatch."

A drop of flop sweat rolled down his nose, right at the point he couldn't get to it inside his helmet. Javier scrolled the lifesuit controls down as cold as it would go. Every little bit would help at this point. No fear in front of killers.

There was an awkward pause.

"How many people are on the ship?" The man's voice was calmer now. "And what cargo are you carrying?"

Javier shrugged to himself. They were going to find out in about five minutes anyway. "Me," he said. "Oh, and four chickens. As for goods, I'm hauling a lot of trees and plants."

"Trees?" the woman's sudden voice was incredulous. Harsh, cold, and vicious, but also incredulous. "What do you mean, trees?"

Javier smiled, swallowed it before responding. "Apple trees," he said, matter of fact. It was a speech he gave at almost every station and sector headquarters. "Pears, oranges, figs, bananas, cherries, hazelnuts, cashews, almonds. Bunch more. Plus fruit bushes, vegetables, hydroponics. And four chickens."

More silence.

She was not mollified. "That's bullshit," she said. "This is a patrol cutter."

Javier took a breath before he responded. "This is a probe-cutter, retired from active duty twenty years ago, and converted to a long-range survey scout."

The man's voice was back. "Who are you?"

Javier shrugged in his suit. "Just a guy on a survey contract for *Concord* Fleet. A private contractor trying to make a buck."

"And all the botany?"

Javier perked up a bit. These people didn't sound like pirates. At least not the ones in the shows or movies. Way too articulate for what he was expecting. "Hobby," he said. "Something to do when I spend two to three years at a time in the middle of nowhere."

Javier could hear the banging on the hatch in front of him. The airlock was about to be opened. With the ship powerless, they had already overridden the airlock bearings and cut the interlocks. And done it faster than most shipyard crews could manage. Damn. They were good.

The woman's voice was back now. She sounded angry. Like a cat denied a mouse. "I've got you on my scanner," she said. "Where are your weapons?"

Javier shrugged. Things were about to get tricky. "I have a pistol in my cabin," he said. "Didn't figure it would do me much good here."

"You got that right, mister," she snarled. "You stand perfectly still when the lock opens. If you're lying about anything, you're a dead man."

Javier braced his foot under a rail put there by the ship's architect for exactly this situation. For good measure, he held his hands straight out sideways, open and as unthreatening as he could. "Got it."

The airlock door crawled open about eight centimeters, about as far as someone without gravity could torque it manually in one twist. Someone fantastically strong. Someone really angry.

A barrel poked through, like a hunting snake. No head appeared in the gap, so Javier assumed a camera on the gunsight.

He remained still. He even smiled. "Hi there."

"Don't move."

"Not planning to."

The hatch creeped farther open.

Somebody on the other side stuck a sensor pod across the threshold. It pinged loudly in the silence.

Nothing.

Javier wasn't used to meeting other people as patient as he was. He had expected them to come barging in shooting by now. Maybe this was a good sign.

The sensor pod chirped.

Javier slowly let out a breath he hadn't been aware he was holding. There was air, so they weren't going to blow the locks and vent his ship into space. Maybe another good sign.

A head appeared in the gap, over the barrel.

"Just you, huh?" It was her.

Javier nodded. "And four chickens."

The edge of anger in her voice was subsiding to exasperation. "What is it," she said, "about the damned chickens?"

Javier held his voice as steady as possible, even when it really wanted to go up an octave. "Some people eat chickens," he said, "and they are quite tasty. But they also make eggs if you treat them right. That means a meal every day for years, instead of one meal and done. I'd rather you not shoot my chickens. Kinda impossible to replace out here."

She swam forward across the threshold, like a Nereid moving in water. The barrel seemed centered on Javier's chest with magnets.

He could see her eyes through the filtered faceshield, barely. He felt like a rabbit confronting a bobcat. He smiled. "Hi."

And then she shot him.

PART TWO

Darkness.

Sensation.

Pain.

Wakefulness.

Javier opened his eyes slowly. Even the dim light hurt.

He settled for a squint.

"Gah. What is that putrid stench?" Javier's eyes came fully open, in spite of the brightness. His stomach would have climbed out of his mouth if there was anything in it. Small victories.

He tried to move. And found his hands were bound behind his back.

"Blood and martyrs," he continued, "don't you people know how to program a bio-scrubber?"

A hand cracked the side of his skull. Open palm, sharp but not damaging. "Mind your tongue."

Javier turned to look up at his tormentor. And kept looking up.

He was pretty sure it was a she, because she seemed to have breasts. Small ones, to be sure, hiding on top of muscles. Lots of muscles. And the bones in the face appeared female. Not particularly delicate. Definitely not feminine.

Brown hair worn short to fit inside a lifesuit, buzzed very short on the sides and spiked into a petite Mohawk. The only thing petite about her.

13

The only vaguely-female touch was the collection of rings, studs, and stones in both ears. Nothing through the nose, though.

And the voice was a studied alto. Sharp, crisp, forceful. Reminded him of a PT instructor from the Academy. The one who liked to sing on twenty mile hikes in full gear. He disliked her already.

Javier's eyes finally focused. Not that bad looking, though. If you liked them 2.1 meters tall and built like rugby players. And scowling.

Javier was having enough trouble not retching to be faux-polite. "Then stop trying to poison me and get me some clean air to breath, lady."

The hand came up again. Javier braced internally for the blow.

"Sykora, enough." The voice cut her off. She looked to her right, scowled, and subsided.

Javier processed the words. Slowly. Eventually. Heavy stun was like waking up still drunk the next morning, fifty kilometers from home, in someone else's clothes. Wearing clown shoes. Been there, done that.

He turned back to the voice and realized he was sitting in a small office, staring at a man behind a desk. An average-looking man. Shaved head where Javier kept his black hair comfortably long. Salt and pepper Vandyke, neatly trimmed where Javier was generally clean-shaven. Average build, average height. So close to Javier's 1.8 meters that they might see eye to eye. That would probably be important.

The man studied him, just as closely. "What do you know about programming bio-scrubbers?" He held a mug of something warm and probably caffeinated. Javier noticed a big, heavy gold ring on his hand holding the mug. The kind you got from the Academy on Bryce when you graduated. And became an officer in the *Concord* Fleet. Huh.

Javier bit back the first rude thought that sprang to mind. Rugby girl would just hit him again. Or worse. "Have you been on my ship yet?"

The man's dark eyes got a guarded look. "I have not," he said. The voice was a rich baritone. Javier could hear the command tones underneath it. This was a man who was used to being in charge, and could pull it off.

Javier leaned forward a bit, until *her* hand landed on his shoulder and *planted* him into the chair. Damn. She might outweigh him, too. "Go smell the air over there and get back to me," he said. "Mind you, stay away from the bee hives and try not to torment the chickens any more than you have to, but go smell how nice my ship is, compared to this poisonous swamp of a death trap you're sailing in, Mister." Javier added the whip-crack to his voice they had both learned on Bryce.

He was rewarded by the man's glance down at where his hands would be, if they weren't tied behind him. Looking for The Ring. It was a rite of passage in the wider universe. Academy graduates. Strangers in strange lands.

The man leaned back and smiled, just a touch. Obviously, the same thoughts had crossed his mind. "I didn't see your ring, Mister." Yup, the universal greeting. Long-lost brothers-in-arms.

Javier shrugged, on firmer ground, if no safer. "My second wife kept it when she divorced me," he said. "Class of '63."

The man nodded, an entire silent, exquisite conversation. "I see. Class of '49." He turned to the woman hovering nearby, her weight just a suggestion now on Javier's shoulder. "Your observations, Sykora?"

Javier noticed her nails. Perfectly manicured, if kept extremely short. Again, working all the time in a lifesuit. He checked her wrist and saw the telltale calluses from an armored suit, the reinforced kind you wore when wrangling heavy equipment in zero-g, or heading into combat. She didn't look like an asteroid miner. Too tall.

She locked eyes with him for a second, as if reading his mind. Not that it was much deeper than a mud puddle, according to both his ex-wives. He winked at her. Her scowl deepened.

"He is correct, Captain," she said. "The ship is extremely clean and well kept. Well-founded, according to the engineering team, although the maintenance logs were destroyed when he smashed the personality computer."

The man, the Captain, scowled at Javier when he looked back. "Along with all the calibration records for the sensors and jump-drives?"

Javier just goggled at the man. "Hey," he said, "You people are pirates. SOP, buddy. Deal with it."

Sykora back-handed him, more of a love-tap than a blow. She growled under her breath.

The Captain tapped his finger, hard, on the desktop, to bring her up short. She glared at Javier anyway. If looks could kill.

Javier decided to ignore her. "So, Captain," he said, "what can I help you with?" He resisted leaning back and kicking his feet out. That might just get him killed.

The Captain glowered at him. Javier could see why he was the Captain when he turned all that charisma on. Power. Presence. The eyes got serious, piercing. The eyebrows flexed like muscles and moved together just a little, like they were pointing at him. Javier felt the man's whole presence centered on him. The voice sounded like a tool, or a weapon. Perfectly crafted, razor sharp, elegant.

"You could fix your highly-automated and customized ship so we could use it. Otherwise, we'll have to part it out and decide if you should be sold into slavery or just killed out of hand. What's your preference?"

Let's see. Lose, lose, or lose. A whole handful of bad choices. Kinda like how both marriages ended up. "How about I fix your bio-scrubbers and then you drop me someplace civilized so I can hitch-hike home? A way to say *thank you?*" Nobody every appreciated his ability to find silver linings.

The Captain was not amused. "Throw him in the brig for a while. Maybe he'll reconsider."

Javier watched, amazed, as Sykora picked him up out the chair, bodily, with one hand and sat him on his feet. "Gladly," she sneered.

Outside in the hallway, the air was even worse. Javier felt like he could walk on it. "How do you people breathe this *squamph?*" He coughed a few times, but that just sucked the crud deeper into his lungs instead of clearing them out.

Sykora didn't help matters. She grabbed him by the wrists behind his back and levered them up until he was on his knees. Through the pain in his shoulders, he did notice that the position compressed things enough that he stopped coughing. Probably not her original plan. Silver linings.

She lifted him again bodily by the scruff of the neck, and shoved him ahead of her. "Move, punk."

He glanced back. "If my ship's dead, can you put me in a cabin over there so I can at least breathe?"

That was good for a cuff to the side of the head. Not enough to rattle anything loose, just enough to shut most people up. Most people.

"Seriously," Javier said, looking over a shoulder, "can I at least fix yours if I have to breathe this gunk? I promise that clean air will make you a nicer person."

His first wife used to give him that same look. Uncanny.

She grabbed him by the collar to halt him, pushed a button to open a hatch, and casually shoved him through, bouncing him off the far bulkhead.

After a few of the stars faded from sight, he looked over a shoulder. "Handcuffs off, please?"

She glared down at the top of his head. "Face the wall," she growled.

Javier stood perfectly still when she unlocked him, and clenched a little as he expected a rabbit punch or another shot to the head, but she stepped back and activated the security field without a word.

Javier leaned close enough to the force field that it started to spark at him. "Remember, Sykora," he called, "clean air and smiling faces." He looked around, found a bed to sit on, and stretched out to contemplate his day.

Kinda sucky, but it could have been much, much worse.

THE VOICE JARRED him out of his daydreams. Probably just was well. They weren't fit for polite company anyway.

"On your feet."

Javier smiled. His princess Sykora had come back to rescue him. Or shoot him. Never a dull moment in space.

He stood up and stayed well back from the security field as she disarmed it and stepped to the doorway. She had to duck to clear the lintel. Javier maybe came up to her chin.

"Hands together in front," she said as she held out a set of manacles. Which was better than a pistol. He put his hands out politely and watched her cuff them expertly.

She pulled the connecting chain until he was almost touching her chest, staring up into her face, which was probably a smarter response than sticking his nose between her boobs. Probably. "Come with me," she said, so quietly as to be almost a whisper.

Like I had a choice? Javier thought to himself. Even four years of Academy training in close-combat drill would make him look like a fool if he tried something. This woman was a killer. She pulled him into the hallway.

Sykora stood him up in front of a tall, skinny, Asian guy. Almost the same skin tone as his, but a different hue. He looked almost as confused as Javier. "Yu, this is…" She paused and stared hard at Javier. "What is your name, anyway?"

Javier stuck both manacled hands out at the man to shake. "Javier Aritza," he said with a smile. Silver linings. Yu shook absently.

"Aritza," she said, tense, "you are going to show Machinist's Mate Yu here how to fix the life-support system and tune the bio-scrubbers."

Javier looked up at her and blinked. "Or?"

She smiled cruelly. "Or I bounce you off the wall for a bit."

He smiled back, warm and sarcastic. "Didn't think I was your type, madam."

Light.

Pain.

Stars.

The wall was cold on his back. And his butt. And he was on the floor. And his face hurt where she had punched him. And his head had a goose egg growing where his skull had bounced off the bulkhead. And bells.

Wonderful. Another concussion. He hated getting concussions.

You felt like you were standing three feet behind yourself and a little to one side, watching everything like it was happening to someone else.

Remote. Hard to process things in real time. Another really bad drunk. Punch drunk. The worst kind.

Javier kinda fish-eyed her as she grabbed him by the front of his tunic and hefted him upright. She looked closely at his face. He might have even talked, although nothing really coherent was going on behind his eyes, either.

Hallway.

Corridor lights.

Pretty music, but that might have been in his head.

Med-bay.

They were the same on every ship in space. Maybe one factory built them all and just slapped on different name plates.

Small room. Three meters by five. Two beds. One big console between them with robotic spider/waldo examination arms that did stuff to whoever you dropped onto the bed.

Javier found himself on his side on the port-side bed. Hands were still manacled.

Cold, proby thingee stretched out.

Bright light in each eye.

Cold something on the back of his head to make the bad go away.

Sting in the shoulder when the spider/waldo thingee bit him.

That was rude.

Oh.

Warm.

Happy thoughts.

Binary chemicals achieved medical significance.

Conscious thought.

Javier sat up with the fading remains of a bad hangover. Or something. Four minutes had passed. She was still there, glowering. With the other guy. You-something?

Javier blinked.

Blinked again.

They were both still there.

"Ow. Was that necessary?"

She leaned in extra close. Even leered. Someone had been chewing wintermint gumdrops. "Necessary, Aritza? No. Fun? Absolutely. Feel free to keep mouthing off to me. Medbay's not far away, as long as I don't do anything the med-bot can't fix before you bleed to death."

Javier tried to concentrate on the freckle on the left side of her nose. Kissing her suddenly at this moment, as much fun as the look on her face would be, would probably get him killed. "I will try," he finally said, with some modicum of normalcy, "to keep that in mind. Where were we?"

He was almost back to competent when she pulled him off the bed and propelled him back into the hallway. Silver linings.

ENGINEERING on the old Osiris-class heavy corvettes was mainly on C deck, with a secondary-level catwalk down on B deck following the curve of the lower hull and allowing an awkward access to engineering spaces. The whole thing appeared to have been designed by circus contortionists who wanted to stay in practice while on duty.

Javier followed the skinny Asian guy through internal airlocks, with Sykora's hand heavy on his shoulder. She was holding him upright while he wobbled forward, as much as keeping him from running away.

Honestly, where did she think he was going to go?

The equipment on C-deck made his heart sink. The Osiris boats were a bad tradeoff to begin with, adding guns and armor to a design that would have been better off with bigger engines to run away from capital ships. Someone had decided to fix that here. But they did it by adding a couple of auxiliary power reactors, one of which seemed to be bolted down exactly where you wanted to be sitting to work on the environmental systems.

Javier considered teaching the engineering crew new swear words, but he decided they probably already knew most of them, if they had to keep this mess running.

Javier watched Yu flag down a petite woman wearing the uniform of the Balustrade Imperial Navy, deepest green with yellow piping. "Chief, we're back."

The short woman kept her red hair medium length. Javier looked closer and realized she must have come from a high-gravity world originally. She wasn't squat, but had a perfectly proportioned body that had been stretched sideways and hung over heavy bones. Not bad, she only came up to his nose, and even then she might have out-weighed him.

She never glanced up at them from her portable computer and appeared to process the situation by reading their shadows on the deck plates. "That's good, Yu," she said diffidently. She glanced up for the briefest moment, studied Sykora. "Will it be safe to have him in here, Dragoon Sykora?"

Javier heard her voice right in his ear. "I'll keep close watch on him, Chief." He felt her pinch his shoulder to drive the point home. As if he was likely to forget.

They moved down a ladder/stairwell to B-deck. Yup. Just as bad as it looked from above.

Javier took a deep breath and turned to the guy. "We're gonna need a triage camera, a number four toolkit, and as many towels as you can scrounge up."

The man looked at him with concern and confusion. "What's a triage camera?"

Javier counted to five in his head. He'd already had one concussion today. "How long," he asked, wincing already in his mind, "have you been a Machinist's Mate, Yu?"

The man lit up. "Oh, I haven't passed the exam yet, sir," he smiled. "I've been an apprentice for four months now."

Javier nodded sagely. This was the way he got another punch in the face. He turned to the giantess. "And you're sure you won't let me in there to do this?"

Her smile was way too pleased with herself. "Absolutely," she purred. "Shall I tell Captain Sokolov you refused to help?"

One. Two. Three. Four. Five. "Will you hold the portable computer with the schematics loaded while I yell across the room?" Javier knew what refusal would buy him at this point. "And if we're gonna do brain surgery by remote control, can I have a comfy chair?"

In response, Sykora pushed him to the deck and leaned him against the bulkhead. "This looks comfy." She did at least pull out a portable computer and flip on the three-dee projector.

Javier reached into the beam and flipped the schematic projection around to face him. He sighed.

"Okay, Yu," he started. "After you remove the six bolts holding the primary panel in place, we'll need to disable the through-put and drain the primary system. You'll be looking for a blue pipe and a manual cutoff valve..."

JAVIER WIPED the sweat from his forehead with both wrists still manacled together. At least he wasn't completely covered in muck and grime like Yu was. And how a black Norwegian rat ended up dead and wedged in the transverse coolant well might end up being one of those mysteries he wanted to ask God about when he died. But the machine was finally working.

He tried to stand, found that his feet, legs, and butt were asleep. He made it about halfway up the wall when he started to tumble over. Sykora nearly dislocated his shoulder when she jerked on the chain.

"Give it a rest, lady," he snarled, forgetting where he was in his tired state.

Sykora was quick to remind him. She grabbed him by the throat with her other hand and spiked him to the bulkhead hard enough to make his skull ring. Again. Yu sidestepped and just kind of stood there with a shocked look on his face as Sykora leaned close.

For a moment, just a moment, Javier considered biting her. It had already been enough of a day. Maybe things should go out with a bang.

"What did you say, punk?" she whispered. She was close enough to kiss, but Javier was dog-tired and cranky. She was close enough for a swift kick, too.

He took a deep breath. "I said I'm tired. I need a shower, a meal, and a nap. Your damned machine is fixed. Can we go now?" Dark and terrible thoughts swirled in the back of his mind right now, not the happy, relaxed place he normally inhabited. This was closer to the bad old days before the Academy. Javier thought he had put all that behind him.

Sykora watched him for a second longer, alpha dog making a point, before she stepped back and moved to one side. "Let's go, Yu."

Javier followed the man out of engineering and up a deck to D. They both staggered like drunks, holding onto the handrail lest they slide all the way back down the sharp staircase.

Sykora led Javier back to his cell and shoved him in. She disconnected the manacles, and flipped an energy bar, the kind that tasted like sawdust and raw sewage, onto the bed before activating the force field.

Javier was just happy that the field was in place. It would keep him from doing anything terminally stupid at this moment. Not that he didn't consider it. "How about a shower?" he asked, just loud enough to be heard.

She smiled, a content little giant princess in her castle. "There's a sink," she said. "The bed has a blanket." And she was gone.

Javier sat on the center of the bed. That wench was seriously messing with his *wa*. He folded up his legs and began to meditate.

PART THREE

JAVIER WASN'T ASLEEP.

He had bathed in the sink and then cat-napped and meditated for several hours. Homicidal tendencies had been pushed well to the back of his mind.

For now.

Not forgotten.

He wasn't that person, any more. They wouldn't make him go back there. Not today.

Escape was primary. Vengeance could come later. But first he had to survive.

A knock at the doorway brought him to the surface. "Javier?" It was Machinist's Mate Yu.

Javier cracked an eye, saw a shadow outside the force field. The cell was dim enough that he was almost invisible on the bed. He started flexing muscles to loosen everything up without visible motion. Sykora was not to be seen.

"Javier," Yu called again, louder. "Time to wake up. Captain wants to see you."

That got the eyes open. For the briefest moment, Javier considered overpowering the slim man and making a break for it, but there was nowhere to go. He was a week's sail to get to anyplace civilized from here, and no boat. Survival first. Still, it was Yu and not Sykora. Silver linings.

Javier climbed off the bed slowly. "Yeah, Ilan," he called, "I'm coming." He stretched everything as he approached the force field. He sighed, mostly due to lack of tea to kick-start his morning. That and freshly-pulled honey made things much nicer in deep space.

Yu shut off the force field with a smile. "Ready?"

Javier looked at him sidelong for a moment. "No manacles?" he asked.

Yu grinned and shook his head. "Captain said to ask real nice and you'd probably behave," he said simply.

Javier felt a chill at the bottom of his stomach. Pirates didn't act like this, not even the romantic ones in the movies. They were cut-throat professional businessmen.

They wanted something.

JAVIER FOLLOWED Yu to the Captain's office and watched him knock. The door slid sideways on silent pneumatics. Javier followed Yu into the room.

Captain Sokolov was at his desk, like before. He looked exactly like a ship's captain was supposed to, according to all the movies. He still had that charisma-thing captains were supposed to have. Javier had never gotten the hang of it. It probably helped to actually like people.

Sykora had apparently decided to get dressed up this morning. She was wearing a *Neu Berne* Field Combat Uniform. Considering her size and mass, it was probably custom tailored. Certainly freshly pressed. It came with a pistol and a short saber. Probably for effect. Probably.

Nobody else was in the room.

Captain Sokolov smiled warmly at Javier and gestured to the seat. "Please, Javier," he said amiably, "have a seat. Yu, don't go far. I'll want to talk to you after this."

Yu did something that approximated a salute in some cultures and skedaddled.

Javier took a long moment to size up Sykora. Not that he intended to do anything stupid. Here, anyway. Mostly just to remind himself not to be intimidated by the giantess with the quick fists. He sat and eyed Captain Sokolov closely. "Captain."

A long moment passed as the two men judged each other.

Sokolov took a drink from his steaming mug. "I woke up this

morning," he began, "and my head felt better." He sipped and watched Javier for a response.

Javier blinked once.

The Captain plowed on. "I wanted to say thank you."

Javier nodded. Still not willing to commit. Something about lack of a shower and hot meal and morning tea and still horribly smelly air caused his manners to be atrocious this morning.

Sokolov seemed to understand. "So now I have a conundrum."

Javier resisted speaking some more. Sykora in dress uniform might mean she wanted to make nice, and it might be appropriate for an execution. *Neu Berne* troopers tended to be sticklers for details. He glanced up at her, lingered, returned. She scowled professionally back.

"I spoke with Dragoon Sykora," Sokolov continued, "and she tells me you handled the bio-scrubber rebuild very professionally, including showing Yu how to fabricate a bypass for a burned out number six lead."

Curiosity got the better of him. "Why can't your Engineer keep those systems running?" Javier asked in the pause.

He was rewarded with Sokolov's awkward glance at Sykora and a deep breath to compose his thoughts. "Dalca is a mid-functioning introvert," he said, pausing to think.

Javier cocked his head. "So are lots of engineers," he replied. "That's why they become engineers in the first place."

Sokolov nodded. "Correct," he said, "and she's quite good. However..."

Javier waited.

"Apparently," Sokolov continued, "the bio-scrubber *bit* her."

"Bit her?" Javier repeated. Understanding dawned. "Ah. So now she won't touch it."

Javier had never gotten anyone to explain it to him better than that. Something bad had happened to them with a particular piece of machinery, it had *bit* them, and they would develop what was, to an extrovert like him, a total neurosis. Introverts made great engineers, most of the time. This was the drawback.

Sokolov nodded sagely. "Exactly. I can't exactly requisition new Machinist's Mates out here, and she can't train people."

Javier smiled evilly. "Good luck then, Captain."

"Which brings me," Sokolov said, "to you."

Javier felt a chill go up his spine. He felt Sykora's smile without looking over.

Javier blinked.

Sokolov at least had the decency to look pained at the words coming out of his mouth. "Normally," he began, "I would sell you off as inmate labor on one of the mining colonies we work with occasionally." A pause to sip at his coffee, reading Javier's face. "In your case, maybe one of the farming worlds where your expertise with plants and animals might be handy."

A long pause. Javier refused to rise to the bait. He wasn't about to let the Captain off his own hook.

"Depending on circumstances and timing," Sokolov finally continued in the silence, "you would be worth twenty-five hundred to three thousand credits to me from such a transaction. I would like to talk to you about honor."

Javier almost snorted out loud. Or sputtered. Hard to tell. Certainly, this was the moment in the movies where someone did a spit-take all over someone else. He drew a breath, careful about how close to the edge he probably was right now. "A pirate, talking honor?"

Sokolov got a very hard look on his face. Captain's Face. "I'm talking about two Academy men under awkward circumstances. And it's not about my honor. It's about yours."

Javier leaned back in his chair, suddenly aware how far forward he had been leaning. A slap might have been less surprising. Well, maybe not, considering Sykora's penchant for mild physical violence. "Mine. Mine?"

"Yours," Sokolov pronounced. "I would like to offer you a deal."

Javier would have liked to have not gotten out of bed this morning. Nothing that had happened had improved that notion. "A deal?"

Sokolov waited for more. None was forthcoming.

"My crew," the Captain began, "are paid reasonable wages. For a ship that wanders on both sides of legality, we do well. I would like to offer you a contract of indenture against your honor. Your ransom, if you will, as an officer and a gentleman. I will value you at twenty-five hundred credits. As a First-Rate-Spacer, you could pay off that debt in seven years as a member of this crew, and then would be free to go."

Javier resisted goggling. Barely. Definitely not what he had planned when he got up this morning. He remembered to breathe. And decided to push his luck. It was what he did best, anyway. Just ask his ex-wives. "What about your Centurions? What do they make?"

Sokolov blinked, slightly taken aback. "My Centurions," he nodded to Sykora as an example, "profit-share." Javier watched him juggle numbers in his head. "In your case, roughly four years, less if we had a big score."

Javier leaned well back into the chair and thought. Lose, lose, and lose. Be a corpse, be a slave, be a pirate. At least pirates dressed well. Maybe he could ask for a fancy sash. You never knew when you'd need a fancy sash. And, worse come to worst, he could sabotage the ship and blow the whole thing to hell if they pushed him far enough. Make the universe a better place.

Javier leaned forward, mentally flipped a coin. Rosencrantz and Guildenstern would be proud. "I have met your Dragoon and your Engineer," he began. "I presume you have a Gunner, a Boatswain, and a Purser. And the medbay is automated enough that you don't need a Surgeon. You could hire me as your *Science Officer.*" *Heads.*

He watched Sokolov do mental gymnastics. The man did sputter, but he wasn't used to dealing with Javier. He would learn. Or not.

Javier waited.

"Why in the world," the Captain finally said, "would a pirate vessel need a Science Officer?"

Javier smiled. "Why, indeed?"

———

CAPTAIN ZAKHAR SOKOLOV, Commanding Officer of the private-service Strike Corvette *Storm Gauntlet, Concord* Fleet career veteran, and pirate extraordinaire, looked down into his mug of coffee as if he could read the future on the dregs contained therein. Apparently, he had hired himself a Science Officer.

And it had been Aritza.

He wasn't sure if that was the smartest thing he had ever done, or the dumbest.

Certainly, a free-lance vessel like his needed every edge he could give it. Would this sarcastic fast-talker be a boon or a bramble? Only time would tell.

He took a deep breath as Sykora returned from escorting Aritza into the hall. The hatch whispered closed.

They held eyes for a few moments, before she shrugged and looked down.

"Yu," he said into the long quiet, "is not sneaky enough to keep a close watch on that man, so I'll settle for regular reports from the rest of the crew."

Djamila Sykora, Dragoon of the pirate vessel *Storm Gauntlet*, combat veteran of ground, sea, and space; giantess; and recreational knitter, came to parade rest just inside the closed door. "I can get close to him," she replied, perhaps a touch defensive.

Zakhar cocked his head. "Djamila," he began, "the first time you met, you shot him. The second time, according to the reports, you beat him up and gave him a concussion. Then you worked him for seven hours fixing the bio-scrubber before throwing him back into the brig." He grinned a little as he paused to take a sip. "If he were a horse, we'd call that riding him hard and putting him away wet. Plus, I've seen the gleam he gets in his eye when he looks at you."

He watched her square her massive shoulders up a little tighter. "I can take him," she said.

"Djamila," the Captain replied, "he's not going to warn you it's coming."

She thought about it and smiled brittlely. "So what do we do?"

Sokolov considered his options. "You and the crew treat him like any other Centurion. And keep a close tab. I didn't promise not to kill him."

He watched her salute, pivot, and exit with all the professionalism he had come to expect from her.

He had a good crew. Would it be enough?

PART TWO

BOOK TWO: SHIPWRECK

PART ONE

JAVIER STOOD in the pirate ship's cavernous cargo bay and considered the possibilities. Torpedoes were big, expensive, and hard to acquire in private practice. Sokolov had reduced the eighty launch silos on E and F decks to twelve tubes forward, six on each side. Only seven were actually loaded.

The remaining space had been opened up for cargo storage, spanned by the original trestles and frames, plus a small flight deck containing a battered transport tug that had started life in the *Daxing* Navy a century ago as an assault shuttle.

Sokolov had been true to his threats. *Mielikki* had been cut into sections and parted out. She had been too customized and automated to reprogram in less than a year and a half anyway, even if they did have someone on crew to do it. Javier certainly wasn't about to help. Whole frames of the little vessel had been cut away to get to the engines, sensors, and jump drives, so they could be unceremoniously pulled aboard *Storm Gauntlet* and stored.

Somehow, however, Javier had convinced the pirates to protect the cargo sections of *Mielikki* containing the arboretum and botany station. It had been wrapped up, insulated, cut out like a plum's stone from *Mielikki*'s carcass, and brought onto the flight deck. Sokolov had even turned off all the gravity plates in the rear half of the corvette so the crew could slide it forward into the foremost port cargo space and link it in to ship's power and the water system. In a couple of weeks, after some more tuning of the life support generators and the bio-scrubbers, he might even connect the hydroponics section externally and let his fish clean the ship's water.

Let them drink fish poop. It would still be an improvement.

Javier keyed the security lock and stepped into his sanctum. Provisional Machinist's Mate Ilan Yu, now his aide, bodyguard, and minder, was close behind.

Inside, Yu grabbed his elbow suddenly. "Are those real cherries?" he asked, wonder in his voice.

Javier smiled as he pulled the primary bin of chicken feed from the shelf. "They are," he replied.

"What are you going to do with them?"

The reality of the situation hit. Javier scowled and shrugged. "When it was just me," he said, "I'd have eaten half and made cherry wine with the rest." When he didn't have any master but boredom. And chickens.

"Really?" Yu asked. "Cherry wine? That's a thing?"

Javier sighed, quietly, mostly to himself. People, again. It was almost as bad as his Fleet days. "It's like this, Ilan. Fresh fruit lasts for days. Dried fruit lasts for weeks. Canned fruit lasts for months. But fermented fruit will last for years."

The tall, skinny, Asian guy lit up. "Really? That's cool. So can we make some?"

Javier shook his head. "Afraid not," he said. "These sixteen little gems are going to the Officer's Wardroom as a treat. Make that fifteen. This one looks bad." Javier picked a red and gold orb the size of a large marble from a branch and inspected its perfection.

He handed it to Yu. "You should eat this one and make sure it hasn't been ruined or something." He had a mock-serious smile on this face.

Yu took the cherry from him with reverence due a priceless religious artifact. "Wow. Thanks."

Javier had his first smile of the day. Or maybe the week. Hard to tell. "Bite slowly, Ilan," he said. "It has a pit in the middle, a little stone. It can damage your teeth, and your teeth can damage the seed. I want to keep it, plant it and grow more."

Yu ate his first ever Rainier cherry with a look of pure ecstasy.

While Yu was distracted, Javier cracked open the bin of chicken feed and rooted around until he found the chip containing Suvi. Good, she was still safe. Nowhere to go, now that her ship had been dismembered, but at least she had survived. He pushed her to the bottom of the bin and pulled out the measuring cup, filled with seeds and vitamins.

In the next space, they found four emotionally-damaged chickens rooting hungrily in the vegetable patch. The first toss of grain brought them all close, angrily scolding him, and each other, and the grass, and everything else.

They were chickens.

JAVIER WATCHED Yu sit down across the table from him and slide his lunch tray into the locks to keep it in place. He felt talked out, after three hours.

Yu was irrepressible. "So, Javier," he paused, an embarrassed look on his face. "Wait, I'm supposed to call you Mr. Aritza in public. You're a Centurion, now."

Javier sighed. This was why he was a civilian now. Stupid, petty rules. "Ilan, call me whatever you want. I'm pretty sure Sykora will slip up and call me shit-head at some point. I'll probably answer."

Yu shrugged. "Captain runs a tight ship," he said.

That kind of ended the conversation. Javier called it a tie and went back to his extruded protein sludge that the mess computer called pudding. His recipe was better, but he used real beets for sugar, instead of cracked industrial chemicals. In about twelve days, he'd have a batch of golden beets ready for harvest. Then he'd show them.

Across the way, he watched another crewmember add his name to the lottery drawing. Every day, the computer randomly selected a crewman from the list to have fresh eggs for breakfast. It messed up Javier's morning routine, but what he was eating was close enough to fleet food, and it would make the crew much more well-disposed towards the new officer.

"So, Ilan," Javier scraped the bottom of the bowl with his spoon. Not bad. Not as good as he could do, but about normal for a fleet vessel, which was pretty good for a pirate. "What's on your mind?"

Javier watched the ground between then start to open.

"Well, sir," Yu said, now a crewman addressing a Centurion instead of two guys having lunch, "what's a Science Officer actually do?" He sipped from a bulb of something. "I mean, besides raise chickens and vegetables and stuff."

Javier thought about it for a moment. Two weeks had already passed. He was already falling back into Fleet routines.

Yuck.

"Today," he said, "I'm going to calibrate the new sensor array they stripped off of my ship, off *Mielikki*. Engineering and Damage Control finally got everything wired two shifts ago." Javier drank some *tea*, wincing at the taste. "Eventually, they'll strip out your old ones and free up hull space."

Yu was entranced. "Are they that much better than ours?"

Javier considered the launch dates of *Storm Gauntlet* and *Mielikki*. "Yu," he smiled to take the sting out of the words. "*Mielikki* was a probe-cutter outfitted for survey work. My survey pod is probably six or eight times more powerful than yours. *Storm Gauntlet* is a warship. Shoot things and move on. I'm used to sitting on the edge of a system for two or three days, plotting the moons orbits for planets on the far side of a sun, before I jump closer." He took another drink. "Much better."

Yu nodded to himself and dug into his food. "Sounds good, sir," he said between bites. "Let me finish this and I'll escort you to the bridge."

Javier was careful not to let the scowl reach his face. Yu was doing his job. All that squank about honor and ransom didn't stop the Captain from assigning him a minder and escort, everywhere he went.

Could be worse, though. At least Sykora had kept her distance.

———

JAVIER KNEW BETTER than to ascribe it to luck. Even bad luck.

Just as he settled into his new workstation on the bridge, Sykora entered and moved to a space facing him from across the bridge. She was wearing a pistol this morning. Unusual. And had a nice clean field of fire at him if she wanted. Not unusual.

Javier decided not to say anything to Yu. She was probably a good enough shot that there wouldn't be any collateral damage if things got out of hand. Not that he was planning to do anything stupid today. Not here.

He watched the Machinist's Mate settle in to the workstation facing his, mirroring Javier's display so he could watch and learn.

Javier decided to find the silver lining and pulled out the headphones. He handed them to Yu as he pushed a few buttons to change Yu's display to a training mode, with his own screen in a corner.

Yu got a panicked look on his face. "What happened?" he whispered.

Javier grinned. "Put them on," he said, "and start working your way through the training simulations." He settled into his chair and toggled through options. "I'm going to be calibrating for the next three hours, and eventually you need to know how all this stuff works, if you're going to keep being my sidekick."

Yu relaxed, strapped himself in, and went to work with the sort of single-mindedness he had shown in the bio-scrubber. Not much imagination, but lots of enthusiasm. Javier had had worse yeoman working for him, back in the day. He looked over as the Captain emerged from his day cabin and relieved the Gunner from the watch.

Sokolov speared him across the bridge with all the seriousness one could put into being The Captain.

"Mr. Aritza," he said, Commanding Officer addressing a junior Centurion on a new deck. "Are we ready to proceed?"

Javier had to resist the urge to salute or something. Too much of Fleet was coming back to the surface. He didn't want to be that guy any more. A glance at Sykora. Or lunch for the black widow in the corner. "Affirmative, Captain," he said, crisply. "Give the word."

Sokolov nodded. "What are our specifications, Mister?"

Javier decided to play along. The Captain was making a show for the rest of the bridge crew, people who were strangers to Javier for the most part, unprepared for a sudden eruption of caustic sarcasm in their midst. "Well, sir," he replied. "How well does *Storm Gauntlet* compare to the old *Bannockburn*?"

Javier watched a small grin cross the Captain's mouth for a second. Only two Academy grads could have that conversation. It set a good tone, considering the rest were likely outcasts and dregs of various navies, put to shore by drink, temperament, or budget cuts. "Without a dedicated Science Officer," the captain announced, "she's probably comparable to the Academy Training Corvette. Perhaps five to ten percent better at shorter ranges. Less so at distance."

So, about what Javier expected for a boat like this. The sensor pods were cheap and durable, and probably older than about half the crew. "In that case, Captain, I would expect to improve on that by a factor of four or five after initial calibration, and six afterwards. If I had access to the kind of tuned automation that had been written for my old probe-cutter, as much as ten."

Javier could hear the gasps and snorts around them, depending on whether or not people believed him or thought he was boasting. He gave the whole bridge crew a carnivorous smile, lingering for a special moment on Sykora. She could have been carved from white marble.

He turned to the Navigator, a big Dutchman who seemed to know what he was about. "If you'd like to watch, we could bring up screen fourteen on the main display." The man nodded at him. "Fifty percent transparency, please. Thirty percent overlay."

The big screen in front of the captain split into two images, almost identical, with the old pod readings on the left and the pod from *Mielikki*, brought up to *Storm Gauntlet's* calibration, on the right.

Javier approved. The man was decisive and professional. Sokolov seemed able to surround himself with good people. Getting them all hung from the highest yardarm would probably make him feel bad. Afterwards. For a little while.

"Captain," he followed up, "permission to hard ping the system to baseline my systems?"

Sokolov played along nicely. "Approved."

Javier unlocked a control on his touch screen with a password, and pressed the revealed button. Like every other default sensor control system in space, it emitted a sound like an old wet-navy sonar system pinging. He smiled. Some engineer, centuries ago, had achieved a personal form of immortality.

He paused and watched his local screen, overlain with a mask as he supervised Yu's training. There shouldn't be anything hard enough to generate a return wave for several light minutes in any direction. This was the boring part he always left for Suvi.

After several minutes, he opened up the configuration console and began tinkering. The system had about eleven hours of passive data to work with. He started adjusting things to the sorts of baseline values he already knew from years with this hardware, as if everything was new. No point in letting them know what he could really do.

A little red diamond appeared on his screen as the computer started washing noise out of the signal. Sokolov was apparently paying closer attention that he let on. He leaned forward. "Mr. Aritza?" was all he said.

Javier was already dialing the signal in and decoding the information. "Stand by," he said.

That can't be right.

Can it?

Huh.

"Captain," Javier said into the pregnant silence. "that appears to be a very old emergency beacon on the fourth planet, which appears to be habitable." Leave it at that. He really needed more information to draw better conclusions. Better to be kind of ignorant at this point and show off later.

Sokolov tore his eyes from the screen to look over. "How old, Mister?"

Javier could read the avarice in his voice.

Avarice? Right, pirates. All about money.

"Sir," he said. Damn, this was just like the Fleet days. Maybe he needed to paint his monitor lavender or something. Just to keep him from getting all serious and stuff. "If the crash date being broadcast is correct, at least seventeen years." But. "However, the power source is extremely weak, and well past its expected lifespan." And the kicker. "You would normally have had to be almost in orbit in order to pick it up, if you weren't looking." Or hadn't just hired an expert on sensor systems to go beyond standard baselines.

Sokolov was doing calculations in his head. "That suggests survivors maintaining it, or at least good maintenance worksystem robots," he said. He turned to the Navigator. "Mr. Alferdinck, plot a jump to get us close. Ms. Sykora, prepare a landing team and wake Smith up to fly you in." He saved the best for last. "Mr. Aritza, you will accompany Sykora's team to investigate the wreck."

Javier goggled at him, completely off-guard. "What do I know about xeno-archaeology?"

Sokolov got that evil Captain's smile going. "The fact that you even know the word puts you ahead of most of the crew, Javier. That's why I hired a Science Officer."

Javier cursed inside as he unbuckled from his seat. That man was entirely too good at this.

On one hand, things wouldn't be boring.

On the other hand, surviving these people long enough to have them all arrested was going to be a task.

Crap.

PART TWO

Javier grabbed Yu and swung by the cargo deck for a quick teaching session.

"Okay, Ilan," he said, "since I'm going to be down on the planet for however long, you're in charge of feeding the chickens. First step, locate them. I'll wait here."

Yu goggled at him briefly, then put on his serious face and headed aft.

Javier let go a breath and grabbed the feed bin. He set it on the counter, cracked it open, and thrust a hand in.

There. Suvi.

He closed his fist and pulled his best friend out, sliding her into a pocket, safe. If they had found her, his life wouldn't be worth a bucket of warm spit.

Yu clomped back into the botany station. "Found them," he beamed. "Sleeping in the apple trees."

"Good," Javier replied. He pointed at the feed bucket. "That's chicken feed. Don't worry about refilling the bucket today. I have more in cold storage." He picked it up and handed it into Yu's uncomprehending clutches.

Ilan looked kinda lost, which was the point here.

"What next?" he said softly.

Javier smiled. "Now you open it up, fill the scoop halfway, close the bucket, and follow me into the forward bay where the fruit bushes are."

He paused as Yu di so, the image of serious scholarship. They headed forward.

Surrounded by fruit bushes and meta-dwarf and columnar fruit trees, Javier gave Yu a serious look. "Okay. Now cluck."

"I beg your pardon?" Yu's face went completely slack.

"Cluck," Javier said. "Like this." He made a sound with his teeth and tongue.

Yu repeated the sound, sort of. A few times.

"Good," Javier said. "Athos will usually find you first. d'Artagnan will almost always be last. Just stand here clucking until all four arrive, and scatter a little grain as you see each one."

Javier stepped back as the first hungry lady arrived in a fluster of wings.

Yu dumped a little of the grain out, and was suddenly ankle deep in chickens as two more surrounded him.

"Good, Ilan," Javier beamed. "Do this every morning around the start of day shift. And make sure you check their water dish in the vegetable garden. You'll probably need to fill it every three days or so."

"What about you?" Yu asked, a little panicked.

"I'm going to be planet-side, probably for a couple of days at least. Enjoy."

Javier stepped out of the room, down the hall, and out of the arboretum.

Suvi was safe, for now. Now he just had to avoid getting killed by crazy dragon-lady.

AFT, on the flight deck, Javier decided he really liked the assault shuttle pilot. Delridge Smith was a gray-haired lunatic who favored Hawaiian print shirts and talked a mile a minute.

The tiny flight deck of the assault shuttle, separated from the aft section by a seriously sturdy airlock, was decorated like a Merankorr brothel, all pinks and pastels, with Terran Caribbean music playing quietly in the background. Javier watched as the man completed a very detailed and thorough pre-flight check, literally touching everything as he went, talking to himself under his breath the whole time.

Javier felt safer just watching.

He felt Sykora arrive.

He still felt safe. Maybe.

She was wearing field gear: light on armor and long on camouflage patterns that slowly moved as he stared. It kinda looked like bread baking, the slow bubbling effect as dots and stripes evolved. He wasn't sure if it was going to make him motion sick if he stared long enough.

Sykora was armed to the teeth, with a knife, a pistol on her hip, another knife, a second pistol in a shoulder rig, and a big, nasty battlerifle slung on her back. He had known street gangs less well armed. Of course, most of them were also less dangerous than this woman.

She was also carrying a familiar-looking backpack. His. She walked up and handed it to him with a simple "Here."

Javier flipped it open and looked inside. Everything was generally in place. He smiled up at her. "Thanks for repacking it cleanly. I told you the only firearm I owned was the pistol in my cabin."

She shrugged. "It was still necessary to confirm." Her eyes conveyed a certain level of distaste, but that might be for someone who didn't own enough weapons to impress her.

He decided to ask, anyway. "Any chance I could get it back, since we're going down onto the surface of a potentially hostile planet?" He even tried to sound charming.

She smiled at him in the way grown-ups do with rambunctious eight-year-olds. "You'll have me," she said serenely. "I'll protect you from the bad men."

Javier was pretty sure Gandhi would have lacked the willpower not to roll his eyes at that one. He wasn't Gandhi, so he did. And then pulled out his sensor remote and toggled the settings to confirm everything was ready to go.

She leaned over his shoulder to look. "What is that?" she said, at least trying to sound nice.

He glanced sidelong, and up, at her, close enough to kiss, or bite. Decisions, decisions. "Short-range airborne autonomous remote," he said as he pulled it out of the pack. It looked like a knobby, gray, grapefruit.

Javier flipped the power on and gave it a soft toss into the air, like a beach ball. It hovered about a meter over his head, rotated a few times as it mapped the flight deck, and began a slow orbit of the space.

Javier pulled the matching portable computer from the bag and powered up the relay controls. The room was mapped in visual, ultrasound, radar, and infrared, with a stack of dials and gauges giving him various readings on people and equipment.

Sykora eyed it professionally. "Is that thing armed?" Of course. Trust the killer to go *there* immediately. Still, a two-meter-tall wall of professional paranoia between him and bad things planetside wasn't necessarily the worst idea he'd had today.

"Not this model," Javier pushed the recall and watched it settle lightly into his open palm. "I rarely set down on a planet without scanning it hard to begin with, so I know where the dangerous carnivores are, usually. This is mostly for working in tight quarters, like cave systems."

She was still an expert. "Or wrecked starships," she said, already adjusting her tactical planning. Scary. Good, but scary.

The pilot rescued him from any further comments as he wandered over. "Any time you're ready, Sykora," he said. "Gonna man the turret going down?"

She shook her head. "This isn't a hot LZ, Del," she replied, counting crew members to make sure everyone was there. "I'll ride with the rest in back."

"Suit yourself," he said. He turned and walked up the big rear landing deck and into the small airlock. As Javier watched, the man grinned at him, waved, and cycled the hatch closed.

Sykora completed her own count and looked around. "Mount up, people," she called, walking up the ramp.

Javier watched around a half dozen people file into the shuttle ahead of him. Two were obviously security goons, armed and armored up like their boss. Two females that looked like scouts. A couple of regular crew he recognized vaguely from Engineering.

Inside, he found Sykora in a jump seat at the top of the ramp. She patted the one next to her. "Aritza," she said, command voice invoked, "you sit here." One seat was as good as the next, so Javier settled and strapped himself in while she watched. She nodded when he was done, apparently satisfied that he wasn't a total landsman. Little did she know.

Sykora pulled on a field helmet and keyed a microphone live. "Gunship One, we are go for launch."

A red light came on, flashing, followed by a horn hooting, and then the ramp began to rise, closing with the solemnity of a bank vault. Interior lighting came up at the same time and the shuttle began to vibrate and hum as the pilot brought systems on line.

A nudge in his ribs, just as he closed his eyes, leaned back, and prepared to nap. "You're going to sleep through this?" Sykora looked shocked.

Javier shrugged, at least as much as he could in five-point harness. "Not my first time in an assault shuttle, lady," he said over the growing racket. "We're probably fifteen minutes to clear the ship from here, forty minutes orbital to match ground windows, and then an hour to get low enough to deploy the wings. Another hour to scout a landing spot and settle."

She scowled professionally at him. "We need to go over the plan for when we land."

Javier looked at her with a lazy smile. "I'm the scientist, you're the big, dumb, gun bunny. I scan the wreck. You shoot things. Not hard at all." He closed his eyes and leaned back.

She poked him harder this time. "That's what you think of me?" she asked. There was a new edge to her voice. "Just another killer?"

Javier couldn't resist. He already owed her. Several times over, if he thought about it. He opened his eyes, let them roam over her whole body, lingering in the girlie places, before he made eye contact. "Yes." And then he closed them again and tuned her out.

PART THREE

SYKORA SETTLED into her drop station, secured in place as the last fuel connection severed with a ping that rattled hollowly through the shuttle.

Djamila seethed.

Like all things, it was internal. In *Neu Berne* society, image and social station were everything. She had learned that early, the daughter of a manual laborer and a former "entertainer." The Navy had promised her an open society, where one could advance based purely on merit and skill. And it had been, but only to a point. She had had to prove herself better than everyone, man and woman, to be accepted.

But she had. Oh, yes, she had. First in her training crèche. Record scores on physical fitness, obstacle course, and survival training. Elite tactical school. Zero-G combat school, where she had earned the nickname "Ballerina of Death" for her ability to move in powered armor in three dimensions, with a weapon in each hand.

She had been the best.

It had even been good enough for a poor, blue-collar waif, with no family connections and no university, to be commissioned as an Officer and a Frieholder. But it could not get her accepted. Not by the elite of the *Neu Berne* Navy.

Not *them*.

They were the scions of generations of service, intermarried almost to incestuous degrees. Money. Power. Connections. The right boarding schools. The right summer vacations at the same wealthy enclaves and terra-formed moons. She could still see their sneers as they *welcomed* her, the poor girl who had risen so far above her station. So far.

She was never accepted. Never one of *them*. She remembered her last commanding officer explaining that she was good enough to promote, but lacked the interest of powerful players to advance her career. She was dead-ended. It was enough to drive her to resign and strike out into deep space, where people like that didn't control her destiny.

And now, sitting right next to her, looking down his nose at her, another one of *them*. Another educated elite prick, from the *Concord* Academy on *Bryce*, no less, who thought she was just a well-trained bulldog bitch.

Captain Sokolov was the only superior who had ever looked at her as a person. He had rescued her from falling into the pit itself when she lost her way, given her a place again, a purpose, a job. He was the Captain.

So Djamila seethed. She considered just smashing Aritza into the bulkhead, like last time. It would be rewarding to pound on him.

But wouldn't that lend credence to his belief that she was just *another dumb gun bunny*? Wouldn't that prove *them* right about her? Excellent for kicking in doors, but not someone you invite to a cocktail party? A well-trained bulldog bitch?

She wouldn't let them win.

Her jaw hurt from grinding her teeth.

Djamila blinked, surprised at the sudden swell of emotions that flowed over her. Normally, she was calmness itself. This runt just somehow pushed all her buttons.

She would have to work on that. And prove them, *him*, wrong.

She smiled hard. Very wrong.

THE RIDE down was smoother than Javier had ever experienced in any assault shuttle. It was more like riding in a VIP transport with an Admiral.

He really liked this pilot.

And the crazy ogre lady had left him alone for the whole trip.

He had been half-expecting more grief from her. Lord knew, he was dancing right up on the edge of rude. It was like poking a sleeping bear, or a missing tooth. Irresistible.

And she had a short fuse. But those military types, all structure and order and pattern, really grated on him. He just couldn't resist. Chickens were still better company.

More than once, Javier had opened his eyes to glance over at the Dragoon, wondering if she had fallen asleep. But the eyes had been open, just lost deep in thought. Probably planning firing lanes and organizing watch shifts. Something very military.

Outside, the whistle of air over the hull was augmented by a soft thump as the wings began to deploy, softly biting into the thickening air. Javier yawned and stretched. He really liked this pilot.

LEMUEL LOOKED up in mild surprise at the sound of thunder. The day had dawned clear and cool, with a nice autumn breeze. There should be no rain.

A glint of light in the northern sky. Movement. It took his brain several more seconds to process the image as the giant, gray-black bird resolved itself into an aircraft approaching, orbiting twice, and then flying east to the grassy plain where the herdbeasts calved in the spring.

It had been years since technology.

A stray though flitted across his mind. *Others* were coming. *Strangers* come to violate his virgin wilderness. He would have to welcome *them* properly. He walked a few steps down the hill to where Anya, Mohr, and Thomas were buried. They had not lasted long enough to see this day.

Lemuel glanced back at the wreckage he had called home for so long, smiled, and strode down the path to the river.

Welcome *them* **properly**.

JAVIER WATCHED Sykora move with an economy of grace. For a woman who was all knees and elbows and shoulders, there was not a wasted motion or a foot put wrong. He still didn't like her, but he could respect pure professionalism when it bit him on the ass.

As long as she didn't actually bite him on the ass.

He smiled to himself and stayed out of her way as he tossed the sensor remote into the air and let it baseline the area around the shuttle.

The air had a strange smell, but every new planet did. It's what

45

happened when you got away from industrial air-processors and let plants and oceans clean things. It was also cool, a sunny day low on the horizon, so either spring or fall, depending.

Javier dialed down the sensitivity on the remote and pushed the scan range out as far as it would go. The original wreck was about six kilometers northeast, tucked up in a small valley drained by a creek. In another twenty minutes, he would have a very detailed map about halfway out. The rest would have to wait until they got around some hills for direct scanning.

There were quite a few creatures nearby, four-legged animals that seemed to be the local version of elk or antelope. Javier turned and located Sykora in the organized mess of landing. Once more, just because. "Hey," he called, "any chance I can have a sidearm for protection?"

The look he got in return could have smashed a glacier. Javier suddenly understood the term 'staring daggers.' "You've got me," was all she said in reply.

Well, then. All-righty. Javier opened his field pack and put on a floppy hat.

Javier found a landing skid that was cool enough and plopped down. He pulled a screwdriver from his kit and opened the side of the portable. When nobody was paying attention, he palmed the chip that had Suvi on it and plugged her into the side of the little computer. It was going to be a tiny shoebox compared to the castle she was used to living in, but it was something. And he could use somebody to talk to right now that he didn't want to see hung from the highest yardarm in space.

Javier muted the speakers and waited. She didn't take long.

Where am I?

Javier typed quickly on the rudimentary keyboard. This was not a conversation to have while surrounded by the bad guys listening in.

Pirates caught us. Trashed the ship. I hid you. You're plugged into the sensor drone's command portable. They don't know about you. Keep it that way. JA

He couldn't imagine she liked the idea, but there wasn't much she could do.

Where are we?

Campeche 7, still. Wrecked starship nearby they want to loot. We have to help.

They're pirates!!!

And we're not dead. Survival first. Vengeance later. Promise.

<pout />

Javier figured it was a draw. Hopefully, Suvi would listen for a while and understand where they were. Having her available just doubled his chances.

And now, the mucking in the mud part.

Unlike all the hard-edged military sophistication around him, his gear was, beyond the sensor remote, decidedly low-tech, almost stupidly so. A magnetic compass. Matches. Pencil and paper for hand-made maps and notes. He did have a small knife, but it was made from a steel alloy and sharpened on a stone. It didn't even vibrate or have a laser-cutting edge, or a mono-molecular razor-sharp blade. Just a knife.

Javier pulled out a nifty little plastic hiking trinket he had picked up years ago. It had a very cheap magnetic compass, a thermometer, and the symbols you should make in the dirt in an emergency, for people searching for you. He clipped it onto the outside of his jacket and marveled. Way better impulse buy at a feed supply store than any candy bar had ever been.

Around him, Sykora's troopers prepared to invade Guatemala.

Javier sat quietly, daydreaming until a tree suddenly cast a shadow over him.

"Are we boring you, Aritza?"

Javier looked up at the ogress, scowling down at him. Maybe honey today, instead of vinegar? What the hell. "No ma'am," he said with a grin, "trying to stay out of your way while your crew organized itself. We ready?"

He was rewarded by the scowl lessening, warming by perhaps a whole degree Kelvin. Nitrogen might melt soon at this rate.

She stepped back, rather than lurk over him. "What's the terrain look like?" she asked, apparently also striving for courtesy. Maybe there was hope.

Javier flipped on the portable's hologram projector. A color-coded terrain map hovered between them, green for trees, brown for grass, gray for rock. Southwest, it just kept gently rolling to a distant sea. Northeast, their goal, the details slowly filled in.

Javier checked a readout to one side. Exactly one transmission source other than the shuttle, anywhere within range. And even here on the surface it was weak. He pushed the remote up another two hundred meters, until it was barely a dot in the clear sky above them. Nothing was going to be shooting at it, fingers crossed.

The wreck suddenly appeared bright on the radar, refined metals covered with dirt amidst scrub on the edge of a forest. It looked like the ship was a small freighter, maybe seventy or one hundred meters long. From the debris field, she had come in pretty hot, plowed through a bunch of trees, barely under control, and broken her back when she slammed down, with three major sections of hull mostly intact, and shards over a fairly compact area.

He glanced back up, but Sykora was intent on the display, not him. She really had nice teeth.

"Any radiation leakage from the wreck?" she asked. And always business.

Javier felt his shoulders shrug. "No more than normal background," he said. "Looks like it landed soft enough to protect the reactors. No load now except the emergency beacon, and it's faint, so they're fading. Maybe another year before they go."

He saw the ghost of a smile actually cross her face for the first time today. "So," she looked down at him, all business again, "something worth salvaging, after all."

"Looks like," he said, unwilling to commit more from the scans. He really didn't know what this ship, this crew did when they weren't all piratey. Maybe they funded orphanages. Space was big. There were a lot of weird people out there.

Javier watched Sykora go full tactical before his eyes. It was like a switch flipped on.

"Base team," she called, a parade ground voice that echoed off the trees, "establish a perimeter. Smith, unlock the guns but don't shoot first." A group of spacers looked up from their tasks and variously kept in motion.

One of the gun bunnies even saluted. "On it, ma'am," he said, all crisp and professional. And ready for Thermopylae.

She pointed in the direction of the wreck. "Pathfinders, north-east and stay sharp. Hostile planet." Two women nodded and faded into the brush, vanishing as he watched. They seemed more competent than he was expecting pirates to be. Much. Who were these people?

Sykora tapped him on the shoulder. "Let's go, Aritza." She encompassed the remaining crew with a look. "Move out."

Javier fell in behind her and tried not to trip over anything as he watched the screen and her butt at the same time. He figured Suvi would warn him if anything really interesting scanned.

48

Lemuel sat so perfectly still that one of the forest creatures scampered right past him, chittering angrily just like the squirrel it vaguely resembled. Completely different form, but just as daft.

Below, on the game trail, two people crept past. No, not people. Females. Unclean harlots. Mistresses of Satan. Succubi sent forth to lead the righteous astray into apostasy. He resisted the urge to spit, lest they detect him.

They passed, silent as the wind.

Lemuel didn't bother to follow them. He faded back deeper into the brush. They would seek the wreck, the destruction, the ark that had brought him to this paradise where no females ruled over men unnaturally. He would watch, carefully. There might be others.

Djamila kept sharp. The tree-analogs here looked similar and fulfilled the same ecological role. That meant the same propensity for ambush and destruction. She glanced up at Aritza's hovering spy.

She'd had him pull it in close, barely eight meters over her head, despite his grumbling. The scanning range was greatly diminished, but she wanted the extra edge. The woods were populated by a variety of creatures, from birds, to lizards, to things like impalas, to things like bears.

As they moved, she had her safety off. The rest of her crew were fast and good. She was still better. She demanded that extra split-second in an emergency. It might mean the difference between life and death.

Djamila stopped suddenly and pivoted in place. It was an old trick in terrain like this. The sudden turn to catch movement from a watcher giving himself away. Nothing. Well, nothing but Aritza nearly walking into her before he looked up from his screen.

"Hey," he looked up, "a little warning?" He looked extremely put out. She chalked it up to working for so long alone. Probably forgot how to be polite around people. Or maybe he was just an asshole, after all.

She considered growling at him, settled for a sickly-sweet smile instead. The muttering under his breath was reward enough. She smiled to herself and set off again.

JAVIER SET his system to scanning the database of transports, looking for a baseline model to compare against. These things always got customized the second day after they launched, as captains and engineers tweaked things. It would be useful to know what they were working with here. And Yu would appreciate Javier finding him a bigger Auxiliary Power Reactor, to free up space for the next time he had to crawl into the bio-scrubbers.

He was so engrossed in the screen that he stopped ogling Sykora's butt as she moved. And walked right into her when she stopped and looked backwards. Fortunately for his day, he avoided bouncing his nose off of her breast.

"Hey," he looked up, "a little warning?" For a moment, Javier thought she was going to punch him, but she smiled instead. He wasn't sure that it was an improvement, but she started walking again a moment later.

Javier kept his commentary to himself. Mostly.

The emergency beacon had been a standard affair, required by law on every vessel capable of interstellar flight. In this case, it had been the cheapest model on the market, broadcasting a twenty-four digit alpha-numeric ID from the manufacturer, rather than the more sophisticated models that included vessel particulars. That, at least, eliminated several classes of vessels, say, things big enough to have customized beacons, or military vehicles. Javier dug deeper.

At least Sykora warned him before she stopped, the next time. It was the smug smile when he looked up, up, from his screen. He grumbled anyway.

"Rest break here," Sykora called to the group. Everyone else relaxed and looked around the area warily. Things were generally just the wrong-enough shade of green to gnaw at someone.

Javier found a dead tree and sat on the trunk. His least-favorite tree returned to shadow his view.

"Aritza, where are the scouts now?"

He looked up at her sourly.

"Please?" she added quietly. Huh. Old dogs and new tricks. That had sounded almost painful. Still, she sounded sincere. It was certainly the first time he'd ever heard her use that word with him.

Javier toggled one of the side gauges into the projector, zoomed, and washed out small animals. Two dots appeared on the map, plus a few others at a considerable distance. It was a good scanner probe. It helped to have Suvi piloting it and refining the data.

"Three hundred meters out and closing, ma'am," he replied. Teeth were teeth. If she could pull hers and act politely, he could do the same.

She nodded and pulled something from her pocket. She started to put it in her mouth and paused. "Cover your ears, Aritza," she said.

He blinked, thought about it for a half-second, and set the computer down so he could jam fingers in, just before she blew a whistle shrill enough to wake the dead. Hopefully Suvi had been paying attention to the audio channel before it overloaded. Everyone else jumped. Except the other gun bunny. He had apparently known it was coming.

A second sharp blast followed the first.

Javier sat patiently until he saw her put the damned whistle away. A string of curse words appeared on the diagnostics readout at the bottom of the flat screen. Apparently, Suvi had learned some new ones along the way.

Movement at the very edge of the sensor range caught his attention. Looked like a bear from the size and heat signature, but it was moving away from them at a slow amble, so he figured it was safe. Maybe remind everyone to make enough noise to scare off local critters. Last thing he needed right now was angry momma bear.

The two women pathfinders made absolutely no sound.

One minute nothing. Next, they pop out of the brush and stand right next to him. And he'd been watching them approach on the scanner, the last forty meters. What the hell did these people do that they needed these kinds of experts, anyway?

Sykora was in her element. "Status report," she barked.

The shorter of the two, the brunette with the nice hips, came slightly to attention. The blond with the long legs caught him staring and winked.

Javier considered his chances. Might be worth trying.

"We found the wreck, ma'am," Pathfinder Brunette said. "Either there were shipwrecked survivors, or there are locals. We found evidence of habitation."

Javier looked up at the three women. "Bear?"

All three blinked down at him. Apparently they had forgotten he spoke.

"Negative," the brunette said. "Fire pit, hand-made pottery, agriculture, closeable door into a cabin that appears recently used."

"But no one appeared," Sykora stated flatly.

"Affirmative, ma'am," the brunette agreed.

Sykora thought for a second. "Three minute break here, then we'll push on." The two women dropped in place and pulled out canteens.

The giant redwood tree turned around and looked down at him. "Aritza, push the drone vertical and do that long range scan trick again. I want to see the wreck." Pause. "Please."

The drone took off straight up, but Javier pushed a button on a screen quickly before anyone noticed the discrepancy.

You don't exist, he typed. *Don't anticipate me. These people are smart and dangerous.*

Sorry.

Javier took it up to 200 meters and hovered. One quick rotational scan, and then he focused in on the wreck. This was where Suvi would help.

Hard scan that thing for me. Inventory everything you can. And don't let anything sneak up on us.

Will do, boss.

He poked the volume button and the screen like he was actually controlling it, but he knew Suvi was flying the remote now. After he escaped these yahoos, he might have to upgrade the remote so she could fly it from whatever ship he poured her into next.

And maybe add a gun.

Let's see: two bears, a small herd of elk-like critters, and he was pretty sure that was the local equivalent of a bobcat. Hopefully it wasn't the local version of a wolverine.

Javier looked up at her. "Path's clear," he said, "you might warn people that there are a few dangerous creatures in the woods."

Sykora smiled down at him. "You mean, besides us."

Javier rolled his eyes in pure reflex.

Ogre-lady trying to be funny might be worse than her as a total hard-ass.

He sighed to himself as he stood up. *Another day, another drachma.*

SUVI WAS TORN. On the one hand, it was good to be awake and doing something. On the other hand, she had been weeks off-line. Things had happened, and Javier wasn't filling in the details.

The tall lady seemed to be in charge. And scary. Suvi really needed her processing core to read the inter-personal dynamics playing out around her. The chip she was on was barely big enough to hold her personality and near-term memory.

As it was, she'd had to off-load some of her consciousness onto the portable. There was certainly space for files, but the processor on that thing was horribly under-powered. She was almost thinking at human speeds. Egads. How did they operate so slow?

She spun the remote in place and pinged. Precious few birds, none of them big enough to threaten her new little flitter-ship. Some fauna large enough to maybe be dangerous, depending on how this planet had evolved.

Over there, some fields had been planted with human-digestible crops, so someone had survived the crash and broken out the emergency seed packet. And it had worked for them, if they'd been here for seventeen years.

Quick pass through the memory files of the remote. The wreck looked kinda like a Kallasky Engineering Mark IX Conestoga. Big, slow, durable. Too many pieces to be sure until she could read some part numbers off the engine, or they found the nameplate.

Suvi counted her humans. Javier, Tall Lady, two "pathfinders" (note: look that term up when connected to better resources. Got no useful dictionary here.), one heavily-armed male, one male and one female without arms, but with toolkits. (note: mark the latter tentatively as engineering crew. Update later. Ask Javier.)

She needed better information. She was missing too much. Javier had said to hide, so she decided to play along. Happy little flying mouse, zooming overhead.

She aimed her microphones down, but Javier grumbling to himself seemed to be the only conversation.

Who were these people?

LEMUEL WATCHED the wreck from a nearby hilltop. He felt sure he was supposed to be overjoyed by the arrival of people. It would be possible to leave this world and return to civilization.

Did he want to?

The ancients had venerated the ascetics, monks living on the edges of the desert, praying and fasting, living holy lives of contemplation.

He had not intended to crash here. But once it was done, he had put in a great deal of contemplation on the Lord's message to him. The Harlot was not meant to rule over men. So she had not. The others had not seen it that way. They had joined her. It was the way of things.

And now, he could return to the world.

But would he have to sacrifice holiness? More harlots had come. One seemed to rule them.

She would have to go.

But the others?

He would have to get closer to see how many of them would trod the path of the righteous. Many were incapable of enlightenment.

The silver bird troubled him.

It flew wrong, was shaped wrong, was wrong. Lemuel knew his eyes were old, but he remembered technology. The silver bird was a device, a thing. It had eyes to watch. He could not sneak up on them unaware. He would have to gain their confidence.

Lemuel silently rose to his feet and took a step down the hillside. It was irrational, but he could feel the silver bird's eyes on him immediately.

So be it. He would be friendly and thankful to his rescuers.

Then he would kill them.

Suvi understood the need for silence, but she really wished she could talk to Javier. Text lacked the subtleties. She settled for highlighting a dot on the display. **That's not a bear.**

She pinged it, hard, once, with every sensor the little flitter-ship had. Yup. Definitely human. Male. Mid-fifties. Pretty good shape if he was a shipwrecked survivor deep into his second decade of local realtime. She displayed his stats.

Javier's voice on the portable's audio input. "Sykora," he said. "Company."

Suvi watched the two armed humans point rifles in opposite directions immediately. The two pathfinder women drew sidearms as well, squatting down and aiming outward. The two engineers dropped to the ground without a word. Javier just stood there.

Tall Lady spoke. "Where?"

Javier glanced at the screen, turned to his right, and waved with a cheery, "Good morning."

Tall Lady was aghast. "What are you doing, Aritza?" she queried. A moment later, she called, "Flip."

Suvi watched her and the armed male change sides of coverage like a ballet, leaving the one called Sykora pointed where Javier was looking and the other covering the "rear."

The strange human was approaching slowly, quietly. He wore robes made of a rough, homespun cotton, probably locally grown from seedstock, and carried a walking stick.

She bounced the flitter-ship up higher for a better view and scanned everything once, and then dropped down close.

Finally, she might get some answers.

———————

JAVIER CONSIDERED THE DEAD FREIGHTER. Definitely came in too hot. Looks like it tore off a landing skid on that rock, which dropped the bow into the ground at speed, which cracked her spine there and there. Probably one you walked away from, unless your number had come up.

Reactor was definitely on-line, banked to minimum load. Heat and light leaked out of an open hatch and the cooling fins were well above ambient temperature.

Somebody lived here. A field of human crops close to harvest. A small drying shed filled with...stuff. Dunno what else to call it. A path down to the stream below. Homey. Javier could see himself living here and enjoying the place. Clean air. No people. Paradise.

That's not a bear.

Good thing Suvi was on the job.

Might as well start the fun. "Sykora," he said. "Company."

Javier watched the armed lunatics go into full combat mode. This was why he was a civilian now. That kind of thinking was just bad. Desperately anti-social.

Sykora was the worst. "Where?" She was probably planning a firefight right about now.

Javier really needed some coffee.

He turned to his right, and waved, "Good morning."

Behind him, he was pretty sure he could hear teeth grind. "What are you doing, Aritza?" Ogre lady snarled at him. A moment later, "Flip."

Great, now she was standing next to him, hovering over his shoulder, big honking war machine ready to lay the smack-down.

I got out of bed this morning for this?

Javier pointed. "A guy. The survivor, I'm guessing. And we're in his front yard, so maybe we should be nice to him?"

Javier slid out of reach and stepped forward. Good old-fashioned Biblical Patriarch stepped into view, complete with a beard to his waist and the sort of stick Moses carried in every video Javier'd ever seen of Exodus. In a dark alley, he might be scary. Here? Faced by a small army? Harmless.

"I'm Javier," he addressed the newcomer. "We saw your signal. Took a while. You are most definitely in the middle of absolutely nowhere."

The man considered him silently. Which made sense. Javier had months where the only person he talked to besides the chickens was Suvi. The old man might have forgotten how to talk. Or, maybe he spoke something really obscure and didn't grok.

What the hell. Javier reached into his pack and pulled out a bar of dried fruit and oats. He opened the bar and held it out as a peace offering. "Food?"

A hand descended from the heavens and drug him back a step before the man moved. Javier hadn't forgotten how strong Sykora was. But, man…

"What the hell do you think you're doing, Aritza?"

Javier turned. Nobody was sneaking up on these people, so he could ignore the guy. "Diplomacy, lady," he said with an exasperated sigh. "Being nice. It's the part of negotiations that doesn't involve shooting people."

She was back to staring daggers. "I'm in charge here." That tone might have put an edge on a dull knife.

Fine. "Fine," Javier said. What the hell. He plopped down, crossed his legs, and took a bite of the bar. Let the gun bunny sort it out.

She snarled down at him. "Now what are you doing?" Javier noted that at no point did the barrel ever waver from dead-center on the new guy. Pissed, she might be. Deadly, without a doubt.

"You're in charge, Sykora," he snarled back, only a little less hostile. "Do it your way."

———

YES, that was the way of things, Lemuel thought. The Harlot was not suited to lead. She knew only violence or seduction. Not the ways of

Men. Here, She was surrounded by sycophants, but for one who was not under her spell. Lemuel found that his purpose was clear.

He relaxed his natural scowl and tried to remember how to smile. The Harlot was a lost cause, so he directed it at the man sitting. "He-he-hello," he stuttered.

He found speech to be a complicated task, once the habit was lost. He spent most of his weeks in silent prayer and the sort of hard work necessary to survive in the Lord's paradise.

The Harlot kept her weapon pointed at him. And her bile.

"What's your name?" she challenged him.

That brought Lemuel up short. He hadn't used his name in…a very long time. He blinked a few times. How many seasons had he been here? Many, doing the Lord's work in the wilderness.

"Answer me," the Harlot continued, her anger palpable.

The Lord counseled patience in the face of the denizens of the pit. "Le-Lemuel," he said brokenly, finding the word deep in his memory.

The friendly male, unbowed by the Harlot, spoke to him from the dirt. "Hungry?"

Lemuel cocked his head. Words were difficult to process.

"Here," the man continued. He held out his hand, holding the bar of food that he had taken a bite from.

The Harlot's fury grew. "Come no closer," she rasped harshly.

The male looked up at her, rolled his eyes disapprovingly, and tossed the bar to Lemuel with a single, "Fine. Catch."

Lemuel managed to keep it from falling.

A sniff. A blue and red thing. Fruit of some sort, dried and packed together, with nuts he could not recognize. Minus a healthy bite out of one end.

Since it came from the male, Lemuel broke off a small chunk and touched it with his tongue. The poisons in this place were subtle, but dangerous. Mohr had died after eating the local fruit in an attempt to go native on this world.

Thus did the Righteous fall from the Lord's Grace.

Lemuel took a very small bite. Better to risk illness than to refuse his one potential ally among the strangers and burn a valuable bridge. He considered his words as he slowly chewed.

"Thank you," he finally found. Language was coming back to him now.

Lemuel considered the lovely taste, fruits that would not grow in this

Eden, nuts from alien trees. His body remembered the taste of honey, so different from the form the local insects made.

Perhaps the Lord was telling him that he could finally go home, after so long in the wilderness.

The Harlot would not be an easy foe.

The words of his father came back to him, across the gulf of vast time.

"Welcome," he said slowly, carefully, enunciating each word with care. "Welcome to Eden."

DJAMILA WAS NOT TAKEN in by the rustic's pose. He had already survived many years on the surface of a hostile planet, surrounded by alien flora and fauna. That made him dangerous. That Eden nonsense bullshit wasn't going to cut it.

And Aritza was going to play good cop. Big surprise there. The man had no sense. None.

Predictable. But she could bad cop with the best of them. Watch this.

"Aritza," she called down to the punk sitting in the dirt, "Is he armed?"

"No." The answer was surprisingly quick. And assured.

"How do you know?" she asked.

"Because," he replied in a voice right at the edge of insubordinate, "the only power sources that aren't over here are in that." A finger pointed at the wreck. "My sensors showed him as a bear until he came into the open."

"And the staff he's carrying?"

"What?" Aritza shot back. "You can't take an old man with a stick?"

Djamila considered kicking him. Aritza was really getting on her nerves.

She scowled her best, most professional, scowl at the native. Yes, she could handle him unarmed. Plus, she was supposed to be nice.

Interstellar law and custom said you always rescued ship-wrecked survivors and got them back to civilization. Even pirates honored that one. Mostly.

So, catalog the wreck. Rescue the local. Figure out if she could make it look like a tragic accident had killed Aritza.

She slung the battle-rifle on her shoulder.

All in a day's work.

JAVIER WATCHED Sykora's face on the sly.

He thought about teaching her how to play poker one of these days, but decided he was safer not telling her she was an open book. The Gunners on B deck were more fun, anyway.

The old man stared intently at him, waiting for the other shoe to drop. Better poker player there. Didn't like Sykora at all. That made him good people.

Might as well cut straight to the messy bits.

Javier levered himself upright and brushed the dirt and leaves and crap off his butt with one hand. He clicked the recall button on the portable and caught the remote as it settled into his hand. Suvi would keep it active. She was very smart. Much better to trust her than the ogre-lady.

Now, the old man.

"So the reason we came here was to salvage the wreck, Lemuel," he said. Simple. Honest. Easy. "We didn't expect to find anyone alive after all this time."

Javier read the signs as he spoke. Two guys at a bus stop, talking about last night's game. He waited for Lemuel's nod, got it, went on.

"Interstellar law says we rescue you at this point and get you someplace where you can get home from." Javier turned as he spoke and looked right up at Sykora's scowl. "Where and how will be up to Captain Sokolov, but you'll be able to save some of your stuff."

Again, the pause as Lemuel processed his words and nodded.

"We're going to inventory everything for value, and most definitely remove the power reactor. What was on your manifest?"

He watched Lemuel scrunch up his face in thought. The eyes drifted off focus and blinked rapidly. A hand came up and scratched the semi-bald pate. Javier heard him whisper *Home* once, under his breath. A very small smile appeared briefly.

The eyes finally focused on his. "Um. Machine parts, I think," Lemuel said quietly. "And trade goods for some colony."

Sykora overrode his next question. "Which colony?" she barked.

Lemuel looked down, apparently embarrassed. "I do not know," he said. "I was a cook and stevedore. Anya was the navigator."

Javier turned to Sykora and gave her his best stink-eye scowl. Then a smile as he turned back to the old man. "So let's go take a tour of the wreck, Lemuel," he said soothingly. "You can point out all the interesting and dangerous parts as we go."

This was going to be like herding cats. Normally, Javier would have said herding goldfish, but carp won't turn suddenly and slash you with their claws. Sykora had that look in her eyes.

PART FOUR

LEMUEL CONSIDERED his options as they ascended into the ship. They were many, but he bestrode a dangerous path.

Javier had introduced himself and made it clear that he could become a friend.

The Harlot had a name as well, but Lemuel had not bothered to remember it. Weren't they all the same, after all?

The others, male and female alike, were obviously under the sway of the Harlot. From the looks and mannerisms, Lemuel could see that they considered Javier an outsider to their group, though they treated him with respect.

That gave him an opening. Did he have the courage to seize it? Was this place to become Megiddo, after all? The Lord had worked in his mysterious ways to place Lemuel here so long ago.

Had he finally proven the strength of his faith? Or had he failed and was to be irrevocably damned by the Harlot?

Lemuel prayed silently to himself as he led the troupe of strangers, invaders unto his quiet paradise, down into the realm of his earliest, greatest challenge.

SUVI WAS HAVING AN ADVENTURE.

The flitter-ship was far more maneuverable than *Mielikki* had been. She could hover, and spin, and bob, and float, and saunter. She missed having a turret she could use, but on a hull this small, it probably wouldn't do more than irritate a squirrel. Not that that was a bad thing.

She had already used a series of ultrasound pings to map the hallway and the first cargo hold they had entered. The humans hadn't heard, but they missed everything anyway.

Now she was studying a small lizard-looking creature on a wall. Maybe the philosophical offspring of a gecko and a chameleon. It blended well, but moved quickly and gracefully. And couldn't have been more than six centimeters long.

She watched it munch happily on the local equivalent of a spider that hadn't heard him coming either. There was probably a moral to that story.

Suvi launched another aggressive series of pings, but nothing moved.

She flitted over to a crate and scanned the weathered coding on the side. The language of shipping containers was probably the first universal stellar language. You could write and speak in any number of tongues and get by, but you had to talk to a very limited intelligence computer to move big things around.

That meant simple codes, with descriptive tags built in, so that someone could point a laser scanner at a stack of containers, scan the whole wall, and inventory everything in seconds. Here, she was stuck thinking at almost human speeds, so it took much longer, and the flitter-ship had a very limited scanning laser, so she had to get close.

But it was fun.

This one contained quality glasswork, cups and vases and such, designed to be sold boutique-style on a frontier colony with some money. The sort of place that had been too poor to take anything initially that wasn't directly related to immediate survival. And had then survived the first few years in the wilderness, and prospered enough that people were ready to have nice things. Suvi added it to the list.

There weren't any great prizes here. No precious metal alloys, or objets d'art, or high-end machine parts that Javier could use to build her a new ship. And this freighter was never flying again without more time in a space-dock than was worth considering. From what she had overheard, the others were mostly interested in ripping out the reactors and engines anyway.

Then she remembered the Black Flag. Being stuck thinking at only human speeds really sucked. These people were the pirates who had jumped them. Javier was a prisoner, of sorts, and that's why they thought she was dead.

Duh.

Gods, she hated slow processing hardware.

Well, that changed everything. If Javier was working with them, he had some sort of deal going, and she was his ace in the hole. She could do that.

Now she really missed all the extra brain horsepower. It would be nice to be able to read these people at the unconscious level, with all sorts of extra scanners and thermometers so she had a solid hold on their biometrics. Hmmm. She'd have to settle for turning up the audio channels and putting in a cutout in case it got loud suddenly.

Time to watch, and wait, and prepare. Javier was going to need her.

JAVIER SMILED BUT GRUMBLED. Having an honest deal with a bunch of pirates was one thing, but it would have been nice if this wreck had had some sort of big score. If he had to work with Sykora for four years, one of them would end up messily dead. No doubt about that.

He was under no illusion that he'd have any chance to escape or communicate with anybody, any time they got close to civilization. Even with a lot of planning. Ogre Lady would just lock him in a broom closet for a day if she had to.

And the old man was going to be no help at all. He seemed lost in a fugue of some sort. Probably spent too long alone here and gone totally nuts. He certainly didn't realize he mumbled, not that anything coherent came out.

And Sykora…Yeah. Don't let her too close behind you. Simple as that. At least he had Suvi watching his back. Not that she could do much, but she was going to make his work a whole lot easier while he was here. And she could keep his back safer.

Javier watched as another box came up on the screen, inventoried, mapped, and tagged. If nothing else, at least they had something to show for all the effort.

He was going to be too busy just staying alive. Being Science Officer could wait.

DJAMILA WAS TORN. The freighter was completely indefensible from even the most rudimentary approach. She had already passed seven places where she would have secured a door, prepared an ambush point, or built a trap. This person, this local with the hard eyes, was a complete amateur. On the other hand, it would make things easier if she found it necessary to arrange accidents for several people down here.

At least one of them deserved it. She was even trying to be nice. Aritza just pushed her buttons. She hadn't even pushed back. Yet.

At least the trip was a success. Based on the manifests alone, if even a third of the cargo survived, they could sell it for a profit, over and above getting a new power reactor. The Captain would be pleased.

She watched Aritza and the local confer on something. It involved a lot of pointing on Aritza's part, and shrugs in response. Much as she hated to admit it, the punk had an easy way with people. Much like the Captain did. She had never gotten the hang of it, and, until now, never really appreciated how useful a tool it could be in her inventory.

Huh. Perhaps the old bitch dog needed to learn a new trick or two. It galled her to think Aritza had something useful to teach her. But there it was.

All right. Observe. Understand. Learn.

No different than taking a fortified position away from bad guys. Figure out their weak point. Come at them sidelong. Get the mission done before they can respond. Tactical 101.

Djamila walked up on the conversation at a measured pace. Quiet. Dignified. Prepared. Open.

Aritza had apparently developed a sixth sense regarding her. He seemed to place her physically at all times, even when he wasn't looking. She felt a moment of thrill course through her for no good reason. No, there was a reason. For all his nonchalance, he was acutely aware of her, even subconsciously, and paying extra special attention.

Good. That meant she had gotten through to him, at least at some level.

JAVIER REGISTERED Sykora before he realized she was that close behind him. Nobody that big should be allowed to move that quietly.

And yet, his favorite tree had sprung up behind him, listening to things without interrupting. It must have galled the control-freak in her to sit passively. Good. Do her good to be in a situation where she wasn't completely in control. Maybe she'd learn to be human occasionally.

He glanced back once. Well, up and back. Seriously, unless she was this close, he forgot just how big she was. Perfectly proportioned woman, just a whole head taller than him. Dancing with her would be fun. Distracting, but fun.

And she didn't say anything. Just hovered in that perfectly poised way she moved. Like she was expecting bad guys to come out of the air vents at any moment, or something. It would involve guns. She did guns well.

But she didn't say anything. Just watched him like a hawk. Weird. Most women nattered. Not her. Didn't even fidget. Might have been carved in white marble. Artemis, by Michelangelo. Huh.

Javier went right ahead with his own nattering. Lemuel seemed a good enough guy. Little lonely. Hard time remembering words. Seventeen years of solo survival on a hostile planet would do that. He himself usually needed a few days in a bar before people made sense again, once he got back from one of his long runs in the darkness.

The cargo was in good enough shape, as the hull had largely held, except where it had cracked on the frames, but that let weather in between spaces instead of into them. Javier figured they would make a clearing and drop the shuttle into it, next trip, so they could pull the reactor and haul it the shortest distance. Maybe the engines were salvageable as well. Hadn't made it that far. And the corvette didn't need them, but there was enough space on the flight deck for another small ship, a gunboat, or a scout.

If he was going to be stuck with these yahoos for a while, he might as well make it as profitable as possible. Buy his freedom, make his escape, whatever.

It would involve these people getting what they deserved. He was sure of that.

LEMUEL FOUGHT to keep his face and mannerisms passive when the eureka moment struck him. For better than an hour, he had explained long forgotten things to the strangers. Well, to Javier. The rest had just trailed along quietly, not touching much, but paying way too much attention to everything around them except him.

By now, he was pretty sure they were pirates. But Javier wasn't one of *them*. Just along for the ride, somehow. Perhaps a prisoner, based on one of his off-hand comments.

Lemuel considered that The Lord might have finally decided he had been tempered enough by the wilderness. Perhaps it was time to take his message to the broader universe. Lemuel had never considered himself a prophet. But it was apparently time.

The Harlot would be the biggest problem. The Lord had put her there as his final challenge before he could bring enlightenment to the galaxy. Well enough. He would overcome her.

She would not be an easy foe. But The Lord had never intended his to be an easy life. And Javier would only be able to help a little. Less, if he was a prisoner and needed to be kept ignorant.

But The Lord would provide.

He continued to answer questions from Javier, even as a supernova exploded in his brain. He could do this. And make it look like a terrible accident.

The Harlot would be first, as she deserved, followed by the three other harlots. And the rest of the Harlot's followers. Only Javier would escape. For now. Perhaps he would have to be sacrificed for the greater good later. The Lord would make His will known when the time was right.

PART FIVE

Suvi flitter-shipped up and over the wreck. After two hours down in the bowels of the dead freighter, she needed a breath of fresh air and some open skies. Even if she was an AI.

Below, Javier seemed happy, overall. Somewhere, recently, a secondary power reactor had made him extremely angry. She could tell by the way his voice grated when it came up. The wreck was going to make it all better, somehow.

Tall Lady, the one called Sykora, appeared pleased as well, so maybe they knew a place they could sell the cargo.

The survivor, Lemuel, was harder to read. She had studied his face. It went from happy to angry and back quickly, but most of the time it was placid. Suvi'd be happy to get her poker-playing sub-routines back on line, so she could understand better all the subtle byplay going on. She wasn't close enough to human to just read them and understand what wasn't being said.

For now, she scanned the few lizard-birds in the neighborhood. Nothing larger than a house cat was within a kilometer of the shipwreck. Somewhere, over behind that hill, somebody named Del was listening to weird music in the background, when Sykora checked in every fifteen minutes. And he was very bored.

Suvi checked her power levels. Enough flight for several hours. More if she kept the scanning to a minimum and sat on a flat rock somewhere, absorbing sunlight. She found a nice spot above the bow of the broken freighter and settled.

The sun felt good on her back. She dialed up the audio sensors to their highest gain and sunbathed while she waited for Javier to call.

LEMUEL WAS on firmer ground now. The strangers had completed their tour of the ship and were making plans to salvage everything so they could haul it back to civilization, including him. The Lord was finally calling him to service.

They sat in the clearing below his crude cabin and broke out pre-fabricated meal packets for themselves. Javier had offered him one, and shown him how to activate the heating element. The smell was nearly overwhelming, as he had not had any meat to eat in many, many years.

None of the animals on this planet could be safely consumed. Even most of the plants were harmful.

Thus had The Lord make his displeasure with Mohr known.

There was a plant Lemuel had found safe, at least for him. Over the years, he had developed something of an resistance to the trace alkaloids in the leaves, if he boiled them long enough into a tea. His dreams were deep and bizarre afterwards, but he was mostly immune now.

Thus had The Lord delivered into his hands the tools of His vengeance on The Harlot.

Lemuel concentrated on his tea kettle, hanging over the fire on salvaged iron bars. As long as the water was boiled hard and rolled, everything dangerous in it was likely killed. He felt Javier's gaze.

"So, Lemuel," Javier asked him, "are the local plants and animals edible?"

Lemuel scowled, mostly to himself. "There are a few safe plants," he said, skirting the trust carefully in his service to The Lord. "The animals are too dangerous to eat. We did not have the tools to understand that when we crashed. Mohr died of the poison. Thomas was killed by a fever."

Javier processed all that carefully. "And Anya, the pilot?"

Lemuel shrugged, skating carefully around the truth. "Her death is why we crashed here," he said, obliquely. "None but her could fly the ship, and the computer was not up to the task."

Lemuel left off the bashed-in skull that had caused Anya's death. They would not understand that she was a Harlot that had deserved death, like so many others that exercised power over him in defiance of The Lord's **Will**.

The whistling steam precluded conversation for a moment. Lemuel felt many eyes upon him. He realized, belatedly, that the simple act of boiling water in an iron pot might be something none but him had ever seen or done. Javier seemed to understand, but he wasn't of *them*.

Lemuel concentrated on turning the simple ritual of tea into a performance.

Let the water boil for several long moments for safety. The local animals had a tendency to flee at the sound. The humans just watched him, rapt.

Pull the kettle from the hanging iron with a cozy he had knitted the third winter, when he began to make his own cloth from cotton he grew and harvested. Rest it on the warm flat rock placed there for just this reason.

Put his largest soup pot next to the kettle on the rock.

Pour a bit of boiled water in and swirl it around to clean and sterilize things.

Pour the cleaning water over the composting pile to keep things damp for the digesting bacteria.

Add several measures of the dried leaves he called *Dream Tea* to the soup pot and pour most of the hot water over it. Retain some of the boiled water to clean the pot later, after reheating.

Stir vigorously for a few seconds to unsettle everything.

And then several minutes of patience as the tea steeped. For Lemuel, a ritual nearly as important as thrice-daily prayer. Cleanliness was next to godliness, especially in this place where so many poisonous things waited to trip the unwary.

Around him, the unwary awaited their fate blindly.

The Lord would welcome them.

———

JAVIER BIT BACK A LAUGH. For people raised on food-dispenser computers, tea-making probably looked a lot like magic. He would know. He had done it enough times, usually for station commanders and admirals.

And Lemuel seemed to have something of the showman in him, after all. Javier watched him rise to the occasion of good performance art.

The tea smelled good, too. Earthy and rich in a way that chemically-processed stuff never had. Javier bit back a moment of frustration and rage at the fate of *Mielikki*. At least he had saved all the botany. And hopefully Yu was keeping the chickens as happy as they ever got.

All in all, things could have been much worse.

LEMUEL FOUND that The Lord had granted his prayers for calmness and patience today.

The tea reached a point of inflection, like a magical infusion of happiness and psychedelic nocturne.

He ladled himself a small cup and tasted it. Perfect. Light enough that he would be happy all day, but not enough to overwhelm him with the sort of sleepiness that had visited him in the early days, before he had developed much immunity.

Lemuel refilled his cup and set it to one side.

He looked up at the surrounding group and smiled. The Lord had indeed provided.

Lemuel gestured with the pot. "My friends, I would like to share with you something of this world that I will soon be departing. It has brought me much joy and calmness over the years. I think you will enjoy it as well."

The others smiled up at him. Even the Harlot relaxed her eternal vigilance and hostility. Lemuel considered that the greatest sign yet. "Please join me in a toast."

Javier held out a mug that Lemuel filled. Lemuel watched him take the smallest taste with a knowing twinkle in his eye.

Truly, Lemuel had found his ally against the Harlot. They would join forces and kill all the pirates, and then go forth and wreak a terrible vengeance on the universe together.

He smiled as he carried the pot around to each of the invaders and shared with them their own taste of The Lord's wrath.

SOMETHING about the whole situation just felt off. Javier couldn't put his finger on it, but Lemuel just felt wrong. All too pleased with himself. Not nearly uptight enough for so many strangers around, or the impending upset to his life. Even rescue didn't explain it.

Javier took just enough of the tea to get a taste, while pretending to take a reasonable drink. He knew better than to try anything on a strange planet.

Yup. Something there. A trace of...*what?* Most of the pirates might have tried various narcotics over the years, licit and otherwise, but probably none of them had made a scientific event of it. Certainly one that certain Shore Patrols still talked about, years later.

Their lives rarely depended on that sort of thing.

His did.

So. Accidental drug overdose, or deliberate? The man's behavior just didn't ring right. Probably not an accident, then. Still, this felt more like a narcotic than a poison.

He should probably do something about it. At least it wasn't that toxic, if this Lemuel-dude was willing to drink it. Slow acting at least, probably not lethal.

It would be impolite to tell the dragon-lady if he was wrong. She'd just shoot the guy out of hand and be done with it. Maybe he didn't deserve that. Maybe he did. You never knew.

Fortunately, Javier was prepared for this sort of thing. These people had no clue what to do on the surface of a hostile world. Obviously, they needed a Science Officer to keep them alive.

Next question, did he want them alive?

Most of them were just folks, doing what they needed to do to get through their day. Not particularly evil or vile creatures.

Sykora, on the other hand...Yeah, he owed her a few. Be interesting to wind her sideways on a good hallucinogenic sometime. Might even make her tolerable. Maybe he should try it. She seemed like she was trying to be nicer than she had been.

Ah, what the hell.

Javier picked up the portable and started typing. He had an expert handy. Let her do the heavy lifting.

Suvi, I know you are in range. Please scan the tea with your laser spectrograph and let me know your results. Quietly.

Javier smiled. One of the new berry species he was exploring had originally been evolved from something called Moroccan Dreamberries. Maybe he needed to spend some time breeding a few crops back into the mother line and see if he could amp up some of the more interesting chemical signatures.

Hell, Sykora might even smile.

Around him, the crew smiled and toasted with the poisoned tea. They didn't seem to notice the slightly metallic taste underneath, but they weren't used to living with this level of paranoia.

Nobody was.

Javier watched Sykora drain her mug in a single shot. It was larger than everyone else's, but she was a big girl. Javier was really, really torn.

He faked taking another sip.

Sykora rapped her cup lightly to get the dude's attention with a "more, please," as well. Please? That was kinda scary, coming out of her mouth without being drug by horses.

As Lemuel stepped around to pour her more tea, Javier surreptitiously poured his cup out on the ground and shifted a heel over it to cover the mud until it soaked into the ground.

His portable computer beeped with a message.

Please tell me you didn't drink any of the tea. Scan identifies trace amides of ergoline present. Expect psycho-chemically-induced hallucinations, possibly with additional soporific qualities. *** DANGEROUS!!! ***

Javier grinned to himself. Rapid acid trip and a nap. Not necessarily a bad thing, if he was in a controlled setting with people he trusted, or locked in a small hotel room by himself. At least it hadn't been bad last time.

This time was gonna be different. Javier doubted that the local was unaware of the effects of his tea on people. So what was Lemuel going to do about it? And, more importantly, what should he do?

LEMUEL WORKED VERY hard to keep a smile on his face as everyone drank the dreaming tea, including the three lesser harlots and the spawn of the unnameable Dark One who led them. Sleep would take them soon, darkness tinged with terror and no escape. Then, he would begin his crusade into the broader universe.

And, as a bonus, the friendly one, Javier, was going to help him kill these people.

From the corner of an eye, Lemuel had watched Javier pour out his tea instead of drinking it. He had known a moment of panic as he stood before The Harlot with all her guns, attempting to be calm while pouring, but Javier had remained silent.

It was a *Sign*.

Lemuel returned to his spot by the small fire and sat the kettle down, listening to the ribald banter flowing back and forth between the strangers. The Dreaming would take them soon. All he had to do was wait, and offer up a small prayer to The Lord for the souls that he was about to send to their final resting place.

Already the tea took its toll. The least harlot was slumped in on herself, precariously balanced with her head down, ripe for the slightest nudge to fall over.

Lemuel smiled.

The heavily armed male was next. Even from here, Lemuel could see his pupils begin to dilate as his speech became labored. In the middle of a word, his brain passed the threshold into sleep. He fell against one of the harlots in green and collapsed atop her in a crude approximation of mating.

Lemuel held his breath as he counted bodies. All were down, save for Javier his friend, and The Harlot who was his adversary's very avatar on Earth. And even she was on the final stages of crisis. He could see the painful realization of failure take hold of her mind, shackled by the twin narcotic hammers of sleep and nightmare, beating away at her walls.

Lemuel knew a moment of total panic as she rose to her knees and drew one of her weapons, pin-prick eyes locked on him like a missile. Before he could move, the weapon came up. Lemuel held his breath.

The shot stirred a puff of dirt between them as darkness claimed her. The Harlot crumpled face down, her very will defeated, the pistol fallen before his Adversary could strike.

Hers would be a quick, painless death. He owed her that much.

Lemuel reached down and picked up one of the rocks that marked the boundary of his fire pit. It was hot to the touch, but he did not feel it. In his mind, he could already see skulls caved in under the fierce impact of this stone. The Lord had spoken to him.

It would be like before. Anya dead on the deck, her blood splattered randomly on the walls in a message he had spent seventeen years trying to decipher. Thomas and Mohr aghast, but unwilling to challenge him. Escape across several systems until they were safe from pursuit and could live out their lives as men, without the creeping infestation of the harlots turning them from the path of righteousness.

Lemuel smiled and hefted the rock. The Harlot would be first to die. She could lead her troop into hell personally. He took a step forward to begin the crusade.

"I wouldn't do that, if I were you…"

JAVIER FELT LIKE A SHIT.

Here, he's spent weeks dreaming of ways to get even with Sykora for all the things she'd done to him. Planning ways he could escape and bring down the full force of the *Concord* Fleet on these bastards, hang them from the highest yardarm, pay them back for Suvi and *Mielikki*.

And now, here he was.

He watched the local dude count them falling with a smile on his face. Okay, so not an accidental overdose, after all.

The rock was a very bad sign. It meant things were about to get stupid.

Javier considered the man. Half a head taller than him. Maybe an extra ten kilos of mass. And right now, the sort of crazy fire in the eyes that just meant everything was about to go to hell. He'd finally figured out that look with his second ex-wife.

Still, Javier was twenty years younger, and had kept up his close combat training over the years. He should be able to take this guy.

Time to save the crew from their own innocent stupidity.

"I wouldn't do that, if I were you," Javier announced in the sort of voice he always heard in the videos. *Never thought I'd be able to actually say that in a real situation.*

He watched Lemuel turn stupidly to stare at him, a jagged five-kilo rock in one hand like a primitive ape's hammer.

"Javier?" the guy was confused, and maybe a bit put out.

"I can't let you kill these people, Lemuel," Javier continued, trying to be soothing. "Drop the rock and we'll make sure you get back to civilization and get the treatment you need. I realize you've been out here a long time and kinda gone stale. We can help."

Javier watched, hopeful, as the crazy seemed to ebb in the guy's eyes, just for a second. Maybe he could talk his way out of this, after all.

And then the fire came back, twice as nuts. "No," Lemuel roared,

"The Harlot must die. All harlots must be destroyed if men are to achieve righteousness. So sayeth The Lord."

Javier watched as the man turned, ignoring him, and reared back with the rock, poised over Sykora's unconscious form.

Shit.

Javier took two running steps and tackled the man before Lemuel could crush Sykora's skull. He landed on top of the guy and got in a couple of good body blows. That just seemed to piss him off.

Javier had never understood the term until now, thought it was a joke. *Rage Strength*. Lemuel took him by surprise. The man flipped him backwards with two hands to the chest, leaving Javier suddenly on his back a meter away.

And then the gorilla was on him. They traded punches. Javier felt his brain rattle around inside his skull. Lemuel didn't seem to notice. Okay, not good.

Javier hooked the lunatic with his foot, twisted them both until he ended up on top. One. Two. Three shots to the side of the head. That just seemed to make him angrier. *Crap*. Was this guy made of brick? That always worked in the movies.

Two big gorilla hands came up and grabbed Javier's throat. Air suddenly became a commodity. Javier shifted, tried to break loose.

Lemuel twisted him, shook him like a rag doll. Suddenly he was face up in the dirt again.

Lemuel stared down with a fiery rage as his hands continued to squeeze. "Why, Javier?" he raged. "She is The Harlot. She is Evil's Mistress. Her kind must be destroyed. You could have helped me, joined me. WHY?"

Movement out of the corner of his eye as things started to get black. Javier smiled into the face of death. Lemuel had longer arms, but Javier could still rabbit punch him in the ribs, keep his attention focused down here, keep him really angry. Not that that was hard to do. Just stay awake a little longer. *I can do that.*

"Because," Javier said calmly, timing it just like in all the movies he'd ever seen, "because it's wrong."

The remote slammed into the side of Lemuel's head at full speed with a thunderous crack. Javier felt the man go slack as he slid to one side under the tremendous kick. Lemuel flopped over and lay next to him in the dirt.

Unlike Javier, however, he was no longer breathing.

Suvi cursed like a sailor as she ran diagnostics on her flitter-ship. Almost everything was off-line, broken. At least she had rolled to a stop face up, although she could imagine a human would have been puking her guts up flipping that many times in a gravity well.

This was the second ship Javier had cost her. He was going to owe her. Big.

She watched him stagger to his feet, take two steps over to the portable computer and start punching keys.

Whatever he was typing, it had better be good. I'm stuck over here and this thing's nearly broken. You owe me.

Suvi pouted.

Thank you for saving my life.

Oh. Well then, that made it all right.

Suvi smiled.

PART SIX

Javier rapped on the closed door twice. Inside, a muffled "Enter," and the door slid aside. He peeked into the small chamber.

Sykora's cabin was stark and nearly bare. A desk, a tall locker shut tight, a bed. No pictures, no color, no scent, nothing. Stark, bare metal. The only hint of personality to be found was a ball of yarn, knitting needles, and something that might be half of a scarf, balled up next to her on the bed.

She was stretched out in her day uniform, ship slippers on her feet, boots lined up at the foot of the bed. She had been reading something on a portable screen, but she powered it off and set it to one side when she recognized him.

"What is it, Aritza?" she asked. There was still an edge to her voice, but it was more tired and less grumpy than last week.

Javier hoped.

He leaned on the door after it closed, unwilling to enter any deeper into her sanctuary than necessary. Without her riding his ass all the time, he had time to do some research on her past.

Neu Berne society had proved to be quite interesting on further reading. He was already verging on impolite, just by being here in her cabin, uninvited, but didn't want to have this conversation anywhere else on the ship, especially not where anyone could overhear.

Javier took a breath.

He'd come here to talk about nice things. Letting bygones be bygones. Stuff like that.

The speech he had planned already sounded wrong, so he tossed it aside and looked at her. Really looked at her. "I wanted to see how you were doing. Medbot said you got an extra hard dose of the stuff that lunatic tried to poison everyone with."

He watched her bite back something sharp and sarcastic. It left a bilious taste in the air, but went unsaid, so it could be ignored. That was already an improvement, considering Sykora. She took a breath, looked down uncomfortably, fought visibly for the words.

Awkward moments passed.

"I think," she said finally, "that the worst has passed." She breathed. "According to the system, I will continue to have chemically-induced nightmares for several weeks, but I should be cleared for duty tomorrow."

Javier nodded. "That's good. We've missed you on the bridge."

She rewarded him with a bleak, wan smile. "I'm sure, Aritza," she said. "Always a party with you."

Javier bit back his own snark. "Not always. Only when I need to lighten the mood. And you can call me Javier."

She studied him for a second before she continued. "Okay." A pause. "Javier." Another pause. "I've been studying the video of the incident and your report. You knew what he was up to, and didn't stop him until it was almost too late. Why?"

Javier sighed. This was why the door was closed. Suvi had edited out her part in things, and otherwise modified the tape to read like Javier was controlling things.

But she'd left everything else as it had been, including his own compliance.

"Because I wasn't sure I was going to stop him."

He watched an eyebrow go up mutely.

"You people are pirates, lady," he continued. "There was a chance we could declare a medical emergency, suffer a couple of casualties, get the rest to medbay, and go from there. Make the galaxy a better place."

"Casualties," she chewed quietly on the word. "Who did you have in mind?" There were no doubts in her eyes, or her voice.

Javier stared at her for a moment, sighed. There was nothing for it. "You."

She nodded, minutely. For someone from *Neu Berne*, that was roughly the equivalent of Javier jumping up and down on the bed and howling various deprecations at the gods.

They both let the moment pass.

"What made you change your mind, Javier?" Her voice and her eyes were much softer now. Not nearly as hostile and agitated as he was used to from her. *Neu Berne* society. This had gotten to be far more personal than he had planned.

"You said please," he said, finally.

At her look of total confusion, he waved a hand. "I don't mean then," Javier said. "Earlier. Something minor and insignificant, I don't even remember what without looking through the tapes. It doesn't matter. You had gone beyond merely civil and were making an attempt to be nice. That mattered."

The look in her eyes was distant, glacial. *Neu Berne* society.

He watched her study him, really study him. The kind of closeness she hadn't bothered with at any point in the previous several weeks. It made him very uncomfortable, but he'd decided to come here, to do this.

"You could," she whispered, "have done something thirty seconds earlier."

Javier nodded. "Yes. I could have. And I could have also waited thirty seconds and shot him in the back with your gun. I'd like to think I made the right choice."

Javier keyed the door open and slid out as soon as it was wide enough. From outside, he gave her a grim grin that softened into a smile as the door closed. He would probably never again see her with her jaw slack in surprise. It felt good.

THE MIND FIELD

PART THREE
BOOK THREE: MINEFIELD

PART ONE

IT HAD STARTED with a tea mug. The best stories usually did. Javier had learned that over the years. There was just something so prosaic, so utterly mundane, and yet so completely irrational about a good tea mug. Wars had probably been fought because of them.

He had certainly considered it.

He had, however, been willing to compromise. Eventually. By declaring victory.

It had been a hard fought contest.

It would begin as always. Javier would be midway through a cup of really good tea, at just the right temperature and strength, and he would set his mug down. Within moments, as if by magic, it would disappear.

At first, he had suspected pixies. Certainly, they would have accompanied mankind into space. And a pirate ship like *Storm Gauntlet* was almost certain to be completely infested with them. Everybody knew they were irresistibly drawn to pirates.

The truth, when it revealed itself, was even worse.

The pixies had minions.

There were several of them, as a matter of fact, carefully disguised as stewards and yeomen from the ship's mess and Officer's Wardroom.

They stalked Javier, wherever he went, stealing half-empty tea mugs.

After moments of panic induced by lack of caffeine, he would confront one of them.

"Where did my tea go?" he would invariably ask.

Those foul, treacherous minions would look at him, all innocent and things. "Oh, was that your tea, sir? Sorry. Would you like me to get you another?"

It had gone beyond a game with them. It had devolved into a full-scale, multi-front war that threatened to involve the whole crew and bring down the wrath of the Captain and the tea gods.

That is, until Javier visualized victory.

He saw it in a vision, like Galahad dreaming of The Grail. He pursued it secretly, obsessively, fanatically. He made offerings to the tea gods, and any lesser deities with whom he might curry favor. He was absolutely non-denominational in this sort of thing.

Until, finally, he achieved Greatness. Completion. Grailhood.

Javier looked down at his new tea mug and savored the first sips of victory.

Bribes paid to the machinists had yielded a hollow cylinder, slate gray, out of a hull-grade alloy that was a near-perfect insulator of heat and pretty much indestructible with any weapon Javier could hold in one hand. Not that he hadn't considered trying. You know, for science and stuff.

Other bribes had led him to Kianoush, a plain and somewhat average-looking woman who worked for the Purser as a logistics tech during the day, while she pursued visions of art in enamel and silver wire in her private time.

She had been a hard sell, a woman with no particular interests in fresh fruit or beautifully cooked repasts that showed his amazing skill programming a culinary-bot. She was, however, a sucker for a good story, especially one that involved evil pixies and stolen tea mugs. And she was willing to trade her work for good stories and occasional reference answers culled from Javier's many years of solitary space-faring and survey work.

From her, he had procured the artwork. Even a little Strike Corvette like *Storm Gauntlet* had a ship's crest, usually only seen in a small logo painted on the wall in the captain's cabin, as well as on the rarely-worn dress uniforms some of the officers maintained.

They were pirates, after all. Spit and polish was not at the top of the list of things. That was usually eating, followed closely by things with guns. Or maybe it was the other way around.

But she had taken that logo, that artistic heart of this thing that was the *Storm Gauntlet*, and engraved it into that mug, using magic he could not fathom without asking the reference computer, and then filled that etching with real, honest to Creator silver, poured while molten, or dipped. He couldn't remember. One of those. Absolutely.

Above it, a name to strike fear into civilians and pulp writers everywhere. *Storm Gauntlet*. A private-service, free-lance Strike Corvette, retired from *Concord* Fleet service after the Great Wars were over and making ends meet with transportation gigs and occasional strong-arm jobs. Like the piracy that had cost him his own lovely little probe-cutter, *Mielikki*, and turned him, through twists and forays, into an officer aboard her.

Some days, he considered explaining to the crew what the term *janissary* meant, but usually decided it wasn't worth the effort. These people were entirely unliterary, to boot.

But he had his mug. And it had the ship's name and logo. Almost complete victory, since it was most certainly one of a kind, at least until some enterprising engineer with access to a power lathe and a CNC laser decided to start mass-producing them.

And they would.

No, he was already several steps ahead of that unfortunate bastard, whoever he might be. Below the logo, that was where the victory lay.

On one side, also etched and filled with silver, his name in bold, block letters. JAVIER ARITZA. Also a name for the pulp writers to make famous. Someday. Hopefully.

On the other side, that thing that would most certainly defeat the evil pixies and their dread minions. A title that was utterly unique in pirateness. One guaranteed to convey to them that this mug was not empty and abandoned, just waiting for them to take it away and clean when he wasn't looking. No, it was meant to be here, with him, for him. Like a candle in a window on a cold and stormy night, marking the path home.

THE SCIENCE OFFICER.

Plus, it would make a really nice memento, one of these days, when he finally managed to escape this ship and these people, and have them all hung from the highest yardarm he could find.

PART TWO

JAVIER WAS FIRST into the conference room today. He needed time and space to spread out the implements of his tea ceremony on the desk. If others were there, he would have had to elbow people out of the way. Plus, it would have taken forever.

Captain Sokolov was known for fast meetings. Javier could imagine getting his tea perfect just as everyone else left the room. No, far better to have the tea ready, bracing him with warmth and caffeine, as the meeting started. He had, after all, transported those very tea plants from the Homeworld itself into space, and halfway across the damned galaxy.

Just because these pirates had made him a slave and cut up *Mielikki* was no reason to give up tea.

And she was still there, at least in spirit. The entire agricultural section of his little probe-cutter had been removed from her corpse like a plum's pit and stowed forward in *Storm Gauntlet*'s huge cargo bay. He didn't get to eat all the fresh fruit and vegetables himself, anymore, but obviously, he had to sample everything before passing it on the Wardroom. You know, quality control. That included tea leaves. His tea leaves. *The kind I'll cut you over, pal.*

So he took over one whole wing of the conference table and committed theater. And tea.

First, the screen was removed from the travel case and unfolded to mark his territory. Pirates tended to be territorial about their tables. Best to set the rules early.

This one was a bamboo frame with cloth stretched over it. Twenty-four centimeters tall and forty-eight long, it perfectly framed the piece of cloth he put down to keep things from sliding. Also so the cleaning crew stopped complaining about water rings and stains.

The portable brazier stood station in one corner. He powered it up and rested the cast iron pot atop it. Freshly distilled water from his personal stores went into the pot to heat. And heating it this way took forever. That was why he invariably ended up staying late after meetings.

The tea caddy came out of the case next, a lovely little canister he had found on some fringe world that had actually been made of bronze. *Who worked in bronze anymore, when you could mine asteroids for the really exotic shit?*

The whisk, the scoop, the cleaning bowl took their places. Javier lovingly cleaned each piece, just as he had putting them away. You never knew what crew member might get their cooties all over things when he wasn't looking. Especially the pixies.

And now, boiling.

Javier scooped his tea into the big industrial tea mug bearing his awesomeness, added just the right amount of water, and whisked it to textbook froth.

Perfection.

The ceremony felt incomplete without someone to hand it to for appreciation. But he was surrounded by pirates. And Philistines.

"There better not be a candle heating that, Aritza," a voice said behind him. A deep, rich voice, attached to an average-looking man with a shaved head and a salt-and-pepper Vandyke.

Javier looked up at Captain Zakhar Sokolov and sighed dramatically. "Battery-powered, captain," he replied in a sing-song voice. This wasn't the first time they had had this conversation. "Engineering built it for me. I'm no longer allowed to play with fire aboard this ship."

"I'm just afraid you'll hurt yourself, Javier," he smiled evilly, "and then where would my investment in you be?"

Javier fixed him with his best stink-eye, but the Captain was apparently immune.

Two others entered right behind the captain. They took seats well away from Javier, as he had intended. The male, Piet Alferdinck, was the ship's Navigator. All Javier knew about him was that he was a quiet, competent professional, who apparently went back to his cabin when he was off duty and read. Javier had never asked what.

He understood the need to escape people and have private time. His was down in the botany bay, raising plants and tending his chickens. They were still better company than the crew. And they kept pixies at bay, like mirrors that blocked demons at doors.

The female was another story.

Two point one meters tall. Muscles on muscles, in places Javier wasn't even sure he had muscles. Above-average looking. She'd be kinda pretty if she ever smiled. If she even knew how. Bright green eyes and freckles. Brown hair buzzed close on both sides and spiked on top. Javier could see nine earrings in the ear facing him. He knew there were seven more on the other side.

It wasn't that he didn't like the *Storm Gauntlet's* Dragoon. He respected her as a violent professional who wasn't just a sociopath, but an experienced and competent sociopath. It was just that Djamila Sykora always seemed to have it in for him.

Granted, she hadn't bounced him off a bulkhead, intentionally, in at least seven months. Close combat training drills in the gym didn't count.

He still owed her.

Javier wasn't sure if she was going to be the first one up against the wall on that day, or the last.

But he smiled. She had at least made a visible effort not to antagonize him. Much. They were more like teenage siblings, now. He supposed he could live with that. Until the time came.

"Okay, people," the captain announced. "Short meeting and then to work."

Javier smiled. Just as his tea had achieved perfection. He could even leave with them today, although he might take the time to clean everything extra, just so they left first and left him alone.

"Two jumps will put us in our target system," the Captain said, bringing up a holographic projector. A small yellow-red star was off-center, with the big purple dot that represented *Storm Gauntlet* coming in from the other focus of a giant ellipse.

"We will come out of jump, do a quick scan of the area, and then move in towards the second planet." He read off a string of galactic coordinates that would have blown right by most people.

Javier had spent too many years doing survey work. The destination sounded familiar, but he couldn't place it.

"Captain," he said querulously, "does this system have a name?"

Sokolov returned the stink-eye from earlier. He did it better.

Fortunately, Javier was immune as well.

"It does," he said after a moment. "*A'Nacia.*"

Javier knew better than to say the first thing that came to mind, or the first profanity. *Are you insane?* was a given with these folks. That didn't stop him from thinking it. Loudly.

"Uh huh," Javier replied, sucking on his teeth and lower lip. He took a long sip of tea as the other three people in the room turned and stared at him.

"What?" he said finally. They were really starting to mess with his *wa* this morning. Uncool.

"I would have expected more of a reply, Aritza," Sokolov said with his head cocked. "Surely you, of all people, have an opinion. You always do."

Javier scowled sourly back at him, and then shrugged. "If you want to raid a haunted graveyard, there's not a lot I can do at this point to change your mind."

Sykora gave him an especially exasperated look today. She was all spit-and-polish commando bad-ass. In her eyes, Javier was constantly in and out of insubordination. Sometimes, she reminded him of his first ex-wife. The green eyes didn't help.

"Lady," Javier said, forestalling her whole argument, "the captain talked himself into it. He can talk himself out of it. Not like you people ever listen to me, anyway."

She arched an eyebrow at him anyway. It was a lovely eyebrow. She really wasn't that bad looking, if you liked amazons. Javier would still have to be even more drunk than her to consider it.

He sat back and sipped his tea instead.

Sykora turned to the Captain instead. "Haunted, sir?" she asked politely.

"Old sailor's tale, Sykora," the captain replied. "One of the last battles of the Unification Wars was fought over *A'Nacia.* It was a terrible affair. *Pyrrhic.* One of those famous last stands for the last of the holdouts against the *Union of Man.*"

"I see," she said. "*Neu Berne* does not cover that particular event, apparently."

Javier resisted snorting out loud.

Neu Berne had started the next round of warfare after that, the one that led to the breakup of the *Union of Man*, the Great Wars that only ended eighty-some years ago. *Neu Berne, The Union,* and *Balustrade* had all pretty much wiped each other out in the process, leaving the *Concord* as the only large political entity left to pick up the pieces. It had inherited galactic hegemony, almost by accident. At least it was far less of an imperialistic power than the others had been.

"So why do you think it's haunted, Javier?" Piet asked suddenly.

Javier blinked. He had forgotten the man was there, he tended to be so quiet.

"Ships that go there disappear, never to be heard from again," Javier shrugged. "Plus, major battlefield, with something like five separate national fleets destroyed there. Lots of ghosts around."

Javier turned to the Captain. "Why?"

Sokolov put on his Captain face, all the charm that reminded people he was in charge. Serious charisma.

"Because we're better armed than the average raider that goes in there," he began. "We're also going to be really sneaky about this, a lesson I learned from Aritza. And we have a Science Officer who's going to keep the ghosts and bad guys away."

Javier snorted, "I can't even keep pixies at bay."

"I beg your pardon?" Sokolov's whole face turned confused.

"Never mind," Javier replied. Pirates, and Philistines. All of them.

PART THREE

CAPTAIN ZAKHAR SOKOLOV sat quietly in his command chair and drank coffee from his battered tin mug. He had seen Aritza's custom-made cup, and considered having it copied, but thought better of it.

Aritza needed something to make him feel like he had some control over his life. Since being captured nearly a year ago, he had managed to carve out a niche for himself as a member of *Storm Gauntlet's* crew. He was well respected, generally liked, and several people, including his chief ground combat officer, Sykora, owed him their lives.

Zakhar refrained from reminding her of that. Touchy, touchy subject.

But Javier also brought a brightness to the bridge, even if he was mostly a complete goofball. He was a competent goofball when he wanted to be. Right now, he needed to be.

Zakhar was mildly surprised at how well the Science Officer was handling the current operation. He had been expecting a running commentary of rude remarks from that corner of the bridge instead of silence. Perhaps he should turn on a microphone nearby and see if the man was muttering them under his breath. Perhaps later. No good would come of it now.

The Navigator, Piet, called the countdown. "Emergence in fifteen seconds," his voice rang out. This was the only time the man was loud. Other times, he was as quiet as Aritza was loud.

Right now, everybody was quiet. Zakhar wondered if Javier had been telling them ghost stories. It was something he would do.

Storm Gauntlet fell back into real space with a lurch that even the gravplates couldn't forestall. Something about the change in physics between universes occurring faster than the machinery could compensate for.

Zakhar settled himself back in his chair. So far, nobody heaving their guts up into a handy trashcan. It happened occasionally, more inner ear and psychology than bio-medical.

"Navigation," Zakhar called regally, "bring the engines on line and ahead slow."

"Belay that order," Javier snarled from his station.

Zakhar jumped as far out of his seat as his belt would allow.

"Nobody do nothin'," Javier continued savagely.

"Aritza," Sokolov barked, "explain yourself. This is my bridge."

"Yes, is it," Javier agreed without looking up from his console screen. One hand snaked out and touched a blue light flashing madly on his console. "And somebody out there just lit us up with a nice, solid weapon lock."

"Have they challenged us?" Zakhar asked, much less angry.

"Not yet," Javier replied. "Or rather, if they have, it wasn't on any of the standard channels."

"Where would it be?" asked the Gunner. Her hands were poised on her controls, but she was waiting patiently.

Javier looked over, fixed her dark eyes with one beady eye of his own. "Whatever you do, Mary-Elizabeth Suzuki, do not deploy turrets or open a launch bay," he said, deadly serious.

Zakhar was surprised. He didn't think Javier did deadly serious.

This must be really bad.

"All hands," Zakhar said, reinforcing the point and letting the bridge computer transmit the message ship-wide, "stand down. We have a situation outside the ship we are investigating."

He closed the channel and looked as his Science Officer. It already felt like one of those days where he was going to owe the man big again. How would they keep him aboard once he paid off his debts and was free?

"Javier," he asked, "what's your theory?"

Javier looked both ways, as if double-checking that nobody was about to do anything. He started to say something when a sudden chime on his console got his attention.

Zakhar felt the emotional lurch as Javier turned back to his screens instead of speaking. The whole bridge seemed to sag, waiting.

He watched Javier pull an earpiece and stick it in. The man listened for a few moments, shook his head, and muttered something under his breath so profane even Sokolov blinked.

"I found their transmission," Javier announced. "It's in Bulgarian, down on one of the lower, older channels hardly anybody uses anymore. That's the good news."

"What's the bad news?" Zakhar asked conversationally.

"It's an automated sentry challenge," he replied.

Zakhar used the same word Javier just had.

Mary-Elizabeth cocked her head at the two men. "Could you two explain that for the mere mortals around here?" she asked with a sarcastic edge that sounded remarkably like what Javier would have used. Obviously, the man was rubbing off on her. The professionalism would be good, but not the attitude problem.

Javier turned to Zakhar and raised an eyebrow.

"You found it, Javier," the Captain said. "You explain it. Do we know if it works?"

"No," Javier blew out a breath. "The only way to know that is when it fires, or fails to. I could live the rest of my days without knowing, thank you."

"Talk, mister," Mary-Elizabeth barked. "I'm getting tired of you yammering. Gimme data."

"Yeah, yeah. Fine."

Javier pushed a button on his console and the main screen suddenly showed a schematic of the local area. *Storm Gauntlet's* purple star sat in the middle, surrounded by other stars of various colors.

"We just jumped into a live minefield," he announced sourly. "I am beginning to map things based on their own signals, while not generating any of our own. Fortunately, we came in dark. The minefield is intelligent, but not fully sentient. It isn't sure if we're a newly arrived asteroid that just wandered into range, or an enemy starship it should kill. On channel 392, it is asking us for the correct authentication code to safely transit the kill zone."

Zakhar watched him pick up his mug and empty it in one go. It was going to be that kind of day.

"Why would sentience be bad, Javier?" Mary-Elizabeth asked.

"Because it would probably just shoot us anyway, Suzuki," Zakhar answered before Javier could.

"Oh," she said quietly. "Can it kill us?"

"Shields were down for the jump," Javier said. "Powering them up most assuredly triggers something, somewhere. There were dreadnaughts at the battle of *A'Nacia*, so there are probably guns big enough here to gig us like a frog."

"Gig?" someone asked from over near the engineering seats.

"The term our Science Officer is looking for is *splatter*," Zakhar replied. "That's a much more accurate, technical term. Boom."

"Recommendation, Captain?" Javier asked politely.

This day was turning into an absolute surprise as other sides of Aritza's behavior came out for the first time.

"Go ahead," Zakhar replied. Internally, he noted how much the two of them sounded like old *Concord* Fleet officers, which they were. The piracy veneer apparently wasn't that deep, after all.

"Can we start shutting down systems? Turn the air temp down so we have longer before we have to dump heat? Power off things that might accidentally generate a signal outside the ship? That sort of thing?"

Zakhar considered it. All things that made sense, since nobody knew what might trigger a lethal surprise. They might not know until it killed them, and then only for a few seconds.

"Agreed," he said. He keyed the general comm live. "Engineering, Bridge. We're going to start powering down some systems to run quieter. Please coordinate with the Science Officer. And tell people to dress warm."

"Yes, Captain," came the polite, diffident voice of Andreea Dalca, the Engineer.

Zakhar looked around the bridge. Command decision time. "Everybody shut down your stations and drop down to emergency crew only. The rest of you are still on duty, so go do paperwork or something."

Zakhar counted ten seconds until the only people on the bridge were himself, Aritza, and Sykora, the Dragoon. He didn't say anything to her. She was going to stay and keep a watch on everything the Science Officer did. At least she had stopped wearing a sidearm on the bridge. Most of the time.

The room went dim as Aritza brought the lights lower. Conserving power now meant conserving heat. He was going to need to grab a jacket out of his day cabin in a bit, but he had enough layers for now.

"Okay, hotshot," Zakhar said to the back of Aritza's head, "how do we get out of this one?"

"I promise you, Captain," Javier turned to look at him, "you will be the second one to know."

PART FOUR

DJAMILA WAS USED to complex multi-tasking. It was practically a requirement to be successful at what she did.

She could, for example, track two different moving targets and fire accurately at both, pistols in both hands and one eyeball following each. She was capable of zero-gravity maneuvers that had earned her the nickname *Ballerina of Death* from her teammates, back in her days with the *Neu Berne* Navy.

Right now, she was flexing individual muscles in her legs to keep them warm and loose, while she sat quietly at a dark console on the bridge and knitted. It gave the hands something to do while the legs worked. The mind was watching Javier Aritza, their much-vaunted Science Officer with his custom coffee cup, pace around a three dimensional projection of the local environment.

When asked, he had explained that pacing made him look at things from different angles in a way that just spinning the projection around didn't do. She could respect that. It was one of the few times the man was a proper professional. Now, if only he could be like that more often, she might actually like him. Hell might freeze over first, but that wasn't her problem.

She looked down as her hands auto-piloted their way to the row marker. The project was well on its way to being a sweater at some point. Much sooner than she had expected if they were going to spend many more hours drifting and tumbling slowly. Pretty soon she would have to break it off as she got to the bottom of the sleeve holes. But not for a while.

As she started on the next row around, she looked more closely at the projection. Djamila wasn't nearly as capable with the sensors as Aritza, but she understood enough to ask competent questions. And he had apparently appreciated trying to explain things to her, because he would get into the middle of a sentence and suddenly break off to go type furiously for several seconds before talking again.

The projection was starting to take shape. Different color stars appeared, strengthened, sharpened.

Apparently, minefields in space were like defensive fortifications on the ground. And she was an expert at those. Defense in depth. Overlapping fields of fire. Enfilade. Variety in range engagements. Lateral support. Stealth. Guile. Ambush.

It took patience to unravel, unlike the soon-to-be sweater in her hands. Watching Javier work reminded her of advanced tactical exercises she had run. Understand the terrain. Understand your enemy's plans for you and his tendencies. Find the weak spot he designed into the system as a honey trap to draw you in and kill you. Unravel the design until you found the hole he missed.

It had been four hours. She had watched Aritza like a hawk. Not because she expected him to actually commit suicide, he was too vibrant to just die so easily, but because she wanted to see him actually sweat. The man was far too lackadaisical.

Plus, he wanted to make sure they all went to jail, or the hangman.

Everyone else had forgotten that, but she occasionally still saw that look in his eyes. Usually when he was looking at her. That desire. That hunger. That hatred. It made her warm and tingly.

Besides, she smiled to herself as she worked, having a good enemy made you better. It made you keep upping your game, in a complex arms race to see who could win, especially two well-matched opponents.

So she studied him. Learned his traits and his tendencies. Watched him work so she knew his weaknesses, even as he worked to understand the long-dead designer of the trap they had entered.

You never knew when information like that would be useful.

From Javier's explanation, the minefield was a hive mind. There was no single controller they could kill to escape. Instead, a small part of the overall intelligence was in each little metal body floating around. It thought slowly, as a result. Patiently. Like a trapdoor spider. Waiting.

She understood that sort of patience.

Around them, dozens of killers floated. Big guns. Little guns. Armoured pods. Things to kill dreadnaughts. Things to kill shuttles. Every one of them powered by the solar wind and designed to last forever. It had been five and a half centuries, so far.

She had looked up the battle. *Pyrrhic* failed to cover the consequences.

Five fleets had all been functionally destroyed. But that was enough for *New London* to win the war and proclaim the *Union of Mankind* to a war-weary galaxy. The last significant challenger to their dream of a universal government had died on the planet below when someone had lost control of a terminally-damaged dreadnaught and it had plunged into the atmosphere, exploding only a few tens of thousands of meters above the ground, over the capital city of an entire Pocket Empire.

According to Aritza, the crater was apparently still visible from orbit, a bullet wound just rising into view below them in the near distance, beyond the minefield, inside the shell of death and destruction the war had left.

Afterward, there had been nobody to turn off the mines. Or the minefield had been laid by the victors as a way of salting the earth. Nobody knew the truth. It only mattered now because they were trapped in it, a small fly stuck in fresh sap, waiting for it to harden into amber. Or trapped in a web, waiting for the spider.

PART FIVE

JAVIER HAD FINALLY FOUND someone to dislike more than the amazon, Sykora. It had been a difficult thing. After all, the minefield designer had never given him a concussion, or worked him into utter exhaustion fixing bio-scrubbers, or any of the other things Sykora had done since they had first met, the first time she had shot him.

But the person who designed the defenses around *A'Nacia*? Here was a prime candidate for his considerable hatred.

Five hundred and fifty years had passed, more or less. The system this designer had built was still intact enough to threaten them. Javier had no doubt that the weapons were fully charged and just waiting to fire. He had sat here and watched the little battle-bots push themselves around with little pulses of energy, so he knew that most of them were working.

At least four different satellites were locked onto *Storm Gauntlet* with cannons of some sort at this moment. Certainly the weapons pointed this direction were things the hivemind that was controlling the field thought were hot enough to crush this ship if she turned out to be an enemy ship and not a rock floating around.

Javier wasn't sure the system wouldn't fire on rocks either. Eventually.

He would have programmed in that behavior.

He had, however, begun to solve the design of the system, sitting here and passively listening. Each satellite in the net broadcast an ID and a location on a regular basis, roughly every second, so the rest knew where each other was and what it was doing.

He had a catalog going. The forty-six closest ones, mapped and classified roughly into ship-killers, shuttle-killers, and scanners that just sat and watched. Some he had no clue what they did.

Their cryptography was weak, but still too strong for him to crack in anything less than a month, even with the navigation computer brute-forcing the signal.

And there were just too many of them out there for Mary-Elizabeth to take out in one salvo. He didn't trust that the shields would come up fast enough to help, or be strong enough to hold out. Someone had planned for dreadnaughts. That meant big guns.

Javier considered the ship's stealth cloak, but that just made it hard to scan them, not invisible. In fact, it had probably been what kept them alive, since they didn't scan like a starship to the stupid brain running things over there.

As soon as they did anything to change that conclusion, they would get boomed. And he was far too beautiful to die like this.

That's what he kept telling himself.

He looked down at his favorite tea mug and decided it had been empty long enough. And he was hungry. And *she* had been staring holes in the back of his head long enough.

Javier pushed a button to save all his notes and stood up.

"You're in charge," he said as he walked to the door.

"Where are you going?" she said, startled.

It felt good to throw her off balance every once in a while. She was just too damned smug, most of the time. Right now, she was furiously packing yarn and stabby things into a small cloth bag and trying to stand as he went past.

"Lunch," he replied, biting off the other replies that were rude, or snarky, or just obnoxious. Not today. He was too tired.

"Wait," she said, abruptly, "I'll come with you."

Javier actually stopped and looked back at her as the hatch slid open, holding his surprise in.

"You have the deck," he said, cruelly, as he stepped backwards and let it close on her surprised face.

JAVIER HAD GOTTEN food from the buffet line and an industrially-manufactured tea-substitute by the time she tracked him down in the main wardroom. Today it was something vaguely approximating previously-frozen burritos and what could charitably be called red rice, heavy on the vitamins and nutrients, light on taste.

He looked up as she walked up, just short of stomping.

"You aren't supposed to just walk off the bridge," she said firmly, professionally, scoldingly.

"What?" he smiled innocently, "you mean I should turn over operational control to another Centurion or qualified yeoman?

She wasn't standing close enough that he could actually hear her teeth grind, but the imaginary image in his head was close enough. He smiled up at her. Way up. Sitting, he was just about looking at her belt buckle.

She didn't respond, but instead slid the chair across from him back and practically threw herself into it.

"What have you learned?" she began the interrogation.

Javier carefully chewed the first bite of his burrito forty-two times, just like his mother had told him to do when he was a kid.

She was gnashing her teeth by thirty-four.

Javier swallowed, set the wrap down, and took a careful drink of the tea, slow to savor the industrial goodness that came of chemicals instead of dried plant leaves that he grew down in his botany hideout.

"Well?" she continued.

"The burritos aren't half bad," he said slowly, "but the tea just doesn't have it today. I would recommend the coffee."

"I meant about the minefield," she replied with a growl, exasperation filling her voice.

"It hasn't killed us yet," Javier said and stuffed another bite of meat-substitute-and-bean-thing into his mouth.

Chew. Chew. Chew.

"So you're no closer to solving the puzzle than before?" she sneered.

"Oh, I know lots of ways to solve it," he replied, eventually. "Most of them end up with us dead."

"Most?"

There was a really strange look in her eyes. One that might have been mistaken for hope, but that assumed that little miss invulnerable amazon giant had the least doubts in her ability to survive this particular situation. Especially when she had to count on Javier to save her.

Probably she just had gas.

"The rest are so completely insane that the Captain would never go for it."

"How do you know until you ask him?" she asked with a smile. Upbeat rationality from her was a new thing. Probably a trick, like telling him to look over his shoulder right before she slugged him in the jaw. Again.

"I'm trying to eat here, lady," he responded, somewhere between a surly growl and an exasperated sigh. It was where she left him, most days.

"You eat, Javier," she said with a smile. "I'll go get the Captain and you can explain it to him.

Javier? Really? Her?

He watched her start to slide her chair back, stop, and stare fixedly over his shoulder.

"Never mind," she said suddenly. "He's already here. You can explain it to him."

"Not falling for that trick," Javier said, stuffing another bite of burrito into his mouth.

"What?" She looked confused. Apparently hadn't had nearly enough caffeine today, or something. She sounded almost human.

He chewed, staring intently at her while he waited for a fist to appear.

"What do we know, mister?"

The Captain was suddenly beside him. Standing there. Really there. It was probably still a trick. Javier watched Sykora like a hawk. And chewed forty-two times. These people just did not understand good digestion.

A tap on the shoulder.

Crap.

Javier looked up, braced to be punched. Chewed. Made a face that boiled all the frustration of the last five hours into a single expression. Modern art. Sort of. Something. He was trying to eat here.

The Captain took a hint and sat down beside him. One of the evil Wardroom minions appeared with fresh coffee. *Why couldn't he get that kind of service?*

He ruminated on his burrito.

Oh, what the hell.

Javier smiled beatifically at the Captain. Go big or go home. Or maybe it should be *Go stupid or go home.* Because this was right up there with the dumbest things he had ever done. At least he was less likely to end up getting shot at or married. Again. Hopefully.

He took a sip of the tea-impersonator and set his mug down.

The whole room seemed to have gone quiet, like everyone was holding their breath waiting for his next words. Yup. Gonna get stupid. Might as well do it right.

"It's like this," he began. Swear to God that everyone leaned a little closer. It was almost like a scene out of a movie. Weird.

"The minefield isn't sure if we're a big rock or a stealthy starship," he continued, a little louder for the guy in the serving line who was leaning in. "As long as we sit here quiet, it probably won't shoot."

Javier looked around, faces were all turning slowly this way. He suppressed a giggle.

"However, if we do anything at all, we might set it off. Sensors. Shields. Engines. Even powering up the jump drive is likely to be enough."

"Understood. What are our options, Aritza?" Sokolov had that whole Captain Badass thing going today. It was impressive to watch.

"I thought about playing games with the gyros to see if we could drift out of range. We could, but it would take about three months if everything went right. Zero margin for error for that long. Unhappy option."

He sipped some more tea. The evil minions brought the Captain more coffee, and ignored him. He scored it a draw.

"Instead, I started looking at the mines themselves. Big, dumb things. Couple of maneuvering pulse jets, banks of solar panels to keep the batteries at maximum charge. Some kind of gun. Either a multi-barrel pulsar, a big-bore cannon, or an Ion pulsar, depending. Enough to gut us like a fish, even with shields up."

"Encrypted?" the Captain asked. Good, solid *Concord* Navy veteran. If you can't kick the door in, pick the locks.

"Good enough. We might crack the code in 30-45 days, if we're lucky. Got a better idea."

"Oh?" The Captain had sense enough to look dubious. Javier's good ideas always tended to be *interesting*.

"Yup. Each mine rotates through a basic signal sequence. Eight and a repeat. Each beep, it also includes a simple x, y, z coordinate, zeroed on the old capital city on the planet's surface. I have no idea what each mine is saying, but it says them in the same pattern. We can use that."

"How?" the Captain looked somewhat askance at him. Smart guy. Waiting for the other shoe.

"We kill one of the nearby mines right after it sends a ping, and start broadcasting the same thing a second later. The hive mind controlling the field falls for it, ignores us, and we can use maneuvering pulses to back out of the field far enough to escape."

"You just said that powering up one of the pulsar turrets was likely to set things off," Sykora said, showing she was paying attention.

"Yup," Javier replied. "Someone will have to go over there with a limpet mine and blow the thing up manually."

"You?" she sneered audaciously.

"Oh, absolutely not," he smiled back. "Well beyond my capabilities. No, we need an expert in EVA and explosives. Somebody crazy. Somebody like the *Ballerina of Death*."

Yeah. That look right there. Smoldering hatred. If looks could kill. Vitriol, distilled down to an aperitif and served with cheese and crackers. That look on her face almost made everything else worth it today.

Javier took another bite of his burrito.

PART SIX

Djamila had insisted Aritza accompany her here, at least as far as the landing bay. It was his brilliant idea that was going to save them, after all, wasn't it? Didn't he want to see it executed right?

The grumbles she got from him were reward enough. If he hadn't put her on the spot like that, she probably would have insisted she handle the task anyway. Nobody else on this ship was nearly as good at this sort of EVA work as she was. Period.

The bay looked strange. Aritza's scheme involved erecting a wall of spare metal plates across part of the bay, a meter back from the inner edge of the hatch.

"*So that the scanners over there don't notice a sudden change in our shape and assume we're about to open fire,*" had been his explanation.

It sounded reasonable. At least as much as anything else coming out of his mouth ever did. As did cranking the door open manually so no power emanations leaked out and triggered a hostile response.

She completed a pre-flight checklist on her suit.

By the numbers. Careful numbers. She had had to leave her radio behind so she didn't accidentally signal anything to the killer mines that would be watching her as she separated from the ship. That would be a quick death.

Instead, one of her people was down here, familiar with the language of hand signals and in charge of her belayed line. There was no way in hell she was going to trust Aritza with that. But she wanted him with down here, uncomfortable, radio-less, forced to talk to himself while they waited to see if she lived or died out there.

He would have a front seat row. That little shit better appreciate it. Especially if he got her killed.

She leaned down to touch faceplates with her assistant. He was ready.

Javier next. He double-checked the electromagnetic box attached to her belt, gave her the thumbs up. She touched plates with him for any last minute instructions before total radio silence.

"Good luck, Sykora," he said simply.

He even looked serious. Awkward, but serious.

"You can't get rid of me that easily," she replied. It felt like a tease coming out of her mouth, even though she intended to make it a sneer. Too late to say something extra.

She saw his nod through the faceplates, followed by a frog-faced grin. So at least he was thinking the same thoughts she was.

Good enough.

She turned, and faced eternity.

A'Nacia was somewhere below the curve of the hull, off to her left.

In her immediate field of view, several bright points of light that represented killer satellite mines. Only one of them was close enough have definition. Javier's target.

It had taken several hours of fine manipulation of the ship's gyroscopes, a tweak here, a surge there, but they had actually brought *Storm Gauntlet* to rest, relative to their target. Not close enough to make the system nervous, but enough that she had a fixed target from which to launch.

Her victim was just a little larger than one of the ship's landing shuttles, a little more than half a kilometer away. And she wasn't allowed to use maneuvering thrusters at all. It would be as pure a dive as she had taken since training, when they held emergency EVA drills and got scored on accuracy jumping across a gap half this size in nothing but a Skinsuit. While under fire.

Here she had her regular armored EVA suit, and a long hunk of line attached to an ankle in case she missed and they had to pull her back. And for when she succeeded and wanted to come home.

She fixed her target in her mind and pushed back against the plate inside the door. Others would probably have turned off the local gravplates and pushed off headfirst. That was a mistake. It went against everything they had trained for, and would throw off their aim.

She was going to take two steps and use the edge of the door as her final push-off point. Speed wasn't the issue here. Accuracy was. In raw space, you followed Newton, regardless of the rules that an interstellar starship violated along the way.

She looked around once, confirmed the rope, the assistant, the Science Officer.

Deep breath for extra oxygen.

Go.

First step. Second Step.

Darkness.

Free flight.

As pure as one could get outside of an atmosphere.

There.

Target acquired.

Coming in slowly, as planned. Others would have jumped too hard, and come onto their target so fast they bounced off before hand and foot magnets could grip.

Damn it.

She was going to miss a little high and a shade right. After setting a new *Neu Berne* record for accuracy at this sort of range.

It would be just far enough away that she would not land on it first shot.

Not having a radio was good. She could give voice to all the profanities she usually just howled in her head at such failures. Space didn't care. It couldn't listen.

Okay. Better idea.

She signaled her assistant to shorten his lead significantly.

She continued to fall. The nearest edge of the machine passed three meters to her left, just below her.

She braced as the line bit.

There.

Pendulum.

Djamila jack-knifed her upper and lower body together quickly, then relaxed. She reached the end of the rope and snapped down and left. She had missed, but only a little and not so much that they had to draw her all the way back in and send her out again.

The image of Javier as a fly-fisher nearly made her lose her concentration. It was a very good thing that in space, nobody could hear you giggle.

Instead, the line touched the side of the satellite and provided a fulcrum point. She swung slowly around the back of the mine, letting the line snug down and pull her in, like an ice-skater pulling her hands in as she twirled.

Contact.

Ferric hull. Generally smooth. Sensor bulbs there, there, and there. Maneuvering pulse thrusters on six points each, at both ends of a smooth cylinder some eight meters diameter and twenty meters long. Ship killer.

She looked around carefully. This was where they ran out of script. Had the designer anticipated this stunt and put a point-defense system in place to clear boarders? It suggested a level of paranoia and sadism well beyond anything else he had done so far, but who could ask someone dead for five hundred years?

Nothing moved. So far, so good.

Djamila detached the limpet mine from her waist and rested it against the hull of the satellite. Low-level magnets would hold it in place enough for her to work.

Stop. Look around quickly, and then slowly.

Nothing jumped out and shot her. Or bit her.

Good enough.

She armed the primary magnets and set the timer to ten seconds. It would be close, but not that close, unless her number was absolutely up.

Quick look around. Nothing sneaking up on her.

Flip the big red switch. Armed.

Push the button.

Run like hell.

This time, she just aimed in the direction of *Storm Gauntlet*. Distance counted way more than accuracy. She needed to be gone fast. If it worked, she was still attached to the ship. They could reel her in like a trout.

Again. Javier as a fly-fisher. She continued to giggle at the image.

Flash of light bright enough to cast her shadow on *Storm Gauntlet*'s hull.

In an atmosphere, something that big would have deafened her for days. And possibly pulped her with over-pressure shock waves.

Another advantage of space.

Storm Gauntlet's hull grew into a wall in front of her. She twisted and jack-knifed until legs were down and she was almost falling. Style counted here, at least with her people.

If you are going to demand excellence, prepare to give it.

She could still see the sign over the exit from the Senior Midshipman's Dorm at the *Neu Berne* Academy. Words to live by. And live well.

She landed like a cat, bounced slightly, put a hand down. But only one. Close enough to stick the landing and get full score from the judges, not that there were any, outside her head. Any that counted.

Djamila detached the safety line from her ankle and cast it back into space. They could reel it in much faster without her attached. She clomped her way along the outside, returning to the bay.

Mission very much accomplished, thank you.

Javier was there when she arrived.

She couldn't resist touching faceplates with him. "So, Mister Science Officer," she asked with a saucy tune, "was that adequate to your needs?"

He looked up at her far more seriously than she had expected. "That was the most amazing piece of free sailing I have ever seen."

Wait? Him? Impressed? Publically?

Crap.

PART SEVEN

JAVIER WAS JUST happy to be out of that damned suit. They had kept his when the killed his ship and took him prisoner, so it fit. That didn't mean he enjoyed it. Nope. Stale, industrial air. Metallic water. Claustrophobia.

Storm Gauntlet's air had gotten so much better since he had been put in charge of keeping the bio-scrubbers tuned, but it was still a pale shadow compared to what he had gotten to breathe on *Mielikki*. Even down in his botany station, it was only a faint reminder. The chickens helped.

Still, the amazon had been successful. If all went as planned, the Captain had flickered the ship's transponders at the right moment and they were now officially part of the minefield, beeping every second and updating everyone as they moved.

And they weren't dead.

Javier pulled on his leggings, tunic, and the extra jacket he had been wearing. It was still cold in the ship.

Of course Sykora was waiting for him when he emerged from his equipment locker. Probably tapping her foot theatrically too, though he hadn't paid that close of attention. He trailed her to the bridge. This was the only view of her he liked, anyway.

"Well done, you two," the Captain announced as they arrived. The air was warmer here, so he had apparently felt safe enough to bring some of the systems on line. That would be good.

Javier was tired of wearing gloves while he worked. Shoes were already too much of a hassle. Hell, some days pants was asking too much.

Still, the Captain was giving them both credit. That would be good for some bribes from the crew. Markers against future need. You know. Stuff.

Javier moved to his station and powered it up fully. The big projection hung in the middle of the room, still.

It didn't look right.

He looked closer.

That was because they were moving deeper into the minefield, not backing gracefully out of range so they could escape.

"Captain," he said wearily. "Are we really going in there anyway?"

Sokolov smiled evilly at him. "You don't think I'd come this far and just walk away, do you? Get to work, Science Officer. There's a whole planet down there for you to survey."

Javier grumbled mostly under his breath as he brought systems live. They still couldn't send out any really good pings from the sensor suite, at least until they got safely inside the shell, but he could start the analysis.

These people were going to be the death of him.

He looked up and encompassed the whole bridge, especially that smiling amazon, in a disgusted frown.

Pirates and Philistines.

PART FOUR

BOOK FOUR: PRISONER OF WAR

PART ONE

JAVIER'S TEA WAS COLD. Not that he was going to get up to get more. And the wardroom minions couldn't brew it right anyway. And if he drank any more, he'd have to go pee.

Plus, they were just about clear of the minefield, so now all the interesting parts would begin, knowing his luck. Because Heaven forbid these people do anything quiet and boring, ya know.

At least he could hammer the neighborhood with the occasional hard ping to see what was going on. The machines around him were dumb enough to think that was a targeting pulse. Sitting blind in the middle of a minefield had utterly sucked.

So, theoretically inhabitable planet below. Had been inhabited once, until a bright fall day in August Standard, five hundred and eighty-three years ago. Nobody had visited since. Or, if they had, nobody had escaped.

Boring looking planet. About half water and half land, randomly arranged by whatever the gods of chance and plate tectonics had found most pleasing recently.

Javier wondered about tsunamis down on the surface, considering the vast amount of extremely large junk in orbit that was likely to fall eventually. Five fleets' worth of warships, plus every raider, scavenger, and pirate, save one, that had tried their luck over the centuries. Gravity was an unforgiving mistress and there was a lot of water to hit.

From here, the wound gouged in the face of the western hemisphere would rise in about thirty minutes. There had been a planetary capital there. Before. Ought to be able to pick up any radiation in a little bit, if there was anything significant. There weren't even lights down there on the dark side, so either the entire population had died, or just their technology.

Javier watched his screens as his data banks slowly filled with interesting tidbits.

He turned to the Captain as he considered taking the time to pee.

"What are we looking for here, anyway?" he asked, in his ten-year-old backseat-whining voice. He was good at that one.

Captain Sokolov barely glanced over as he watched the screen. "Money."

Okay. Yeah. The obvious answer. Translation: I have no clue what's here, we'll steal everything not nailed down, or anything that we can pry up.

Pirates and Philistines.

Still, it beat being dead. Or working as an agricultural slave on some forgotten, misbegotten backwater. At least the pirates had a sense of humor.

Centurion Djamila Sykora, Ship's Dragoon, walked in.

Most of them.

PART TWO

ZAKHAR HAD LEARNED to watch what was going on in Aritza's head by the way his hands moved when he typed things on the console. Usually, it was a lazy, one-handed motion, two fingers and a thumb roaming the whole face to find keys and buttons.

When he got excited, or nervous, he used both hands, striking with precision and all ten fingers. *Concord* Fleet Academy training. When Sykora was around, back to one hand, slowly banging things out, like he was driving nails with his fingers.

If they both weren't so good, and, more importantly, so professional about it, he would have had to physically separate them a while ago. As it was, she was generally on his left and stayed away from the Science Officer on the right, with most of the width of the bridge between them.

Not that it would do him any good. Zakhar had seen how fast Djamila could move when she wanted to.

So Zakhar watched the Science Officer's whole outlook change, just in the set of his hands, when she walked in. He doubted that anybody on this ship, excepting possibly Aritza, would even recognize a reference to Pavlov, but he couldn't help himself. It was like a bell rang.

On the big projection, he watched the real time face of the planet slowly turn. They had already done something nobody had ever done. At least, that anybody had ever mentioned. If they could sneak in and out of here, he might have to bring back a bigger ship, maybe one of those monster cargo carriers, all hollow box, and see how much loot they could steal.

The old ships weren't going to be worth much as salvage after this long, but there would be logs, and sentimental value in things like personal effects and ship's crests, vintage fighters left alone on abandoned docks, etc. That would be worth something to collectors, especially since he had the market cornered.

Hell, Javier might make enough off his Centurion's share to buy his freedom, if it went really well. Maybe he could actually hire the man. He certainly wasn't about to just give back the trees, Javier would have to buy them. *Tell him that later.*

And then Javier's back flexed. Zakhar couldn't think of a better term to describe it. If he had been a cat, it would have been that moment when they arch their back and puff all the fur out.

It had that same feel to it.

He considered saying something, but he was afraid Aritza would realize that he was being watched so closely and clam up more. It wasn't as though he wasn't liked and respected. Javier was just a loose cannon on a pitching deck. A good Captain paid attention.

The profanity, only sort of quietly muttered over there, got attention from more people than just him. Several heads turned.

Javier repeated the word. Louder this time. He still hadn't looked up from his screens.

Zakhar watched Javier's head come up so that he was staring at the bulkhead beyond his station. Then it cocked to one side. Then it bent back down. Looking at the screen.

Javier repeated the word a third time, this one more of an incredulous whisper.

It was amazing how much of a conversation you could have, inflecting a single profanity different ways.

Javier turned, realized he had an entire audience.

"Captain," he said mildly, "you won't believe this..."

Zakhar agreed internally. Little that happened on this ship, especially when either of those two was involved, was believable to outsiders. And sometimes to crew.

He fixed Javier with his Command Eye. It made him feel like an evil wizard, eyeing his realm. And it usually worked, on the rest of the crew.

"Mister?" he replied, aloof, supernatural. *The Captain.*

"So *A'Nacia* has a single moon," the Science Officer began, pitching his voice into storytelling mode.

That was never a good sign with Aritza.

"I'm aware of that," Zakhar continued. Easier to just let Javier run.

"It's not as big as the homeworld's is, but it is still significant," Javier kept up his patter. "And because it is there, there are LaGrange points. Nice, happy little pockets in the gravity web where something will stay put after you leave it."

"Navigation 101, Aritza," Sykora called from across the way. She was apparently feeling feisty today.

"And as a rule," he continued, ignoring the *agent provocateur*, "I scan those as soon as possible, looking for things other people thought might be interesting enough to park there."

"Go on," Zakhar said. Javier had his own pace for this sort of thing.

"Most of the ships out here are just pieces or shells. Nothing that looks really valuable until we board some of them and take inventory. However, there is something interesting in the trailing LaGrange point."

"Define interesting," Zakhar's bad feeling had nothing to do with horror movie results. Javier was too much a sarcastic jokester.

Javier's smile probably would have chilled a lesser Captain to the core. He kept expecting the man to crack his knuckles ominously.

"Well, sir," Javier's smile grew, "there's a ship over there. It's an older model, but even the design is a century *later* than the battle that was fought here. After the minefield."

"So somebody else did the same thing we did and got here earlier. And?" Zakhar felt like the straight man here, but anything else would just slow it down. Nothing was dangerous or shooting at them, or Javier would have been acting more professional.

"It has power," Javier said simply.

"Oh."

There really wasn't much more to say at that point.

PART THREE

"ONE OF THESE DAYS," Javier ranted gloomily, "I'm going to learn to keep my big mouth shut."

"Ooh, can I sell tickets to that?" Sykora smiled down at him sweetly. "I'd be rich."

That woman had a knack. She just seemed to know instinctively where all his buttons were, and how far she could push them without making him do something about it.

He decided to talk to her boobs instead of her face. Craning his head back got old, anyway.

"For you, maybe never," he said. "What would we do if you retired?"

"You'd do something stupid and get yourself dead inside a week," she added a layer of sugar on top.

"Children," Captain Sokolov said. Quiet. Firm. Commanding.

Javier refused to listen to that part of his lizard-brain that had been trained to salute even when he was dead asleep or falling down drunk. Bad precedent. The man might come to expect it. Then where would they be?

They were, right the moment, back down in the loading bay, waiting for the engineering crew to finish extending the boarding tunnel, mate it, and override the airlock on the other side so they could board. It felt like they were getting ready for a picnic. Kind of looked like it, too.

Captain Sokolov was there to see them off. Sykora had a smaller-than-normal group of her killers, armed for invading small planets. Javier's occasional assistant and sometimes minder from engineering, Machinist's Mate Ilan Yu, was present.

Sykora's two pathfinders for planetary work were also there: Sasha: the short brunette with the nice hips, and Hajna: the skinny blond with the long legs. Nice girls. Cut-throat card sharps.

Javier took inventory. Since they were expecting power, heat, and hopefully air over there, at least after some repairs, everyone was only wearing skinsuits today instead of the big armoured suits like Sykora had used to kill the mine.

To various loops and belts Javier had attached bits and pieces he had rifled from his planet-side gear. The little bag with low tech stuff like a magnetic compass (currently useless), matches (no scrub to burn), paper and pencil (good for mapping), a small metal knife (it didn't vibrate, or have a laser edge, or collapsed monomolecular edge, or anything cool), and his handy little hiking trinket that combined a very cheap magnetic compass, a thermometer, and the symbols you should make in the dirt in an emergency.

The only thing high-tech he was taking was Suvi.

Externally, she looked like a small gray grapefruit, covered with knobs and things. Externally, she was just his short-range autonomous sensor remote, with an extra surprise. When the pirates had taken his ship, *Mielikki*, he had managed to smuggle out the AI who ran it, and pour her into the remote. And kept her his little secret ever since.

Since then, he had upgraded her electronics about as far as he could without people asking suspicious questions. She didn't have her original memory core, but all of her personality could fit now and she had pretty much all of her log files and enough books to keep her busy for a few years at least.

He looked around to make sure he had space and then tossed her into the air as he pulled out the matching portable computer. It would take her about thirty seconds to re-baseline the bay in visual, ultrasound, radar, and infrared, with a stack of dials and gauges giving him various readings on people and equipment.

There had been enough time to upload what he knew about the ship over there, plus some of the mission parameters, so she was at least as prepared as the rest of them. And probably smarter.

The engineering crew coming out of the boarding tube brought him out of his fugue with a jolt.

"We have a seal over there, sir," the woman said, addressing herself to him instead of the Captain standing next to him or the Dragoon beyond that. When had he gotten put in charge?

Still, this was a technical task, and they were nerdy people. He at least spoke in a language they could follow, some of the time. Unlike little miss amazon killer here.

"That's good," he replied, absolutely at a loss for her name. "Status over there?"

"Didn't get too deep into their diagnostic system, but we're pretty close to level," she said. "Gravplates are dialed down to about one quarter, so be careful or you'll bonk your head. Air reports breathable and acceptable pressure, but stay prepared anyway. Temperature is only a few degrees above freezing water, so you'll want to dial your suits up now."

Javier glanced around. The people surrounding him were almost scary competent. Paying attention. No questions. No complaints. Already setting switches and dials, based on the word of an engineer they barely knew.

He put actions to thought and turned his temperature up to a balmy twenty-five degrees. A beach would be nice about now.

Javier checked all the gauges and dials on the remote's control board, watched them adjust themselves for the environment over there and smiled to himself as he started typing.

Good morning. Ready to go? JA

Affirmative. Can we steal it so I have someplace nicer to live?

He suppressed a snort. If the pirates around him found out about Suvi, his life wouldn't be worth warm spit. That was why she was hidden in the remote. They forgot about the device most of the time, and he could work on it without arousing suspicion.

Let's wait for these chickens to actually hatch?

<pout />

Yup, it was going to be one of those days.

He looked up to see Sykora watching him from across the way. She would be in charge as soon as they stepped onto the other ship. As well she should be. You never knew when you were going to find monsters out there.

Just because mankind had been exploring the galaxy for more than four millennia and not found anybody didn't mean there was nobody to find. Just that we hadn't gotten out far enough, or soon enough, or something. And not all monsters were aliens.

"Ready, mister?" she asked.

He looked at the heavily armed people in the party. "Can I have a sidearm, just in case we run into monsters?" he asked. It was mostly pro forma at this point.

"Aritza," she smiled calmly down at him, "I'm the bogeyman."

PART FOUR

Suvi watched the hatch grind slowly open, at least slowly to her, and directed her sensors into the other ship.

275 degrees Kelvin, so warm enough to keep water liquid and not rupture things. Atmospheric pressure at the low end, roughly two thousand meters equivalent elevation. Gravplates set to one quarter standard. Not as light as Homeworld's famous moon, Luna, but she would have to hop across the gap in freefall and dial everything down so she didn't mash into the ceiling.

Piece of cake.

She watched Sykora, the big woman Dragoon, *the dragon lady*, nod to Javier. He pushed a button on his little console that normally handled the flight controls. Now, it just displayed a happy face in her cockpit and started up mood music for flying.

Today, she was flying an early heavier-than-air aircraft known once upon a time as a helicopter. Hers wasn't as loud as those primitive machines, although she had considered adding sound effects for verisimilitude.

Like the two pathfinder women, Suvi went in first.

It was a boring place. Industrial design heavy on gray, with square corners that actually looked welded instead of cast. *How droll.*

The hallway from the airlock was relatively short. The dimensions were human, 2.5 meters wide and tall. Coarse texture on the deck plating for traction under gravity. Boring walls.

The whole ship appeared to exist on a single deck, laid out long and narrow, pointy at one end and flared at the other, from the pictures Javier had uploaded.

Suvi flitted to the place where this little hall emptied out onto the longer hall that ran down the central axis of the ship. In her mind, she echoed Javier's question. *Why couldn't we just bring it aboard the pirate ship to open it up?*

She replayed Captain Sokolov's comment: "Because I want it go boom outside the ship's armoured hull." He reminded her of her first Captain, Ayumu Ulfsson, back before the probe-cutter *Mielikki* even had a name, back when she was just a hull number scouting for *Concord* fleets during the Great War. Maybe it was the Academy training. It hadn't stuck with Javier, but it had with Zakhar Sokolov. It brought back some of her earliest memories.

Suvi smiled.

From the long hallway, she could see more than two thirds of the ship. She added dimensions and schematics to the information she was displaying on Javier's screen. To the right, the hatchway that probably led onto the bridge. At the rear, a huge, armoured bank-vault of a hatch. Obviously engineering. You wanted things going boom back there to stay back there.

Someone had painted a really strange logo onto the wall a little forward of the crossway. At first, Suvi had dismissed it as art, but from here, it looked official, and kinda important.

For fun, she locked her targeting brackets on the image and beeped Javier's console extra loud. Through the tiny fish-eye lens he had installed on the control portable, she could see several people jump suddenly.

Suvi giggled.

She missed having access to *Mielikki's* data banks. That thing looked like a symbol, but it was outside her current knowledge base. She would have to rely on the much-dumber computers running *Storm Gauntlet* to hopefully have an answer. *Mielikki* would have known instantly.

She missed being a starship.

A few moments passed. She watched the group consult. Guns came out. Javier apparently was arguing with them, but there was too much noise for the little microphone to wash it all out. And she didn't want to listen to an argument today.

Javier surprised everyone by walking away from the group and entering the boarding tube. She could hear him clomp up the walkway towards her, followed a few seconds later by the big woman, Sykora, and the rest. The profanities bouncing around in the cool air seemed interesting. She filed them away for future use. You never knew when they might be useful.

Suvi watched Javier enter the ship through one of her cameras. She put his picture on his screen to say hello while the rest of her attention scanned the hallway.

She could hear little radio emissions bouncing around the ether. Javier had never bothered to load cryptographic software onto the remote, so she couldn't listen in to whatever conversation the strange ship was having with itself. It didn't sound particularly exciting, from the strength and frequency of the transmissions.

And Storm Gauntlet *was WAY too stupid to be able to do something like that all by itself.*

How could humans get around the galaxy in a ship that didn't think? I mean, sure, they had before good AI's had come along. But still, she was way smarter and way faster, and rarely fat-fingered a control. Whatever.

Javier stopped beside her, looked her in the eye with a smile, and cracked open the faceplate to his skinsuit. He took a shallow sniff, cold air being detrimental to organic lungs, and nodded.

According to her readout, the air should smell acceptable. Boring, without all those complicated trace signatures that plants, and soil, and chickens gave off, but not lethal and not particularly uncomfortable. To someone accustomed to *Storm Gauntlet*, probably a breath of fresh air, literally.

Humans were weird. But, hey, it paid the bills.

"Aritza," the big woman boomed, across the air and the radio, "what the hell do you think you are doing? This ship could be dangerous."

"Nope," Suvi heard him reply with a chippy glibness. "Not with that."

He pointed at the logo as he spoke.

It was a blue circle, reasonably thick, with a green ellipse painted across that. Overall, exactly fifty-two centimeters tall and fifty wide.

It had been painted by a human, rather than an AI. AI's were too fussy for that level of wobbliness.

Okay, most AI's. I might have done it in a lighter green, and added some sparkles to the paint. And maybe a few stars for effect. You know, ART.

From her knowledge of human eyesight, it might appear to be a planet with rings. Weird looking rings, but rings. There were a lot of weird-looking things out there. She had been a galactic surveyor for years. She could testify.

"What is that?" Sykora asked over the clamor as the rest of the boarding crew caught up.

"Something the *Neu Berne* military programs probably didn't cover," Javier said quietly, forcing her to lean down to listen.

She hated that, according to Javier. Suvi got the impression Sykora might be grinding her teeth right now. Certainly, she took a breath before she answered.

"Oh?"

"I only know it because I spent a weekend at a religious retreat a while back with the modern incarnation of those people," Javier said evasively. "Weird folks. Generally harmless, but weird."

"Pot, kettle," the short, brunette pathfinder injected into the conversation as she arrived. Sascha was an extremely smart woman, from what Suvi had been able to surreptitiously observe.

Javier made a face at her.

"I got over it," he snapped sarcastically. "Anyway, that is the emblem of a group of pacifists from a very long time ago."

"Pacifists?" Sykora asked, dripping sarcastic honey on her words.

Suvi loved to listen to the tone and inflections the woman used. It was so different from Javier's, or anyone she had known in the *Concord*. One of these days, she needed to convince Javier to take her to *Neu Berne*.

Sykora did something with her hands. Suvi watched Sascha and Hajna, the other pathfinder Javier played cards with, take up station looking fore and aft, guns drawn. The others stayed back in the side hallway, prepared to run or fight.

As far as Suvi could tell, Sykora was the most dangerous thing on the ship right now.

Javier watched, bemused.

"Pacifists," he repeated. "Shepherds of the Word."

"Which word, Javier?" Hajna asked, kneeling beside Javier and covering the aft hallway to engineering.

"Aritza," Captain Sokolov's voice came suddenly over the radio. "What are you talking about?"

Suvi got a head start and transmitted the image of the logo back to the ship. They would think he had done it. He would back her up, later.

A moment of silence passed, breaths baited.

Suvi imagined the Captain asking his ship's computer for more information. She envisioned an ancient butler, shambling along looking through a musty library for an ancient book. She giggled.

"Javier," the Captain continued, "are you sure?"

"Sure enough," Javier responded. "Plus, it's been a very long time, so it's not like there's anybody here to bother us."

"Agreed," the Captain replied. "Sykora, stand down for now. Those people really were pacifists. Pay attention for surprises, but you should be safe from booby-traps."

PART FIVE

Javier refrained from smugness. Outside. Inside? Different story. After all, Dad loved him best. See?

That thing on the wall had brought back a lot of memories. Most of them things he'd rather not remember, these days. He'd kinda forgotten how ugly things had gotten in his life after his first ex-wife left and his career with the *Concord* Navy started to ramp down with the budget cuts.

Out of work. Out of married. Down on his luck and himself. Amazing he had survived. Even gave religion a try at one point. For a long weekend. Those people had just been too weird to be believed.

He was much better now. Even Sykora really only occasionally got him mad enough to go back there. Okay, weekly. But that was down from daily. Hourly. Whatever.

The Shepherds of the Word. The Prophet of the People. The *Union of Man*. Things from the history books.

That painting there meant that this ship had, at one time, belonged to one of the actual Shepherds, one of the close followers of Rama Treadwell himself. The Prophet who had preached a universal brotherhood of man that should be reflected in a union of worlds. *The Union of Worlds*.

The battle that had destroyed *A'Nacia* had been, in its own bizarre way, the culmination of Treadwell's life and teachings, twisted though the outcome had been. Even after he simply disappeared from history while

131

traveling in deep space, his words had resonated. Some people had thought that that disappearance was what triggered the Unification War.

Javier wasn't sure. He was kind of sketchy on that history anyway. After all, it was just about 650 years ago. And the Battle of *A'Nacia* was nearly 600 years ago, at the other end of the Unification War.

The Shepherds had faded, down the centuries, until there were only a few small monasteries tucked in out of the way places that were too damned cold and frowned on gambling and drinking. Silly people didn't understand what made human organizations successful.

For luck, Javier touched the painting. He spun in place and scanned the hallway, correlating naval architecture with what he had learned in school.

Skinsuits didn't allow it, or he would have cracked his knuckles.

"Right," he said, mostly to Sykora. She and Ilan Yu were the only two looking at him, anyway. "Bridge at that end. Two cabins right behind it on one side, office and stores on the other. Wardroom and Rec room behind the hallway, most likely. Big engineering section back there."

"Recommendations?" Sykora asked. There was no doubt she was in charge here. None. Devil take the hindmost if you asked her.

"We have power," Javier replied. "Heat would be nice, and I want to see if the environmental system is up to handling a dozen people." He smiled extra evil at Ilan. "You'll get to practice on a very old system."

"Joy," Ilan replied with a tired sarcasm. Still, it was his job, and he was pretty good at it over on *Storm Gauntlet*. This should be a much less complicated system to fix up.

"Very good," Sykora decided. "Drone first, then pathfinders, then me. Civilians behind that and one guarding the rear."

Javier shrugged, pretty sure he and Ilan were the civilians. Still, let the gun bunnies absorb any incoming fire. Better that way. He pushed a button and let Suvi take point. She would protect him better than Sykora. She'd already proven that.

So he ambled along. Sykora's skinsuit just emphasized how nice her butt was. He could follow her around, pretending to pay attention to the remote, while Suvi was actually doing all the work. Too bad the rest of the Dragoon was so much less fun.

The words on the door didn't really catch his attention. It was just another one of the side doors headed back to engineering. There were a lot of them. Turned out the ship was a little longer than he had expected. Or had smaller rooms.

After a beat, his brain clicked. *Cryonics Lab.*

"Oh, crap," he whispered, forgetting that he was arm's length from a keyed-up, heavily-armed lunatic.

She spun in place and drew her pistol in one motion, even before he could say anything to stop her.

Next thing he knew, she had it pointed between him and Ilan, safety off, prepared to unleash complete mayhem. Or what she probably called Tuesday.

"What?" she whispered hard at him. There was nobody to shoot. She sounded disappointed.

Rather than speak, Javier stuck out one hand and touched the little brass plate next to the door. He tapped it twice for emphasis.

"You don't suppose..." He let the rest of the sentence trail off into the surf of its own accord.

"How old did you say this ship was?" she asked, standing a little more erect and holstering the weapon. She was no longer eye level with him.

He looked up and shrugged. "The design dates back about five centuries or so. I'd have to look at the deck plate on the bridge for her actual keel date."

He thought about it for a few seconds. "Really freaking long ago."

She looked at him hard. Javier nearly jumped in surprise when she shrugged back at him. "Anyone in there isn't going anywhere, anytime soon. Let's get engineering ship-shape."

Hopefully, she wasn't relaxing around him. He'd have to do something stupid, or personal, or both, if that happened. Little miss amazon ramrod never relaxed. He would bet money she slept at attention, although he had no intention of ever finding out.

"Move it, people," she called out.

Suvi was already hovering at the hatch to engineering.

Javier knew she was just waiting, as she could have triggered the mechanism herself. But a remote wasn't supposed to be that smart, so she played along.

Javier just pretended as though anything he pushed on the console actually did something. He made a mental note to ask her what actually happened, next time they were alone. It was probably something pretty silly, knowing her.

Sascha had to open the big armoured hatch to engineering instead. Hajna and Sykora covered her with weapons out. He and Ilan just stood around. The guy at the rear walked backwards with a cannon pointed up the hall.

Some people.

Like all good, military-grade starships, engineering was separated from the rest of the hull by a fairly solid internal airlock. Fires didn't breath deep space, and if something went wrong back there, sometimes that was the only solution. Sucked to be an engineer at that moment, but they kept emergency breathers in every drawer for a reason.

Suvi passed through the airlock first. Javier typed away on the keyboard as she provided a running commentary.

Not as big as I was expecting.

Older design. Significant technological leaps during the Great War. It's what made you possible, young lady.

Still, it looks rough. Unpolished.

He had to agree. What she showed inside there had an almost amateur look. Maybe civilian was the word. Almost every starship he had been on in three decades was either active-duty military or retired surplus. There were certain rules of architecture that every navy followed. Physics were physics.

This looked like something thrown together from parts someone had salvaged from a junk yard. While drunk.

Of course, if they had been as serious about the whole vow of poverty thing in those days as now, they might not have had the funds to build custom ships to spec.

Not that poverty had been the breaking point with him, that weekend he had spent at the monastery. No, it had been that stupid requisite vow of chastity. And sobriety.

Javier could see the jumpdrive. Big, honking monster sitting there in front of twin pulse thrusters. That thing over there was probably an auxiliary power reactor, just from the color. Air scrubbers all along that wall. Way smaller than he expected, so either more efficient design than he thought, or smaller crew.

"Looks good," he said finally. "Everything accounted for. Environment safe. Only wandering monsters are out in the hallway."

That got him a sour look from all three girls. Of course, he wasn't holding a gun on a closed hatch. In a ship that was centuries old, stuck inside a minefield. Did they think they needed the whole van Helsing routine?

"Sascha and me next," Sykora commanded. "Hajna with Aritza and Yu last."

"Aye, sir," replied the girls and the gun bunny, on cue.

Javier nodded sloppily. Her, he might salute, just to piss her off. He might even do it right, just to show her, exactly once, that he could.

He refrained. Barely.

He typed instead. *Company coming. Stay sharp.*

Si, commandante.

See? That, right there, was how you did snark. He was so proud of his girl.

Javier thought about going back up to the Cryonics facility while the amazon was elsewhere, but decided that the gun bunny would just interfere and stop him before he could do anything interesting.

Might as well wait.

He was quickly bored, waiting the three minutes for the two women to cycle through the airlock.

Anything you want me to do while we wait?

Not that wouldn't give you away. Look for rat droppings. That will be the clue that the environmental systems are compromised.

Fresh or dried?

After this long, anything you can see is a problem.

It would, however, give Sykora something to shoot. That would probably improve her humor. Silver linings.

It seemed like forever before he and Ilan finally made it onto the big deck. It was noticeably warmer back here. Not warm, but the various machines seemed to be turning over regularly to provide power from the solar batteries. And the life support systems had been left on. That was a good sign.

Or a bad one. Hard to tell. Still, Javier had three armed women handy. Not exactly a harem, but this wasn't exactly his idea of a bordello. Generally.

"Ilan," he said, shaking himself from his reverie and dragging the machinist's mate along with him, "this is the environmental system. I'm familiar with the theoretical design. You get to learn it. Don't do anything stupid. Yet."

"Gosh, sir," Yu replied with an equal-parts sloppy and sarcastic salute, "I shall endeavor to live up to the standards of excellence you embody."

Javier did a double-take, just to make sure the man was kidding. You never knew with engineers. He might have gone all professional and stuff. Bad juju.

Javier gave him the stink-eye, just in case, and then headed in the direction of the APU. It seemed to be putting out a baseline.

What, however, needed a baseline? Life support would barely require a quarter of the juice flowing out. The other options made him nervous. More nervous. Almost as nervous as his paranoid cohorts.

Okay, maybe not that bad, but bad.

Mentally, he made a list as he cracked open an access panel and shined a pocket light in. *Storm Gauntlet's* Chief Engineer, Andreea Dalca, could probably have it tuned and humming in half an hour. She was that good. One of her people would probably take a half-day, just to be sure. They might need to string a power-line over from the big ship, if what was using the juice was what he feared. Not a good thing to interrupt.

Engines were next. Primary tanks were long since drained, but could be filled up pretty quickly by cracking hydrogen from the water tanks that showed mostly full. In a pinch, Javier had once hijacked a comet and used a small pulsar to cut a section out to melt for the water.

If all else failed, there was a whole planet below. Water would not be a problem. Whether the fusion torch would work, that was a different question. And not his concern. Let Dalca's people solve it. Tomorrow.

"Javier, I thought you said this would be hard," Ilan mock-whined from the corner.

"Nope," he replied with a smile. "Sledge-hammer stupid. Brute force machine."

"I know," Ilan smiled. "Wash the screens, flush the primary coolant and recycle it. I don't have all the tools I need, but this won't take more than an hour. Why do we use bio-scrubbers?"

"A quarter the size, Ilan," Javier noted, "and about a thousand times more efficient. This air would get pretty stale after a month."

Javier looked around at the jump engines and the thrusters. "Ship like this is designed to sail point to point in small jumps, and land on a planet every two to three weeks, or dock with a station. Not to make long sails like *Storm Gauntlet* does. And it would still have a very small crew doing it."

"Well," the machinist's mate said smugly, "I can fix this easy enough."

"Good," Javier said. "Make a list of what you think you need and then go do the same thing on the APU. I expect we'll need to bring over a portable generator or run lines across the way so we can bring it off-line and work on it. Don't worry about the engines until the Chief comes over and inspects them."

"Roger that, sir."

Javier turned and realized that all three women were staring at him. Not hostile. More like open-mouthed shock. It was a weird feeling, surprising this particular group. Felt good.

He forgot, sometimes, that they never saw him in his engineering and fix-it mode. *Concord* Fleet officers were trained for this sort of thing as a matter of course. Hell, fixing the bio-scrubbers on *Storm Gauntlet* when he first arrived was the original reason he hadn't ended up as a slave on a farming world.

He smiled innocently at Sykora. "Nobody to shoot here," he needled. "Orders?"

PART SIX

Javier stood outside the hatch and took a deep breath. Ilan and the male gun bunny had been left in engineering to clean things up. He had the three women with him, four with Suvi, as he contemplated the little brass plaque hung at eyeball level.

Cryonics Lab.

To Sykora and Hajna and Sascha, just words. They weren't trained in this sort of thing. Hell, almost nobody was, these days. The technology was used so much less today than it used to be. Mostly for medical purposes, in a total catastrophe. Ships didn't need it, as life support systems were so much better now and Jumpdrives could hop so much farther in one go.

He took a second deep breath.

"Why are you nervous, Aritza?" the amazon asked, her voice almost blowing warm air in his ear.

He did not, quite, jump out of his skin. He did turn and look her in the eye, from a distance of about eight centimeters. Biting her seemed rude. Kissing her, more so. Both would be equal amounts of surprise as payback. Maybe tomorrow.

"What's on the other side of this door," he said, just loud enough for the three to hear him.

Safeties clicked off in the ominous silence.

"Oh, put them away," he half-snarled. "There's nothing in there to worry you. You're the bogeyman, remember?"

That nearly got him punched. By more than just Sykora.

They did holster the weapons, though, so Javier could relax.

Suvi took up watch above and behind, where she could see down the long hallway and over any of the bodies in the way. She was prepared, in case she needed to rescue him. Again.

Javier turned back to the door and placed his palm flat on the access plate. Given the circumstances, he could see someone actually locking it, but that would be an oversight, not a design feature.

The hatch clicked back a centimeter into the room and slid out of the way on powerful pneumatic sledges.

Javier reached out a hand and caught Sykora before she could complete her step forward.

"Not yet," he whispered, almost intimately as she rounded on him. "Let it breathe."

"Breathe?" she asked, almost as quiet.

"It has been closed up for a very long time. The air is likely to be a little foul with volatile trace elements."

"What's in there, Javier?" she asked, turning her head to scan the room beyond.

Javier? We're back to Javier, are we?

"Not what," he said, a little louder, for the other two to hear as well. "Who."

"Who?" That got her head spun all the way back around to face him. A hand was on the pommel of the pistol, ready to draw and fire.

Javier leaned forward and sniffed carefully at the breeze blowing softly into his face. A little rank. Extremely dry. Cold, where the rest of the ship had been merely cool. Right about what he had expected, from the things he had read, once upon a time.

Some days, he hated being right.

Javier walked forward instead of answering, one hand still on Sykora's arm, but more as a guide than a restraint. As if he could actually stop a woman like that if she set her mind to something.

She trailed along anyway, half a step behind him, probably prepared to throw him into the dragon's maw to give her the half-second she would need to draw and kill it. It was how she thought.

The room was larger than he had expected. Or rather, the walls were where they should be, but less space was taken up.

Based on the size of the ship, he had expected two, or possibly three big boxes in here. Sarcophagi. Coffins.

There was only one, tucked back into the corner, although he could see the power couplings for two more coming out of the walls.

One was enough.

Javier walked to it quietly, hearing the slight hum of the device in the still air, feeling it in his feet when he got close and stood over it.

Ancient kings on the Homeworld had been buried like this. Big black box, three meters or so long, two wide, one tall. This was metal instead of stone, and the inscriptions on the sides were medical instead of propaganda.

The goal was still immortality.

He glanced over at the three women to make sure they were still with him. They were, but their faces showed growing apprehension. They were beginning to understand things, at least a little.

He heard Suvi shift a little forward just inside the door, where she had a good view of the room and could still interfere if someone tried to sneak up on them. They had cleared the ship room by room, but Sykora was a stickler for those sorts of details and he wasn't in the mood to argue with her. Not right now.

Javier leaned forward for a better view. The top half of the sarcophagus lid was clear, covered over with a thin rime of frost. It was active. Whether it had worked was a different story.

He reached down pulled off a glove. He would need the body heat.

That warm hand wiped away the layer of frost ice from the glass.

Inside, the face of a young woman, instead of a desiccated mummy. She was dressed in a simple black shirt, with the same logo worked on both sides of the collar.

Javier blew out a breath he had forgotten he was holding.

"That's who," he said, quietly, reverently. Without a nav computer, he couldn't even begin to guess the odds of success. Machines like this were supposed to be used for much shorter periods. Months. Maybe as much as a year, in a pinch. But centuries? The mind boggled.

"Who is she?"

Javier wasn't sure who spoke. It was a quiet whisper, almost an intrusion into the realm.

"She is a Shepherd of the Word," Javier said simply.

PART SEVEN

Zakhar looked down at the coffin. This was why they paid him the big money, so he could be in charge at moments like this. Life and death decisions. Command.

His Science Officer stood to one side, consulting quietly with the Chief Engineer. Andreea Dalca was a broad, compact woman, a product of high-gravity world. She was a first rate engineer, and a complete introvert. How she and Javier got along so well was a mystery for the ages. But it worked.

Right now, they were deep in a very esoteric, technical conversation. He followed about a third of it. Nobody else in the room probably got a tenth.

Sykora and her two pet pathfinders were here as well, staying mostly out of the way in a corner. The room wasn't crowded, and he wasn't sure they would leave if ordered, given the situation. It was certainly unique for him. Best let it slide for now.

Out in the hall, he could hear others moving around. Mostly Dalca's people, doing the sorts of maintenance tasks any ship accumulated, even at rest. Given the age and state of the ship, they were already money ahead if they could get it to any port. If they could locate the right sort of collector or museum, they might be rich.

That would bring a new set of problems. He would burn that bridge when he got there. They had a much more interesting problem today.

What to do with the ship's owner?

Andreea and Javier seemed to think that there was a good chance she could be revived with no long-term damage. At which point, she became his problem.

Zakhar hadn't set out to be a slavemaster. He was a *Concord* Fleet veteran, retired, damn it. They had saved the galaxy when *Neu Berne* had set out to conquer it. That it had been done before his birth didn't reduce the fact that they were supposed to be the good guys.

Javier looking at him that way didn't help. It was a reminder that they were brothers, of a sort. Men who took the oath.

Unconsciously, he found himself playing with his class ring. *Concord* Fleet Academy, Class of '49. An Officer and Gentleman, by Act of Congress Enshrined.

If he thawed her out, he would have a brand new kitten. What was the ancient saying? If you saved a life, you were responsible for that life. He could order the plug pulled instead, but he didn't want to know which of his crew would actually obey that sort of order. Or how much of his crew he would lose, on a personal level, if he became that sort of Captain.

There really was no doubt what his answer would be. Javier and Sykora had to have known that. But they had been in complete agreement that he had to come over and make it. This was only the third time they had ever done something like that.

So here he stood.

Zakhar tried to remember what little he knew about the founding of the *Union of Man*, and the ancient Prophet, Rama Treadwell. Not much. *Union of Man* history had never been his thing, growing up. Too busy with racing speeders and sports teams.

He knew even less about the religious order known as Shepherds of the Word. Something about a group of wandering mystics looking for their lost Prophet in the depths of space, and carrying the Word like missionaries to all the worlds of the *Union*.

Javier had said that the Order still existed in a few places in the *Concord*, or the quieter corners of the worlds that had once belonged to the *Union of Man*. Before the Great War. Probably a museum somewhere on *New London*, if he cared enough to look. Maybe someday.

He leaned forward again to look down at this woman. She looked young. Sleeping peacefully, like the princess in the ancient fairie tale, or the strange little man who walked down into the fairie mound and lost centuries when the morning came.

Zakhar estimated her age to be in her mid-twenties, barely out of her childhood, although he had been commanding an armed pinnace at that age. Officer and Gentleman.

What to do with this kitten, after he found her by the side of the road and took her home?

Command.

"Javier," he said firmly, projecting his voice clear into the hallway. It was a skill that made Captains. "How long to thaw her out?"

He noted how serious the man had become. Nothing like the normal class clown. That usually meant bad things. Today, it just meant serious. Like he was thinking the same things.

Javier had once been in command. He knew.

"Given the lack of a Ship's Surgeon," Javier replied, "I would recommend wiring the box to a portable generator and moving her close to *Storm Gauntlet's* medbay first."

He paused there and looked down at the coffin. Zakhar could see the wheels spinning in his head, calculating options and timelines. Were all Concord Fleet officers like that? Probably. Came with the territory. The Good Guys.

"After that," the Science Officer continued, "I think we bring her out just about as slowly as the box will let us. Not like we're rushed for time here."

"You volunteering?" Zakhar asked gruffly.

The man shrugged eloquently. "You got anybody else?"

"No, mister, I do not," Zakhar said. Command voice. Command decision. "You will take charge of the rescue."

He turned to his Engineer. "Andreea, you are in charge of getting the ship ready to fly if possible. It's too big to transport out inside *Storm Gauntlet*, and too valuable to section up unless we have to. Questions?"

She never once made eye contact. She never did. Sometimes, he felt like he should keep his shoes extra polished, just because she would be looking at them instead of his face.

"No, Captain," she said quietly. "I estimate we will have a complete status in eighteen to twenty hours."

"Good enough," he replied. "Javier's kitten first, Andreea."

He turned and started to leave the room. Sykora fell into step with him, to his right and half a stride back. Just like always.

"Kitten?" she whispered as they walked. "What are you planning to do with her?"

143

"I'll know that, Djamila, when he succeeds."

"Aye, sir."

PART EIGHT

JAVIER FELT like the greater of two evils. Any two evils.

The Purser's people had emptied out a nearby storage room for him, giving Kianoush Buday, his tea mug artist, a chance to see the whole affair unfold as he had several crewmembers sled the big sarcophagus over and then connect it to ship's power.

It dominated the empty room, laying there like this was a state funeral.

He was the Science Officer, so he was in charge, right? Said so right there on the side of his mug. This was Science. Javier can handle it.

He looked at the hatch, as if it was transparent. Medbay was just across the hall, door locked open and machines on standby, in case something went wrong. He hadn't bothered to tell them that if something went wrong during the thaw, she would be better off never waking up from whatever dreams had filled her long night. They wouldn't understand until it was too late.

As far as he knew, nobody had ever been successfully kept alive this long under cryo. Not because the theory was flawed, but because there was no reason.

You found the survivors or you didn't. She had had to be a prisoner of war, in a war that had ended five hundred and eighty-three years ago, to even be a candidate.

Javier sipped his tea and ruminated. How could you explain to someone the rise and fall of the *Union of Man*, the Great War with *Neu Berne*, or the rise of the *Concord*? Depending on how long she had been here, would she even know about the latter two?

What do you do when you wake up, Rip Van Winkled out of five centuries of history? Everyone you knew wasn't even a footnote any more.

And then, to top it all off, you've been captured by pirates.

Javier was a well-treated and well-respected member of this crew. But he never forgot that he was here paying off a debt as a slave. Honor. Duty. But still a ransom.

If he brought her out of the fugue, wouldn't she be just another slave? And did she have any skills that could make her valuable? Or would she be so hopelessly out of date that all she had to fall back on was a strong back on a mining colony?

Javier looked down at the sleeping face and realized that she might find a fate worse than being an agricultural slave. It was still, to some extent, a man's universe.

The hatch opened before he could sink too deep into a funk. A body slipped in, closed it quickly. The lock keying into place got his attention.

Sykora.

He fixed her with a questioning stare. She had no business on this deck right now. None.

She was impervious to his look as she strode into the room and stood across the box from him. She stared back.

The quiet hung.

Usually, the air crackled with negative energy when he was around her. Today, nothing. Just silence.

She spoke first.

"Have you decided yet?" she said quietly. It was a tone he had never heard from her before. Calm. Serene. Inquisitive.

"Decided what?" Javier wasn't going to play whatever game she was up to. Not right now. He would just keep score. There was always tomorrow.

"If she lives or dies," the tall woman replied. She had a hard look on her face.

"I don't make that decision, Sykora," he said. "Sokolov does."

"No," she refuted him simply, "he decides what happens after that. You decide if she ever wakes up."

Javier's eyebrows threatened to crawl backwards over the top of his head. He tended to forget that underneath that tough killer exterior was a first-rate mind. Until she did things like this to remind him.

He would have been happier not being reminded.

"You look down and see a woman," she continued, "and wonder if she can find a place in this world, or if she would be better off not having to make that choice."

Javier shrugged, unsure where she was going but unwilling to gainsay her.

"You were raised to think of women as weak," Sykora said. "The *Union of Man* was the worst, but the *Concord* is not much better. In *Neu Berne* or *Balustrade*, women are the equal of men, in all things."

"And?"

She leaned forward, almost conspiratorially. "If that was a man, would it be a question?"

He leaned in as well. "Would a man be at as much risk of finding worse things in life than being a slave in a mine?"

She looked down, considered the peaceful face between them. "Is it a fate worse than death, Javier? I've seen men and women indentured to brothels. As slaves go, they tend to be better kept than those in mines, or farms. It is a business, after all. She might be happier if that happened to her."

"Oh, I know," Javier replied finally. "There are a number of places the Captain might sell her. Me? I'd head to one of the big worlds and ask for a finder's fee from one of the big universities to cover the expenses. They would love to have someone who lived that long ago, just to talk about what the world was like."

"And what makes you think the Captain won't do that?" she asked him, harsh vitriol creeping back into her voice.

"Because I'm a slave, Sykora," he said flatly, harshly. "Dress it up all you want in fancy language, but I owe a bonded debt to that man. One of these days, maybe, MAYBE, I will be in a position to pay it off and get my own life back."

"And are you treated poorly, Mr. Science Officer?" She leaned closer, getting right down into his face.

He leaned closer as well. "You killed my ship, cut her into parts so that I'll never get her back," he snarled hotly. "You drag me all over the damned galaxy doing pirate shit, so that I'll hang with you if we ever get caught by someone big enough to do the job. And I am not a free man, Sykora. You could walk away from this ship if you wanted. Just walk out the hatch at the next station we visit and never come back." He tapped his finger on the top of the box as he spoke. "I do not have that luxury."

"You were a mouthy punk who pushed as hard as you could, when I met you," she snarled back, nose almost touching his, voices so low that someone at the doorway might have mistaken them for lovers. "You were offered the choice to be here or somewhere else, somewhere where you could have escaped if you wanted. You chose to stay. You do not get to complain now."

The room was suddenly tiny.

"So I should just trust that you people will do the right thing?" he growled back. "That Captain Sokolov really is a good guy and it will all turn out? Based on what?"

She stopped and drew a breath.

It broke the spell.

She leaned back, flushed. She blinked.

"Because it is not your decision to make," she said quietly, tapping on the sarcophagus. "It's hers. Anything else makes you just as bad as Sokolov."

If she had just slapped him, a good open-palmed right hand to the face, he probably would have been less surprised.

Javier bit back any retort that might have come out of his mouth. He leaned back as well, drew a breath deep into his chest, tried to burn off the surge of adrenaline that threatened to overtake him.

They stared at each other for several moments, neither moving.

Javier nodded, mostly to himself, partly to her.

He reached down and flipped open a panel by his right knee. Inside, a big red button. Obvious in its intent and purpose, scribed in half a dozen written languages, just in case.

He leaned into it, watched it start flashing slowly. Off. On. Off.

He straightened up and looked at the tall woman standing across the sarcophagus from him.

"Who are you?" he said querulously.

She straightened out to her own great height, towering a whole head above him in the tiny space.

"I am a woman who will not take any shit in a man's world, mister."

Javier nodded. That was about right.

PART NINE

It had been nine hours. Javier was keeping himself awake with heavily caffeinated tea and regular potty breaks. He had napped some, early on, with Sykora, of all people, keeping watch while he did, lights dimmed and all sound off.

This day had gotten completely and utterly weird.

Now, there was nothing to do but wait.

The sarcophagus had a timer function, but he had cranked the system down to the lowest setting to bring the woman out of her sleep. He figured that would do the least amount of damage, and let her recover best.

If the theory of this machine was the same, she was slowly being refilled with the same synthetic blood that had been keeping her alive for so long, with the anti-freeze elements slowly being weaned out. The longer she had to recover, the better. At least in theory.

Any Ship's Surgeon, even the drunkard that Sokolov had apparently fired three years ago, would have made him feel better right now.

Javier wished he had Suvi handy to talk to, but that would raise too many questions from the crew as well. And he really wasn't prepared to deal with Sykora again any time soon, not if her latest gambit to drive him crazy was going to look like this.

He sipped his tea and thought dark thoughts.

The hollow thump caused him to blink. He didn't think he had been asleep. Hell, with this much tea in him, he wasn't sure when he would next sleep.

Thump. Right. Activity. Progress.

The sarcophagus suddenly started to hiss, just like a tea kettle reaching the boiling point.

Javier was out of his chair and across the room in almost one bound.

The machine had broken the internal seal.

He could smell the gases it was releasing. It smelled like a pickled artichoke he had eaten once, at a parish fair.

The room picked up the faintest hint of fog, even as the air circulation system kicked itself into overdrive and sucked the strange vapors down and away from him, probably to vent into space.

Below him, the glass slowly retracted into the belly of the system, like a vehicle window rolling down, with the faintest puff of dust.

Javier held his breath, mostly out of anticipation. He vibrated, but that was the adrenaline mixing badly with the caffeine. He rocked back and forth on his feet, like a kid waiting for his turn to open birthday presents.

Javier stopped when he caught himself.

I am a professional. I am this ship's Science Officer. I need to act like a grown-up. At least for a little while.

He looked down at the girl asleep with bemusement.

Up until now, she had been a problem to solve. First, transporting her intact from the other ship over here, and then getting the power switched over. Finally, defrosting her like a ham.

He hadn't taken the time to actually look at her.

Her hair had been tucked up under a knit hat to keep it away from sensors and probes, but a few stray hairs peeked out. Redhead. With a splash of cute freckles across her nose and cheeks.

A very feminine face, soft across prominent cheek bones and a soft jaw. Skin that his mother would have called porcelain.

He couldn't see much more of her, other than the black shirt with her Order's logo on both sides of her throat. A Shepherd of the Word. An honest-to-goodness missionary.

She wouldn't have been old enough to know the Rama Treadwell himself, the ship wasn't that old. But she would have remembered the *Union of Man* in the early days, before entropy and bureaucracy set it. Before the dream had soured.

Not that he would tell her. Let her find that out on her own. Wasn't that what Sykora had said? She deserved the chance to make her own decisions, rather than having them made for her, however well-meaning those decisions might be.

Eyelids fluttered.

Breath restarted with a gasp, drawing cold air hard down into her lungs.

Pretty blue eyes opened. They didn't focus, but he didn't expect them to.

He leaned back as the lid of the sarcophagus cracked along the edge and slowly began to pivot up and away. It was a well-designed system he had no intention of interfering with.

Inside, she was wearing a full bodysuit, made from some stretchy black material and covered with a mesh of sensors and tubes that had kept her safe and alive. A little more solid than he liked his women, but in relatively good shape for a woman who had just set the galactic record for a nap.

"Can you hear me?" he said in a quiet voice. Everything from now on was going to be intuition and luck.

He was rewarded with a couple of blinks.

"You are safe now," he continued in his best bedside soothing voice. "Let me know when I start making sense."

She turned in his direction and came back from a thousand kilometers away slowly.

Her whole vocabulary seemed to consist of blinks and alternating deep and shallow breaths.

Javier had had days like that.

"Good morning, sleeping beauty," he said, unable to help himself.

She croaked at him, so there was sound as well. She made a face, too, trying to find the words, or the concepts of the words.

"What can I get you?" he asked, leaning a little closer. That seemed to help, as her eyes began to focus on his face.

"Water," she whispered back at him in a bone-dry voice.

Well, crap. That I can't do without leaving you alone in here. Shouldn't do that.

Javier looked down at his mug of slightly warm tea.

Oh, what the hell. She's human.

He handed her his prize tea mug carefully.

"This is tea, young lady," Javier said, carefully enunciating and hoping he was making sense. "It's still a little warm, but also kinda chewy. Hope you like it green."

He helped her wrap both hands around the metal cup and then let her tip it backwards slowly, sipping some of his prized green tea in small dribs.

After a few sips, she lowered it and fixed him with those bright blue eyes.

"How the hell did you get here?"

Javier smiled. This was going to take way longer than just one pot of tea.

PART TEN

Zakhar sat and watched Javier take his first sip of tea, after working his way slowly through the act of making it. It had seemed like meditation in motion, watching him move, almost like a robot.

The man looked exhausted.

The rest of the room sat dutifully quiet as well, although Zakhar was sure they were bubbling over with questions.

Javier finally sat his mug down.

Interestingly, the first person he made eye contact with was Djamila. Something subtle passed there. Something deep and intense.

She nodded back to him.

Whatever it was, it must be good. Zakhar wondered if he would ever get that story.

"Four hundred and eighty-eight years," Javier said tiredly, answering one of the first questions, and by extension, several others.

He took another drink.

"Her name is Wilhelmina Teague," he continued, "and she was born on *New London* in the early days of the *Union Of Man.*"

Zakhar let the room hang for a few seconds, but Javier was apparently done for now.

"What does she know?" Zakhar said quietly. The rest of the room appeared to be in some level of shock. It was one thing to envision that stretch of time, but it was something else entirely to have it there on the table in front of you.

He watched Javier shrug. Again, the eye contact with Sykora. Another message passed.

"She knows how long she was in there," he said. "She knows that the minefield is still intact, but doesn't know how we survived it. I don't plan on telling her."

He took another drink of his tea. Zakhar waited patiently.

"Right now, she's asleep in medbay, being monitored by the robot. She didn't want to sleep. We talked for nearly three hours, but she's got no reserves to draw on. That will slowly change over a month or so."

Zakhar nodded. About what he had expected.

Javier was taking all this way too seriously. It was possible that the man was planning to steal the ship and try to escape with it. Unlikely, but he had to consider the option.

"Andreea," he turned to the Chief Engineer, "what's the status of the ship?"

She never looked up from her little portable computer as she spoke. She never would. "We will have to transit the minefield to get far enough away to test the Jumpdrives, but they appear to be in good order. I'm sure the calibration is off by an order of magnitude or more, but we can fix that after one test jump. The ship was rebuilt to run with only one crew member, but I wouldn't trust it without at least an engineer, a machinist's mate, and a navigator aboard. It is in remarkably sound condition, all things considered."

Zakhar smiled. He knew a collector who would probably outbid everyone for such a ship, more so for one with such a history. And would keep quiet about the provenance of such a prize, at least until they could come back and do a more thorough job of looting the system.

He would be rich. They all would be wealthy.

His eyes fell onto his Science Officer. Javier might even make enough to buy his contract out on his share. Not the trees, but some things were negotiable. He did, after all, owe the man his life and his ship. They would have been dead ten seconds after the jump without him. And dead again in the minefield without his patience.

He would miss the man. Not that he would ever admit it. Javier had made *Storm Gauntlet* a better place.

Zakhar turned to his Navigator. "Piet, what are the Astrogation computers like?"

The big Dutchman smiled grimly. "Five hundred years out of date, Captain," he said quietly. He did everything quietly. "I have taken the liberty of downloading the data to storage and replacing it with as much data from our own systems as I felt prudent. There is additional space for whatever course you wish to plot from here."

"Good job, everyone," Zakhar let his warm smile embrace them all. It almost felt like the old *Concord* Fleet days with this crew, especially when they were humming along like they were now. Although Javier and Djamila NOT bickering was a point of concern. Still, those were indeed problems he could trade up for.

"I know this has been much harder than we normally encounter, but it will all be worth it."

He took a sip from his own half-forgotten mug of coffee.

"Javier," he said, "when she is awake again, I would like to meet her."

Again, the look exchanged with Sykora. What the hell were those two up to?

"First thing on my list, Captain," the Science Officer replied, "right after breakfast. I had the medbot give her something extra to sleep, so she will be awake in about eight hours, famished."

This time, Sykora nodded first. Something was going on and he had a feeling that it was a secret those two would take to their graves.

"Until breakfast then," Zakhar said in his command voice. Would he ever get that story?

PART ELEVEN

JAVIER ESCORTED Wilhelmina with one arm, like a proper gentleman and everything. He was pretty sure she was up to the walk, but best not to take chances. Not today.

She was dressed in an outfit Kianoush had picked out for her, from things carefully stored over in the little ship.

Black pants baggier than was the style these days. A tight, long-sleeve shirt, also in black, with a gray sleeveless tunic over it tabard-style and a black leather belt. The same logo from both sides of her collar was emblazoned on her right breast, about the size of a goodly grapefruit, embroidered into the cloth.

The hair, once released from confinement and cleaned in a long, hot shower, had turned into a strawberry blond braid down to her shoulder blades in back, with cute little bangs in front.

Standing in her stocking feet, Wilhelmina had turned out to be a few fingers taller than Javier. Not in Sykora's range, but probably the third tallest woman on the ship. He would have to line them up to be sure.

Javier felt like the hero escorting the magical Princess to meet the King. There was something to that. Not that he would ever say that out loud to Captain Sokolov. Man might get fancy ideas, and then where would they be?

The Officer's Wardroom had laid out for a special affair this morning.

It almost looked like a State Dinner, with fine china and silverware Javier hadn't even known the ship still had, left over from the Fleet days.

Off to one side, Captain Sokolov and Sykora sat at a small table, obviously cleared and organized for such an affair. Javier led Wilhelmina to a chair across from the Captain, and seated her like they had trained him in the Academy days. It was amazing how quickly all those classes in deportment were coming back to him.

He was going to have to do something stupid and crass. Not now. But, later. Now was too important.

Javier slid into the seat across from Sykora and smiled at her. She nodded back with a smile. This was going to be even weirder if she was going to be nice to him and everything. It might be time for a few good practical jokes on the woman, just to keep things light and stupid. Friendly Sykora was too much like Trapdoor Spider Sykora.

But right now, Wilhelmina. Her time. Her luck. Her fate.

Javier did a triple take when he realized that someone had brewed tea and steeped it already. His awesome mug was in place and steaming vaguely.

He tried to say something suave about his tea, but it came out more like a Tamarin, babbling and pointing ineffectively.

"Pixies," the Captain smiled his evil smile.

That did NOT help the matters in Javier's head.

The two women silently looked at each other, and then the two men. Javier felt an eyeroll coming on. Fortunately, Wilhelmina didn't look anything like his second ex-wife, or that would have been just too much weirdness for one day.

"Ms. Teague," Captain Sokolov began instead, "I am Zakhar Sokolov, Captain of the *Storm Gauntlet*. Welcome aboard. You've met my Science Officer. This is my Dragoon, Djamila Sykora."

She shook hands with both across the table. Her manners were up to the test today. Javier kept his running commentary inside and smiled. The tea was even done right. *Wonders.*

"Thank you for rescuing me, Captain Sokolov," Wilhelmina purred. "What would be the fastest and safest way for me to get back to *New London*?"

Oh, did I forget to mention she was a genius-grade intellect?

Javier smiled, remembering what it felt like to talk to her, even newly awakened. Him playing jacks. Her playing the ancient oriental game of

Go. Her draining him of information until she finally had to sleep, and let him recover. She didn't look like an intellectual vampire.

They never did.

Javier watched the Captain make a moue as he considered his response.

At no point had the word *pirate* come up in the previous conversation, but she was a very, very sharp woman.

"I realize," she continued blithely, "that I represent an unexpected complication in your salvage operation, but I am prepared to work for my passage."

This time, the Captain's eyes darted to his Science Officer. Javier took a sip of a really good cup of tea to hide his smile.

Any response was defeated by the arrival of breakfast, served by the wardroom stewards.

Javier had a moment of panic as he considered that the pixies and their evil minions might be planning to poison him, but they would have done that already with the tea. So, this should be attacked like a proper final supper before the execution. Word to deed.

"Where did you get fresh eggs?" Wilhelmina said with wonder.

"I raise chickens," Javier replied around a piece of marmaladed toast.

She put her fork down and turned to stare at him. "You RAISE chickens?"

"When you feel up to it, I'll take you down to the arboretum and introduce you to them."

That got him a look. Pirates didn't have arboretums. Most pirates. They certainly didn't keep chickens. Not in any of the stories she would have known.

Javier smiled. That would be an even longer story.

"Why *New London?*" Sykora asked as they got back to the task of eating. "Why not someplace like *Bryce*, the capitol of the *Concord?*"

"I considered that, Dragoon Sykora," Wilhelmina replied.

"Please, call me Djamila."

"Djamila. Thank you. Please, call me Wilhelmina."

She took a sip of coffee to organize her thoughts.

"I was born on *New London*, five hundred and eighteen years ago, if the clocks are to be believed. I began my journey there, seeking to follow the footsteps and mission of Rama Treadwell. I would like to see my hometown, just once, before setting out on my mission again."

"Mission?" Sykora asked.

Wilhelmina smiled. "Did they ever discover what happened to Rama Treadwell?"

"No, they never have," Sokolov replied quietly.

"Just so. I am a Shepherd of the Word, Djamila. I might be the last of my kind, at least until I can train others."

"But the Unification succeeded," Sykora said, confused.

"No," Wilhelmina replied firmly. "*New London* conquered a goodly chunk of the inhabited galaxy and proclaimed a *Union of Man*. That lasted until someone else decided they should conquer the universe and enforce their own definitions of good and evil on everyone. Rama Treadwell's dream was a place where all people were free to define and encompass their own destiny. Not just the wealthy, or the lucky. Every man. Every woman. Every person. From what Javier has told me, the *Concord* is trying, but even more in need of the words of the Prophet than ever."

Both Sokolov and Sykora turned to look at him. He stared back, challenging them to say anything. Prudence got the best of them.

"We're trying, Ms. Teague," the Captain murmured.

"We're all trying, Captain," she replied with empathy. "It is a hard road. But one that must be traveled. We must bring the light to even the darkest corners and darkest hearts. That is what Rama Treadwell taught."

And that, was most certainly that.

Minutes passed in companionable silence as they ate.

The Wardroom stewards cleared the plates and brought fresh coffee. Wonder of wonders, a small pot of steeped tea, even done right. Obviously, pixies.

Javier wondered when the ambush was coming.

"So, Ms. Teague," the Captain broke the silence, "If you are set on traveling to *New London*, that represents another complication. We aren't likely to be in that sector any time soon. The closest we are likely to get in the next six to nine months is *Meehu*. Once in the near future for supplies before we return here to *A'Nacia*, and then again after a second trip."

"I can work for my passage, Captain, both here and after I make it to *Meehu*," she said quietly. "It won't be the first time. Ships are always looking for good crew. I have several degrees, including accounting. And, after a time to return to proper form, a strong back. I can learn most things quickly."

She took a sip of her coffee and glanced sidelong at Javier. He fought a losing battle to keep the grin off of his face.

"One other thought," she trailed off.

"Yes?" Captain Sokolov took the bait.

"Javier tells me that you don't currently have a Ship's Chaplain."

He smiled. The looks on both of their faces was worth every bit of what was going to be coming to him for this.

PART TWELVE

ZAKHAR TRIED to hide his surprise.

Djamila stomping into his office was a new experience. She was the most professional soldier he had ever known. Yet here she was, practically gnashing her teeth, assaulting the floor plates with her boots.

Starting with breakfast, today was just turning out to be all sorts of special. Zakhar could only imagine what fun Javier would bring, at this rate.

Before she even stopped moving to salute, he pointed at the chair. "Sit."

As she did, Zakhar experienced some level of juvenile payback, watching her realize that the chair had already been adjusted to her height. The look on her face was priceless.

Normally, the first thing she did when her butt hit a chair was manipulate it for her so-much-longer legs. She was the tallest person on the ship. Nothing fit.

Unless you knew she was coming.

Zakhar refrained from smiling at her. Command face.

He let her stew for a few moments, composing herself from being knocked off kilter.

"I have a problem," he opened the bidding strong. Jacks or better.

Her eyes got that cagey look that told him far more than just responding would have done. She really was up to something. And Javier was involved. Helping, perhaps.

Perfectly crazy.

He waited, but she had closed down and was happy to call. At least this round.

"I have found a lost kitten by the side of the road," he continued, watching her like an owl might observe said kitten.

"Yes. Kitten," she replied, all clammed up.

Apparently, this was not how she had expected the conversation to start out. Probably wouldn't be the conversation she expected to have. Tough.

"Normally," he continued, drawling out the syllables, "I would happily add such a kitten to the list of trade goods for sale at the next station or land-fall."

The way she flinched said far more than words. The chair actually creaked with the stress of her suddenly gripping it with one hand.

He dangled that last part for an extra moment.

She wouldn't take the bait.

"I have the impression, from more than one crew member on this vessel, that people would prefer that I make an exception to the normal rules, at least in this case."

She nodded slowly, warily.

It dawned on Zakhar that his Mistress of Close Combat had learned some useful things about political maneuvering over the last few years. Probably from watching him. The Djamila who had joined his crew, once upon a time, would not have been able to hold her tongue right now. She would have been ranting at him, as was her style, in the privacy of his office, never a word whispered about it later.

This new woman had gone quiet, reserved, poised.

What the hell was going on?

"So," he continued, "should we get out of the business entirely?"

He left it hanging.

"There are times," she whispered, finally breaking her silence, "when it is appropriate to bend the rules."

WHAT?

For a moment, Zakhar was nearly convinced that he had a doppelganger sitting in his office.

This woman embodied a life following the hardest rules and order. It provided her context, and, often, solace.

He took a sip of coffee to prevent the absolute shock spreading across his face at her words.

"For her," he finally said, after he could swallow his shock and his coffee.

"For her," Djamila replied, barely above a whisper.

What the hell was going on?

"What about others?" he said warily. "Javier Aritza, for example."

The open palm slamming onto the top of his desk was loud enough to make him nearly jump clear out of his chair. Zakhar made a mental note to check the surface for a dent, later.

He would have broken his hand, hitting something that hard. She probably hadn't noticed.

"That little punk had it coming," she hissed savagely. "Still does."

Okay, then. That settled that question. For a moment, Zakhar had been afraid that the two of them had patched things up and secretly started dating. Crazier shit had happened in the last seventy-two hours.

"So the rule is generally sound," he nodded, drawing the words out, "but not in this instance?"

She nodded back, dropping back into her quiet place, breath still a little ragged. He watched her fight her heart rate back to normal.

Between Javier getting serious and Djamila getting flexible, Zakhar wasn't sure the vessel wasn't completely overrun by Aritza's pixies. It made about as much sense. Perhaps more.

"Why?" he said flatly.

He was still the Captain. This was his deck, his vessel. But it only worked with a good crew. And something had changed.

It was like an infection, brought aboard by the Shepherd, without her ever saying a word.

And he would have never believed it, had he not been there.

Djamila took a deep breath, held it, released.

He wondered, briefly, if she would even tell him. Something was going on with her and Javier. And two less likely co-conspirators he had a hard time imagining.

The pause stretched. He could see the thoughts and words racing around in her eyes.

"Djamila," he said quietly. "It's not enough, even for you. I need to know why."

He heard her breath catch. The room had gotten that quiet.

"Opportunity," she whispered back, so quiet that he might have not heard it, had he not seen her lips move.

He fixed her with a quizzical stare, unwilling to speak and break whatever spell had taken this warrior woman and suddenly made her... something. Not vulnerable. She didn't do vulnerable. Human, perhaps? Had he ever seen her *merely* human?

"I'm here because you gave me a chance, when *Neu Berne* was done with me," she continued, still barely audible. "Andreea had run out of chances with the *Balustrade* Navy. For others, it was the same way. Aritza is working off his debt-bond, but even then, he has had an opportunity that he wouldn't have had, if we, if you, had sold him to some colony as slave labor."

"And Wilhelmina Teague?" he asked into that vast gap that had suddenly opened between them.

Djamila paused, composing her thoughts. For moment, her guard was down.

The look in her eyes was almost pain. From a woman who prided herself on being tougher, harder, meaner than anyone else. Always.

"When she's little," she said in a tiny voice, "her daddy takes her on his knee and tells her stories about princesses and dragons. And she grows up with those fairie tales. Sometimes she remembers them, and wonders what her life could have turned out like if it hadn't gone down the particular path it did. How it might have been different."

Zakhar sat quietly, marveling at a side of Djamila Sykora he had never *imagined* existed. He sat perfectly still, unwilling to break the spell that had come over her.

"And Wilhelmina is a magical princess, sleeping for centuries and then awakened."

The image of Javier Aritza as the dashing hero waking the princess with a kiss almost made him laugh out loud. Being the Captain was enough to hold it in.

What the hell was going on?

"We," she said quietly, "you, have the opportunity to do something from a fairie tale. You can rescue the princess like the fairy godmother, or put her back to work scrubbing floors, like the evil stepmother."

Zakhar had been called many things in his life. Officer and Gentleman. Captain. Warrior. Pirate. Other things less savory, sometimes only in the voices he heard when he tried to sleep.

He had never been an evil stepmother.

For a moment, the silence just hung. He seriously considered actually hiring that woman as Ship's Chaplain, if for no other reason than to see what *Storm Gauntlet* might turn into. He had already seen sides to Aritza and Sykora he never dreamed he would.

What other surprises might the future bring?

Zakhar realized that Djamila was hanging on pins and needles, watching him.

Again, not vulnerable, but human. Perhaps vulnerable. Especially if she suddenly saw him as a fantasy king and Javier as a heroic prince rescuing damsels.

He nodded to her.

She breathed out and deflated a little.

"Thank you," he said quietly, solemnly.

She nodded and rose. After a moment, the spit-and-polish Sykora made her appearance, ramrod straight and perfectly poised. She snapped off a salute, pivoted, and exited the room, once again every inch a recruiting poster Dragoon of a pirate ship.

Nobody would ever believe him, even if he had someone he could tell this story to.

Zakhar keyed the comm built into his desk. "Kibwe Bousaid," he said, activating the system to locate his aide, wherever he was on the ship and beep the nearest comm.

"Bousaid here," the voice came back after a beat. Rich, warm. A man with a background in radio. How had he ended up on *Storm Gauntlet*? What was his story? Zakhar realized that he had never asked.

He never did. They were pirates. Some things were better left unknown, and the rest were frequently far more mundane than esoteric.

"Sokolov. Please locate Ms. Wilhelmina Teague and ask her to join me in my office."

"Will do, Cap'n."

Zakhar leaned forward and rested his chin on his hands.

How had any of them gotten here?

Some time passed before a knock at the hatch. He opened it, expecting his aide and Teague.

Javier stood there.

"Two minutes?" the man asked hopefully.

Zakhar nodded and watched the next round of craziness ooze into his day.

Javier sat without asking, as was normal with the man.

The look of surprise on his face was almost as good as it had been on Sykora's.

"So she's already been here," the Science Officer said as he adjusted the chair.

Zakhar nodded. This round was going to be two of a kind or better to open, and Javier was a better player than Djamila. Let him start the bidding.

"Did she get an answer she liked?"

Zakhar had to pause and deconstruct that question. It made no sense. Unless the two of them were up to something.

The two of them.

Together.

What the hell was going on?

Zakhar cocked his head sideways and looked at the man before him.

"Why?" he asked, every inch the Captain right now. He felt the deck threatening to slide out from under him.

"I have two speeches prepared," Javier grinned back at him. "Didn't want to waste your time rehashing things if you had already made that decision."

Whatever it was, Zakhar was suddenly unsure if he should keep Teague around forever, or get rid of her immediately.

The ship had changed. He wasn't sure it was a good thing.

"She's a most amazingly interesting woman, when you actually get to know her," Javier said, apropos of nothing.

Zakhar paused, considered, studied.

"Teague or Sykora?"

Javier gave him a frog-faced grin that made his eyes almost disappear.

"You spend time talking to someone like her," the Science Officer continued, "and learn things. Sure about her, but also things about yourself you have forgotten over time. They come back and you remember them again from when things were good."

"I see," Zakhar said, unwilling to commit to more just yet. He didn't, but it was a useful placeholder until he did.

"I remember a quote," Javier said, again wandering off on another tangent that made no sense. "*We do things not because they are easy, but because they are hard.*"

"And what would be the hard choice here, mister?" Zakhar growled quietly, two old Bryce Academy school chums having lunch.

If only.

Javier grinned.

"It's not that hard, really," Javier replied. "Teague already knows her ship is salvage, and she's okay with that. You send her to *Meehu* with the ship when it goes, and she makes her own way from there. She'll be fine."

"And what's the hard choice?"

Javier paused and swallowed. His eyes got very cold.

It was a look Zakhar was familiar with, from his own mirror. A man making hard choices.

"When you sell her ship, the crew will get their shares, the officers theirs. And I'm betting you'll find a very happy buyer, since we just did the impossible and found a working ship five centuries old, with a fantastically awesome story. Am I close?"

"Close enough, mister," Zakhar said.

Javier studied his face for a moment.

"I would like Wilhelmina to get my share."

Zakhar's stomach felt like it had been punched. He would have bet that Aritza couldn't have topped Sykora today in surprising him.

And lost.

Moments passed. Two men staring at each other across a desk.

"Why?"

"Something she said made me remember who I always wanted to be when I grew up."

"Teague or Sykora?"

But Javier just smiled at him.

IMPASSE

A KNOCK AT THE HATCH.

Zakhar had a chime, but it was rarely used. People preferred the tap. More personal, perhaps.

He pushed the button to open the hatch.

Aritza stood in the door with a clipboard in one hand and a mug in the other. He entered and plopped down in the chair without invitation.

Zakhar looked up at him silently, waiting.

"The other ship is away with Wilhelmina and Sykora aboard," he said. "Just made their first out-system jump en route to *Meehu*. Should take Piet about eight days to arrive there. Are they really going to hire a big freighter to come back out here?"

"They are," Zakhar nodded. "We'll use the same trick to get the freighter inside the minefield as we did to get the other two ships through."

Sykora was likely to get good at the technique of killing mines by hand. If he didn't get her killed. Or she decided to kill both he and Aritza for making her do it.

"Why not hire a minesweeper?" Javier asked.

"I don't want to share my toys, mister," Zakhar growled across the desk. "After I've taken everything I want out of here, then maybe we'll talk about hiring a minesweeper. Right now, like you said, it's a haunted ships' graveyard."

He watched Javier shrug and take a drink before setting the mug down on his desk. It was an old battered porcelain mug from a bakery on Merankorr.

"Where's your fancy mug, Aritza?" Zakhar asked. Come to think of it, he hadn't seen the man without it in some time.

Javier looked down at the mug for a moment, and then looked up at him with a smile.

"I sent it with Wilhelmina," he said, "as a memento of her time here. Wanted her to remember all this in a good way."

"I see." Zakhar craned forward to look into the mug. "Is that coffee?"

"Yup," he said, taking a sip. "Trying new things."

Javier stopped and looked extra serious for a moment.

"I also wanted to thank you for sending Wilhelmina off with enough money to do something good with her life."

"It might have been enough to buy out your contract, you know," Zakhar said quietly.

He watched the man shrug eloquently.

"It wouldn't have been enough to ransom my chickens and my trees."

Zakhar smiled a tight, tiny smile. "Figured that out, did you?"

Javier rose with his own smile and made his way to the door.

"You people won't get rid of me that easily," he said as he departed.

Zakhar scowled alone at his desk, pondering the new sides of his Science Officer he had discovered.

What was the secret he and Sykora shared?

Was Javier staying a good thing or a bad thing? Was he starting to like being here, enough to hire on after he was free? Or was he waiting until he could see them all hang?

And what mind games would they start playing tomorrow?

THE GILDED CAGE

PART FIVE

BOOK FIVE: WILHELMINA

PART ONE

THE VOICE COMING out of the comm was such a surprise that Javier nearly set his workbench on fire with the welding laser.

"Science Officer to the bridge," Captain Sokolov growled from speakers on several walls.

Javier took the time to disarm the laser and set it down carefully. He really didn't feel the need to explain to the Chief Engineer how he managed to set off the fire suppression system.

Again.

He stood and scratched a spot on his kidneys as he stretched and weighed the urgency in the captain's voice.

The desktop was a mess. But the man had sounded a bit cross. Worse than usual, even.

Javier couldn't remember what he might have done this time to set the captain off. After all, Sykora wasn't back from her trip yet, so he really didn't have anybody to bicker with.

Too bad he couldn't figure out how to keep her gone permanently. He might even like it on this ship, regardless of his status as a highly-valued slave.

Javier considered adding a fancy sash to the basic ship uniform of slacks, undershirt, buttoned-up tunic, and occasional jacket.

They were pirates. Weren't pirates supposed to wear a fancy sash? They did in all the movies.

I wonder what uniform I could convince the crew the ancient Janissaries wore. Probably get Kianoush Buday to work up me something swanky. She'd be tickled.

Still, Sokolov hadn't asked politely. And he didn't sound like today was going to involve him using the word *please* a lot.

Javier flipped a coin in his head, studied the results, and started gathering key electronics components into his hands and sliding them into his pockets. For now, Suvi's little flitter was scattered all over the place, part of the shell here, optical sensor turret brain sitting to one side, lifter controls physically removed and sitting on a shelf.

The key components: her secondary processor, radio encryptor and transmitter, and backup memory storage, were what he wanted right now. He was in the process of upgrading the flitter's processing power, and adding more horsepower to the controller portable, so his secret AI assistant could think faster.

It was amazing what kinds of spare parts you could scavenge on a ship this size, just by paying attention.

Suvi was still a little pissed at not being a starship anymore, with all the power of a nav computer to think with and store movies and books and stuff.

But when Sokolov and his pirates had captured the two of them, Javier had just barely managed to sneak her memory and personality chip off the vessel, and then pour her into the only thing he had to hide her in, his short-range airborne autonomous remote. The one that looked like a big gray grapefruit, covered with sensors.

It wasn't his old probe-cutter, *Mielikki*, but Suvi could hide in the remote, safe from the pirates. They would have killed him if they knew about her, and turned her into a slave, too. Another slave. The flitter was as close as he could get her to starflight right now. And she had saved his ass more than once in the little flier.

"Now, Aritza," Sokolov growled from the speakers again. Apparently, he knew his Science Officer a little too well.

"Coming," Javier yelled back, stuffing things into pockets and moving to the door.

PART TWO

Zakhar Sokolov sat in his command chair and stewed.

Externally, he maintained the façade of *command*.

Aloof. Charismatic. Demanding. Durable.

The Captain.

Storm Gauntlet was on her late first shift. Normally, he would come off duty in another hour or so and go hit the tiny gym at the back of E-deck for some sweat and mobility. That wasn't going to happen today. At the same time, Javier Aritza, his Science Officer/botanist/pain in the ass slave/Centurion would have come on duty at that time.

With Djamila Sykora and Piet Alferdinck away on a mission, he was down to a very small group of centurions to stand watches, which meant he actually had to do it, instead of delegating like he normally did.

And it wasn't going to get any better.

Sokolov looked over to his administrative assistant and comm tech, Kibwe Bousaid. The man had the size and bulk to be a successful soldier or dragoon, if he had any trace of killer instinct in him. Instead, he was big, and soft, and quiet, an introvert with a passion for paperwork. And he was probably worth his weight in exotic metals as a result.

"Bousaid," he called across the bridge, waiting for the man to look up. "When the science officer and the chief engineer get here, you'll be in charge."

Bousaid nodded, powered down his station, and stood up.

Sokolov hadn't planned to interrupt what his aide was doing, but he recognized the sense of purpose the man brought to any task, so he stood as well. Bousaid would sit in the command chair, deadly serious, and be *In Command*, when he could have just kept working at his station and answered any rogue questions that came up.

Sokolov shrugged and moved to one side. They were all pirates, usually by choice, with one exception, and even Aritza had chosen to be here, when push came to shove. They all could handle their jobs with a minimum of adult supervision.

The main hatch cycled open to one side of the bridge.

Zakhar looked over and pointed at Aritza, then at his chief engineer, Andreea Dalca.

"Primary conference room," he said, moving that direction. They both stopped and turned around to head back up the hall.

JAVIER SUFFERED a moment of despair as he considered the old battered table in the conference room. The last time he had been in here for something important, he had arrived early, taken over a whole corner, and committed a petite tea ceremony while waiting for the rest of everyone to gather.

Now, it was a much smaller group, and no warning. Javier plopped his old battered coffee mug on the tabletop and settled into a chair.

He watched Sokolov blanch slightly when he saw the other side of the mug, which, based on the amount of hot coffee inside, would currently be a beautiful young woman with green hair, and no clothing north of her belly-button.

Javier smiled.

He hadn't been the person who picked it up from the tourist shop in a brothel on *Merankorr*. He'd just found it down in the officer's wardroom about a week ago.

And kept it.

It wasn't as good as the custom team mug he had sent with Wilhelmina when she and Sykora left, but it still was very obviously his now, which kept the pixies in the wardroom and galley from stealing it when he wasn't looking.

They did that. Well, used to. Obviously the captain had worked his command magic on them at some point and made them stop. He had even said so. Not in so many words, you know. But it was all captainy magic. Bad juju.

Sokolov didn't waste any time today on polite questions or fripperies. Also, not a good sign.

"An hour ago, we received a message, transmitted from well outside the minefield, by someone who knew where the safe boundaries were located."

Inside, Javier snarled to himself, remembering all the *fun* to be had when this ship, this little private service strike corvette, *Storm Gauntlet*, had first come to *A'Nacia*, the Haunted Star, and gotten trapped in an ancient mine field like a fly in a spider's web. How much *fun* it had been figuring out how to save the ship, and her crew, when he'd really just wanted to say *I told you so.*

But in the end, they had rescued a princess from a dragon, fixed her starship, and sent her off to live happily ever after. Not bad for a bunch of pirates.

Still, there was something about the tone of the captain's voice. Something ominous and dangling, like any good bait.

Oh, what the hell.

"From whom, Captain?" Javier asked.

He wasn't going to like the answer. Might as well get it over with.

"Wilhelmina Teague."

Huh?

Apparently, Captain Sokolov had been sand-bagging, probably just to see the way Javier felt his face screwing up sideways in confusion.

Inside Javier's head, little warning buzzers and klaxons were going off as the reactor that was his brain scrambled itself and began to shut down. Or words to that effect.

Whatever.

"I'm sorry," Javier replied as he fought to keep his brain on-line. "I thought you said Ms. Teague."

"It gets better," Sokolov growled sarcastically. "She's in the smallest deep-space yacht you've ever seen. Apparently, she stole it.

"And where are Piet and Sykora?"

"They've been captured and are being held for ransom."

Well, so much for a quiet day.

PART THREE

JAVIER WATCHED his sensors and readouts like a hungry raptor. Not that there was anything he could do if something went wrong as they slowly transited the minefield back out to deep space. No, if that happened, they'd be dead so quickly they would probably never know what hit them.

He had mapped all the mines around them. Big purple triangles marked the ones that could probably gut a battleship at this range. There were a lot of those.

Out beyond that, a pretty, pink star, because that was how he thought of Wilhelmina. Not that he had really seriously considered trying his luck with the woman. His grandfather had always warned him never to chase a woman smarter than himself.

You can't catch them. And worse, what if you did?

She was one of those. Brilliant, decisive, incisive. Several different college degrees in a variety of fields. And totally freaking nuts, but at least in a good way.

She was a Shepherd of the Word. A missionary. Probably the last of them. From what he had seen, years ago, the sad, modern remainder of the order had none of the spark of the early missionaries like her.

Rip van Winkle.

At least she was nice to look at. Half a hand taller than he was. Not as tall as Sykora, but tall. Maybe a little squishier than he liked them, but five centuries in cryo-sleep would do that to you. Nothing a few months of effort couldn't fix if she wanted to.

Warm blue eyes that didn't miss anything. Cute freckles. Ready smile.

Javier smiled to himself. It would be nice to see her again.

Not that he'd been bored or lonely. He was still the new guy to many of the folks on this ship, and none of them had any misconceptions about marriage or white picket fences. But there was nobody aboard the ship that could discuss Kierkegaard or Schumpeter. And certainly not while roaring drunk.

Well, maybe Sokolov, but who wanted to get drunk with their dad?

No, it would be nice to see her again.

On the console, a single bright green light, with a helpful ping, interrupted his train of thought before it really got going.

"Aritza?" the captain asked carefully.

"You remember the range you considered safe? Sure we wouldn't trigger any mines?" Javier replied.

Sokolov nodded. "Was that it?"

"Oh, no, sir," Javier smiled innocently. "I'm eighteen percent more paranoid than you are. But we're clear."

Sokolov's glowering scowl was almost worth getting out of bed this morning, all by itself. That man was one of the few people Javier had ever met who could pull it off.

"Engines ahead three quarters," Sokolov growled. "Kibwe, keep Teague updated with our ETA."

"Aye, sir."

Javier smiled. It would be nice to see her again.

Even if she was coming with bad news.

THERE WERE days when Zakhar regretted not having sold Javier to an agricultural colony somewhere. Sure, they'd all be dead right now without him, but that man seemed to know exactly how to annoy people. He was like a sliver under the skin. Not painful, but something you could not ignore.

Still, today was the day to play nice. He needed the goofball even more than usual now, and was going to have to ask for the sort of favor that would forever change their relationship. Even Javier would figure that out soon enough.

After all, the man was an excellent poker player. Almost as good as his captain.

Zakhar wondered where they might have ended up if they could have been friends, instead of…whatever they were. Slavery was technically illegal on most worlds. And Javier wasn't exactly a slave. Close, but not exactly.

Technically correct was always the best kind.

Debt bondage was perfectly legal. A handful of years and Javier's debt should be paid off. If they managed to loot *A'Nacia*'s orbital graveyard properly, he might even cut that to less than one.

Zakhar considered what this would cost him personally. The two men were both Academy graduates from Bryce. Officers. Gentlemen. Anywhere else, they would be friends. Brothers in arms.

But Javier still occasionally got that look in his eyes, when he thought nobody was looking. The one that said he was visualizing most of the crew hanging from yardarms in a public square.

Perhaps not all of them. Just Zakhar and Sykora and a few others.

Today was not that day. Javier had a smile on his face, almost a goofy one. Presumably, the thought of Djamila Sykora being held prisoner and threatened with execution had cheered him up.

Zakhar sighed internally, where nobody could hear it, and considered the bait he was about to dangle in front of that man.

Even Javier would listen.

She hadn't changed.

Well, she had, but it had been to apparently spend a lot of time hitting the workout machines and doing pushups and sit-ups in the morning. Javier supposed that her time with Sykora might not have been a total waste after all. *THAT* woman was all about running for three hours in full pack before breakfast, just to wake up in the morning.

Javier was practically allergic to that level of effort. Pushing his luck was usually enough exercise. He could hit the machines and the treadmill a couple times a week and be fine.

Wilhelmina looked good. No, freaking fantastic.

This meeting could have been done on *Storm Gauntlet*. She had a conference room the right size and purpose for this sort of thing. But instead, he and Sokolov had waited for the two ships to get close enough to dock, and then crossed over to the little vessel to meet.

Just the three of them.

Normally, Javier would have been iffy about this sort of thing, but Wilhelmina had been living aboard this vessel for several days, and had a nice perfume that had worked itself into every bit of fabric visible, from the pilot's chair at one end of the room to the comfy sofa he had settled into.

Javier looked around him with a critical eye. He had lived in efficiency apartments larger than the interior of this ship. Rectangle-shaped when looking down from above, chopped at angles at belly-button level, to slope in to a roughly-pointed nose and stern, like a long, blunted diamond laying on its side. Two engine pods sticking out the back, with a jump-drive tucked between them, right behind and above the primary power unit.

Inside, a single room. Pilot station at the bow with a single chair. Sofa on one side wall, kitchenette on the other. Fold-down table and bench for eating. Storage closet on the starboard aft, head on the port aft, not far from the airlock entrance. Everything a muted seaweed green tone.

That's why it smells so nice. She sleeps on the sofa.

Javier smiled to himself, stretched out, and crossed his legs at the ankles.

Wilhelmina had greeted them both with a hug and a peck on the cheek before retreating to the pilot's chair. Sokolov ended up pulling the kitchenette bench down and perching on it rather than sitting too comfy next to Javier.

The three of them made up corners of an unhappy triangle.

"So where did she screw up?" Javier asked, to open the conversation.

He was an expert screw-up, but he also treated it professionally going in. Little miss Amazon war-babe was too spit and polish to pull off the sorts of risks he took for granted.

Wilhelmina was apparently thinking the same thoughts. She had pressed her lips together to suppress a smile.

"Perhaps a failure of paranoia," she replied.

Javier blinked. He blinked again.

Was that even possible with Sykora?

He thought about it some more. Reconsidered everything he knew about the dragoon, aware that the other two people were now staring at him.

Nope.

"Did you even make it to *Meehu?*" he asked finally.

Wilhelmina's shoulders came down. Javier only now realized how tense she had been, seated over there, when it bled out of her.

What was making her nervous? Him? Really? Weird.

"We did," she began after a brief pause, apparently to order her notes in her head. "Sykora had made some contacts with local fences to find a buyer for my old ship. The four of us: myself, Djamila, Piet, and Afia, had just finished dinner and were headed back to our hotel when we were ambushed. Djamila was stunned unconscious while the rest of us were captured."

Javier watched her stop and take a breath, eyes flickering back and forth at some bad memory.

"How did you escape?" Javier asked quietly.

"I didn't," she replied grimly. "I volunteered to deliver the ransom message to Captain Sokolov."

Javier looked around the cabin again. It smelled nice, but it wasn't the ancient explorer they had set out for *Meehu* in.

"What happened to your ship?" he asked simply.

"It's still there," she said. "We had paid for a full month docking fees, expecting to need some time to find the right buyer. But it was too slow to get here, so I hot-wired the fastest runabout I could steal and ran as fast as I could. He still thinks it will take me three or four more days to get here to contact you, so we have at least that much a head start."

"He?" the captain asked suddenly.

Sokolov had been so quiet, perched on that bench, that Javier had almost forgotten him. And he didn't look surprised. Maybe she had already told the captain part of her story, and the rest of this was for his own benefit.

"Captain Abraam Tamaz," Wilhelmina said simply.

But that look, right there, said it all.

One time, Javier had farted really loudly, the morning after an especially-bad rice-dinner-and-all-night-drinking session, and really stenched up the conference room in the middle of a centurion meeting. Sokolov got that same look on his face. Sour disgust, mixed with a dollop of angry, but holding his comments in and not venting them all over the crew.

Too busy being *The Captain.*

"You know the guy," Javier said to the captain.

It wasn't a question.

"*Storm Gauntlet*'s former Executive Officer," Sokolov replied. "A few years before your time."

"Bad feelings?"

"Tamaz wanted us to be more of a pirate operation and less of a business enterprise."

"More?"

Javier had a hard time politely wrapping his tongue around that word, considering his place in this *enterprise*.

"More," Sokolov smiled winter itself at him. "Send out a distress signal, and then massacre whoever shows up to rescue us. Raid small colonies, slaughter everyone, and steal all the hardware to sell to other colonies. *More*."

For just a moment, Javier was able to pierce the captain's veil and see the high-wire act the man had to walk every day, keeping an expensive former warship in raw materials and fresh socks, while not always having legitimate cargo to transport. The type of piracy Sokolov practiced was sometimes a lesser evil.

Javier experienced a moment of true empathy for the man. Then he carefully wrapped it up in tissue paper and put it in a box in his mind. That box he stored on a high shelf in a closet. And locked the door behind him when he left.

Sokolov and the rest of that man's crew were still all going to hang from a *Concord* Fleet yardarm one of these days. Hopefully in low gravity. Javier would see to that when he got free.

And then a little light bulb went on, just like in the cartoons.

Sykora a prisoner, being held for ransom. He and the Captain having a private conversation with Wilhelmina. *Why* the three of them were having this meeting on her vessel, instead of aboard *Storm Gauntlet*.

Witnesses. Loose tongues.

Risk.

Poker was one thing. It was a game of will and perception and luck. Javier made nice spare change off the crew playing poker, especially the engineering deck. Those people were amateurs.

Captain Sokolov was playing chess now. Probably a multi-level version Javier had seen in a bar once, with pieces representing fantasy armies on the ground, while other armies fought in the heavens and underworld. Too much like work, but some people liked it.

Everything clicked.

They wanted his help. Needed it. Absolutely relied on it to pull off whatever crazy stunt they had planned. To rescue Sykora.

Huh.

Javier actually looked both directions, like crossing the street, and then at Wilhelmina, and then Sokolov.

Time passed.

Captain had a hard look on his face. Javier imagined his own mirrored it. Wilhelmina sat perfectly still and quiet as she watched.

"I'm in," Javier said into the quiet whisper of the air systems.

Just like that.

ONE OF THE advantages to being The Captain, as Zakhar saw it, was generally being able to pick the field of battle. One of the disadvantages was that he occasionally forgot that behind that facile, fast-talking tongue on his Science Officer was a first-rate mind.

Something had happened to his crew when Wilhelmina Teague had first been found, trapped in cryo aboard her ancient ship inside an even-more-ancient mine field. Even before she had been rescued and defrosted.

He couldn't explain what, or why, but it had.

Sykora had become emotional and flexible about rules that used to be iron-clad. Almost human, at least for a few days. He'd never seen that in all the years he had known her, but she got over it quickly, like a bad flu.

And Javier had volunteered to walk away from enough money to possibly buy his freedom from slavery. Almost acted like a grown-up, for even longer.

The two of them had even stopped bickering long enough to make common cause.

Over Wilhelmina.

Zakhar had considered hiring Teague. It had made his ship a better place to have her around. But it had also disrupted everything in unsettling ways. He was not a man enamored of sudden, chaotic change.

He locked eyes with his Science Officer.

"I haven't asked yet," he growled.

It didn't help that the two of them tended to think along similar paths at times like this, an outcome of the years at the Academy on Bryce, followed by active duty careers with the *Concord* Navy.

Brothers in arms.

"You will," Javier replied, now in his serious voice.

"What will I ask, Aritza?"

"We're going to go rescue Sykora. You want my help. You want me to do something nobody else on this crew can do."

"And you're in, just like that?" Zakhar asked.

"You wouldn't understand why," Javier replied coldly, as if from a great and remote mountaintop.

Zakhar agreed with that assessment.

He carefully pulled himself back from an unnecessary emotional confrontation. Aritza and Sykora had taken their hatred to a new and dangerous place because of Wilhelmina. Before that, it had almost turned into a teenage sibling rivalry. With him as the father in a sitcom.

Now they were comrades in arms themselves.

Unsettling.

"We could use words like honor, or duty," Javier continued, his tone dropping to almost a whisper. "You own my ransom, so you have both a carrot and a stick, should you choose to exercise it."

"And you'll volunteer to help rescue her, just like that, and then come back to *Storm Gauntlet* as if nothing happened? As if you weren't thinking about your own freedom and an open door? Or taking this runabout and disappearing?"

"That's right," Javier said flatly, glancing over at Wilhelmina in some random and unexplainable way.

Just what the hell had happened between Aritza and Sykora?

Zakhar had the feeling he would go to his grave with that question unanswered. Perhaps God would be willing to explain it for him, if he made it there.

Zakhar looked at the woman as well.

She was carefully not moving, as if to not disturb the emotional balance of the room. She had changed as well, but he hadn't spent that much time around her from the time she was defrosted until she had left, in order to baseline her behavior now.

Older than he had first thought. Possessed of a stillness he attributed to her being some kind of missionary, a Shepherd of the Word. Whatever that meant now, five centuries later.

Brilliant and broadly educated. Charismatic, and entertaining, and exotic all at once.

Poised.

"Wilhelmina?" Zakhar asked simply. "You're sure about this?"

She nodded once. "I am, Captain Sokolov."

"Aritza," he continued, turning now to the other thorn in his side. "Wilhelmina has asked me to send you with her back to *Meehu*, to help rescue Djamila. As you said, your return here is a matter of honor. Something between gentlemen of *Bryce*. Will you honor it?"

Javier stood up from the sofa, suddenly every inch a *Concord* officer, probably more so than he had ever been when he had worn the uniform.

"I will, captain."

Wonder of wonders.

Zakhar stood as well. Two short strides put him close to the man. He stretched out a hand.

Javier shook it.

"Good luck, Javier," Zakhar said quietly.

"Thank you, sir."

Javier considered things, smiled.

"Cavalry will be three days behind you," Zakhar said firmly. "Tamaz is not someone I would miss. Nor would the galaxy."

Zakhar turned and found Wilhelmina close.

He started to say something, but she engulfed him in a hug. Zakhar had forgotten how much taller she was until she leaned down and kissed him on the cheek.

"Thank you, Captain," she whispered in his ear.

Zakhar smiled at her and walked to the airlock door. He glanced back and watched the emotions in the room swirl.

Being a pirate was so much easier.

PART FOUR

Wᴵʟʜᴇʟᴍɪɴᴀ ᴄᴏɴsɪᴅᴇʀᴇᴅ the scene after Captain Sokolov departed, leaving her and Javier alone.

Javier was far too nervous around her. Had been, from the first moment she could remember anything after waking up from a nap that had lasted four hundred and eighty-eight years.

She considered approaching him, initiating physical contact. She knew he found her attractive. Most men and many women did: tall, vivacious, and redheaded.

But there was an air of cold reserve around the man, like a fog, shielding him.

They locked eyes across two meters of space. Whatever it was, that remoteness, that coldness went all the way to the bottom of his soul.

In the end, she retreated, ceding him the field of battle. This was too important. The captain's chair beckoned, warm and protective. She moved next to it, but didn't sit.

Javier had taken up a spot next to the bench where Sokolov had sat by the time she had turned around.

The silence stretched, uncomfortable and taut in ways she hadn't been expecting.

Wilhelmina had spent nearly six weeks aboard *Storm Gauntlet*, recovering herself and preparing. She still felt like a butterfly emerging from a chrysalis, but the crew had treated her well, far better than she had expected, especially once she'd realized they were pirates, at least in their spare time. Six weeks had been a lot of time to recover, and to prepare.

After all, how often do you lay down to sleep, and wake up five hundred years later, hale and hearty? But the crew had accepted her, almost adopted her.

Javier had been goofy and witty, but also protective. He had seemed to like girls, but kept the space between them carefully professional, not that she hadn't considered making the effort. He was a good looking fellow, dark and well-built.

But there was a gulf now. And she hadn't said or done anything, except return.

She *had* returned without Djamila. And the wars between those two were almost legendary, to hear the crew tell it. Especially Javier's assistant, Ilan Yu.

Wilhelmina considered the emotional chasm between them.

"Did I make a mistake?" she asked finally, leaving all the linguistic options open to interpretation. He was one of the few men she had ever known who could use it as an artistic palette.

"No," Javier replied, his tone flat and hard, but not angry at her. "You did what was appropriate. What comes next will be *necessary*."

The emphasis on that last word sent a chill up her spine. This wasn't the Javier she'd known. He wore the man's shape, but there was another soul there. Something deeper, unseen. Almost malevolent.

Wilhelmina considered the fairie tales her grandmother had told her once upon a time, in the dim recesses of history. Javier struck her as a Doppelgänger now. The shape was right, but there was a stranger sitting before her. He reminded her of no other man so much as Sokolov.

Perhaps that was what it meant to be an officer of the *Concord* Navy now. Hard men, facing a hard universe.

Had she turned Javier back into the man he used to be? Before he was happy?

"I need your help," she said finally. "Tamaz is a bad person, surrounded by bad people. I wanted to gather good men to my banner."

It almost sounded like a recruiting speech, but five months ago she had still been Shepherd of the Word, assembling good men and women in the cause of civilization. That everyone who had heard her speak that last night had been dead for hundreds of years didn't change anything. There were still monsters in the darkness, and civilization needed paladins to protect it.

Even the most unlikely of paladins.

She smiled at Javier. He had puffed up a bit, as if he could read her mind.

"The Word has been forgotten," he replied softly, almost apologetically.

"No."

She shook her head in harsh negation, eyes locked with his.

"The speakers have been forgotten, Javier," she replied, moving slowly closer to the man. "The Word will never be lost."

"Why me?"

She let go some of the tenseness in her back. They had just moved past the hard part. Javier was willing to help, to go on this quest. Wilhelmina felt like Queen Isabella, or Eleanor of Aquitaine, or Elizabeth One.

She could do this.

"Two reasons. First, Tamaz doesn't know you, and I'll be in disguise. We can get closer to him than anybody else on the crew could. Second, I wanted someone I could trust with my life."

She watched one of his eyebrows arch, rather eloquently.

"It took more than a week to get to *Meehu* in that old ship, Javier," she said. "Djamila and I had a *lot* of free time to talk. You came up a lot."

His face got even more distant and cold. He understood *what* the two women had discussed.

She sighed inside.

"I wanted to say thank you, Javier," she continued. "For letting me live. For giving me the chance to continue my mad quest. For sending me on my way with your share of the treasure, when it could have bought your freedom from *them*."

Them was obvious.

He said nothing.

Wilhelmina cursed inside, unsure how to break through, to reach him.

Moments of emptiness passed.

"Are you ready? Time is wasting, Javier," she said hopefully into the vast, emotional space.

They were close enough to dance, if he would just relax.

Some mad fire finally lit in the back of his eyes.

"If we're going to rescue Sykora, I don't even had an overnight bag, madam," he smiled up at her finally.

"I stole enough clothes for both of us, you know" she tried to leer back at him. "You won't have to slut walk home."

"That works," he said as he turned and moved away from her. "I need to grab a couple of things from the ship. Fifteen minutes and we'll be in free-flight."

It felt good to flirt with the man, even if there was some manner of icy bulwark between them. Wilhelmina would just have to figure out how to melt it.

Djamila had never once suggested anything other than hard fire between she and Javier, and Wilhelmina knew there were no other crew members he was more than occasionally involved with. She had checked.

Could a relationship based on hatred be as fulfilling as one based on love?

Javier paused at the airlock hatch and studied her face.

He nodded to himself, turned, and disappeared through the opening.

Wilhelmina let her long legs collapse, dropping her butt into the captain's chair with an explosion of air from her lungs.

She'd had men reject her advances before, for a variety of reasons, but never once because it might get in the way of his vengeance.

She would need to work on that.

PART FIVE

It was the dead of night shift.

Sleep eluded Javier. Or rather, the dreams would not let him sleep. And there was no booze aboard the little vessel that could help him relax enough to pass into darkness and stay deep.

The lights were low.

Javier didn't need to be awake. The ship was in the middle of a jump that would finally drop them at the far distant edge of the *Meehu* system, one or two jumps out from their target, but not for another three hours. If they missed the alarm clock, the ship would just sit there, waiting for someone to tell it what to do next.

It wasn't intelligent, not like Suvi, but the vessel was automated enough that someone with no experience could figure out how to make it fly. If she was as smart as Wilhelmina.

Javier sat in the pilot's seat, spun around backwards to he could rest his feet on the edge of the inflatable bed that had been hidden inside the sofa. Where he could watch Wilhelmina sleep.

Where he could brood.

With the bed inflated, there was no other room in the space, so they had ended up sharing it. It was like sleeping with your sister when you were kids. Even dead asleep, his lizard-brain kept him from rolling over and snuggling himself up against her bottom. That she slept nude didn't help. He was wearing orange sweat pants and a purple t-shirt with *Surat*

193

Thani Angels printed on the front. Apparently, they were a professional, minor league skyball team from a far-distant sector.

Javier watched her chest rise and fall as she breathed. Even her nudity barely distracted him, which said a lot for his state of mind.

None of it good.

More than once, he considered their next hop. It would be simple enough to bypass *Meehu*, make a hard run lateral across the sector, and get back to the civilized part of the galaxy in just over a week. He wouldn't have his chickens, or his trees, but he had Suvi. They could start over, fresh.

But to do that, he would turn into the thing he despised most: a pirate.

Javier had given that man, Sokolov, his word. All Javier had now, besides Suvi, was his honor, hard-fought coin of the realm. He wasn't going to just throw that away, even in his own mind. Not for those people.

Wilhelmina had at least backed off, sensing his troubles with her feminine ways. Not that he was much more complicated than a mud puddle, according to his second ex-wife. But he wasn't himself.

They had made it through two full days of each other's company, living in each other's pockets. As honeymoons went, not bad.

Now the hard part. *Meehu Platform.*

Something woke her.

Wilhelmina rolled onto her side to look at him. The change from her normally red hair to a dark chestnut brown was jarring. It made her look like someone else, which was the goal, but it also made them strangers, sharing a bed and nothing more. That might not have been the worst choice.

"I'm sorry," she whispered.

For what was left unsaid. It could cover any multitude of sins, real or imagined. Who knew what Sykora had told her? Or rather, how much?

He nodded. It wasn't her fault he was being like this. She was just the reminder. How far they had fallen from imagined glory. What he had become. What still awaited him when he got back to *Storm Gauntlet.*

Some of the cold bled out of him. He felt his shoulders lower.

Wilhelmina patted the empty spot beside her. She stretched in distractingly-interesting ways. He noticed. She noticed.

"Come to bed," she said in a tone that left little ambiguity.

"I'm still not sure that's a good idea," he replied.

"This isn't about you, mister," she said, iron steeling her voice. "I haven't gotten laid in either six months, or five centuries, depending on how you want to count it. I have needs and you're going to help. I have no interest in anything more serious than a good roll in the hay, right now."

Javier nodded. He even smiled a little as he stood up and started to strip off his t-shirt.

This was a woman who got him.

PART SIX
BOOK SIX: NAVARRE

PART ONE

Abraam Tamaz smiled at the view, laid out before him like a buffet.

The room was plain. Gray walls, fluorescent lights, metal floor.

Sterile. Antiseptic.

The woman before him was not beautiful in the classical sense. She was 2.1 meters tall and built more like a man, with broad shoulders and muscles and thighs that masked the lovely, small breasts and trim waist in a cloak of false masculinity. A strong jaw and boring nose were redeemed by a spray of cute freckles. He could count nine holes in her left ear, where bangles had been removed. Her hair was the unmistakable hue of mud, clipped very short on the sides and normally standing upright in a vaguely-stylish mohawk.

Today, it was slicked back with sweat and pain.

Tamaz stepped back to get a better look at this woman, this prisoner, his prize.

She had been carefully, lovingly strapped to a modified hospital bed, her feet on his left and her head below his right hand. An intravenous drip in her left arm kept her hydrated and mildly hallucinating. Not bad, just enough to keep her tractable.

A strap was across her mouth. Not to keep her from screaming. She would never show pain. No, this was to keep her from unknowingly biting her tongue off in her agony. She might need it later.

Enough straps had been employed to keep even Djamila Sykora from moving more than two millimeters, to say nothing of getting free. He would have it no other way. Were she to escape, they would probably be forced to kill her, if for no other reason than to keep her from killing all of them.

Still, her angular, nude form was perfection itself. He paused to marvel at the taut, rippling stomach. The only men he knew with abs like that were professional models. Even the identity tattoo on the side of the ribcage closest to him was the beautiful statement of a powerful, independent woman.

She seemed to be composed of nothing but formidable muscle. Abraam Tamaz prided himself on being strong and fit, but he knew that she could out-lift him in any method, any machine he chose, as well as outrun him in full pack, and probably out-shoot him with any weapon, although that would be a matter he would have liked to test, if he could have trusted her with a loaded pistol.

Still, he lusted over this woman, all the more so because such perfection was denied to him. Oh, he could take her, but she would never know, right now. And while there were drugs he could introduce that would allow her conscious thought while he did so, she would still not give herself willingly.

At least, not yet.

Tamaz studied the wires coming from a device above her head. He traced them to little disks attached to her ears, her forehead, her neck, her nipples, her belly, her wrists, her ankles. They almost looked like tiny vines sprouting from her body. Except these were pouring electricity into her body, instead of nutrients.

Not enough to drive her mad. Oh no. Not her.

At least, not yet.

Just enough to…call it negative reinforcement. She would not come willingly. She might yet be broken to the bit, given enough time.

He was a patient man.

Tamaz nodded to the man who had been lurking nearly invisibly behind the device at Sykora's head. The man had a look of the mad scientist about him, shaved-bald head, spectacles for reading, squishy paunch, white lab coat.

In his mind, Tamaz always referred to the man as Igor, regardless of his medical degrees and schooling. After all, once you have been stripped of such honors for ethical and criminal convictions, can you really still call yourself a doctor?

Tamaz supposed that made him Dr. Frankenstein.

He always preferred Blackbeard, himself, especially once his rook-black hair began to silver in a way that seemed to make him more attractive to the fairer sex.

He looked down sourly.

Not that she would ever smile at him.

Igor turned a dial on the front of his machine. Tamaz was astounded, as always, when the nearly subconscious hum faded. The machine made him tense.

Sykora relaxed as well, but that was an end to the electricity torturing her nerve clusters. Her muscles softened from the absolute tension they had held. Even her nipples faded from their peaks.

Tamaz nodded again.

Igor opened a small vial of liquid beneath Sykora's nose. Even from here, it was foul enough to wake the dead.

Sykora stirred.

Her eyes had blinked occasionally, while under the rush of electrical pain, but that had been an autonomous function.

Now, there was cognition in there, slowly dawning.

Tamaz watched as those brilliant green eyes came to focus on the ceiling above her. After a moment, she found him standing there.

The opposite of love is not hatred. It is apathy. There is no apathy there. Now we just need to transform the passion.

Djamila Sykora came back to herself, back to him, from whatever place she retreated to in the face of his onslaught.

"It is not too late, my love," he crooned to her softly. "You have it in you to end the pain. All you must do is surrender to me."

She was not broken yet. But he knew that. The subtle way her lip and nose curled into a sneer around her gag made that evident.

But he could still try. She might yet acquiesce, before things were required to reach the ultimate stage.

Her Prince Charming, her Captain, would come soon to rescue her.

He could not bear to leave her in the hands of someone like Tamaz, where her purity might be sullied.

No, it would simply be necessary to kill Zakhar Sokolov. And to do it in front of her.

Make her watch, make her plead, make her suffer. Combined with the torture and the drugs, that should be enough to break her.

A broken Sykora would not be as good as a willing Sykora, but he could settle for half a loaf, especially one as magnificent as her.

"Sokolov is coming for you, dear Djamila," he continued, in the kind of voice you used on frightened animals.

Her eyes flared as the words penetrated her inner being.

Was that hope? Fear? Love?

Whatever it was, bringing it to the surface was just one more step on the path to breaking her, to taking her, to owning her.

Tamaz physically stopped himself from licking his lips at the thought of a pliant Sykora, offering up her core, her self, her womanness, to him.

Soon. Very soon, his vengeance would be at hand.

Tamaz nodded at Igor, silent and unobtrusive as ever. The man spun the dial back into the sixth setting.

Tamaz felt a spear of lust pass through him as her toes curled under, her back tried to arch, her nipples reached for the heavens. But never a sound passed her lips.

First I will have my revenge on Sokolov, my love. And then you.

PART TWO

MEEHU PLATFORM. An ugly, geo-synced, misshapen metal donut orbiting an otherwise-worthless planet of the same name, in an unfashionable corner of space where the *Concord* tended to bleed into vagueness and three other political entities lacked the oomph to exert their will.

Javier didn't know the place all that well, but word got around. There were always stories about a place like this.

Mostly, the tales were far more exciting and exotic than the reality would turn out to be. Pirate stations always sounded cool, but usually turned out to be rather seedy, like the bad part of a bad town where you were likely to be rolled for spare change.

The *Platform* was a few degrees better than that. Maybe. It was certainly run by a fearsome oligarchy of merchants-cum-pirate/smugglers who understood the need for a place where there were some rules, and where people could relax, without worrying about the authorities showing up. They weren't the kinds of rules you found in nicer establishments, but there were rules.

Meehu Platform's claim to fame was the level of absolute ruthlessness behind the enforcement of the code of conduct. If you broke the rules, you paid a fine, scale dependent on your error. And you might also be banned from the station for a number of years that usually turned out to be longer than most people wanted to wait. Rarely was anyone executed. You tended to run out of paying customers if you did that.

And *Meehu Platform* was all about paying customers.

If you had a need, and the cash, almost nothing was impossible to acquire. Chickens had taken him some time, once upon a yesterday, but that was because they weren't illegal. It was simply that nobody carried them in stock.

Someone had gone off to find them and retrieve them, so they could sell them in turn to a wandering scout on a *Concord* Fleet Survey contract.

Javier smiled to himself. Everyone had assumed that he'd never been here, because they hadn't bothered to ask him.

Behind him, he could hear Wilhelmina finishing the last touches of her outfit, but he was concentrating on the station ahead of them.

I mean, how many people are crazy enough, or dumb enough to return a place like Meehu Platform *in a ship they stole from here in the first place?*

That would work to his advantage. People here were supposed to be smart. Nobody would be that dumb, so the authorities wouldn't pay that close attention if he didn't draw their attention.

Javier had spent a great deal of time, over the last few days, working on electronics. Suvi was rebuilt. Or rather, her little flitter was faster, smarter, and had enough spare storage to keep her in movies and books for about a year at the speed she usually went through stuff. A couple of centuries for him.

At the same time, Javier had exercised his paranoid demons by running through the little yacht's engines and computers. The system on the ship was stupid. He had owned smarter dogs. But he had traced every line of logic in the computer and identified all the places where a cop might look for serial numbers or other identifying marks. And a few other spots where he would have looked. And then finally he had asked Suvi to attack it from the electronic end.

All was fixed. She had even found a file that simply told a police computer where to look for a serial number that had been hand-etched with some sort of power-tool by the original owner. It didn't, anymore, after Javier had gotten into the engine well himself and flash-welded over it. Sure, a forensic specialist could probably tease the numbers and letters up, but if they were already that suspicious, he was a dead man.

"What do you think?" Wilhelmina asked invitingly.

Javier turned and looked up at her. And then remembered to pick his jaw up off the deck. Twice.

Tall. Long legs poured into pointy-toed, high-heeled boots that came up past her knees. In a color of sparkly, bright purple that was almost mesmerizing to look at. More mesmerizing than she was

Cream-colored tights that showed off the powerful thigh muscles she had obviously been working on since her long nap.

A belted tunic, dangling just past her bottom as she slowly spun in place, showing off. He would have sworn it was chamois, it had that feel. It was the color of doves in a fog.

Around her waist, a fancy sash/girdle/belt/thingee in a black so dark that is seemed to absorb light. Because he had convinced her that pirates always wore fancy sashes. Every movie agreed on that.

Glossy black leather bandoliers attached to a brass ring that rested exactly between her breasts, at the level of her nipples, and focused the eyes on the deep V of her top, straining to hold those breasts in. She had nice breasts, struggling to be free.

It took several moments to remember she had a face. A layer of makeup base had washed out all her freckles, making her seem vaguely Egyptian, an effect she heightened with the brown eye-liner and color. Blood red lips that made her look like a night creature. Mixed with the now-dark hair, she was someone else. And most men would never make it that far north, anyway, to actually see her face. He certainly didn't feel that great of a need.

"Ahem," she said, not exactly disgruntled, but obviously feeling a bit objectified as he stared at her tits.

Tough, lady. You're about to visit a station full of people who will want to kill us. Get used to being a moll.

Javier smiled. His own outfit was nowhere near as impressive. He wanted them paying attention to Wilhelmina Teague, or *Hadiiye*, as she was now going to be known.

He smiled even broader. Very few people in this sector would know enough Turkish to realize her name roughly meant *Guide*. Fitting for a one-time Shepherd of the Word.

"Very nice," he replied. "Nobody will even remember what I look like."

"He might like boys exclusively, you know," she answered tartly.

"Men are visual creatures, Hadiiye," Javier leered expansively. "Even then, he'd lust."

She blushed, even through the makeup.

Javier knew that the Shepherds took a variety of vows: poverty, obedience, chastity. That sort of thing. But she had also explained to him, lying in the darkness, covered with sweat, that those were generally more suggestions designed to keep a proper seeker on the path, rather than rules designed for monastic lifestyle. She could still enjoy a good steak, or a good tumble, but those were things for the body, not for the soul.

He disagreed wholeheartedly. They were very good for the soul.

"Stand up, you," she said finally with an impatient snap of her fingers. "I wanna see."

Javier rose.

He had refined her original vision for a blood-thirsty pirate bad-ass, but not in the direction she had intended. It was more like a troupe of Shakespeareans done in street-gang motif.

Twenty-ring lace up boots in glossy neo-leather, with curb-stomping soles and hull-metal toes. Bright red laces all the way up and double-knotted.

Knee-length britches out of dark maroon corduroy, with heavy leather combat padding along the outer edge in case someone out of a Chop-sockey movie kicked him.

Sixteen centimeter tall leather belt around his middle, with a canary-yellow sash tied around that. Much fancier than hers. Just because.

Sleeveless doublet in that same maroon corduroy, but with two rows of buttons that ran from the inside of his hips to the middle of his collar-bones. Underneath, a startlingly white long sleeve shirt.

The woman across from him had pointed out that he had the shoulders to pull a doublet off. Javier just had rarely felt the need. But this was Halloween. He could do this level of costume partying for a few days and not feel silly.

Not very silly.

Just for the hell of it, a cloth was tied around his head, with a *Neu Berne* Assault Marine logo in the middle. Sykora would appreciate that last bit. He needed a little bit of silly on his side, to balance things out before they got too dark.

A dress sword and flash pistol balanced themselves on either side. Javier could barely use the pistol. And if it came to blades with anyone who knew what they were doing, Javier was a Christmas turkey waiting to be carved on.

Hadiiye, Wilhelmina, whistled, gesturing for him to turn in place as she had done.

"Honestly," she said with a wink as he finished. "You should consider that as a permanent look."

Javier gave her his best stink-eye scowl, but kept himself from drifting back into that *hard* place where he had been.

"It would be wasted on the rest of the crew," he said. "And you won't be around to reward me appropriately."

She blushed again. Harder this time. But didn't comment.

"So if I'm Hadiiye," she asked after a beat, "who are you?"

"I am *Navarre*," he announced with an air of dangerous menace. "The first King of Navarre, back on Earth, was an Aritza."

"I didn't know that."

"I did learn a few things in history class, lady," Javier replied.

He took a deep breath and felt the seriousness begin to take hold of him, like darkness creeping in at sunset.

"When we get there," he continued, edging ever-closer to that black place in the back of his mind. "I'm going to need you to either be dead serious bad-ass, or total bimbo, but I need you to decide right now, so I can plan accordingly. Any slip-up in front of those people gets us killed."

Javier watched her eyes and then saw her take a deep breath, almost meditatively. She rose to her full height, towering almost as far over him as Sykora did, but there were fourteen centimeter heels involved with Hadiiye. Her eyes closed for several seconds.

It was like watching ripples on a still pond as the energy flowed outward from her belly-button to the tips of her bright red fingernails.

"I am Hadiiye," she announced in a voice that had been cast in bronze. "Killer. Assassin. Death-dealer. Commend your soul to God before you try your luck, bucko."

She had gone for bad-ass. He should have known.

Javier let a single raised eyebrow ask the next question.

"The galaxy was no safer for a single woman traveling alone five centuries ago," she purred silkily with an evil smile, just oozing *big cat predator*. "Not everyone took no for an answer. At least, not the first time."

He felt a chill in spite of himself.

PART THREE

THE GOONS HAD PICKED them up as they entered the joint. Wilhelmina counted them.

No, damn it. Focus. Hadiiye counted them.

Five, one obviously the official bouncer, two more at the bar, and two others scattered about the room, trying to look innocent as customers.

Hadiiye did not hang on Navarre as they walked. That would have been the bimbo version of this costume.

Hadiiye was a killer. She had to act the part: blades secreted in three places, plus one on her belt; a smaller flash pistol than Navarre carried, tucked into a hidden holster, against her left kidney, where she could get at it quickly.

She was as much body-guard as gun moll here, with a dose of eye-candy designed as the second layer of distraction. Her nipples pressing against the soft cloth of her tunic certainly worked in her favor, but she honestly couldn't help herself.

This was so much fun.

Shepherds of the Word were always serious people. Constantly learning, traveling, proselytizing. They were not supposed to do things like this, dressing up in costume so they could pull off a caper on a criminal enterprise.

Hadiiye caught the appreciative looks from the five men, either staring at her chest or crotch. Navarre had been right. She would have to pay off on that bet.

But honestly, what did she know about the baser examples of men?

Well, okay, maybe that was a bit arrogant and superior, but here were several examples of exactly what the Word was intended to rectify. Hadiiye might have to kick their asses up and down the block a few times, just so Wilhelmina could preach to them, once they were properly disposed to listen to her as a person and not stare at her as a side of meat.

Wilhelmina sat quietly in one corner of her mind as Hadiiye scowled at the men. They were seeing her undressed and probably bent over one of the tables in this restaurant, with them taking turns.

She envisioned them hanging from hooks in an abattoir.

Apparently, they picked that attitude up as she moved.

Javier walked up to the bar and leaned against it.

No, damn it. Navarre.

A flunky appeared from a door behind the bar, cold and arrogant as he considered these *tourists* who had obviously wandered into the wrong joint.

Navarre could handle him. Hadiiye turned to study the rest of the space. And the men subtly adjusting themselves as if violence was imminent.

Because seriously, if you needed five to take on the two of us, your boss needs to hire better goons.

And that was what they were. Goons. Second-rate, muscled thugs guarding a restaurant that specialized in French cuisine. On a station dedicated to being a criminal marketplace. In the middle of nowhere.

Hadiiye smiled to herself, then let it encompass the men around her. Once upon a time, a young Shepherd named Wilhelmina had taught close combat techniques to younger students, mostly girls, preparing them to go out into the oh-so-dangerous galaxy and preach the Word. She had the reach for it, too, with legs longer than some people.

Behind her, the bartender grunted something rude.

Navarre responded in French, which apparently surprised the bartender almost as much as it did Hadiiye.

"I don't care what you think, peasant-boy," Navarre growled softly. "Your job is to send a message to Captain Tamaz. If you can't handle that, I'll have one of these puppies here do it, instead."

Around them, the punks tensed, but that was the way hackles came up at being insulted, rather than about to attack. Indignant shock.

"What message?" the bartender asked with an accent better suited to one of the harsher slums of Paris. How had he gotten out here, so far from Earth?

But then, how had Hadiiye? They were all far gone from home.

The assassin fixed her steely eye on each of the men in turn. It wasn't exactly a dare. It was worse. It was a woman simply laughing at them as the junior varsity.

"My name is Navarre," the once-and-future Science Officer said condescendingly. "I want to talk about the woman from Neu Berne. He'll understand. Right now, we are going to have dinner at Galileo's. Good day."

Navarre appeared in the corner of her eye, already moving towards the door at a sharp clip. Hadiiye smiled once more at her prey and followed the man out the door.

PART FOUR

"How DID you know where to go to find him?" Wilhelmina asked. She was still Hadiiye, but they were in a lovely bistro specializing in traditional Italian peasant food. There was enough music and chatter to keep their conversation private as long as they were careful.

The food was excellent.

"While we were inbound, I made a few calls. You were in the shower," Javier replied.

Except it wasn't Javier. It was still *Navarre*, a hard, cold, pirate son-of-a-bitch that looked more like the man who had stood on her deck with Captain Sokolov than the goofball who had awakened her from a magical sleep.

At least she had finally gotten her kiss.

"You know people at *Meehu*?" Wilhelmina was shocked.

He hadn't mentioned anything. She had been prepared to wing it, knowing they had a few days to scout before Sokolov would arrive.

This creature named Navarre wasn't waiting.

"I've been through here before," he replied, in a tone that didn't suggest further questions on the topic.

"So what's your plan, Navarre?"

She was still a little lost in this century. Certainly, humanity hadn't changed much. But she'd never been a criminal element before. Fun, but a bit unnerving. Navarre was an interesting, if unsettling companion.

"We have a two or three day head start," the hard man across from her replied. "He won't start getting prepared for Sokolov just yet, probably figuring that the captain couldn't react so quickly. We're going to get close to him first, find his weaknesses, and exploit them."

Navarre leaned forward and put both elbows on the table, resting his chin on crossed fists. His eyes grew even harder.

"It will probably be necessary to kill people before we leave this station, Hadiiye. Are you at peace with that?"

"I think so."

"No," he replied flatly.

It was the tone that chilled her. Up until now, this had been a game of dress up, for a party. She sensed a line suddenly drawn in the sand at her feet.

"*No?*"

"You will either say *yes*, or you will stay on the ship while I handle this. I have to trust you completely, unquestioningly. Pick. Right now."

The last several days were gone, just like that. The last six weeks. The friendship. The comradery. Staying up late and fooling around. Everything.

Gone.

Doppelgänger.

There was no Javier. Only Navarre. Where had he come from? Would she ever see Javier again?

Already, she missed him.

"I trusted you with my life," she said quietly. "My soul."

"No. Sykora did that. You were just the result."

Huh?

Wilhelmina thought back to the long conversations with Djamila, over tea, listening to the ancient ship chug through the darkness while Piet and Afia slept. She had missed something. Something critical between those two, Javier and Djamila.

Lovers in hatred.

Wilhelmina considered her options.

The Word conveyed the value of all lives. At its very bottom, the cornerstone of Rama Treadwell's teachings was the very egalitarian nature of happiness. All beings deserved the freedom to define and obtain happiness on their own terms, in their own way, free from censure.

Thus had she been taught. Thus had she taught.

And yet...

212

Sophisticates frequently fell into their own logical trap: the *Fallacy of Pacifism*. They forgot that the Vow of Peace contained within it the promise of violence in defense of others.

Shepherds of the Word were expected to engage with their words, but they were also equipped to use their hands, if all else failed.

Wilhelmina looked around the room once, aware that Javier was waiting for an answer. To an outsider, it would look like Hadiiye actively looking for threats to her being. But this was much deeper.

There were no tourists here. Not in the sense of fat, happy, middle-class travelers on an adventure. That kind did not come to *Meehu*. Even accidentally.

Instead, there were kids, folks barely past their teens, who had either run away, or been chased out. There were middle-aged people who had lost it all and had to start over. There were older people trying to hang on to something, facing only a cold and lonely death ahead.

Very few of the people she could see here probably intended this as their destination, their lot.

But then, who did?

Wilhelmina framed the words, passed down from Rama Treadwell and his intellectual descendants a very long time ago, but Hadiiye spoke them aloud.

"Paladins are men and women of the *Sword*, Navarre."

There. Commitment.

I will kill people for you, for Djamila, for Sokolov. I will use violence to try to make the galaxy a better place, not by imposing my order upon it, but by using my will to thwart would-be conquerors, bad men, villains.

Navarre studied her for several moments silently before he drew a breath and nodded.

For a moment, she saw a depth of pain in Javier's eyes she had never imagined existed. Something terrible and bitter. Obviously, he was good at hiding things from people.

Would it better to let it lie, or help him heal? Would he welcome the suggestion?

A change came over Navarre as he glanced to his right over her shoulder. Subtle, but critical.

Hadiiye shifted her weight invisibly and let one hand fall off the table to rest close to a blade balanced for throwing, hidden in her right boot top. Something prickled in the air, like the smell of ozone.

"Captain Navarre?" a man asked carefully.

Hadiiye looked about, but nobody else was paying attention. She glanced back at the figure.

Oily, in a slippery way. Well-dressed man in dark pants and matching jacket. Businessman who knew how to wear the suit, instead of the goons at the other restaurant who let the suits wear them. Hair cut short, brown on top and graying on the edges. Conservative and quiet.

Hard, but in a deadly, accountant kind of way, rather than being a killer.

Not like her.

Across the table, Navarre relaxed a touch, perhaps from absolute zero to merely liquid nitrogen.

"Indeed," Navarre said, gesturing to the table. "Please, join us. Have some wine. Let us talk like civilized beings who find themselves at an uncivilized crossroads."

There was the Javier she remembered. Smooth, charming, eloquent. Even hiding behind that hard face.

These bastards had no clue what they were up against.

The man nodded appreciably and pulled a chair out with one hand, all manners in a place that could barely spell the word, let alone practice it.

Hadiiye felt his eyes pass over her once. Wilhelmina would have smiled. Hadiiye scowled instead, intent on her role as a moll, a sidekick.

A killer.

She felt him dismiss her, barely lingering on her cleavage, before he turned his attention fully on Navarre.

"I do not believe we have met before, Captain Navarre," the stranger said carefully. "My name is Marcas Almássy. I work as an agent for Captain Tamaz. I understand you wish to speak with him."

Navarre had lowered his hands and leaned back from resting his chin on his knuckles. He reached out now and took hold of a half-filled wine glass as a waiter materialized with a second glass and a new bottle.

Moments of silence passed as the waiter expertly cracked the new bottle, poured, and disappeared, without a word spoken. Obviously, this wasn't the man's first visit. Good to know.

"I understand," Navarre finally said, slowly, carefully. "That Captain Tamaz has recently come into possession of a person. A woman, exceptionally tall, formerly of *Neu Berne*, now a freebooter."

Almássy paused, sipped his wine appreciably, and considered the tableaux.

"And where might you have heard something like that, Captain Navarre?"

She watched Javier, *Navarre*, lean closer, conspiratorially.

"Someone talked," he almost whispered with a chilly smile. "Someone always talks."

Hadiiye held her breath as the energy rippled between the two men. She remained aware of every patron and every wine glass in view, confident that the two men with her would cover her blind flanks if something happened. Both were professionals.

The room remained amateur.

"And your interest in the woman?" Almássy inquired with a smile.

Crocodiles might learn something from this man.

"Entirely personal," Navarre replied succinctly. "Old business. Unfinished."

For a moment, she watched all of Javier's hatred bubble to the surface. There were actors who could probably fake that sort of thing, but they were few and far between. And they would be hard-pressed to match something like this. Perhaps only a master Shakespearean could manage.

"And were you interested in negotiating a bounty for her?"

Hadiiye nearly choked at the price the man quoted. It was a significant proportion of the extravagant fortune Sykora had thought she might get for the ancient freighter with the amazing history.

Almássy and Navarre leaned close, two old merchants at the bazaar, getting down to brass tacks. She wondered if the man owned one of those old-fashioned accountant hats, all bill and no lid.

He had that feel to him.

"Oh, no," Navarre smiled, catlike. "I was much more interested in obtaining front row seats when you executed her. That would satisfy me. And my backers."

"Backers?"

Hadiiye saw the man's concentration crack for a second of utter confusion as the implications of the word settled on him like a winter mantle.

Navarre wasn't a lone wolf who wouldn't be missed if something happened to him. Others might inquire. Unknown others. Potentially dangerous others.

She considered it a masterful job of misdirection, until she saw the light in Navarre's eyes. If a supernova was white hot summer heat, this was the exact equivalent in winter.

The accountant saw it as well. He retreated, emotionally as well as physically, leaning back as far as his chair would comfortably allow.

Moments passed.

Navarre considered the man as bobcat might consider a field mouse.

"I think," Almássy responded finally, "that you would be better served to discuss such a matter with Captain Tamaz directly, Captain Navarre."

"I suspected as much."

"Perhaps you will be able to come to the club, Sevenoaks, this evening? Captain Tamaz will be handling some business there in about six hours. I am certain he will be quite interested in making your acquaintance."

Navarre rose slowly from his chair, his hand extended. Almássy did the same.

"I look forward to it, Mr. Almássy," Navarre said. "Until then."

And then the man was gone.

The emotional power of the room dropped precipitously, even as the space seemed to grow warmer.

They were alone again.

Hadiiye smiled tightly at her partner.

"Navarre, that was a most amazing bluff."

He fixed her with a cold stare.

"Bluff?"

PART FIVE

THE LITTLE, unnamed, stolen ship was a useful base while they stayed at *Meehu Platform*. For the time they would be here.

Javier scanned the single room once, taking note of several little things he had left, precisely located, that would have been moved by someone rifling the place for clues to his identity. It was second nature when he had to deal with people. Any people. Even ones he liked. In addition, he had left Suvi's sensors on, so she would have flashed a red light at him if anyone had come in.

The space was still secure. He entered, the hard woman one step behind him.

Javier took off Navarre like an old, comfortable cloak and hung him by the airlock hatch, along with the belt holding the sword and pistol. The ship felt warm, almost enough to leech the cold from his bones and soul.

He turned to find her standing in the middle of the room as the hatch closed.

They studied each other, across a gulf far greater than it had been when they left.

"It's safe to be you," he said.

It wasn't an apology, but it was headed in that direction.

"Are you you?" she replied.

Javier considered any number of responses, some of them tart, some angry, a few goofy.

It was a fair question. It deserved a fair answer.

"Close enough. For now," he replied.

These two women had taken him to his dark places. It wasn't her fault. Sykora had started him down that road when they met almost a year ago. Wilhelmina when she first came into his life, and then again when she came back.

"So what do we do now?" she asked, looking unsure for the first time since they had left *Storm Gauntlet*, days ago.

"Now we sleep," he replied, popping buttons and taking off the doublet. "It will be a long night, with a bunch of punks who like to think they're tougher than everyone else by staying up all night drinking shots of engine coolant."

"Really?"

"Really," he said, starting to unlace the boots. "After a nap, more food to absorb the booze."

"What about Djamila?" she asked evasively.

"We don't know where they're keeping her," he replied. "Or how to get her out."

He paused, looked up, fixed her with a hard gaze.

"Yet. We do know she's still alive."

"You're sure?"

"Yes," Javier replied. "He would have offered to sell me footage if they had killed her already."

She took a step sideways and sort of collapsed into the captain's seat.

"So we'll waltz in there?" she asked. "Just like that?"

"Unless you know a way to hack into their security systems and steal all the information we need," he replied, tugging a boot off.

"And Tamaz will fall for it?"

Javier smiled at her. It was a brutal smile. His mind was in a brutal place.

"If he doesn't," he said, "then we're dead."

"And you plan to sleep at a time like this?"

His smile became more rueful.

"I'm surprised you aren't better accustomed to sleeping whenever you got the chance, as slow as that old barge of yours was."

"That was different," she replied, pulling off her own boots and making fists with her toes. "That was boredom. I was never risking my life."

"Wilhelmina," he said sharply. "You were risking your life every time you jumped into hyperspace. Every time you got out of bed. Maybe you should consider how risky this universe is and start paying attention."

"I am paying attention," she shot back, edges of panic creeping into her voice. "But three months ago I was a missionary. Now I'm an assassin. And I have nobody but you to get our mission done. I'm scared."

Javier considered the woman sitting there.

For the last several hours, she had been merely a piece of furniture to maneuver around. An art object that happened to move. He had gotten so lost in himself again that he forgot people around him.

They had feelings. Wishes. Dreams. Fears.

That many years in deep space, alone but for a clutch of chickens, had helped smooth over some of the rough spots, but there were still holes. Landmines he occasionally stepped on. Less so now, but still there.

Fighting a war with Sykora had both sharpened those issues, and made them recede a bit. He had stopped being introspective when he had a foe worth the name.

Now he had Wilhelmina, who might be a…what? A friend? A comrade? A lover?

All of those. None of them. Something. Nothing.

He stood up and held out a hand. She rose as well and took it mutely.

Javier considered his options.

"You trusted me with your life," he said, feeling the warmth of her skin. "Even when you didn't know it."

He was close enough to her to smell the underlying flowers of her perfume that suffused the room.

She looked down at him, confused, and nodded.

"I'm going to do the same," he said. "There is a secret that is worth my life, if Sykora and Captain Sokolov ever find out."

He watched her eyes grow a little bigger, but she remained silent.

Javier smiled. It was warm this time. Maybe for the first time in weeks. Months. Years. Lifetimes.

"Before I was a slave," he said. "I was an explorer, doing survey work for the *Concord* Navy on the far fringes of civilized and terraformed space."

He studied her face. She had withdrawn some, not so much distant as closed. She nodded again, as a placeholder while he spoke.

"I had a lovely, little probe-cutter for a ship," he continued. "It had been retired out of *Concord* service, demobilized, and was destined for the breaker yard. I got it cheap, fixed it up, and reprogrammed the AI aboard to be much more human and interesting than she had been when she was in the fleet."

Javier felt a pang of anguish and rage stab him in the guts as he thought of his lost starship, of *Mielikki*. Of how much he owed Zakhar Sokolov and Djamila Sykora. He did not, could not, let the emotion show.

"When I was taken by Sokolov's crew," he continued. "I told them I had destroyed all the personality and programming circuits. I lied."

She blinked in surprise. Obviously she had heard part of that story at some point. Probably from Sykora.

Vast oceans of emotions and questions played across her face as she stayed perfectly silent.

"Instead," Javier said, "I smuggled her out in a bucket of chicken feed, and then poured her into the only thing I had that was remotely like her old home."

"Her?"

He pointed at the autonomous sensor remote, resting on a shelf where he had placed it when he finished all the upgrades he could manage without building her a bigger body.

"Wilhelmina Teague, I would like to introduce you to my former first mate, my comrade in surveying, my friend. Suvi, please say hello to Wilhelmina."

On the shelf, lights clicked on and the sixteen centimeter, gray, grapefruit-looking globe rose into the air with the faintest of hums.

Because he was holding her hand, Javier felt the sudden surge of adrenaline as Wilhelmina's muscles clenched.

Her era held nothing like the AIs of the present day. There had been smart systems, extremely autonomous and capable, but they did not compose music. Or write poetry.

They did not dream.

"Doctor Teague," Suvi said warmly. "It is my pleasure to finally get to meet you. I have been looking forward to this for so very long."

PART SIX

SHE WAS BACK to being Hadiiye.

Javier had explained how to wear the identity like a costume, intricate and realistic, but never once exposing your inner self while playing the role.

She wondered if she had ever seen Javier not playing some role. She considered asking Suvi sometime, when he wasn't around.

Sevenoaks turned out to be a noisy nightclub, located well away from the other two establishments she had visited with Navarre. It wasn't a pretty place, filled with well-dressed folks showing off in a complicated mating ritual.

No, it was much rougher, filled with crew off of various ships docked at the station, perhaps at a two or three to one ratio, male to female, plus a variety of what were obviously locals and professional entertainers, here eight or ten to one female.

The first person to grope her bottom in this place was going to end up eating teeth.

Just for good measure, Hadiiye pasted a hostile snarl on her face and followed Navarre as he slowly made his way through the press. It was not a full rugby scrum, but there was unavoidable-but-polite jostling. Her height and obvious attitude problem helped clear her path.

Away from the dance floor, the crowd thinned out. Sevenoaks wasn't particularly cavernous, but it made good use of space, with a bar along each side wall, and a series of four rising levels, like steps for giants, climbing towards the back of the club.

She could see booths up there, filled with older patrons, while the kids were down here. Apparently, there was a kitchen around here as well. She saw several people eating dinner, or at least snacks more complicated than instant bar food.

Not that she could hold another bite at this point. But she was good for drinking, especially with men who had never gotten drunk with a missionary before. In some places, there was nothing to do but drink with the locals. You got to be good at holding it.

Almássy, the accountant, rose from a booth above them and back a few tiers as they approached the rear of the club. There wasn't a toll gate here, but several bouncer-looking goons in black muscle shirts made it obvious where the invite-only section began.

Seeing dancers and patrons move against that was like watching waves lap at the beach, with clean, dry sand beyond them.

Navarre walked right up to the bouncers. She stayed a step and a half back and a half step to his left, where she could see over his shoulder, prepared for trouble.

The music wasn't that loud, but she watched Navarre gesture silently to one of the bouncers as Almássy approached, instead of speaking. The man got a nod from the accountant, nodded back, and they were on dry land.

It was quieter here, as well. Wilhelmina would have appreciated the architectural design that went into the ceiling and load-bearing pillars to shelter them from most of the noise. Hadiiye concentrated on people, mostly seated, mostly ignoring her.

The crowd here was different, as she had thought, but not really older. More mature. Perhaps more professional. Much more dangerous. These were captains, and senior officers from various ships, mingling with bankers and fences, if the suits were any clue. Hard men and women, doing deals.

There were no working girls back here.

Almássy shook hands with Navarre and ignored her for the most part. She followed the two men up a set of shallow stairs to the top-most tier, against the back wall of the club.

From the elevation, she guessed there was an entire set of suites or conference rooms below them, but she didn't know this place well enough to guess if they were cribs for a brothel or conference rooms for more complicated, private deals.

Hadiiye didn't care nearly as much as Wilhelmina might have.

They were led to a horseshoe-shaped booth on the fourth tier with the best view. She recognized Captain Tamaz from her previous *encounters*, as well as Adam Erckens, the man's first mate.

Wilhelmina hadn't really had a chance to study Captain Tamaz before, and certainly hadn't paid attention to the sorts of detail Hadiiye required now.

He was tall, even sitting down. She would have guessed he had a centimeter on her if they were both in stocking feet. His black hair was long and tied back in a tail. It had streaks of silver that would have made him distinguished, but for the cruel mouth and harsh eyes.

Captain Tamaz was clean-shaven, but she could already see a shadow on his jaw. This was a man who might need to shave twice daily.

Hairy men didn't do it for either her or Wilhelmina.

Erckens sat next to his captain in the black leather booth. If Tamaz captained a rugby team, and he had that look, Erckens was the muscle in the middle of the scrum. There was nothing soft about the man, from the auburn flattop to the scarred hands resting on the tabletop.

He had the build of a man who spent a lot of time and energy on the right nutrition, the right drugs, and the requisite number of hours at the gym daily.

Fanatic, in all the wrong ways.

Hadiiye's tits sheltered her. None of the three men at the table appeared to even notice she had a face as she approached. The one woman sitting with them looked closer, but said nothing.

She was a stranger, dressed like a banker but still in good shape, if thickening with age. Hadiiye would have guessed her to be in her well-preserved fifties. She could see the older woman's beauty slowly aging, like the best wines, even as she wore little makeup and kept her hair buzzed to perhaps three or four millimeters long.

Her eyes, though. They had the intelligence of an alpha predator, but the warmth of a human, something missing from the three men here. Four, with Navarre.

Tamaz nodded, mostly at Navarre.

"Captain Navarre," he said carefully with a semi-formal nod. He did not rise, but the body language suggested it diplomatically as he gestured for them to join his party.

Dominance games. Two springboks about to joust for supremacy. Local boys unsure of the stranger and willing to play nice for now. At least until he showed weakness. Sharks waiting patiently.

Wilhelmina was aghast, deep inside, as Hadiiye used her well-honed perceptive skills so ruthlessly.

Tough.

"Captain Tamaz," Navarre replied, equally politely.

Bodies shifted around, making a space for Navarre to sit next to Almássy, with Erckens between him and Tamaz.

The woman chose to slide out of the booth and stand.

"Tamaz," the banker said. "I will check my inventory and get back to you in a day or so. I'm sure we can deal."

She looked up and eyed Hadiiye from close up, almost a head and a half shorter but massing a similar amount.

She nodded with the ghost of a smile, and departed without another word.

Hadiiye could have slid in, but chose to remain standing.

Bodyguards, professional ones, didn't limit their movement like these men did. She could probably successfully assassinate Tamaz, if she was suicidal. There were enough guns around her that she'd never make it out alive.

That wasn't necessary. Yet.

For all the noise on the dance floor, it was quiet enough to talk here. Hadiiye suspected a sound-dampening field, but didn't bother looking for it. It would be concealed, along with pop-up stunner turrets a bar like this would certainly invest in.

"I do not believe we have met," Tamaz said, dangling his tone like bait.

Useful, if you wanted to catch a megalodon.

"I rarely work this sector, Captain Tamaz," Navarre replied. Not evasive, but not particularly descriptive. "This was a special trip."

His smile could have sliced bread.

"And your interest in the woman?"

Navarre's smile turned winter.

"I owe that woman more pain than you can possibly imagine," Navarre purred.

"Professional," Tamaz asked, "or personal?"

"Or?"

"I see," Tamaz said succinctly. "Almássy tells me you inquired about a front-row seat for her execution."

"She's cost me too much money," Navarre said. "I can't afford to buy her from you outright."

"Oh ho, so it is professional."

"No," Navarre replied. "With Sokolov, it's professional. With her, it's very much personal."

A single raised eyebrow asked the obvious question. Navarre nodded, warming slightly to the man.

Hadiiye tensed, wondering if this was the point where things would get out of hand, or whether Javier was about to change sides.

Did he have a side?

"They cost me a very expensive, very custom ship."

"I don't remember you, Captain Navarre," Tamaz said sternly. "And I would."

It was Navarre's turn to raise an eyebrow.

"You served with Sokolov? With Sykora?"

She watched Tamaz lean back and smile, almost preening.

"I was *Storm Gauntlet's* Executive Officer," the man announced. "Before I decided to go make my own fortune five years ago. They dreamed too small for me."

"Five years?" Navarre asked. "Then my backers would have no beef with you. Only them. Him, mostly."

"So you aren't really that interested in the woman?"

Hadiiye saw something in the man's eyes. She wasn't entirely sure what it was. Wilhelmina might have discounted it. Another man would have missed it entirely.

Hadiiye was a woman. A hard, brutal, lethal woman. Keyed up for violence and studying all the men about her as victims in waiting. But still a woman.

There was something oddly possessive about the way the man spoke, the way he smiled. Something at odds with the situation. Both Javier and Navarre would miss it.

Hadiiye decided to gamble.

"You could always let me have her," she said with a slow drawl, just loud enough to be heard, just cold enough to convey a very painful point.

Every head turned her direction. Eyes met hers and stayed, for the first time, instead of wandering down her front.

She had just become a person instead of an object.

The tension shifted, bled sideways. Navarre scowled, blinked, processed, grinned. *Good.*

Tamaz studied her closely. His eyes took her in entirely, from the high-heeled fighting boots to the bronze-ringed gap that showed the shadows of her breasts as she breathed, to the long, long arms ending in blood red nails.

She smiled, catlike at him, watched him lick his lips unconsciously. *Better.*

"Interesting," Tamaz said.

Either he was a better poker player than Javier, or he had just bought the identity of Hadiiye.

She wondered if either Javier or Navarre realized how much Tamaz was in love with Djamila Sykora.

"After dealing with Sykora," Navarre said into the silence. "I went and got my own version."

"Is she as good?" Erckens suddenly spoke up, having been silent until now. He had a tenor voice. It might have been pleasant, if it wasn't dripping with frat-boy innuendo and lust.

"Maybe," Navarre said. "She's killed everyone I've wanted her to, so far."

Maybe, Navarre? You don't think Hadiiye could take Sykora?

Wilhelmina spoke up from her quiet corner, offered a memory of Djamila working out. The muscles rippling as she lifted huge weights, did hand-stand pushups against a bulkhead, punished the sparring dummy Wilhelmina held for her.

No, probably not. You three, however, would be meat.

Hadiiye settled for a predator's smile. Big cat.

She *had* killed everyone Navarre had asked her to. That turned out to be nobody as yet, but perhaps he would demand Tamaz and the other two be first. That would please her, after experiences with these men that she would never tell Javier or Djamila.

"Killing Sykora isn't really necessary," Tamaz purred.

Again, that soft undertone. Wilhelmina, the Shepherd of the Word, spoke up, offered all the experience of a doctorate in human psychology. Helpfully pointed out the set of the eyes, the posture, the way the lips held that smile.

He wasn't going to kill her, but he was never letting her go. He was going to break Sykora. Shatter her. Make it impossible for her to say no to him.

That would be enough. Tamaz was a glass-half-full man with Sykora. Not just simple conquest, but also willful acceptance. Something Djamila would never give him willingly.

There was no more dangerous creature in the world that a thwarted lover plotting his revenge.

Wilhelmina wondered about Javier's posture. It was different, but not different enough. The opposite of love is apathy, not hatred. Javier was not apathetic here.

Navarre watched Tamaz and the others for a second. He nodded, mostly to himself.

"In that case, gentlemen," Navarre said. "We probably can't do a deal. My apologies for interrupting your evening."

He began to slide out of the booth, but Tamaz stopped him.

"Actually, Captain Navarre," he began, much more politely. "We might be able to. Sokolov ought to be here in another few days. We can certainly find a happy common cause around his death."

He dangled the bait skillfully.

Hadiiye watched the play of emotions across Navarre's face. She knew Javier well enough from across a poker table to see how much of it was false detail. Hatred. Hope. Vengeance.

Navarre cocked his head.

"Sokolov's coming for her?" he asked, voice dripping with anticipation. His smile gained several degrees of warmth.

"I sent a messenger to draw him in," Tamaz replied. "She had a slow ship, so we have a bit of time to prepare."

"She?"

"One of Sykora's crew. She'll scamper home and undoubtedly bring the cavalry, like it was some boring melodrama. They will expect a trap. I will serve them up one they can escape. They will rescue Sykora. I'll use her to kill them all."

Tamaz was preening again. Butter would not melt in his mouth right now.

Navarre reached out a hand and grabbed the glass of wine that had been in front of the woman banker. He made a production of toasting Captain Tamaz with it.

"To vengeance," Navarre said seriously.

The others scrambled to grab their glasses and rattle them together awkwardly. "To vengeance."

Hadiiye scanned Tamaz and his crew expectantly. They might have Sykora, but they were toasting retribution with Javier Aritza, even if he was portraying the role of Captain Navarre.

Who was doomed here?

PART SEVEN

BOOK SEVEN: DJAMILA

PART ONE

It wasn't *Mielikki*, but it was still an improvement over that short-range airborne autonomous remote Javier had hidden her in when the pirates first captured them. A girl could stretch her legs out in here.

Suvi completed an inventory of her upgraded suite of toys. The new remote was eighty-three percent faster to process and had nearly forty-three times as much non-volatile memory. Javier had even added a whole library of new movies and musicals for her to watch when she had time.

The shell had been reinforced, as well. After she had cracked her egg killing the bad man, the remote's frame had never been the same. She could compensate, but having to was a pain. The new shell was much tougher, with a layer of charcoal gray painted hull metal padded underneath with nearly a centimeter of good sprayed-foam material, double wrapped in cloth. She was hurricane-proof now, too, instead of just rain-proof. Bigger batteries, more lift potential, refined sensors.

It almost made it worth it.

Still, she missed being a starship. She'd have to convince Javier to buy or steal her a ship one of these days, upgrade the hardware, and pour her soul into it. Oh, to feel the solar wind on her face again.

At least she'd finally met Dr. Teague. Finding out Javier had given that woman all of their reward money from the mine field treasure above *A'Nacia*, that he'd added years to their sentence of servitude, that had hurt. She had been all set to hate the woman, especially after finding out that now she wanted their help to rescue the big, mean dragoon, Sykora.

I mean, really, the nerve of some people.

But Wilhelmina had turned out to be good people. Really nice. Probably good for Javier in ways Suvi couldn't manage, unless they built her an android body with big boobs.

Pygmalion be damned. A girl could dream.

Dinner and talk and stories and plans, plus a lot of food. Javier obviously trusted Wilhelmina with his life, with both their lives, so she must be good people. Really nice, too.

And now, a costume party. Well, for the organics. Actually, no, her too. Nobody would realize that the little remote had a person inside.

And other surprises.

Suvi cycled her attention back down to the new entries in her encyclopaedia entitled *Q-section.* Javier had added some new capabilities when he updated the hull of the new remote. It wasn't her old dorsal twin pulsar turret on *Mielikki,* but she could still take down a moose with the little pop-up pulse turret she had now.

Were there any moose in space?

Suvi made a note to update her xeno-biology and seeding histories to look for programs to introduce large ungulates on terraformed planets. Or, alternatively, to locate bio-equivalent creatures on non-seeded worlds. You never knew when you'd need that kind of information handy.

Q-ship. A very boring-looking freighter in a war zone, sailing happily along as bait for an enemy raider. Armed and armoured, but hidden. Prepared to absorb lots of damage. All set to sink the poor bastard who thought he was all that and a bag of chips.

Suvi envisioned dancing a happy jig before she climbed down into the flight seat of her little flitter, at least in her mind, and started the power-up sequence to bring her little assault fighter on line.

Scanners: active. Currently tracking one target: Javier, currently costumed as Captain Navarre, with a little ping transmitter in his belt-buckle that apparently even Wilhelmina/Hadiiye didn't know about.

Flight systems: warming up. I can outrun a cheetah. And out-marathon a saluki. And out-climb a Stellar's Sea Eagle.

Fear me, I am awesomeness itself.

Batteries: ninety-nine point three percent. No solar power around here to recharge, so I'll have to rely on standard indoor fluorescent lights. Estimate nineteen days to critical discharge, two if I use the guns on anything. Assume trouble.

She made another note to have Javier relocate the standard plug-jack closer to her waldo claw, so she could find a power socket and get to one hundred percent without relying on him.

Cavalry needs to be able to cavalry, damn it.

PING!!!

Suvi nearly dropped her iced tea. Well, she envisioned one in her hand so she could almost drop it. Then she added a cup-holder on her console, to hold her new glass, and finished her power-on sequence. Javier would only push that button when he was ready for her to follow them to the bad guy's lair. And since Wilhelmina/Hadiiye didn't know about it, that meant Suvi needed to come running.

She popped up off the bench, oriented herself with one last hard ping of the little runabout's interior, and flew her nose carefully into the airlock control button.

She needed a bugle. Well, an external sound system so she could play the bugle.

Cavalry needed to cavalry.

She added it to the list.

He's gonna owe me big after this, anyway.

PART TWO

Hadiiye was astounded at the amount of alcohol the three man had put away while she and the accountant had watched. It was staggering. Seven empty bottles of the hard stuff were lined up carefully along the edge of the table. Dead soldiers awaiting proper interment.

About midway through that performance, someone had decided to send a goon over to protect Captain Tamaz while he got really, really drunk with his new friend, Navarre. Hadiiye kept one eye on the newcomer, just as he watched her.

Insurance policy, really.

The new guy, the body guard/bouncer, was one of the biggest humans Wilhelmina had ever laid eyes on. Dark brown hair, nut brown skin, nearly black eyes. He would have been half a head taller than Sykora, were she here, and massed her by at least four stone, maybe five. Wilhelmina was even more amazed when the man moved.

It was obvious that the man had studied ballet at some point. He was too big to be any good, but she couldn't think of a single martial art she had studied, on any of the worlds she had ever visited, that would teach you how to keep yourself so perfectly poised and centered as you moved. Plus, she recognized the way his hands and feet moved.

Those skills had been pounded into an eight-year-old version of her, once upon centuries ago.

So, trained as a dancer, moves like a jaguar. Callouses on his hands from striking things repeatedly. Close in, he would be murder. Stay far away and shoot at him instead.

He looked like a breaking-boards-and-heads kind of guy.

Hadiiye wondered if he had ever studied one of the descendants of Aikido or Judo. She smiled to herself.

There's more than one way to skin a cat.

Externally, she and the new guy kept a polite façade. She was here to protect Navarre. He was doing the same for Tamaz and Erckens. All three were oblivious, drinking, toasting each other, laughing, and carrying on.

Oh, the terrible lies and stories men will tell when they're drunk.

In vino, veritas. So they say.

Only the accountant, Almássy, was relatively sober, matching the rest of the men roughly sip to bottle as they went.

"No," Captain Tamaz slurred out loudly. "I insist. You will believe me after that."

Hadiiye had no idea what the men were on about. She'd been mostly filtering out their words and watching the room. Navarre was too canny to start anything here. But suddenly everybody was in motion, sliding out of the booth towards her and standing up all wobbly.

"Come, my friend," Tamaz continued. "You will see the truth of it. They are all doomed. DOOMED!"

The drunks erupted in a symphony of cheers and giggles. It was weird, even by normal standards, if there was such a thing on a pirate space station.

You could tell a pirate by how well he walked, blind-stinking-drunk. Tamaz had the look of a man who could walk across a high-wire between buildings in a cross wind, right now. Everything seemed to be battened down perfectly water-tight as he strode down the stairs, glancing over his shoulder at the rest of the group as he went.

Javier was much more fluid and relaxed as he moved. Hadiiye chalked that up to all the food they had eaten earlier. She wondered if the others would realize how sober he was.

Hadiiye made eye contact with the burly bouncer and indicated silently that he should be up front and she would be at the back. He thought about it for a moment, shrugged, and got moving. There wasn't really a good choice at this point. She was obviously a stranger, so would encounter friction at every waypoint, while he could ease them through. She was just along for the ride.

Now she just needed to figure out where they were going to take her.

PART THREE

Deep inside, where nobody could see, Javier smiled.

Captain Navarre was a happy, cheerful drunk, making toasts, telling jokes, and egging the other men on, like any best buds freshly-met in a bar. Life was always a party.

But let's face it. Until you wake up three days later, in different county, wearing someone else's pants, you're bush league. Bonus points if you have a Shore Patrol hat on at the time.

It was a shame he never got to keep those hats. It would have been an awesome collection, all things considered.

But he was here to do a job. An ugly, ill-conceived thing, but one he was perfectly suited for. After all, it just might involve that crazy Amazon bitch ending up dead, and not be his fault.

How much better could it get?

"But how did you manage to keep her quiet?" Navarre asked. Well, slurred. It was a wet, messy sound, but all drunks have that same sloppy accent when two and a half sheets to the wind. It might be Shakespeare to them.

"Bah, she is pussycat," Tamaz roared back, slamming back another shot of something pink and then hammering down his shatter-proof shot glass. "And I use her to kill rest of them."

"Really, Abraam," Navarre replied with the utter seriousness only a drunk can manage. "A pussycat?"

"Come, my friend," Tamaz continued. "You will see truth of it. They are all doomed. DOOMED!"

Navarre nodded. As Tamaz started to move.

It made perfect sense. Tamaz wanted to go walksies. We shall go walksies.

All three drunks made it vertical. The accountant was there. Killer-babe was there.

And who are you?

Navarre was looking at someone new, from about the center of the other guy's chest. Definitely a him. Pecs but no boobs.

He leaned back, craning to see the man's face, all the way up there, and nearly toppled over backwards. A hand, a gigantic paw really, slashed out and caught him easily by the front of his doublet, held him effortlessly, tugged him carefully upright.

Navarre stepped back and executed a perfect Court bow. Deportment classes had not been a waste. He could do this even dead drunk.

Or faking dead drunk, as he was now.

In the middle of his motion, obscured by moving parts and backs of heads, Navarre clicked a small button hidden inside his belt buckle. Javier smiled.

One silent Ping for mankind.

"Thank you, good sir," he slurred, rather louder than required, and then staggered after Tamaz and Erckens.

Damn. That guy was big. And fast. And looked smart, too. Good thing this was only the scouting portion of the trip. Probably need some heavy artillery to take him down. Or just blow the whole damned section open to vacuum. Make the dude a space dragon or something.

Right now, Navarre and Javier were both just looking forward to seeing Sykora again.

THE FEET KNEW THE WAY, having navigated it enough times that the mind could focus elsewhere. Abraam Tamaz felt the joy of absolute power wash over him as he went to visit his love, waiting for him like a songbird in a gilded cage.

And traps, traps within traps. Doom within spirals of destruction.

Tamaz did not trust this Captain Navarre fellow. The timing was too close. A helpful stranger arrives just as his grand trap for Sokolov was about to slam shut?

What were the odds that the fates were conspiring so brightly on his side? They had never loved him so much before today.

Thus, traps within traps.

Tamaz smiled up at Morghan, his own personal Kodiak bear, as they passed through another set of hatches, closing on the edge of the station. He could be as drunk and relaxed as he wanted with that man about. Utter loyalty. Unbelievable ferocity. Absolute sobriety. Navarre might have brought along a killer, the woman had that look about her, but nothing could stand against Morghan.

Around a long hallway, ever-so-slightly curved, the ship's main personnel hatch came into view, carefully guarded by two of his crew. Tamaz smiled to himself.

That was power. Right there. Crew on duty instead of drunk off their asses like their captain.

Tamaz stepped to one side and gestured his new friend to precede him.

"I give you, the starship *Salekhard*," he said grandly, knowing the title would be lost on them.

After all, how many people would recognize the name of an Imperial Russian prison camp for exiles in the far wilds of Homeworld Siberia? Or guess how appropriate it might be...

In through the double airlocks and onto his ship. Tamaz found himself jostling up against the woman Navarre had brought, as they waited for the airlock doors to cycle. He resisted the urge to reach out and caress one of her breasts.

They were quite lovely.

He was the captain, it was his ship. But it would be rude. Especially if Navarre might truly be a possible ally against Sokolov, and not a plant or a spy. He could always kill the man and have the woman later, if that was the necessity of things.

He settled for a deep draft of her perfume. Sykora never wore perfume. The old Sykora. Who knew what he might convince her to do, once he owned her body and soul.

Once she existed only to please him.

The thought was more intoxicating than any narcotic might dream of being.

He turned to lead them deeper into the ship, accidentally brushing against a warm, full breast as he went, supreme in all things.

HADIIYE WAS SLIGHTLY BEMUSED at the situation. Wilhelmina wanted to gouge his eyes out. But then, Hadiiye hadn't been touched by this man or his first mate.

Rape existed on a spectrum, not a point. They had stayed generally at the emotional end, with enough groping to make their point, without ever getting truly physical.

Wilhelmina the psychologist wondered if either Tamaz or Erckens even really liked women, or needed frightened little girls or boys to get excited. Certainly, they hadn't gotten aroused by the situation, but rape was a crime of power, not passion.

Wilhelmina had simply not let them have power over her.

Hadiiye was willing to geld them with a dull spoon for her anyway. It would be an improvement to the species, to keep them from propagating.

Especially when Tamaz got that look in his eye.

One of his hands twitched, like it was going to go up her skirt. Hadiiye might even let it be, considering the situation, the location, the company.

Or she might pull a shiv and touch his cheek, right below the eyeball, just to get his attention. She didn't owe any man anything. Except pain and a slow, lingering death.

She smiled at Tamaz as he changed his mind. She even suffered the space violation with a light smile as he leaned forward and inhaled her scent. The way his eyes rolled back, half-closed, was fascinating.

He certainly wasn't thinking about her.

Food for thought.

Salekhard proved to be a medium freighter as they tromped her decks. It was built more durable than hulls from her time, but five centuries of technology and metallurgy will do that.

There was far more crew than a freighter this size would normally carry, but she was expecting that. This was a pirate, after all. Play possum until someone got close, and then turn into wolf in sheep's clothing.

From her recent studies, improvements in jump drives and life support systems meant that a crew of twenty to thirty would be normal on a vessel of this scale. She had probably already seen twice that count, just crossing half the linear distance and going up three decks.

They certainly weren't going to shoot their way in, if they wanted to rescue Djamila. Hadiiye was patient. Navarre would have a plan.

The party came to rest at a closed hatch. It was like that moment when the tide turned, pooling all the water to stillness in a bay, just before it started to run back out. She missed the smell of Dundee.

Tamaz gifted them with his warm, drunk smile, a canary in his mouth, at least metaphorically.

"And now, my friends," he said, summoning his best diction from the depths of his drunkenness. "Now, you will see the power that I wield. The glory. I give you, the dragoon, Sykora."

He turned and theatrically pushed the button to slide the hatch into the wall.

Hadiiye was last into the small room, crowded with five other bodies around the table.

No, six. Strange little man tucked into a corner, crowded back from the killers around him as if they had a sour smell. She sniffed. Nothing but the musk of big men and her perfume.

Probably not something that turned the little man on, either way.

They jostled around, finding a calm point. Again, tides swirling, eddying.

In her heels, Hadiiye was taller than anyone in the room but the big guy, so she could see over shoulders and didn't need to press forward.

Hadiiye suppressed any gasp, any emotional response, any clue that might suggest she was more or less than she seemed. They had arrived at a moment of life or death.

Djamila.

The dragoon was tied naked to a modified hospital gurney. Trussed, really. Immobilized by someone who was extremely serious about his business and not just exploring his kinbaku kinks on a long woman.

And wires everywhere. Every good nerve cluster appeared to be getting a jolt of electricity, except the one between her legs.

So, pain, but at no point pleasure. About what she expected from these men. Brutality, with no understanding of what made a woman tick. Especially not one like Djamila.

Morons.

Not that she would help correct their misunderstandings, but it was certainly ammunition for what she had planned for them.

Lit cigarettes and bolt cutters came to mind.

Hadiiye stepped back. She had seen what she needed. Her job was to bodyguard Navarre and keep him safe, especially here in the pits of hell.

Navarre stepped close to Djamila, leaned over, got very, very still. He could probably smell her sweat from there.

"You see, Captain Navarre," Tamaz gloated. "I have succeeded where all others have failed. The woman is mine."

She watched Navarre's head turn to look at Tamaz, his face unreadable but closed.

"Would you like to say hello to her?" Tamaz asked innocently.

Hadiiye felt the room around her grow cold. She suddenly understood why Tamaz had been so easy about inviting them into his lair to see his prize.

It was a trap.

Masterful, really. Bring them here where they couldn't escape. Bring Djamila out of her tortured state, present the strangers, see her response before she could collect herself.

Navarre, they would kill out of hand. There was a very good chance Wilhelmina would end up on a table just like this one, if something went wrong.

Her death might linger over years.

There was nothing of Javier in the man before her. Captain Navarre was supreme, regal. He was vengeance, personified. He had a voice that could etch metal.

"That would be lovely," Navarre drawled, acid dripping on every word.

The other men had grown suddenly tense, respecting the possibility of violence on close quarters. Very few people would make it out of a room like this alive, most likely, if something bad happened.

Navarre stood perfectly still. Calm, poised, almost happy. She watched him look down at Djamila again, smile with the warmth of an owl sneaking up on a field mouse.

"Please?" he continued, putting true emotion into his voice as he looked at Tamaz.

Captain Tamaz nodded to the weird, little dumpy man in the corner, who leapt forward and began jiggering with a machine by Djamila's head. Hadiiye has taken it for a bio-monitor at first glance.

It was apparently the source of Djamila's pain.

She watched Djamila's body grow limp and relaxed as the electricity subsided.

Tamaz worked his way around to the other side of the table with the doctor, leaving him a clear view of Navarre's reaction.

And, coincidentally, moving him out of the way if Erckens and the giant needed to get physical in a small volume. Hadiiye let herself fade back just a bit more, and turned slightly to the side, in case she needed to get at a hidden knife quickly. Not that it would probably matter, but anything in a maelstrom.

Even from here, the smell of whatever they put under Djamila's nose was putrid. Almost raw ammonia. Certainly, it got through.

Djamila opened her eyes slowly. She came to herself and looked up at Javier/Navarre, leaning over her, leering.

"Hello, princess," Captain Navarre said cheerfully.

The big guy tensed. Erckens tensed. Hell, all of them puckered up a little.

Djamila, bless her soul, actually growled up at Javier, around the gag in her mouth.

Navarre was looking away from her, at Tamaz, when he straightened up, so Hadiiye couldn't see his face. But the emotion in his stance, his body language, was pure triumph.

"Whatever you have planned for her and Sokolov," Navarre purred loudly. "I'm in."

Wilhelmina reconsidered whether bringing Javier here had been a good idea, after all.

PART FOUR

THE BED WAS COLD.

Not physically. Wilhelmina had thrown the covers down to keep from completely overheating as Javier slept. The man was a portable furnace.

No, emotionally.

The need for Navarre and Hadiiye to remain in character all the long way back to their own ship, having seen what they needed to see and made friends enough with Captain Tamaz.

Navarre silent in thought and triumph. Hadiiye silent in worried fear.

There was no love lost between Javier and Djamila. She knew that. She had hoped that his own decency would overcome his hatred, at least long enough to save Sykora from a fate worse than death.

She was beginning to question that assumption.

Javier barely snored as he slept beside her.

There had been little physicality between them, save the one time. It was normally almost like sleeping in a bed with her brother, when they were still children.

Tonight, it was like sleeping with a soon-to-be ex-husband, trapped in a bed and unable to go sleep on a non-existent couch.

The ship was too small to get away from him.

Had she really brought them all this distance, just so he could get his revenge on Sykora personally?

The thought sent shivers down her spine, in spite of herself, or Djamila's stories, or that look in Javier's eyes.

And that vial. Tamaz's frumpy little assistant had pulled the glass tube, filled with a bright green liquid, from a nearby refrigerator, for Tamaz to show off to his new, drunken friends.

Wilhelmina had studied the social sciences, the liberal arts. She had degrees in sociology, psychology, history, and accounting. She barely knew anything about medicine, beyond the basics of field first aid on primitive planets.

The conversation between Tamaz and Navarre had quickly gone over her head. But that was to be expected from someone who once owned a steel coffee mug with *THE SCIENCE OFFICER* etched into the side. It had made good memento. Wilhelmina wondered if it would be a terrible reminder if they failed.

Tamaz's plan was simple.

Empty the vial into Sykora with a needle.

Ransom her off to Sokolov as a carrier.

Wait twenty-four hours for a plague to vector its way through *Storm Gauntlet*'s crew.

Death. For everyone but Djamila.

Tamaz and his friends had already deserved whatever punishment could be meted out. Now they deserved a first class trip to hell.

Hadiiye looked forward to punching their tickets.

Javier stirred.

A hand snaked out under the sheets, caught hers before she could twitch it away.

She was trapped.

He opened his eyes.

Javier, not Navarre.

"Are you ready to talk?" he asked her simply.

"Do you have anything to say that I'll want to hear?" she replied with far more edge that she had expected when she opened her mouth.

He stared at her for several seconds.

"Djamila Sykora is almost everything I hate about deep space," Javier began with a shrug. "Stick-up-her-butt rules-follower who is constantly belittling everyone around her for not measuring up to the impossible standards she sets."

Wilhelmina nodded, unwilling to trust her reply.

"But she's just an asshole," Javier said. "Tamaz and his friends are *evil*."

Something changed in his face. In his hand as well, pressed up against her side and twined with her own.

"Once upon a time," he continued. "I was one of the good guys. It didn't work out, for reasons we won't go into here. But nobody deserves that."

What *THAT* was, she left dangling, just as he did. This was yet another side of an already complicated man, one she had certainly never met before.

Wilhelmina wondered again if she had ever met the real Javier Aritza, or just the many roles he played to keep the world at bay. She could tell that there was someone underneath that façade but there were enough flashes to keep her guessing.

She felt his hand give hers a squeeze.

"I'm not doing this for her, `Mina," he said simply. "I'm not doing it for you. I'm doing it because it's right."

Oh.

She wondered about future conversations she might have with this man about the nature of evil.

What was *evil?*

Javier Aritza did not frequently strike her as an especially deep philosopher. Certainly not a pre-eminent existentialist.

And yet.

He was willing to simply step past all of his hatred for Djamila, and do the right thing, because Wilhelmina Teague had asked.

Because she needed paladins.

"So what do we do now, Javier?"

Instead of answering, he let go of her hand and rolled out of bed. She watched his butt in those old sweats as he took two steps to the piloting station and pressed a button.

"Curveball, this is Mother Hen," he said into the radio. "What is your status?"

"Primary scouting complete, Mother Hen," Suvi replied instantly. "Transmitting now."

The console chirped as a file arrived. Javier sat down to read it.

In spite of the cooler air in the room, Wilhelmina climbed out of bed and looked over Javier's shoulder as he quickly digested the document.

He looked up with a sardonic smile.

"This would be easier to do if you were wearing any clothes, `Mina," he observed tartly. "Men do find your breasts distracting."

She considered responses for a moment with a sly smile.

This Javier was much closer to the man she had been expecting, a week ago. Nicer. Friendlier. Softer.

Navarre might prove to be an interesting lay, but he wouldn't be nearly as much fun in bed as Javier.

"So I can't tempt you?" she replied teasingly.

"You're already tempting me, woman," he said. "But time's tight if you want to do this. I can always have you for dessert, afterwards."

Wilhelmina blushed, smiled, and turned to look for a shirt.

That would be a promise to keep him on track. She could always threaten to withhold marital favors if he got them all killed.

Hopefully that would be something to bring Javier back to her.

PART EIGHT
BOOK EIGHT: PALADIN

PART ONE

THE STARS around her were wonderful. Suvi was home again, however temporarily, as the little flitter silently cruised through deep space outside the station, working hard to sneak up on the pirate freighter, *Salekhard*, with Javier and Dr. Teague in tow in suits.

Suvi considered Javier's plan with mixed feelings.

When she was *Mielikki*, this trick would have never worked on her. But then, in those days she'd also been a small warship, built to *Concord* Fleet standards and expected to operate like an officer and a gentlewoman. She'd been literally wired into every hatch, every vent, every everything on her former ship.

Salekhard was just an old tired freighter. At least she looked that way to someone looking in from the outside. Probably the big, bad wolf if you got too close. Q-ship.

But that was the mean people aboard. *Salekhard* was just an old iron ship. No brains, no personality. No AI cousin aboard.

That was probably for the best, considering *Salekhard* was in service to evil. Suvi wouldn't have to figure out a way to kill her. Javier could do this thing and they'd be off.

Suvi wished she could talk to Javier and Wilhelmina right now, but his orders had been extremely specific. No radio transmissions until he said otherwise, when they made it to the other side. Suvi looked around at the deep black of empty space instead.

Not being a starship anymore had always been painful, but now it hurt doubly so. She was back in deep space, pulling what Javier called a second-story-maneuver.

A length of line connected her to Javier and then to Wilhelmina, floating silently behind her on a tether like strange little balloons in their space-suits. He could communicate with her via hand signals, if he had anything useful to say, but right now, it was just silence.

Oh, sure. Traffic all around them. A place like *Meehu Platform* was never quiet. There were ships coming and going every hour of every day, sometimes stacked up three deep in nearby orbit awaiting a docking bay.

The comm was never quiet either, but Javier wanted them to think like cat burglars, and he didn't want any transmissions close to *Salekhard* to possibly warn anyone what they were up to.

Seriously, Javier. Who's going to see this coming?

But she kept her own counsel. Suvi'd been an officer and a gentlewoman, a scout, a pilot, a warrior. She'd never been a thief.

It was kinda cool.

She gave a little burst of power. Not much. Mostly to redirect herself down and sideways, just enough to tug Javier and Wilhelmina into line with the secondary engineering airlock she had picked out two hours ago.

A game of galactic billiards.

Contact imminent.

Suvi flared her lifters just enough to counter the mass of the two humans behind her. Bring them in to almost a dead stop relative.

It was all in the English you put on that ball, folks.

Javier landed like a cat. Wilhelmina was…

Oh, crap.

Has this woman never done an EVA? That looked like a gymnast in gravity.

Oh, right. Human reflexes. This was something you trained for. Nobody was born with it.

Well, Dragoon Sykora might have been, but that just proved the rule. That woman was scary good.

Radio? No. He'd been specific.

And he can't reach her.

And I'm out of position.

And…Hey, what are you doing, Javier? That's my tether line. Stop pulling me closer, I need to go get Wilhelmina and bring her back.

Suvi let her lifters go slack before she pulled him off the hull as well.

He had magnets, but they were for walking, not holding them both down if she red-lined things. The last thing she needed was both of them floating loose out here, where someone might look out a porthole and raise an alarm, even in dock.

She waited while Javier grabbed her body with both hands, tied the line to his belt, and then pushed her softly at Wilhelmina. She felt like a game-winning free-throw, spinning slowly backwards.

Nothing but net.

It's a damned good thing I don't get airsick, bucko, or I'd have to blow electronic chunks all over you.

And worse, Javier missed.

She was going to fly right by Wilhelmina, about a half meter out of reach.

Now what do we do?

Javier tugged on the rope and snapped his arm to one side.

Great, now sideways torque as well? Are you trying to make me heave here?

And then it dawned on her. As the whip snapped her to one side and around Wilhelmina's back.

And I'm wrapped around her like a lasso.

Oh.

Right.

Maybe he *has* done this before.

I'm going to sit here very quietly and pretend like I planned it that way.

Perfect.

THE AIRLOCK DOOR slid open with a minimum of noise. Javier preferred it that way.

In dock, he knew engineering would generally be on minimum shifts with everything powered down. Unless they were rebuilding something big, in which case it would be wall to wall people and noise and he'd be caught in about two minutes.

Darkness.

Well, dimness.

Engines shut down. Jump drives off. Auxiliary power reactors on baseline. Life support dialed down as the ship drew fresh air off the station. At least, fresher air.

Stinky with a different set of trace volatile organics, at a minimum.

Salekhard was a freighter. She wasn't flashy. She certainly wasn't fast. Victims came to her.

From the drunken conversation with Tamaz, the ship had lost a pair of cargo holds during the massive up-gunning refit that turned her into a Q-ship. Space lost had been turned into banks of generators and batteries. The center of gravity of the engineering crew had shifted well forward when that happened.

Engineering was a ghost town.

Javier grinned.

Starships in space were never shut down, but humans were humans. You set your bio-rhythms a particular way and left them there. Eight hours of duty in a twenty-four hour shift. Couple three hours for food. Couple hours personal recreation. Time for training and school recerts. Eight hours down to sleep.

Even in station, you'll keep to that pattern, with time thrown in for parties and business.

For *Salekhard*, it was the middle of the night.

The perfect time to break in.

She wasn't a navy ship, with snappy, matching uniforms for everyone, color-coded by department and rank. Tamaz might be a sociopath, but he wasn't ex-fleet.

Crew tended to either wear what they came with, or what they picked up at stations like this. In between, they would have the sorts of pants and tunic the quartermaster could sell you cheap. At that point, the only real difference between ships in space was color, because a cheap acquisitions officer was going to buy a block of sizes of everything in a single color.

On *Salekhard*, that was brown. Boring, mud-colored brown.

Fortunately, this was *Meehu Platform*. Everything was available for a price, including boring, mud-brown disguises.

Suvi went into the vast space first, quietly pinging all of engineering to map it.

Nothing.

Lights dialed down to reduce power load and save money in dock. Critical systems well lit, but the rest shadowed. Standard operating procedure.

Javier followed, mud-brown with a gym bag in one hand. Wilhelmina came last, still wearing those damned high-heeled purple combat boots under her pants.

For a moment, the evil conscience on his left shoulder suggested she should wear them to bed sometime. Nothing else, just the boots. Even the good conscience got a goofy smile on his face at that image.

Javier had Suvi's flight controller remote, hanging like a satchel to one side, just in case, but she was flying the remote. Some of his buttons apparently made happy sounds play in her cockpit, or little unicorns and toy dinosaurs race across the console. He certainly wasn't flying the craft.

"Suvi," he whispered, just loud enough for her to pick up. "Find me the entry hatch off the top-most catwalk gangway."

Instead of answering, she bounced straight up, almost silently.

Javier was reduced to sneaking over to a set of stairs and mounting them. He wasn't as quiet, but he didn't need silence. Around him, *Salekhard* groaned and creaked as systems came on and off, generators, air, and cooling systems answering the call for power or going back to sleep.

Space was only silent on the outside. On the inside, it never shut up.

Engineering had three decks of verticality. Mostly, that was the thrusters. *Salekhard* could hold a lot of mass, so the ship needed a tremendous amount of initial thrust to push it along. Doubly so when climbing out of the local gravity well to reach a safe jump range.

That just meant the rear third of the ship bulged strangely. And you were a ways off the deck plates when looking down from that second catwalk.

Javier looked at the hatch Suvi'd found.

At least freighters followed a simple naval architecture. Either you had one main arterial corridor down the spine, with the cargo holds hanging to either side off that like ribs, or two corridors down the outsides, with individual cargo holds on the centerline.

Salekhard had central holds. That also served to mentally divide the ship into thirds. Either you were forward, with the important people close to the bridge, or aft with the engineers. Stevedores got stuck in the middle. And ignored.

It was the dead of night. In a hallway as far from the important parts of the freighter as they could get. Javier didn't really feel safe, but he figured the odds were in his favor.

"I lead," he said quietly before opening the hatch. "'Mina second. Suvi, try to stay back a little farther as an ace in the hole."

Wilhelmina nodded. Suvi flashed her running lights on and off. Javier took a deep breath and palmed the button.

The hatch opened slowly.

Nobody.

He blew out the breath and started walking. Behind him, utter silence so intense he had to turn and look back to make sure both women were still behind him.

Okay, good.

He didn't bother with a weapon. He wasn't that good to begin with, and a firefight here would screw everything quickly. Plus, both girls could take care of themselves. And hopefully him.

Instead, he was the pathfinder today. He might have had a lot to drink, but seriously, that was nothing.

Hell, the other two men might still be in bed for a number of hours, trying to recover.

Amateurs.

Javier counted his steps. Internal passageways on a ship like this didn't have happy little colored lines for tourists to follow. But there were only so many ways to build a vessel.

He turned to port and went down a side hall that wrapped around the front of engineering's bulge.

No fancy castings or curves. Just basic cubes welded together at a mostly-automated ship yard, knocking out parts twenty-four-seven and then assembling them like three dimensional jigsaw puzzles later. Corridor, cargo hold, cabin, suite. Weld A to B. Repeat with C.

Javier let his monkey brain drive. Overthinking was bad here.

If he was right, the correct hatch was about here.

Javier looked around.

Yup. That stain on the wall. The one shaped like the Blessed Madonna. The one that looked like a pulse-pistol burn scar. This was the place.

He signaled to the girls to get close, unsure if opening this hatch would trigger an alarm somewhere other than in his head.

Certainly, the clock would start running.

He reached out and pushed the button.

PART TWO

The pain ebbed.

Djamila felt the barriers around her soul coming down. The physical world grew close.

Tamaz must want to torture her again.

Certainly, the last time had been the most intense. Djamila was beginning to wonder if her sanity was finally breaking. She had actually imagined Aritza here, helping Tamaz break her.

If she was going insane, that would be the shape hell took when she got there.

That smell brought her back the rest of the way. By now, it was beginning to be impressed on her nervous system as *home*. Djamila wondered if she would carry that association to her grave.

Her eyes opened to painfully bright light. She could focus. Something was wrong.

She could move.

Tamaz was standing over her, leering at her, lusting after her, even after all these years. The first mate was with him, standing back and to one side.

She would have only one chance at this.

Djamila exploded off the gurney in a flash of movement, trusting her instincts to guide her.

She grabbed Tamaz by the front of his shirt and slammed him backwards into the bulkhead hard.

Djamila had no expectation she would get out of this room alive. She just wanted company on the trip to hell.

Abraam Tamaz would be a fine companion.

He didn't struggle as much as she expected him to. He barely resisted as she got her hands around his throat, lifted him bodily, and began to crush.

It would be good to kill this man.

Why wasn't he fighting? Had she knocked him out against the bulkhead?

No, his eyes were open, boring into hers from so close.

And why wasn't the first mate trying to stop her? All she really wanted right now was to die in battle.

Was that too much to ask?

Pain. There. Yes. Good. I'm alive enough to feel pain. This isn't a torture-induced fantasy overtaking my sanity. This is someone pinching my earlobe hard enough to hurt. Not pulling, just pinching.

What?

"Djamila," Wilhelmina Teague's voice penetrated her haze. "I need you to listen to me. Please come back to me."

Come back? Where else would I be?

No, better. Why would Wilhelmina Teague be here in my illusion? She doesn't deserve to die with me. Perhaps to have vengeance, though. That would make sense.

The pain became a pull. Djamila felt her head turn, being turned, being drug around to one side. Someone was there.

It wasn't Aaron Erckens, after all. It was a woman. A very tall woman. A familiar looking woman.

"Djamila Sykora," the stranger said. "Please listen to me. Please hear me. Please come back to the present."

The present? The present was a torture chamber on Abraam Tamaz's ship, slowing losing her sanity rather than finally give her soul to that man. It was impending death, perhaps taking Zakhar down with her, because she was too stubborn to simply allow herself to die on this table.

She would make them kill her. Right here. Right now. It would be a good death.

But that face looked familiar.

I've seen you somewhere before.

And then the woman leaned close and kissed her lightly on the lips.

What?

The shock broke through the final haze around Djamila's brain.

"Wilhelmina?" she asked, slamming suddenly back into the present.

But if that's Wilhelmina, then who am I choking?

Djamila turned her head back as the pull on her earlobe lessened.

Aritza.

Briefly, she considered finishing the job. It wouldn't take much. A little twist, some lateral torque. A quick and painless death.

Aritza deserved it.

And yet, he had saved her life. More than once.

And he wouldn't be here without Sokolov's permission. That mean was Zakhar coming soon.

The Captain should have been the one to awaken her, if he was here. Aritza was standing in.

Djamila let Aritza's feet touch the deck again.

"Hello, Princess," he said again. "Maybe I should have wakened you with a kiss?"

Djamila nearly killed him anyway for that. Wilhelmina pulled her ear sideways as she started to.

Djamila let her head come around. Aritza could always suffer a tragic accident later.

Wilhelmina handed her a bundle of clothes and a black wig.

"Put this on," she said.

Djamila let the moment direct her. She wasn't up for more than pure reaction at this point. Obviously, they had a plan.

Djamila realized she was still nude. There was a towel in the bundle. She used it briefly to dry herself.

Aritza was busy ogling her as she did.

You're just as bad as they are, bastard.

She dressed quickly. Brown pants. White t-shirt. Brown tunic. Her own ship slippers from *Storm Gauntlet*, the ones custom made for her long skinny feet.

"Are you you yet?" Aritza asked simply.

Djamila considered the answer. She had been in another world for some time. Days, possibly weeks if he was here now. Her survival had required retreating into the unpassable mountains in her mind and waiting out the winter.

Her rescue force had arrived with spring. They wanted to know if she could handle herself.

If she could fight.

Djamila felt a snarl take hold of her face.

She wasn't dead yet. Of course she could still fight.

She nodded at him professionally, unwilling to trust her tongue just yet.

He smiled. And surprised the hell out of her.

"Here," he said.

Djamila was suddenly holding a late-model pulse pistol in one hand.

Automatically, she confirmed the safety, the power pack, the grip, the sights.

"Now what?" she asked him.

Aritza had obviously planned this. Let his plan run forward until she understood it enough to improve it. He was a science officer, not a killer.

Not like her.

"Now we escape," Wilhelmina answered.

"Not quite yet," Aritza said.

Djamila watched him walk to a small refrigerator unit in a corner and squat down. She did not understand the vial of greenish liquid he pulled out, but Wilhelmina's gasp of shock told her many things.

"First, I owe that man something."

The harsh look on Aritza's face matched the feral anger burning deep in her soul. Perhaps he was a killer, after all.

PART THREE

HADIIYE HAD to explain it to Wilhelmina. Hadiiye already grasped the fundamental point Navarre was making. Wilhelmina was aghast at the possibilities.

Navarre was a hard man. She knew that. She had seen it first hand, along the way here.

This was something else entirely. This was verging on evil itself. This wasn't fighting fire with fire. This was burning the whole damned world down and starting over.

This was Ragnarok. Twilight of the Gods. This was Navarre as Surtur.

So, Javier was a specialist in the old Norse mythology cycles, as well?

And Hadiiye was going to help. It fell to Wilhelmina to put a stop to it.

There were some things that were simply too evil to contemplate. This was one of them.

She started to speak. Hadiiye stopped her, reminded her that they had to escape first.

Wilhelmina subsided. For now. They had a long road to go to escape this trap. And a shipful, a stationful, a galaxyful of pirates to escape.

Still, Navarre had taken all four vials. He had the big one, plus all three of the little ones that were apparently the antidote. That had to count for something.

First they would escape *Salekhard*. Then they would discuss the ethics of biological warfare.

SO FAR, so good.

Navarre kinked his head to one side, then the other. He opened his mouth wide enough to pop the jaw, then closed it.

There would be a couple of really good hickeys on his neck tomorrow, assuming he lived that long. But at least Hadiiye had kept the dragoon from killing him.

Today, anyway. She still had that light in her eyes, that hatred, that barely-in-control rage.

It made him warm all over.

He got a nod from both women, indicating their readiness. They both had pistols, although he had no idea how good Hadiiye might be. Sykora was the ballerina of death, so he had no worries there. Not right now.

Tomorrow? That would settle itself.

Home first.

The little flight controller came active and showed him the hallway.

Suvi was following orders and had found a quiet intersection where she could see partway back to engineering and all of this corridor. And she was at least generally listening to the joystick controls, aware of who the audience was today.

Things were still quiet. And dim.

You would think, plugged into station power, that a captain would leave the lights on full. They weren't going to cost that much, especially once your docking fees would already cover part of it.

But some people were just too cheap for their own good, always cutting corners instead of doing it right. *Storm Gauntlet* came to mind, at least when he had first boarded her, but those corners being cut had saved his life. Probably. Maybe not. Who knew where he might have ended up if they had sold him to an agricultural station as labor?

Water under a burned bridge.

Javier opened the door. Navarre would had done something grand and obnoxious here. Javier wanted to sneak out the back door just like he had come in. He had to take charge here, so they could get out alive.

Into the corridor.

Nothing.

Two killer girls steps behind him silent. Eerie.

"So glad I upgraded the auto-pilot on this thing," he stage muttered to the women as he typed.

Suvi hopped to the next intersection and looked around.

Emptiness.

Javier followed, remembering to look both ways before crossing this dangerous street.

Now they were back in the main corridor, a straight shot aft to engineering.

A nameplate on a door caught his attention.

Burakgazi.

He only knew one person with that name. A short, skinny engineer with a heart-shaped face who had gone off with Wilhelmina to keep that old ship running.

That was too much for coincidence. He pushed the button to open the hatch.

Yup. Score one for the good guys as she looked up from a bunk.

"Javier?"

"Rescue, kid," he replied. "Move."

She was up off the bed in a flash.

Javier looked around.

There. Alferdinck. Navigator-extraordinaire.

Javier pushed the button.

"Piet, let's go," he said into the opening space.

The tall Dutchman didn't ask, just moved.

Javier parked Suvi in place with a quick command and turned to the girls.

"'Mina," he said. "You lead. Take everybody to that engineering hatch but don't go through. I'll bring up the rear with better sensors, so nobody sneaks up on us. Go."

Two extremely nice bottoms flowed by him. Well, three, but Afia's wasn't even in the same league as the taller women. It wasn't the time or place to really stop and appreciate Wilhelmina or Sykora, but they were still nice. Even if he couldn't imagine two women less alike.

"What are we looking for?" Suvi typed on his read-out.

"Nothing," he typed back. "Any bad guys will be coming from the bow. The girls can handle engineers. Let's go."

Javier had gone two steps when the alarms started.

"Warning," a woman's warm voice filled the corridor. "Enemy

boarding parties at large. All crew shelter in place. Security teams to red alert."

Well, crap. Still, better than he had been expecting. Probably a video monitor in a hallway somewhere, or they would have seen Sykora leave the bed. Of course, that assumed anybody but Tamaz got to watch her. That would be like him. Probably an alarm on the other two crew.

Wilhelmina and the others were outside the engineering hatch.

Wilhelmina pushed the button as he approached, but nothing happened.

"They've locked it," Sykora said harshly, obviously blaming him for everything. "Now what?"

Javier held his snarky comment inside. They would gain nothing but lost time right now.

"You remember my first remote?" he asked the dragoon, pointing at Suvi back over one shoulder.

Sykora just nodded, her eyes a little bigger than a moment ago as she realized the new one was much larger.

"You were sad it wasn't armed, as I remember," he continued. "I fixed that with this version."

"Who let you have a weapon?" she snarled quietly.

Javier pointed to the one in her hand.

"Probably the same people who wanted me to rescue you," he retorted.

She refrained from commenting. Or doing anything stupid. Probably for the best. She might be fast. Suvi would be faster. And didn't particularly like Sykora.

"Everybody step back behind me," Javier said, fiddling with buttons. "I need to pretty much overload the turret to do this."

Hopefully, the stunt pilot was listening. He didn't even have controls for that turret programmed on his console. She would have to handle everything. Besides, it was her ship now.

A bright red targeting reticule appeared on one of his screens, blinking lightly. Oh, yeah. Stunt pilot to be sure.

Javier felt like he was flying a World War One Red Baron game. It had that feel to it. Maybe that was what she'd programmed for herself.

He made a note to ask her later. She had access to most of history to look things up.

Right now, he moved the impact point up and left a little.

"Everyone close your eyes," he called over the wailing sirens.

He did the same as he pushed the button to fire.

A light strobed through his eyelids.

Javier blinked. A new message appeared on his console

Warning: onboard power at 9 percent. Please charge as soon as possible.

Nine percent? But that would mean...

Javier looked up.

He had meant to blow the locking mechanism apart, so Sykora could crank the door open manually.

Suvi had damned near blown the thing off the rails.

So much for sneaky. Everybody on the ship probably felt that one.

"Sykora leads," he said. "'Mina follows. I'm last with the remote."

Nine percent power? Wow. But that was still good enough for the rest of the day, assuming nothing bad happened from here.

Or rather, nothing Sykora couldn't handle with a pulse pistol.

Which was nothing at all.

PART FOUR

ABRAAM TAMAZ CAME awake at an alarm beeping madly.

He was tired, he was groggy, he had drank way too much Sambuca last night. His head rang with the pounding of large industrial machines making fender panels again, on the inside of his skull.

It wasn't the duty alarm. That had a much different tone. And it wasn't a system alarm. They were docked to a station. What kind of emergency might strike them here?

The world did not want to come into focus.

He knew it should make sense, but the alcohol had evaporated into a lovely fog this morning, making his head feel like a field in Flanders on a quiet, fall day. Nothing but bundles and rumbles of clouds moving about.

He staggered to the console and pushed the red button to silence the alarm, mostly on auto-pilot. Two still did not want to work with two to make any number, let alone four.

The sideboard was close. Tamaz grabbed a dirty glass and poured in a dollop of bitters and a finger of rum, followed by a good zap of soda water. He swirled the mad concoction around the glass a few times to stir it, then slammed the whole thing down the back of his throat in one go, letting the fire burn all the way down and sort out the mess it found in his stomach.

That seemed to cut through the fog. He felt sunrise slowly begin to burn away the clouds that had taken root in his head.

Tamaz blinked furiously a few times, willing himself to conscious thought. It was a hard road this morning.

Why was he awake?

Thought grew slowly concrete, but he got there.

The alarm.

The laboratory.

Someone had opened the door without putting in the correct code combination. Nobody but he and Igor knew that combination. Nobody but the two of them had any reason, any business whatsoever, going in there.

Tamaz lunged suddenly at the console. He took three tries to enter his password correctly into the keypad, coming dangerously close to locking himself out and forcing him to reset the entire authentication suite from files in his personal safe.

There.

That was the alarm from the lab. Bring up the camera.

She was gone.

His love, his treasure, his little titmouse in her gilded cage. She had flown.

Someone was going to die for this.

Slowly, painfully. Someone would take years understanding the depths of his vengeance. Who?

Quickly, Tamaz cycled through cameras.

There. In the hallway. Several figures.

NAVARRE!

I would have given that man Sokolov's head on a stick as a holiday present.

It was all a sham. He was here to rescue the woman, not avenge himself on her. Not like Tamaz would do.

Frantically, he toggled the comm until he found the channel he wanted.

"Security station," he growled. "We have intruders aboard. Lock down all access ports to the station and scramble your teams. I want them alive."

Let that bastard make his way forward. Most of the crew would be at the front of the ship. And waiting.

"Acknowledged, Captain," the man replied. "Stand by."

Tamaz watched the man begin to push buttons on his own console.

Somewhere, heavily armed men were moving towards armaments

lockers. Death would not be quickly coming for Navarre and his woman. Women.

Tamaz watched the group approach the starboard axial corridor on deck one. That made logical sense. It gave them access almost all the way to the bow airlocks if they moved quickly enough.

What? Why are they headed aft? What was in engineering?

Tamaz slapped his hand on another red button and held it down.

"Warning," a woman's computerized voice filled the corridor. "Enemy boarding parties at large. All crew shelter in place. Security teams to red alert."

Normally, that was recycled on a loop when they had played dead and allowed another vessel to try to take them. Wolf in sheep's clothing. Let them think the crew was in a total panic, but also it let his crew know to lock themselves away from trouble, because the hunters were armed and stalking.

Tamaz opened a secondary drawer close by and pulled out a larger pistol than he normally carried. This was a stun-only model, a neural whip designed to overload someone's brain, without actually killing them.

It would just put them down, so he could capture them for play later.

Navarre was not allowed to steal his toys. He would keep the other woman as a prize.

But they were all going to die for this.

PART FIVE

"Are you sure about this?" Javier heard one of the women yell. He wasn't paying enough attention to tell them apart right now. Around them, flashing red lights and a painfully overloaded siren wailed.

"Do you want to be here when Tamaz arrives?" he yelled back, pounding down stairs, almost flying, and letting his feet touch about one in three as he went.

Suvi cheated and dropped straight down the outside of the stairwell. She would beep if she saw anybody, but her gun was pretty much just for show at this point. Still, it had saved them a lot of time at a moment when the sands might be running out.

Sykora probably could have passed him if she'd wanted to, but she was too busy looking everywhere to move around him without falling on her face. And how Wilhelmina ran down stairs in fourteen centimeter heels was a mystery for the ages. But she did.

At least Piet and Afia kept up.

Javier hit the main deck as a hatch opened one level above them, at the far end of the open space, from the forward sections. Men poured through it. Javier didn't take time to count. It was enough.

The pirates opened fire wildly, beams ringing off stairs and rails and metal but not hitting anyone. Not yet.

Sykora was apparently in her element now. Javier was facing enough of the right direction to see her pop off three shots in rapid succession.

The first one blew up a significant chunk of railing on the catwalk, right about dead center of the guy moving behind it. He survived because the metal exploded instead. The second and third hit the two men in front of that other guy. They got drilled dead center, from fifty meters away, both shooter and target moving rapidly in three dimensions.

Seriously, that woman was scary.

Javier raced across the open space toward the open airlock hatch, three steps behind Suvi. Fire erupted behind him.

After a moment, Javier could identify when the girls were firing versus when the boys upstairs opened up. The pulse pistol had a higher pitch than the rifles the boys were toting. It took him a second to identify that sound.

Neural lash.

Crap. Someone over there was playing rough.

There was nothing like getting tagged with a beam of coherent sound designed to scramble all your brain cells. Easy way to take prisoners, especially the kind you might sell on the open market later.

Not that Javier figured Tamaz would be selling him, if it came to that.

Another round of incoming fire.

For one giddy moment, Javier considered venting all of engineering to space. It would end the threat of the neural lash, at least until someone went back for something heavier, something that would work without atmosphere. And he'd be long gone by then.

Javier made it to cover and turned back to check on everyone. Afia had apparently been in his hip pocket the whole time. She was already past him and back to the far deep end of the airlock. Piet was right behind that.

That left the girls.

They had both paused midway to provide covering fire for the rest of the crew. There were already half a dozen men down over there, but more were pouring into the room from other doors every second.

Wilhelmina moved first, apparently responding to commands from Sykora. That one was a black widow spider. 'Mina's movement drew several men from cover to take a shot.

Sykora got most of them.

Did that woman actively worship Death, or something? Were these human sacrifices to appease her harsh mistress? How could anybody be that good?

Sykora was off like a jack-rabbit as everybody over there ducked, perhaps cowed into submission by the havoc she had just wrought. The body count was certainly impressive.

Javier watched her move. The ballerina of death.

Slow-motion.

She had a smile on her face that looked almost orgasmic for a moment.

Someone got lucky.

Sykora's hair haloed around her head as a beam found her.

Her face screwed up in pain, slackened into nothingness.

She toppled, fell, slid, halted.

Javier was off without hesitation.

"Cover me," he yelled frantically at Wilhelmina as he ran past her into the valley of death.

There was no time for thought, just action.

Zig.

Fade.

Beams.

Drift.

Race.

Javier slid into home with the game-winning run, grabbing Sykora's pistol and firing three shots randomly before stuffing into a pocket as he grabbed Sykora's belt and used her mass to anchor him in his slide.

Somewhere, Wilhelmina was pouring fire back up-range at the bad guys. Nothing fancy, just keep them ducked.

No time to think. No time to breathe.

Javier hoisted the massive woman up into a fireman's carry and staggered to one side, fueled by adrenaline and fear. Tamaz would not be a pleasant captor. Not like Zakhar. Not even like Sykora.

Somehow, he made it to the airlock.

Wilhelmina went to close the airlock hatch, but he grabbed her hand before she did.

"Keep firing," he said.

'Mina nodded and leaned out, randomly potting panels and catwalks as quickly as she could pull the trigger. The charge pack wouldn't last very long at this rate.

It didn't need to.

Javier dumped Sykora full out before him. He squatted long enough to peel an eyelid, both eyelids.

Unconscious, but not permanently scrambled. Hours recovering, instead of months.

It happened, from time to time. Instead of just fuzzing everything, the beams would hit something important and scramble it like an egg. That was like suffering a medium-sized stroke. Curable, but months in rehab learning to walk and talk again. Most unpleasant.

It was his lucky day. Or hers. If you could call it that.

Javier would have liked to take the time to put on a proper space suit on Sykora for what was coming next. This would shortly qualify in the top ten dumbest things he had ever attempted.

They'd all be dead if he took the time.

Outside, the room grew quiet.

Javier considered his options. None of them were good. Conversely, not all of them were suicidal.

"Navarre," Tamaz yelled from somewhere outside. "I'll give you credit for style and balls. You almost pulled it off. If you surrender right now, I promise to kill you and the girl quick. I know Sykora is done. Let it go."

Wilhelmina muttered a word under her breath that would have made Javier's career-navy father blush.

Javier nodded at her, with a hard smile. He reached into the bag and pulled out the vial of green liquid, weighing its immense gravity with one hand.

"What are you doing?" Wilhelmina whispered fiercely as she glanced over at him.

"It's not enough to escape them, 'Mina," he murmured back. "It's not enough to rescue everyone. He must be stopped, destroyed."

"There's no other way?" she asked.

"Do you want him to keep doing this to people like you and Sykora?"

He watched the flicker of pain cross her face. He knew there were stories untold about Tamaz. He could guess the script.

Add that to the bill.

Wilhelmina ground her teeth for a moment and closed her eyes.

Javier wondered if it was a prayer, but Hadiiye looked back out of them when they opened.

"Paladins are men and women of the sword, Javier," she said calmly.

It was almost frightening the way she could do that. But it was enough.

Javier took a second to locate his target.

There. Primary air intake vents for the life-support generator. Suck in all the bad air, pass it through a hydroponics system to feed the fish and plants, push cleaner air up into the ship. Repeat. A lovely, efficient design.

Javier took a step and snapped his arm forward, gunning for the runner coming around third in the bottom of the ninth.

His aim was perfectly timed, dead accurate. The vial impacted on the vent cover with a satisfying thump.

And fell to the deck unharmed.

Javier muttered something that might have made Wilhelmina blush. He dug for the pistol in his pocket, pulled it out, and began to sight.

"Navarre?" Tamaz called. "What's it going to be?"

Apparently, he had missed the vial flying in the dimness and haze.

Javier felt Hadiiye's hand on his before he got settled.

"Can you use that thing?" she asked.

Javier shrugged. "Probably."

"I thought so," she continued.

Javier watched her raise her own pistol in one motion and fire a single shot that dead-centered the vial. It shattered, spewing a greenish slop that was quickly sucked into the vent.

That was the lovely part of a pulse-pistol, as opposed to a disruptor. It used a force bolt instead of heat. Rupture, without the risk of cooking the green liquid and killing all the nasty bugs floating in it.

Javier watched just long enough to be sure, and then slammed the airlock door closed.

"Afia," he said, turning. "Deploy the emergency cocoon and get Sykora into it first. You and Piet next."

He turned to the control panel and emptied three shots into it in a rapture of smoke and sparks.

"What about the suits?" Wilhelmina asked.

"Can you get one on in thirty seconds?" he replied.

"Watch me," she said, pulling her tunic over her head.

Javier would have liked to watch more as her nudity unfolded, but there was no time. He stripped as well.

PART SIX

THE LITTLE RUNABOUT was quickly packed to the gills as people poured out of the airlock. Javier watched Piet and Wilhelmina carry Sykora's body to the bed and carefully lay her out.

He went straight to the flight console and brought everything live.

"How much time do we have?" Afia asked from his elbow. With him sitting and her standing, she was barely taller.

"You planning on coming back to *Meehu Platform* anytime soon?" he replied.

"Not on your life, sir."

"Me, neither."

Javier pushed a button that triggered the emergency overrides on the docking mechanism.

Every station had one. Usually, the station master would use it to push back a ship in danger of exploding, to keep it from venting nastiness into the interior and killing lots more people than just the crew.

You could set them off from inside a ship if you had to. If you suffered an emergency. Or needed to flee and didn't mind angering the stationmaster.

Somewhere nearby, bank vault doors were slamming shut and atmosphere alarms would be going off. People were going to be pissed.

Javier was in a stolen ship, fleeing a criminal enterprise, in the middle of a running gun fight, after using biological weapons. He really didn't care if they were going to give him a parking ticket after this.

The runabout lurched harshly before the gravplates could compensate.

"Piet," he called to *Storm Gauntlet*'s navigator. "I've calculated a course. Take us out that way as fast as she'll go."

"Roger that," the man replied, flowing into the seat.

Javier watched just long enough to confirm they were in safe hands, then he went to stand next to Wilhelmina, seated next to Sykora.

"How is she?" he asked.

"Been kicked by a Missouri mule," Wilhelmina replied. "Lucky for us she's tougher than one. Groggy now. Coherent in a few hours. Should be right as rain tomorrow. Assuming we survive."

"We'll survive," he said.

Javier turned around.

"Piet, how long to max acceleration?"

"Oh," the Dutchman replied sarcastically. "I was supposed to wait for that order?"

Javier smiled back at him. "Nyet, Gospodin. All ahead everything. Full speed crazy."

Javier consulted the watch in his head.

"Where are we jumping to, anyway?" Piet asked.

"Nowhere," Javier replied. "Just running."

"Javier?"

Wilhelmina looked closely at him, one hand holding Sykora's.

"'Mina?"

"How soon until we know?"

And that was the crux of it. How soon?

"We're a speedboat. He's a jumped up freighter. Let's find out."

Javier stepped close to the console. He watched Suvi land carefully on her charging ring.

After the mad dash here across open space, he knew her batteries were almost drained. But she had also saved all their lives, doing something no mere human could pull off. Like pulling a full emergency cocoon across the space between the two ships, straight to the runabout's airlock. Faster than anybody on the freighter or the station could move to intercept them.

One step ahead.

He smiled at Suvi as the little charging blinky thing stuttered. He imagined that was Suvi smiling and winking at him. He winked back.

Javier pushed a button to open a comm channel.

Winter's mantle draped itself across his shoulders as he inhaled.

"*Salekhard*, this is Navarre," he said calmly, coldly.

"I'm going to kill you, Navarre," Tamaz replied instantly.

"First you have to catch me, you amateur punk," Navarre replied, sticking the knife in and starting to twist it. "Good luck with that."

"You cannot run anywhere that I cannot find you," Tamaz continued. "And I will never cease hunting you. You have my honor on that."

"You have no honor, Abraam Tamaz," Navarre sneered. "You are the scum crusting the bottom of the barrel, after all the rotted fish have been dumped in a back alley. Right now, everyone knows you've lost her. But then, you never could keep a woman, could you?"

Navarre closed the channel with a vicious push. Virtual buttons lacked that hard tactile feedback that would have been nice now. He wished he could slam down a phone receiver, like the old movies did.

It would be more satisfying that way.

He turned to survey the crew around him. And nearly suffered the shock of his life.

Piet was watching him with a jaw dropped open. Afia's eyes were huge. Even Hadiiye was shocked.

"Piet," he growled, trying to glaze over the gap between himself and the rest. "How long until we reach those coordinates, if we don't slow down?"

The navigator just stared at him.

"Piet," he snapped his fingers. "Wake up."

"Right," the man said, tearing his eyes around to the console.

Moments passed.

"Assuming we just blow right by it," he said after a space. "A little less than two hours. Five if you want to slow down and park there. What is it?"

"A hole in space, Alferdinck," Navarre replied.

He wanted to be Javier right now. He really did.

That wasn't possible. Not today.

Today, he could only be Captain Navarre. Killer. Pirate bad-ass extraordinaire. That would have to do.

Right now, he was the captain of this little runabout. The way the rest looked at him right now left no doubt.

Time to make the best of it.

"Afia," he said, turning the vitriol in his voice down to normal conversation levels. "Could you take charge of making us some coffee? There's time before the next act."

"Coming up, sir," she said quietly.

It would be good coffee. Afia liked it dark, the same he did, especially on a day like this. The others could add cream or something to cut the bitterness down to levels tolerable for mere mortals. He wanted something monumental. This was a day for grand gestures.

Like stealing a prisoner out from under Tamaz's thumb.

Le Beau Geste.

"Contact," Piet said suddenly as a chime sounded on the console. "Looks like *Salekhard* has finally managed to detach from the station and is slowly accelerating out after us. He has weapon's lock, but won't be in range anytime soon."

"He had to behave," Navarre responded. "We could leave the place like bank robbers."

"Not complaining, sir," Piet replied. "Way happier here than there. I've got sensors and comm covered for now."

Navarre was pretty sure that this might be the most words the normally-quiet Piet Alferdinck had ever spoken to him in one setting.

"Tamaz saying anything interesting?" Navarre asked quietly.

The mad energy was beginning to ebb. The tide of the day had pooled, turned, threatened to run out of the harbor dragging him with it.

"Not unless you want to learn to curse in a few new languages, sir."

Sir? Yeah, I suppose I did just become a sir to them. I've gone from a slave on their ship to an officer in charge of things, responsible for their lives, to breaking them out of jail and rescuing them from a date with the hangman.

When the hell had he turned into one of them?

Navarre's eyes caught Djamila Sykora on the bed. Wilhelmina had covered her with a light blanket. He could see her closed eyes going back and forth, trapped in some nightmare from which she would awake to find she had traded her fate with Tamaz to a new fate with him.

I wonder which one would be worse, from her point of view?

Still, he was one of them. He was in charge. He would captain this mess to the bitter end.

Now it remained to see if he was Bligh or Christian.

Navarre reached down and activated the comm. He made sure it was a standard navigation channel this time, so everyone in the system might listen in.

"*Salekhard*," he growled. "I'm still waiting to dance. Or are too big of a coward to even come out to fight me, Tamaz?"

Across space, Tamaz gasped with rage, and then continued his stream of never-ending invective.

Navarre quickly grew bored. Javier would have at least been impressed that the pirate could go that many words between repetitions. There was a skill to that.

Tamaz was still an ass.

Navarre shut off the comm for now. It served no purpose now but to goad the man on further.

He had probably done enough already. If not, it would be there waiting.

Afia served him a mug of coffee.

"So where's the rabbit?" she asked innocently.

"Rabbit?" Navarre blinked down at the tiny woman.

"I've played too much poker with you, sir," she said. "You aren't bluffing here. So you have a rabbit you're going to pull out of a hat soon."

Navarre smiled cruelly at her, let it warm some.

"You saw that vial of liquid, Afia?" he asked conversationally. "I don't suppose you saw where I threw it?"

"No, sir," she replied firmly. "I was busy helping load the dragoon so we could abandon ship. What was it? I saw green."

Wilhelmina rose from the bed to join the conversation. She looked tired.

"It was a biological agent, Afia," she said. "Captain Tamaz was going to infect Djamila with it and then send her back to *Storm Gauntlet* to infect the rest of the crew and kill them."

The woman's dark eyes got large. "Seriously? Plague?"

"Correct," Navarre said. "Plague. We ruptured the liquid into the air intakes for *Salekhard*'s life support blowers."

Afia Burakgazi was an engineer by trade, an expert in the care and feeding of complicated mechanical systems. Navarre watched her eyes flicker back and forth as she traced the equivalent systems on *Storm Gauntlet*. Their Strike Corvette home was a purpose-built warship, instead of an up-gunned freighter, but the equations were similar.

"Biological weapon," she muttered. "Vaporize it into the wet air off hydroponics, feed it with all the right nutrients, blast it all over the ship. Infect everyone in under an hour unless they shut the whole system down."

"They can't shut the life-support systems down."

Her normally dark skin paled as she stared mutely at him.

"How do you know?"

Navarre felt a cruel smile overtake him.

"They could have, but that would have required them to vent everything and pipe in clean air from the station. And we know they didn't do that..."

"Because they detached from the station and are chasing us," Afia finished in a whisper.

"Will they even realize they're dying?" Wilhelmina inquired.

Navarre shrugged.

"We didn't go into details, 'Mina," he said simply. "Knowing the kind of man Tamaz is, it would be something extremely painful, but fast acting. He would want to kill everyone on *Storm Gauntlet* quickly enough that he could board her, fill Sykora with the antidote, if she wasn't just the carrier vector to begin with, and then steal the ship. He'd have a brand new warship in his fleet, as well as his revenge on everyone. Letting people linger runs the risk that someone cures it, or Sokolov blows the *Gauntlet* in place."

"How long do you suppose, then?" Wilhelmina asked.

Navarre counted the clock in his head.

"Slightly over two hours since exposure," he said. "Piet, how soon until they catch us?"

The navigator tore his eyes away from Navarre and consulted his console.

"We accelerate faster," the man replied finally. "They've got bigger engines so I would guess thirty percent higher top speed in this solar wind density. Maybe four more hours if nothing changes at their end and then..."

Navarre watched him stop talking, his concentration somewhere else. One hand came up to an ear.

Navarre hadn't realized that Piet had an earpiece in, listening to Tamaz on the comm all this time. That took intestinal fortitude, considering the company.

"Sir," Piet said. "You need to hear this."

He reached over and punched a button on the console, dialing up the sound.

A howl of pain filled the cabin.

It was a wail, an angry *ban sidhe* calling for your soul, wordlessly, mindlessly screaming. It took a second for Navarre to realize that a human throat was making it.

Navarre let the chill etch itself into his soul before Javier took over again, relegating the pirate persona back to the dark places inside where a man like that normally resided.

Javier looked individually at his crewmates. Navarre would have scowled at them. But Navarre was gone. He gave them a hard, purposeful smile instead.

His eyes linked with Wilhelmina. He felt warmth there, but it was across a distant sea, lost across horizons.

"Paladins," he whispered, just loud enough to be heard, "are men and women of the sword."

PART SEVEN

JAVIER STOOD to one side of Sokolov's desk and watched the blackness of deep space out a porthole.

Salekhard was gone. Obliterated. Shattered under a rolling salvo of *Storm Gauntlet*'s guns. Purification by immolation. But at that point, it really was just putting down a lame horse. Tamaz and his mad dogs were already dead.

Locals would mark it down to a turf battle between pirates. Those were common enough in places like this. Tamaz had gambled and lost. That was the price you sometimes paid.

"Everyone pays that price eventually, Aritza," the captain replied.

Javier hadn't realized he had spoken aloud in his musings.

"And we might have been able to salvage her," Sokolov continued, almost hopeful.

"No," Javier said firmly. "Better the purging fires. Let hard vac and radiation cleanse the carcass. Anything else risks too much. Who knows what else that bastard had cooked up?"

"So now what, Mister Science Officer?"

"Now?" Javier mused. "We send Sykora and Wilhelmina to complete their mission and sell that ship. Plus we sell the stolen runabout. Then we go on with our lives."

"Are you ever going to tell me the whole story about what happened, Aritza?"

Javier smiled ruefully.

"Not this side of hell, Zakhar. Not this side of hell."

THE BLACK HAIR WAS DISCONCERTING, but she was still beautiful. Javier still saw traces of Hadiiye in the way she moved, but this was Wilhelmina standing before him.

They were alone in his cabin.

He held out a hand, almost shyly.

She took it, almost as carefully.

Silence passed as he sought the words.

"I want you to do something for me," he said finally.

"What?"

"I want to send Suvi with you, 'Mina. She can help protect you out there, and she deserves a chance to escape. I'm going to be stuck a slave for years at this rate. She should live."

"No," Wilhelmina smiled softly at him. She could be a stubborn woman.

"No?"

"No. We talked, her and me."

"You what?"

"Suvi and I talked, while you were with the Captain. I asked her. She wants to stay with you."

Javier turned to face the remote, resting quietly on the charging ring.

"Are you freaking nuts?" he asked.

Suvi's running lights came on.

"You need way more protecting than she does, boss," his first mate, his comrade in surveying, his friend said.

Javier refused to cry as he engulfed Wilhelmina in a hug.

It was good to have friends.

JAVIER WATCHED Wilhelmina walk down the airlock tube to the little runabout, just like last time. And just like before, he would never see her again. Although he had made arrangements with her to be at a specific bar on a specific day, five years from now, with a rose in his lapel.

Just in case, you know.

Afia Burakgazi and Piet Alferdinck were already aboard getting ready, like nearly a month hadn't passed since the last time they had tried this. Luck was better the second go round.

He was alone in the airlock.

A tree suddenly appeared behind him, almost silently.

Javier turned.

Djamila Sykora. Dragoon. Ballerina of Death. Angry, angry woman.

She was almost close enough for him to stick his nose into her cleavage. He almost did, anyway.

He looked up.

There was a mad hatred in her eyes.

It was good to be home.

"I've heard most of the story," she growled under her breath.

"Those parts were lies and innuendo," he replied, feeling the heat rise up in his stomach, like bile turned to napalm.

"I have no doubt, Aritza," she snarled. "Especially around you. I want to know why."

"Why what?"

"Why did you agree to it?" she said. "Why risk your life? Why not just walk away? You might like Teague that well, but not Alferdinck or Burakgazi."

"Why did I risk life and limb, freedom and forever, on you, Sykora? Is that it?"

"Exactly, Aritza. Why?"

Javier reached up with his right hand and grabbed her by the shirt front. There was nothing remotely man or woman here, he wanted her down at his level.

He pulled. She came.

They ended up nose to nose, snarl to snarl.

"Because nobody gets to kill you but me," Javier rasped.

Sykora stared hard at him for several seconds, delving as deep into his soul as he went into hers.

He watched the hatred burn in those eyes. That mad, burning rage that overwhelmed every bit of rational thought, of care, of survival. He saw the primal creative energies of the universe. Creation myths unfolding. Pantheonic wars playing out.

Götterdämmerung.

She lunged forward suddenly and kissed him hard on the mouth. It was passion without romance, fire without warmth.

A promise of forever.

Lovers in hatred.

"Deal," she said.

THE PLEASURE DOME

PART NINE

BOOK NINE: MERCENARY

PART ONE

JAVIER HAD NEVER BEEN one for gear lust.

It had never been about fast cars or fancy starships, with the sole exception of Suvi and *Mielikki*. The rest of the time, whatever was necessary to get him to the next gig, the next station, the next bar was enough.

But that was before he laid eyes on the Land Leviathan.

Starships were cool and all. As were AI systems smart enough to compose music and poetry.

Hell, he even knew one like that.

But the Land Leviathan marked that point where you were truly living in a galaxy wealthy beyond ancient dreams of avarice, regardless of what anyone else thought on the topic. For the longest moment, he considered how he would go about stealing it.

"Why are we here, again?" Javier finally asked Zakhar Sokolov, seated next to him in the backseat of the VTOL limo as they slowly descended on the giant metal train from above, a tiny eagle chasing a monstrous snake across a salmon-colored desert wasteland.

Ten square cars, each sixty meters on a side and at least half that tall. Connected like a train, except rumbling slowly across the sand and rock on treads at least four meters tall instead of rails. From where Javier sat, it looked vaguely like an ocean liner, with the top of each of the ten sections dedicated to a different task, including a landing deck, a swimming pool, an amphitheater, and something that looked suspiciously like a barbeque pit big enough for a whole pig.

Stealing it would be difficult. He could see a big, honking gun turret up front, and two smaller, flanking ones at the rear, plus six air-defense cannons on the sides. The last car had a semi-open bay at ground level, containing a variety of ground and skimmer combat vehicles, including at least two that looked remarkably like main battle tanks from one of Suvi's favorite video games.

Clearly, someone had let their paranoia get the better of them. Or seriously considered the sort of gear lust that this level of cash expenditure would engender in someone like Javier Aritza.

And this wasn't a rolling resort, even if it looked like one.

No, this was somebody's personal land yacht. Complete with a crew and staff of three to five hundred. One of the most expensive vehicles ever manufactured on the surface of any planet.

Chicken feed.

The man seated beside Javier stirred. He might have been napping. All the more reason to wake him up.

"Because someone wanted to hire a bad-ass mercenary named Navarre," the man replied, stretching. "And she seems to think I'm one of the few people in the galaxy able to locate the man."

Javier nodded. It was true. He was.

Zakhar Sokolov. Captain of the private service strike corvette, *Storm Gauntlet*, a vessel meandering back and forth across legality as situations demanded.

Average, if you met him on the street. 1.8 meters tall. Ordinary build. Shaved head with a salt and pepper Van Dyke. Mid-fifties lines on his face. Nothing interesting at all.

At least until he turned on that *Captain thing*. Then he was all charm and bad-ass.

Javier had never gotten the hang of being a command officer. Liking people was probably a requirement.

A bridge too far.

"That explains why I'm here, Zakhar," Javier volleyed the conversation back across the tiny enclosed space. "Not you."

Javier watched the man who was technically his superior officer, possibly his owner, depending on how you wanted to slice things, chew on his next sentence, like a cow with good cud.

Whatever lies were coming must be pretty amazing.

Since Javier, posing as Navarre, had rescued his own mortal enemy, Djamila Sykora, Zakhar Sokolov's *Dragoon*, at *Meehu Platform*, Javier's relationship with Sokolov and the rest of the crew had changed. It had really started at *A'Nacia*, when he saved all their butts from the killer-robot mine field, and then rescued Wilhelmina Teague from eternity, before he made the rest of them rather wealthy.

The crew no longer really considered him a slave they had captured. Even an honored one like a modern Janissary. No, these days he was just another officer in charge, just another Centurion.

The Science Officer. And all that implied.

Those folks he generally liked well enough to let them out of his revenge.

But he hadn't paid off his debt bond to Sokolov. And he still hadn't killed Sykora.

"That comes after we meet with the contact," Captain Sokolov said simply. "You and I are going to need to have a conversation. Without the rest of the crew around."

Javier bit back the sarcastic riposte poised on the tip of his tongue. The last one of *those* conversations had sent him to rescuing Sykora from her captor, when he could have easily fled across deep space and made it home and left the woman to her well-deserved fate. And he could have taken Suvi with him, still tucked quietly into her handheld scout probe, even if now it was the size of a soccer ball.

He hadn't, because he had given his word as an officer and a gentleman of Bryce, according to the statement on the commissioning papers each man had received upon graduating the Academy and becoming officers of the Concord Navy, once upon a long time ago. Literally, his ransom, to use the archaic term.

Going back on that, even with people like this, would make Javier the one thing he despised most in the galaxy.

A pirate.

One of those conversations, Zakhar?

Javier held his tongue, and his peace. They were on the final approach to the last car of the Land Leviathan.

Soon enough, he would know the truth.

Hopefully, he wouldn't have to kill as many people this time.

Unless they were pirates.

JAVIER REALLY DIDN'T WANT to go anywhere as *Navarre*, even in his own mind, but the situation demanded it. Someone wanted to hire the psycho who had killed Abraam Tamaz and his entire crew of the Q-freighter *Salekhard*. Singlehandedly.

This wasn't going to be a tea and crumpets kind of meeting.

If he didn't owe Zakhar Sokolov so much money, he might have refused. Zakhar might have even let it go.

But there was a lot of potential money on the table. Maybe enough to get his freedom and buy his botany station back in the deal.

No chicken should have to spend one day more than necessary with pirates. Even nice ones like *Storm Gauntlet*.

They landed with the soft blush that told Javier most passengers boarding like this were screamers when something happened they found unwelcome.

Up close, the Land Leviathan made all of Javier's dreams of avarice suddenly junior varsity. It got worse as his eyes progressed from place to place.

Entire walkways, everywhere he looked, appeared to be plated over with gold. Granted, most younger solar systems had enough of the material that it had almost no value in and of itself except as decoration, but people still used it as a measure of wealth. Of Power.

Of the ability to just have tons of the stuff as ornament. Simply because it was gold.

They were met at the landing by a hard man in a well-tailored suit, and two killers in loose, black outfits. Javier knew the type. One dressed up to impress you with his culture. Two more to kill you if you got out of line.

Hard people. It was a hard business.

Navarre came to the fore as Javier handed the man in the suit his smaller belt, with the holster for a pulse pistol and a fighting poniard. This wasn't that kind of meeting. He hoped.

He settled for walking in the man's wake, Sokolov trailing, with the two others behind that.

The desert planet was hot, so he had cut down what he thought of as the Navarre costume.

Twenty-ring lace up boots in glossy neo-leather, with curb-stomping soles and hull-metal toes. Bright red laces all the way up and double-knotted at the top.

Knee-length britches out of dark maroon corduroy, with heavy leather combat padding along the outer edge in case someone out of a Chop-sockey movie kicked him. The socks were much lighter fabric today, and only as tall as the boots, rather than covering the knees.

Sixteen-centimeter-tall leather belt around his middle, with a canary-yellow sash tied around that.

Up top, the sleeveless doublet in that same maroon corduroy as the britches, but with two rows of buttons that ran from the inside of his hips to the middle of his collar-bones.

He had skipped the white shirt he would normally wear underneath and left the top part of the doublet unbuttoned, showing off muscles and hairy bits. Time well spent in the gym over the last six months.

And just for the hell of it, Javier had kept the cloth tied around his forehead, with a *Neu Berne* Assault Marine logo in the middle.

It was a look. It had even worked to convince people that he was a sadistic killer.

Killing a lot of people at *Meehu Platform* had helped.

But those people had been pirates. They'd had it coming.

The long walk finally ended somewhere around the third car back from the prow. Javier had lost track of the number of times they had exited a section into heat, crossed a catwalk, and entered the next. He probably should have been paying closer attention, but Navarre was an unwelcome guest in his head.

If only there was some other way to do this, without pretending to be *him*.

The last surprise today was probably the least surprising, if he'd have given it more thought and less brooding. There weren't that many people who even knew about Navarre.

And there she was.

The only time they had met had been on *Meehu Platform*, when Javier as Navarre was busy getting close enough to Tamaz to rescue Sykora.

Stewart Lace.

Javier had looked up her name later, after Tamaz was dead, to make sure he wouldn't have a problem with her.

She was still dressed like a banker and still in good shape, if thickening with age. Mid-fifties, perhaps, from the lines about her, so around Zakhar's age, and a decade older than Javier. A little more solid than he liked them, but still very well-kept.

Her beauty had that slowly-aging thing going, coming down from an amazing starting point, like the best wines, even as she wore little makeup and kept her hair buzzed to perhaps three or four millimeters long.

Her eyes were what did it. They had the intelligence of an alpha predator, even as they smiled rather warmly at him.

Javier wondered if she had started out as a lawyer or a prostitute forty years ago, and how she had managed to retain some level of humanity for this long. She wasn't really his type, Javier liked his women skinnier, but she was probably one of the few he had ever met who could have a good conversation over breakfast, afterwards.

He doubted that was why she had brought him here.

She rose as they entered the cozy little salon, done up in soft pastel fabrics and paint. Peach. Aqua. Seafoam.

Silk sofas and antique wooden side tables. Money.

"Captain Sokolov," Lace said as she shook his hand. "Captain Navarre. I'm surprised you didn't bring your dangerous sidekick."

"She's guarding the ship," Javier said with a noncommittal growl.

Technically, the woman was referring to 'Mina, but she was hopefully gone away and safe. Converting the galaxy up from being heathens into civilized folk. Sykora could probably be convinced to sub for her, in a pinch. Especially if she got to beat people up.

Djamila Sykora lived for that.

"I see," Lace said. "Please, join me."

Javier had to suppress an inappropriate giggle. The room had been set for tea and cucumber sandwiches.

Seriously. Antique, bone china. Small plates with cucumber and dill-cream triangles of bread.

All those classes in deportment, back at Bryce Academy, all that preparation to be here now as *Navarre*, and here he was.

Both he and Sokolov managed to drink with pinkies out. Concord Fleet Officers, and all that.

Javier could see the woman smile knowingly as she watched them.

So, surprised you got someone with more manners than Abraam Tamaz, lady? Two of them?

The only thing he got out of the small talk was that she didn't own the Land Leviathan, but was representing the iron snake's owner in this deal. So stealing it was probably right out. And buying it outright would take the annual budget of some medium-sized planets.

Javier made a note to check his investment portfolio sometime. Most of it had been cut to pieces when Sokolov's crew had dismembered Suvi.

The rest was hidden in civilized places where Sokolov's pirates wouldn't let him go without adult supervision. And he had no intention of letting that bunch of yahoos anywhere near his bank account.

That could wait until he got free and had to start over.

"I've been doing some research," Madame Lace said finally, placing her teacup just so and leaning back with a vague smile. "Captain Navarre didn't seem to exist before the incident on *Meehu Platform*. And seems to have disappeared afterwards."

Javier felt Sokolov tense, ever so slightly.

He was personally neither here nor there.

The moment stretched.

"And?" Javier finally said.

Her smile turned a few degrees warmer. Not actually warm, but less predatory.

It was just the three of them, with hard-man and his two killers somewhere outside.

Either she trusted her defensive systems, or didn't think violence would come up in the conversation.

"And so that entire operation appears to have been an elaborate con job," she said. "Designed to get someone close enough to Captain Tamaz to rescue a hostage, escape safely, and lead him to his death."

She paused, in case one of the men wanted to speak, but Sokolov had clammed up.

"Close enough," Javier finally demurred. "I would have phrased it: *...and kill him like a rabid dog.*"

"I see."

More pause.

"The galaxy is a better place without people like Abraam Tamaz," Javier finally offered.

"Indeed, one could make that case," Lace said, her eyes boring in on Javier. "And if I hadn't been there at the time, Captain Navarre would have probably disappeared from all human cognition, wouldn't he?"

Javier just sat and watched her for a few moments. Navarre would have said something cold and biting into the gap. Wanted to. Was at the tip of his mind, offering the words.

Certainly, that would be one path forward.

Just turn into Navarre full-time until he paid off his debt to Sokolov and got his life back. It would make things simpler. Cleaner.

And it would take him back to where he was before. Years ago. Put that blackness back in the center of his soul, instead of stuffed into a locked closet, where it belonged. Remind him why he had two ex-wives.

Not for you to unlock, lady. Not for any of you.

"So," Javier ventured, shoving Navarre to one side. "Did you need princesses rescued or dragons slain?"

Navarre was still more of a *Kill the princess, rape the troll, burn the treasure* sort of person, anyway.

Stewart Lace studied Javier closely. More closely.

Like she could see the two men at war inside his head.

She smiled with just the right level of empathy. Neither of his wives had ever managed that.

"A little of both, actually," she finally replied.

Javier felt an eyebrow ascend of its own volition.

"There exists a box," Lace continued, holding up her hands to encompass a space just large enough to store a pair of tiny stiletto heels with frilly puffs on the front. "Through a complicated chain of conversations, my principal has been asked to see to the destruction of the contents of that box. They will pay well. There is an even greater bounty if the contents can be recovered instead."

Javier leaned back and scowled. Navarre was close to saying *I told you so* in his head.

Anyone wanting Navarre wasn't going to be particular about collateral damage. That man had a reputation, at least with the bystanders.

There hadn't been any survivors.

"How much?" Javier asked, cutting to the chase to see how serious these people were.

The number she quoted as an *opening bid* nearly made Javier drop his tea cup. He could suddenly see while Sokolov was here.

That man had a vested interest in making sure the money passed through his hands first.

Javier's cut would still get him within spitting distance of buying his freedom. Another year, or another score like that, and he could probably buy back his chickens and his botany station outright, as well.

Outwardly, Javier nodded calmly. Opening bid. Still several rounds before they got to the final hole card and the serious money.

"Where is it?" he asked.

That much money could only come from someone with planetary wealth at their command. The sort of people who could build a Land Leviathan and occasionally pack it up and take it to a new planet when this one got boring. People who owned whole planets, whole systems, in fee simple.

Dangerous people. Usually quite vicious because nobody has ever been allowed to tell them *No* in their entire lives.

"*Shangdu,*" she replied with a biting smile.

"I'm not familiar with that planet," Zakhar spoke up suddenly, in an earnest voice out of place with the man's normally growliness.

"It isn't a planet, Sokolov," Navarre replied, spitting the words out like a grain mill. "It's a starship.

At Xanadu did Kublai Khan
    A stately pleasure dome decree…

Shangdu is the correct Chinese place name."

"I see," Zakhar replied icily, giving Javier a dose of stinkeye for quoting ancient poetry at him in public.

Javier, in turn, gave Lace a dose of the stinkeye.

"Even bigger reward for recovering it?" he asked.

"Indeed," she agreed. "And I can get you the introductions to get you aboard, depending on your plan. Thoughts?"

"I would like to spend a day or so aboard the Land Leviathan," Javier replied. "Let us have dinner, and spend more time hammering out details. We can come to some consensus tomorrow."

"Excellent," she said, rising. "I will get you situated, and we will convene for dinner in about five hours, gentlemen."

Javier rose, and followed Sokolov out and through the nicer parts of the vessel.

Someone wanted to hire Navarre. Someone probably expecting a mass casualty incident that they could disavow later.

That would be rude. Doubly so on one of the modern age's largest starships, a private playground for the wealthiest elites.

A great way to make a galaxy full of blood enemies.

Javier couldn't do that. Navarre couldn't make him.

But still, he was looking forward to visiting *The Pleasure Dome.*

Again.

PART TWO

ZAKHAR WAITED until he and Javier were nominally alone. The conversation could probably be recorded or transmitted, if that lady banker cared enough. Zakhar had no intention of discussing anything truly incriminating in a place like this.

He was already here hat in hand. No reason to give her or them anything more with which to blackmail him.

This salon was part of a private suite. Two bedrooms off of a central area that was somewhere between hunting lodge and salon. Comfortable, expensive furnishings just masculine enough to make it look tough, but just feminine enough to make it intellectual, rather than barbaric.

Zakhar watched Aritza walk to the bar along one wall, pour a finger of something, and slug it back in a single, hard motion. He would have to wait to see if the alcohol helped or hindered.

Instead, Zakhar pulled up a comfortable-looking leather chair and settled himself into it. Less confrontational, he hoped.

"I got most of the story from Shepherd Teague, before she left," Zakhar said, drawing Javier's eyes and then his whole body around.

Javier's look was non-committal.

"I doubt it."

He poured another finger of something, but held it this time, looking like a prop.

"I have concerns about this proposed operation," Zakhar concluded.

Aritza looked angry. But he also looked human, which was good. According to Wilhelmina Teague, Navarre had turned the man into a monster from the cold, empty darkness.

"Such as?" Javier finally drawled sarcastically before finishing the second shot and pouring another.

"She specifically asked for Navarre," Zakhar replied. "Based on what he did at *Meehu Platform*."

Javier just eyed him, so Zakhar plowed ahead.

"That's not the sort of reputation I desire," Zakhar continued. "That's not the sort of person I wish to be known as."

"You're a pirate, Sokolov," Javier snarled without ever raising his voice. "And a slaver. I don't think you've got a lot of ground to stand on, here."

Zakhar stopped himself from jumping up to confront the man. This was why he had sat before he spoke.

"I've done indefensible things, mister," Zakhar agreed. "I'll grant you that. But doing to *Shangdu* what you did to Tamaz is not something I will allow."

"It would be worth a tremendous amount of money, Sokolov," his Science Officer, his *slave*, fired back angrily. "Enough that you'll be that much closer to being done with me."

"I don't care, Javier."

"Well I do," the man growled, stopping to slug back the next finger of whiskey in the glass. "It's that much closer to me being free."

Zakhar watched Javier pour another.

"Anything to get away?" Zakhar asked.

"Damned straight," Javier replied.

"You could have escaped, Javier," Zakhar countered. "More than once."

"You don't get to win, Zakhar."

That shot vanished into Javier's mouth.

He watched Javier pour another finger into the glass, two, heavier this time. He hammered it back in a single, ugly gulp and fixed angry eyes on Zakhar.

"You have my ransom, Sokolov, my word of honor as a gentleman," Javier continued in a nasty, vicious voice. "You will get your money. And there is nothing you can do to stop me. If this deal is too much for your squeamish stomach to handle, then you and I are going to have a problem."

"Javier, it is evil," Zakhar said, nearly pled. "Nothing more. Nothing less. If you feel that strongly, I'm willing to walk away right now, and credit what would have been your share of the deal against your debt. I will not do evil."

An offer like that, and Javier didn't even blink.

"You don't even know what evil is, Sokolov," Aritza sneered at him.

That brought Zakhar out of his chair.

"Oh, no, Aritza. I understand evil," Zakhar snarled quietly as the two men were nearly nose to nose. "I've *been* evil."

Javier stared at him for a moment, and then laughed.

The son of a bitch laughed.

Zakhar stood there, rigid with rage, not trusting himself to keep from strangling his Science Officer. Or punching him.

Javier smiled, turned back to the bar, and grabbed a second highball glass, pouring a shot of whiskey in.

"Good," Javier said with a canary-eating grin as he handed Zakhar the glass and tapped the two together. "Because we're going to do this my way, and see if we can pull off the caper of the century without a single person getting hurt."

"And Navarre?" Zakhar asked, suddenly finding himself on squishy ground.

"Navarre was appropriate to dealing with Tamaz and *Salekhard*, Zakhar," Javier said. "On *Shangdu*, most of them will be children with a lot of money but not the sense God gave a goose."

"And the rest?" Zakhar asked.

"She might be the most dangerous person in the galaxy."

She?

PART THREE

AT LEAST, Javier thought to himself, watching his assistant/minder/bodyguard, Ilan had turned into a pretty competent Machinist's Mate. And the man could keep the chickens fed and safe for a week, and the botany station from catching fire, while Javier had been down on the planet.

Ilan sat across from him now, happily munching a *sandwich*, of some sort.

"So why did it take four days to do your deal, sir?" Ilan asked around a bite.

Javier considered the *casserole* on the plate before him. Industrial cheese. Previously-frozen vegetables of uncertain ancestry. Meat-like substance.

At least the rotini noodles tasted right. It was really hard to screw up rotini. Not that he felt like challenging the cooks around here, or anything.

Javier contemplated his fork like a man considering seppuku. Which wasn't fair to the wardroom cooks. They were just working on a much smaller budget than Stewart Lace.

He sniffed at the casserole anyway.

"Sir?" Ilan hesitated.

"Could have been done in two, Ilan," Javier sighed. "But they had real, fresh cream."

"How fresh?"

Ilan put his sandwich down and grabbed his glass of *something* to drink. Not a good vintage of wine, nor an exquisite Scotch-style whiskey.

"They keep four cows in a small petting zoo, Ilan," Javier said.

Even a man who kept chickens in deep space could be awed at the cost and effort to keep cows.

"You mean, like, real ones?"

Ilan's eyes got big. And this was the man tasked with making sure all of Javier's fruit trees and vegetable gardens got watered regularly when he was off having adventures.

Javier enjoyed being bribed with top notch food to consider doing a job he had already accepted in his head in the first five minutes.

"Yeah," Javier agreed. "Real ones."

Ilan started to say something, changed his mind, and fell uncharacteristically silent.

Javier watched him grab his plate and glass, stand up, and vanish as if his ass was on fire.

Weren't many people could do that to Ilan.

Javier waited.

Sure enough, someone had silently planted an oak tree on the deck behind him. That made it even fewer.

As tall as he was in the torso, Javier was still only looking at her belt buckle when he turned to glance behind him. *Storm Gauntlet's Dragoon*, her master of close combat.

Djamila Sykora.

The Ballerina of Death.

Javier let his eyes roam northward as she stood there.

It had been a year since they had met, the first time she had shot him.

Two point one meters of woman, built like a rugby player with muscles in places Javier wasn't even sure he had places, and he was in better shape than most of this crew.

Dressed today in black slacks, maroon shirt, and a black tunic. Black combat boots with a polish clean enough that Javier could have used them to shave with.

Powerful thighs, reasonable waist, V-shaped torso with small breasts atop big pecs.

The bones in her face were female. Not particularly delicate. Definitely not feminine.

Brown hair worn short to fit inside an armoured lifesuit, buzzed very short on the sides and spiked into a petite Mohawk. The only thing petite about her.

The only vaguely-female touch he could see was the collection of rings, studs, and stones in both ears. Nothing through the nose, though.

She still reminded him of a PT instructor from the Academy. The one who liked to sing on twenty-mile hikes in full gear.

"Captain tells me we have a job," she announced quietly, standing there at a parade rest that made Javier's feet hurt just thinking about it.

The voice was a studied alto. Professional. Polite, even.

She must be trying really hard to be nice today.

"We?" Javier drawled up at her, Athena atop Olympus.

She took that as an invitation and settled into Ilan's abandoned chair with the precision of a combat drop.

Sykora was like that.

Surprise of surprises, she actually leaned forward, rested her elbows on the table, and rested her chin on her fists with a slight grin.

Javier hadn't known she had that posture programmed into her operations manual.

"Someone hired Navarre, Aritza," she said plainly. "That means they would be expecting Hadiiye as well."

"She's gone, Sykora," Javier smiled cruelly back. "Obviously to a better place. What makes you think you could replace her?"

"Doctor Teague was good," Sykora agreed. "With a little training and practice, she could have easily found a place on my combat force."

"This isn't a raid, Dragoon," Javier let his face grow serious. "If we do our jobs correctly, nobody will even get hurt. Can you replace 'Mina as an actress?"

He really loved the angry scowl he could bring out on that woman's face. Made getting out of bed in the morning worth it, all by itself some days.

Her eyes narrowed to angry slits.

"What did you have in mind, Aritza?" she asked.

It was obvious from her tone that she was willing to go toe to toe with anyone on the ship, to prove she was better. Even if she had to spend two weeks in a crash course, twenty-four hours a day. She was the kind of woman who wouldn't accept second place.

Javier leaned back and smiled.

"How are your tan lines?" he asked deceptively.

"My what?"

301

She leaned back as well, but that was surprise and defensive body posture.

Javier had guessed that she might have a soft spot in her personal armor right there. Comments and things about body image were the clue.

Javier let his smile turn feral.

"*Shangdu* is the personal yacht of one woman, who has turned it into a flying resort for the wealthiest, the most elite in the galaxy," he said. "It has a casino, and a couple of clubs and restaurants, for the hundred or so guests she allows at any time. But *Shangdu* is best known for the lake in the middle of the ship."

"Lake?"

"Lake," Javier agreed, watching doubt creep into those eyes finally. "A body of water in a rough elliptical shape, two kilometers long and a kilometer wide, with a nice island in the middle."

"Kilometers?" she sputtered. "But that's…"

"A little over six square kilometers of water," Javier said. "Average depth ten meters. Nearly ten kilometers of beach around the outer edge."

"And tan lines?" she asked, slightly hoarse.

"Most of the time, your entire costume would consist of a single piece of light cloth, a little over a meter long, and half that wide, wrapped around your hips and held in place with a small, gold clasp. A professional won't have any tan lines at all."

Ye gods, could that woman scowl.

Javier wanted to pinch himself, just to make sure she hadn't just turned him to stone with that look.

"You want me to be your doxy?" she hissed.

Javier leaned forward and rested his own chin on his hands, eyes wide and innocent.

Just how far are you willing to be pushed before you hit me this time, lady?

"Hadiiye was a stone killer, Dragoon," he replied mildly. "Pumping biological weapons into the life support system might have been my idea, but she fired the shot that did it. She killed them all."

Javier watched the Dragoon process that bit of information with a hint of surprise.

Sykora had been out cold, and 'Mina obviously hadn't said anything to her later on, letting Navarre take all the credit.

"I have no doubt you could do the same, push comes to shove," Javier continued. "But she was also very serious about being eye-candy on that operation. About using her tits and ass to distract people, keep them off-tempo. Wilhelmina's first doctorate was in psychology. If you want to play, you'll have to sell sex to rich degenerates. Whether you execute the sale afterwards is entirely up to you."

"Whore myself," she snarled under her breath as her eyes seemed to turn red.

"Perform your portion of the mission with the sorts of excellence you demand from everyone else, regardless of how personally distasteful you might find it," he fired back, barely any louder, or warmer.

She hissed. Nothing more. Snarled silently, lip curled and nose scrunched ever so cutely.

"My last mission, you'll recall," he continued, "involved rescuing you from being tortured to insanity, and then killing everyone aboard that ship for you. I can do things I find distasteful."

Bingo.

That strike went home.

It was amazing how blind someone might be to their own, personal short-comings.

Javier made no bones about his own screw-ups. Embracing them had let him discover how to be happy, happier anyway, than the driven, hard-ass, drunkard who had blown up a career in the Concord Navy and two marriages.

Little Miss Perfect over there had never come to grips with that sort of thing. Had never locked herself and her psyche in a dark closet for a long weekend and really examined herself. And done it sober.

Probably not many people could do it and retain their sanity.

Of course, Javier never really claimed to be sane.

He looked her in the eyes with a cold smile.

There.

Gotcha.

That flash of angry green light.

Realization that Javier Aritza might have drawn a line in the sand you weren't willing to cross?

Javier figured she'd go silent and internal at this point. She frequently had in the past when pushed this hard.

She might not even realize she did it, vaulting away into herself to have some conversation with her own angry ghosts.

Javier put his head down and attacked the casserole like there was a fuse burning somewhere close.

IT TOOK everything Djamila had not to reach across the table and punch the man so hard he concussed against a bulkhead. She could do that, even seated.

And the way he just ignored her and ate grated all the harder.

Wasn't it enough that he thought of her as *just another dumb gun bunny*? No, he had to add insult to injury and make her a common whore?

Djamila flashed back to one of her brother officers offering to pave the way for her to be promoted out of her last dead-end assignment. To use his wealth and connections to get her into a better berth.

If she would just do this one little thing for him...

The top of Aritza's head showed where his hair was very slowly receding, and just beginning to turn gray. He would probably still die with a full head of hair.

If he didn't push her so hard all the time, it might even be of old age, too.

For the longest moment, Djamila considered letting this one go. Just staying back with the ship, presumably while someone else served as Aritza's bimbo. Either of her pathfinders, Sascha or Hajna, would be perfect in the role.

Letting it go? Let the Science Officer win a round?

A year ago, inconceivable. Utterly incalculable.

Djamila felt the cold in her limbs meet with the fire in her belly, like a volcano running into the ocean to generate a wall of steam.

But Wilhelmina had taught the Dragoon something about herself, on those two long missions they had shared. Those late night conversations when the other two crew members had gone to sleep.

About not always having to win. About letting go of old angers, old rivalries, and learning to like herself.

Even Teague hadn't used the phrase *"love herself"* but talked about liking who you were first.

A first step on the road to discovering happiness.

The rest of the crew accepted her as the most dangerous, most driven creature aboard. Morning PT. Laps around the ship in full gear. Close-combat training daily with a rotating cast of crew members.

Being the best.

And this bastard wanted her to dangle everything out for whatever wealthy men found a woman of her physicality arousing? To measure her value to the mission, to the ship, in bed?

Djamila flashed back to the tiny, ugly smile Aritza had given her before he looked down.

He knows.

Aritza had found a weakness in her soul, one even she hadn't know about until he drew blood.

Was counting on it.

Wanted her to quit now and let one of the pathfinders take her place as Hadiiye, so he wouldn't have anyone around to stop him from acting like a juvenile delinquent. To maybe let him sell them all to the hangman while he worked out a deal.

In her memory, Wilhelmina smiled up at her, one of the tallest women she had ever met outside of her own extended family.

Will you let others judge your worth, Djamila? Or can you establish your own scale?

Djamila felt the cold give way, warmth flooding outwards to her very fingertips.

Aritza was close to finishing his lunch.

"It will take about two weeks of work to get my tan even," she said simply, snapping his eyes up to meet hers. "I'll presume you want my hair dyed into the Egyptian look she was using before?"

Yes.

That little flare as the pupils got bigger for a moment.

Adrenaline. Unconscious shock that couldn't be faked, couldn't be hidden. Even with an expert poker sharp.

I'll play your little game, Aritza.

Let's dance.

PART FOUR

JAVIER SMILED as the ship's Purser looked up with a scowl verging on an eyeroll so hard the man might pull something.

"No," Ragnar said in a flat voice.

"Captain already approved it," Javier countered, smiling.

"Don't care," the Purser stated.

"And I've got a budget," Javier continued, keeping his lilt light and breezy.

"Matrons of Hell, now what?" as a hand went up to massage a sudden headache.

As Purser on a semi-piratical voyager like *Storm Gauntlet*, Ragnar Piripi was the ship's Quartermaster, and the crew's personal banker. The man who counted everything. Twice.

He even looked like a banker, being tall and a little skinny, with mid-length, curly hair a graying platinum blond. His uniforms were always understated, and a perfect fit.

A quiet, nerdy, pirate accountant. Water to Javier's fire, frequently.

Javier produced an actual piece of folded paper from a jacket pocket and handed it to the man across the slightly-messy desk.

Ragnar handled it like an audit summons, fingers lightly gripped at opposite corners so he wouldn't get anything on his suit.

"Not as bad as I feared," Piripi murmured after a moment. "We should be able to pick most of this up at our next stop."

"Can't," Javier grinned. "Need an inventory count so I know how much we need to acquire by other means, or can manufacture out of stores."

"What do you mean, *can't*," the Purser huffed. "Fine. The sapphire won't be a problem, assuming you have a means of coloring the industrial glass we normally use for monitor screens. There is no rhodium on this vessel at all, as far as I know, and maybe a tenth of what you have listed for platinum. I believe we have enough indium for whatever devilry you're up to now."

"Yup," Javier agreed. "Cryogenics and life support systems still use the stuff. Since the way old days. Oh, and I'm going to need to borrow Kianoush for a week or three."

"Dare I ask why?" Ragnar snarked.

"Science, man," Javier grinned. "I am the Science Officer, after all."

"Yes, I suspected as much."

JAVIER FOUND her in her usual cubicle, precarious stacks of *things* and *stuff* everywhere, leaving only a small spot for her to move her piles of paper around.

Bankers and accountants never trusted electronic files. Javier had spent enough time lying to computer systems to understand and appreciate that. You can't magically update paper without physically touching it, like you can do to a database somewhere.

Especially when you have your own sneaky, little AI handy to do the work.

Kianoush Buday's ancestors had originated in that part of the Asian landmass known poetically as Persia. *Fars*, in the ancient tongues.

She had brown hair, brown eyes, and brown skin, in various shades. A little pudgy from sitting down all day and cutting corners on proscribed exercise. Normal looking. Maybe almost plain.

Until you got her onto art. For a good story about evil pixies, and all the art supplies, he had traded her the work to create his original Science Officer mug that had gone off to have more adventures with 'Mina.

Now she got to top it.

"Good morning, beautiful," Javier hummed as he snuck up behind her.

"I heard you tell Ragnar we were about to have another adventure," she replied, carefully stacking three piles in different directions before turning her chair to look up at him.

Art really did bring out her dimples.

Javier handed her a transport chip with a grin.

"Haven't loaded it into the core yet," he said. "Wanted your opinion on a few things first. Plus, I'm pretty sure I'll have to go steal most of the supplies for you."

One chiseled eyebrow arched eloquently. No words. Not even accusations. Just a knowing grin.

Maybe a slight shrug with her cheeks.

It was a good thing she preferred girls. Even with that smile, he really didn't need a third ex-wife.

Kianoush loaded the chip into a reader and called up the CAD/CAM package that filled most of it.

Javier smiled as the woman dove in and started studying the design. If pressed, he would have to take credit for everything. Certainly, there was no way in hell he was explaining to everyone that Suvi had done the research and the design.

At least he had studied it close enough to answer the sort of questions an artist was going to throw at him. Even one like Kianoush.

"Lovely design," she finally surfaced after five or eight minutes. "Corinthian?"

"'Ish," Javier agreed. "Liberties were taken for modernity and such. It's art."

"Uh huh."

She pushed a button and there it was, hanging in the air. Another button, and the image was slowly rotating between them.

It was a helmet, of sorts. Done in the ancient Hellenic style, with long, solid pieces protecting the cheeks, leaving only a T for eyes, nose and mouth. Wings ascending outward from the ears. A crest on top would have been done in horsehair millennia ago, eight centimeters wide and ten tall, but Suvi had done it all in thin wires, wrapped together three at a time, out of yellow gold.

The rest was supposed to be forged in platinum. Except for where she had added three round sapphire gems on each side, starting at the forehead and trailing down the cheeks. The small one on each side was still bigger than his thumbnail.

"Platinum, huh?" she asked with a leer. "Got enough rhodium to plate all that?"

"None, you witch," Javier smiled back. "It's the blue gold around the eyes I needed your opinion on."

Those eyes got canny.

"That's really supposed to be blue gold?" she inquired sideways.

She spun back and started typing furiously.

Javier loved being able to stump an expert jewelsmith, however rare that occurrence was.

"Did you want to do this the right way, or close enough to fool anybody but a metallurgist?" she asked, spinning back to face him.

Javier shrugged vaguely.

"You said you didn't have any rhodium," she replied with a shrug. "Throw in some ruthenium and a few other things for a real alloy, none of which we have on board. Alternatively, we could plate it over with yellow gold, and then indium, and apply heat. Won't be as good, but will fool the average fool."

"Can you do the work?" Javier asked carefully.

It would raise too many questions if he got in there and started programming. Like, it would take him months to get the various machines to behave, since there was no way he could load Suvi in and let her control all the machines that would spit out the finished product in three days.

"You get me the base materials," Kianoush smiled. "Piece of cake."

She did have a magical way with an auto-furnace and a laser lathe. Let her handle it.

Now, where the hell was he going to find all this crap?

PART FIVE

ZAKHAR REALLY DIDN'T HAVE to watch the sensor station readouts from his day office. Javier had trained enough people to Concord Navy standards. And there was a team on standby in case the man needed a rescue.

Zakhar had no intention of telling his Science Officer that the Dragoon was leading that team.

She had offered to help in the field. And been turned down flat. Vicious, in fact, when rude would have been the norm.

Part of that was Navarre, less far away from Javier's everyday psyche than he had been for months.

But part of it was also the situation at hand.

Space was huge. Even something so dense as an asteroid field was mostly empty space. *Storm Gauntlet* was poised nearby, shields on but at their lowest rating, and sneaky cranked up as high as it would go.

Javier was *over there* with the Assault Shuttle, pretending to be an asteroid miner. Parked close to a large rock that had looked promising on his scanners. Del Smith was his only company, although Sykora and her EVA team were all suited up in *Storm Gauntlet's* flight bay, with individual impellers at hand, against sudden need.

Zakhar had seen the flash of hatred in Javier's eyes when Sykora had offered to accompany him. Nobody else was looking the right way at that exact moment.

One of them wouldn't come back aboard alive, if they both went.

Zakhar wasn't sure which.

Normally, their rivalry was verbal. Vicious, yes, but not bloody.

Something had changed.

Nobody would talk, but he could see it. Some level of polish had come off of Javier's bonhomie veneer in the last two weeks. Thinned, perhaps, revealing an ugly darkness underneath.

Zakhar had always known it was there. Shared experience of both men having come out of the Bryce Academy and the Concord Navy. He could read the signs in the man's eyes.

Zakhar wondered if Djamila had finally found a chink in the man's armor.

Somebody really might end up dead in the cold vacuum of space.

"Bridge," he said, keying the systems live. "What's your status on the Science Officer?"

"Scanners are Nine and One, sir," a voice replied.

Nearly perfect signal. Very little degradation. About as good as it would get with this much rubble flying around.

"Wanderers tracking?" Zakhar asked.

"Javier parked us upstream, sir," the woman continued. "Using us and our shields as a rainshadow against anything flying faster than his rock."

"Keep me posted," Zakhar closed the channel.

Huh.

You would think Aritza had done this before, given the speed with which he had set everything up. Find a young, close solar system in a supernova neighborhood. Locate a field of big rocks. Maneuver in tight. Hide behind *Storm Gauntlet*. Dig out an armoured lifesuit and get to work.

Solo.

But something within his experience, apparently.

Zakhar didn't figure he'd ever get that story out of the man. Just like so many others. Pirates tended to not ask each other where they came from before. Usually, the story was too banal, rather than too rousing.

Boring would be nice, about now.

SUVI MADE sure that every maneuver she pulled was accompanied by back-and-forth radio signal to the controls in Javier's suit. By now, she had gotten the hang of making it look like he was flying the soccer ball-sized probe remote.

Everything was heavily encrypted. Even with the full power of a navigation computer behind it, cracking the codes she was using to talk would take *the beast* a couple of decades.

She probably shouldn't call the ship that. But it was big and dumb. Simple programs that wouldn't fool anyone with their sophistication. Just barely enough to fly and fight and do stuff, but nowhere as cool as she had been when she was a starship.

There were days she considered regretting letting Dr. Teague go alone, when Javier had been trying to send Suvi along.

She probably could have been a ship again.

But then there were days when she got to practice strafing runs on a moon just big enough to generate its own gravity field, but not enough that she would crack anything if she pogoed off a rock accidentally.

<Ping!>

Ouch.

Suvi envisioned a radio in the console of her imaginary Sopwith Camel so she could turn the noise down. The Red Baron stopped zigging and zagging behind her, and took up a spot on her wing instead.

Let's see. Scanners currently set to pick up deposits of metals in the platinum group and...

Oh, my...

Suvi reached out and changed the radio to channel six. Javier was busy talking to Del, the crazy, old man pilot who liked to listen to Caribbean music and had decorated the flight deck of his assault shuttle like a *Merankorr* brothel, to hear Javier describe it.

Not that she'd ever been in a brothel. Or even to *Merankorr*. She had secretly considered building herself an android body, one of these days, just so she could walk around on the surface of a planet, but being a probe was too much fun today.

She listened for a few moments.

Boys. Talking about girls. Really? Two grown men couldn't have a better conversation while doing deep-space asteroid mining, than to talk about girl's bottoms?

Suvi sent a scrolling message across the bottom of his display.

Channel eleven, please?

Three was *Storm Gauntlet*, and Captain Sokolov. Four was the private channel between the beast and the shuttle. Eleven was where she had set the encryption to stooooopid levels.

"What's up, kid?" Javier asked.

Kid? I'll have you know that I'm eighty-four years older than you are, mister.

Still, most of those years had been boring. Serious. MILITARY.

Not like the years with a goofball like Javier, learning how to play poker.

Yeah, fine. Okay. Maybe.

"Good morning, Captain," she said as she poured honey over the blade.

His tone got serious in a heartbeat.

"Talk to me, Suvi," Javier intoned.

"So, you were looking for a lump of ore that would refine down to around ten kilos of platinum, randomly mixed with the usual bunch of sundry, related elements in the platinum group, right?" Suvi smiled and pushed another new button on her console to transmit her sensor log.

Off her right wing, according to only her sensors, the Red Baron was patiently flying, waving at her to hurry up so they could get back to playing. Suvi waved back. Unlike the Baron, she wasn't using all five fingers.

"Mary, Mother of God," Javier whispered over the radio waves. "Damn it."

"What?" Suvi cried. "I'd think you'd be happy. There's enough here to set you up."

"Suvi, that's a unicorn," Javier whispered in awe.

A what? Oh, damn it, why won't he build in a bigger library. And a faster one. It is not funny, having to stop and look things up, mister.

Yeah. Okay. Big horse. Horn in his forehead. Mythical beast. I don't get it.

"I don't get it," Suvi said after a beat.

"Suvi, I needed kilograms of metal," Javier replied. "That valley you're in runs to kilotonnes of the stuff."

"And?" she asked. "It might be enough to buy our freedom."

"Suvi," he rasped. "If we give it to Sokolov, yes, it might be enough to buy our freedom, especially after this next job."

"And?" she continued, exasperated.

"If we don't tell them," Javier replied. "There might be enough there to buy you a new body, young lady."

Oh? Oh. OH!

"Oh."

313

"Yeah. Find me a chunk of ore with enough of everything, and cut it off with your pulsar," Javier said. "The gravity on this rock is low enough that you should be able to push it up and get it headed in this direction. I've taught you enough snooker to make you look good. Ping me when we get clear of that valley, and I'll bring Del over and we can dock."

"Sí, Commandante."

Suvi envisioned goggles on her forehead so she could pull them down, stand the Sopwith on one wing, and dive back into the canyon, with an evil, three-winged overlord chasing her and ranting in German behind.

PART SIX

THE ROOM WAS JUST dim enough to add atmosphere. Javier caught himself holding his breath as he looked around and let it go. Kianoush was as much a showman as he was, and she was making a grand production of this, even if it was only the primary conference room on *Storm Gauntlet*.

Armoured transport cube half a meter on a side sat on the table in front of Kianoush as she stood and watched everyone settle. It was done in a matte black finish so dark that reality seemed poised on falling in, and it made such a strange contrast with Kianoush. She was in baggy, blue pants and a ratty, gray sweater that had tiny holes burned in the front. And white gloves, but Javier suspected those were just for grandiosity at this point.

It felt more like a game show, where she was intent on drawing out the tension.

Could you make an art show burlesque? The woman seemed intent on testing that question.

"Earth," she intoned seriously. "Second millennium before the Common Era. Roughly nine thousand years ago. A tiny peninsula on the north shore of the Mediterranean Ocean, known later as Greece. End of the Bronze Age, just as the world was turning to Iron. A smith in that era might have made a helmet that looked like this. They would have worked in bronze and gold, and it would have been an object worthy of a king."

Javier appreciated the buildup, but he already knew all this. He glanced to his right. Sokolov, Piripi, and the Dragoon were rapt.

But then, the others had only heard rumors so far. But everyone had seen the fantastic coffee mug Kianoush had made for him, once upon a time.

What they didn't understand was that Kianoush was an *artisté*.

And a jewelsmith, but she really did understand people. Way better than Javier did.

No, that wasn't true.

She just liked them way better than he did, not counting Suvi. And 'Mina.

Kianoush popped open all the latches holding the lid down, one at a time.

More buildup. More striptease. More burlesque.

She had custom-built the box too, once the helmet was complete.

"Ladies and gentlemen," Kianoush announced, and then smiled. "And crew. I give you the *Crown of Athena*."

And there it was, just like Suvi had designed it. Platinum body sheathed in a mirror-flashing of rhodium. Six sapphires on the cheeks, outlining the eyes. Blue gold around the facial opening, highlighting the wings, and forming the base of the crest. Suvi hadn't added those latter touches. Obviously, Kianoush had taken liberties.

She had taken the right ones. It was gorgeous.

"May I?" Sykora asked politely.

She could be very friendly when Javier wasn't involved.

Kianoush moved around the table, delicately handling the heavy trophy, the Corinthian helmet, as she did. She put it into the Dragoon's hands.

"It won't fit you," Kianoush said with intent.

Sykora turned a sharp eye on Javier.

"My skull is no larger than yours," she accused.

Javier smiled beatifically.

"It was designed for a woman an entire eighth smaller than you, Sykora," he replied, his eyes finding a spot on an invisible horizon. "A rather delicate, wiry, foul-mouthed, goofball of a pilot I once flew with. She had a thing for art similar to Buday."

Sykora handed it back to Kianoush with a moue of disgust on her lips.

"Thank you," Javier said to his partner in crime. "I wish there was a way you could show her what you had done. She would have gotten a charge out of it. I plan on saving a ton of pictures and video, in case I run into her one of these days."

"So, Aritza," Sokolov finally spoke. "We've agreed to Lace's deal. You've mined an asteroid and made an *objet d'art*. Sykora is in disguise. What's the next step?"

Javier stopped and really studied Sykora.

Most of the time, she was an alabaster statue standing in his way, frequently wired with an electric fence that would bite you if you got too close.

He had known a few women like that in his life.

But now, there had been a serious transformation.

She had been true to her word. Her skin had gone from washed-out ship-pale, to a nice, even bronzed tan. Her short hair was dyed a chocolate brown so rich that the mahogany was verging over into black cherry.

Sykora was even wearing makeup. Had been for about a week now, in retrospect. A base layer that washed out her freckles. Black eye-liner that extended a fingernail-width beyond her eyes to each side. Blood red lipstick. Matching fingernail polish. Probably the toenails matched, as well.

And she smiled at him.

Javier wasn't sure if he should be frightened or appalled.

'Mina's chest was much larger, both relative and absolute. She was also curvier everywhere. And knew just how to kip a hip sideways and drop a shoulder in a way that disarmed men. And most women.

Her eyes could communicate want, need, vulnerability, and fire. All at once, too.

Sykora did not have that. And she was a head taller. Stronger. Harder.

She didn't have the sexiness that Wilhelmina had just oozed, but a man who liked a fit woman would likely be drooling all over himself when she walked by.

That would have to do.

At least she would protect him from any other assassins. That much he could absolutely rely on.

"We'll meet up with Lace," Javier said, ruminating aloud as Kianoush took a seat to watch the potential fireworks. "She'll provide the documentation and cover story Hadiiye and I need to get aboard *Shangdu*. You'll drop us then and hang as close to the big resort ship as you can hide while we take a commercial flight over, case the place, and plan the next step of our caper."

"Why the helmet, Aritza?" Sykora asked.

For once, she sounded inquisitive, rather than accusatory. Of course, her life depended on them pulling this off, too, so she needed to be in on as much of it as he wanted to share.

"We'll have just pulled off a major score," he smiled up at the woman who was about to become his bodyguard, his conscience, and his minder. "We need someplace to hide while we wait for our fence to make our deal. A place like *Shangdu* is perfect for this. Plus, we need someplace to safely stash a modern-day, priceless antique. Either they let us have access to her major vault and we can see how to crack it, or she's changed her ways and everyone has their own safe spot and we'll have to find the one belonging to our target."

"She?" Sykora spike the word.

"She," Javier agreed. "Our host. The woman who owns *Shangdu*. The *Khatum of Altai*. Who is also hosting the Jianwen Emperor. Or, as close as the modern era gets."

"Jianwen?" Sokolov asked. "Or am I better off not knowing?"

"Zhu Yunwen," Sykora turned to the Captain to explain.

Javier felt his jaw drop open.

"Second Ming Emperor," she continued with a wink back in Javier's direction. "Ascended the Chinese throne young, was soon overthrown by an uncle and supposedly killed in either the revolution or a subsequent palace fire. Rumors always persisted that he had escaped, disguised as a monk. The third Ming Emperor spent years sending out voyages of exploration trying to prove the man was dead."

Javier willed his eyes to return to their normal size. It was painful.

Her smile didn't help.

"Are we assassins now, Navarre?" Sykora continued with a knowing smile.

"No," he replied to her obvious disappointment. "If we're lucky, we'll never meet the man. This guy fled with the family chop, a variety of personal papers, and the genetic records he or his descendants would need to challenge the current rulers, back home. We're hired to destroy the box, or steal it, but not to injure the man."

"Interesting," she said. "So just waltz in, bluff your way to the heart of a conspiracy, and make off with the prize?"

"It's happened before," he smiled coldly back at her. "You spent most of it unconscious."

That brought the scowl back to her face. Which put a smile on his.

"You're good with this, Javier? Djamila?" Sokolov asked, playing the role of dutiful father figure.

Sykora glanced at Javier for some sign. She got it and nodded to the Captain.

Javier shrugged.

"I'm sure Lace's principal wants a mass casualty incident here," he said, sounding harder than he intended. "Else why go to the effort to hire Navarre and not someone easier. Whether the money man has other enemies on *Shangdu* and is looking for a cover story for his own assassin, I neither know nor care. These people are rich, spoiled aristocrats. I want to fly so far under their radar that this turns into a caper for the ages."

"Anything else I should know?" Sykora asked him.

"Yeah," Javier finally admitted. "This is not my first trip to *Shangdu*, but that was a while ago and nobody in the crew should remember me."

"And the *Khatum*?" she continued. "Will she remember you?"

"Black widow, even then," Javier fired back. "But I was too small for her to notice."

"Navarre isn't small."

"No, but he plans to be the absolute definition of sneaky."

PART TEN
BOOK TEN: XANADU

PART ONE

Javier smiled as the shuttle docked with the big resort ship. He had flown on first class ships that weren't as nice as *Shangdu*'s cargo lighter, to say nothing of the private ship reserved for the very elite. Brightly painted walls. Thick carpets underfoot. Even a touch of spring flower scent pumped through the air system.

Heaven. Or, more likely, money.

He was in the full Navarre costume, with the weapons belt, but mostly that was appearances. Anything else and people might have wondered. Hadiiye was also armed to the teeth, but she was a weapon, even naked.

And if Sykora's version of Hadiiye's costume wasn't as distracting as it had been on 'Mina, it would still do the job. Javier had been hard pressed to remember a woman that big in that good of shape. Ever. Even volleyball players at the Academy usually settled into middle-aged squishy after a decade or so.

Not Sykora.

Never Sykora.

The hatch opened and a Purser awaited them.

He probably had another title. One far more interesting. He still looked like an accountant.

But you needed that level of professional paranoia about your paperwork, when the net worth of your passengers outweighed many planets.

"Captain Navarre?" he smiled, stepping close with a hand out.

Javier handed him the two travel document packets and a hundred credit note.

It wasn't a bribe. That would need to be several magnitudes of order larger, if Javier was serious.

No, this was simply a tip in advance for good service, for a man who had it in his power to be an absolute shit if he decided he didn't like you.

Pursers could get that way.

The bureaucrat quickly scanned both packets, compared physical descriptions, ogling Hadiiye briefly, since her nipples were about on a level with his eyes.

"No armaments on board," he said simply.

Javier already had his belt off and in hand. Hadiiye was a beat behind. Another man detached himself from a wall to collect them and hand over a luggage ticket. They would get them back when they left. Hopefully.

"Let's see," he continued, scanning things. "Luggage was checked ahead. You have some personal effects. And one non-standard shipping container that warrants inspection."

Javier smiled cruelly. The shuttle's crew was nearly invisible in the background, getting everything settled and ready for unpacking. Similarly, ship's crew were moving around in the large, airy foyer beyond the Purser.

"I would prefer if we could inspect it in a private room, sir?" Javier asked lightly.

"That is highly irregular," the faceless bureaucrat replied.

"Understood," *Navarre* said firmly.

Eyes locked for a moment.

As contests of will go, barely anything. Still, it was necessary to establish a tone as a dangerous yet polite visitor.

A nod.

"Come with me."

And he turned and started walking.

Javier dipped to grab the big, black case. They had a cover that needed to be maintained.

He had stolen the helmet, according to all the rumors Stewart Lace was busy planting in the stream. Hadiiye was his bodyguard, not his maid.

Javier had considered bringing along a crew member to fill the role of personal assistant and gopher, but there wasn't really anybody with the acting chops to handle such a chore: long term and always on.

He would need to rectify that, one of these days. Especially if they got a rep for pulling capers like this.

Maybe he needed his own crew of petty criminals. No, then they'd have to learn the choreography for the big Bollywood productions. I mean, if you're going to do it, why stop small?

Maybe he just needed to start small and find a couple of folks who could dance.

The office for the inspection had the feel of one of those small boxes where cops stashed shoplifters while they interviewed everyone else and wanted to sweat someone. Claustrophobic. Industrial. Banal.

The Purser took his obvious spot on the far side of the small table with an expectant air.

Javier smiled as he rested the box on the table and popped open the six latches holding the lid. He paused to pull his own pair of white gloves from a pocket and don them before lifting the bright helmet clear and holding it in the air.

"Oh, my," was the bureaucrat's response.

He leaned forward to inspect it from almost close enough to fog the platinum, before leaning back and eyeing Javier speculatively.

"I see," he continued. "And the purpose of your visit to *Shangdu* goes beyond merely rest and relaxation?"

"Indeed," Javier grinned back. "Having arrived, our fixer is contacting their fixer, and arranging for the buyer to come aboard, make payment, and take possession of the trophy. Everyone agrees that this is one of the safest spots in the galaxy for such a transaction. Neutral ground, as it were."

"Very good," the man said, pulling out their paperwork and stamping it. "Will you be in a position to notify us when the buyer is due?"

Javier shrugged meaningfully.

"That sort of thing is outside my realm of control, sir," he said with just the right amount of nonchalance. "I will share as much as I am at liberty. I understand that your systems might be available to secure this package while we wait? For a price, of course."

The Purser fixed him with a hard stare, but Javier was confident that his cover would hold. They would have picked up any holes long before now and simply not let him aboard.

"I will make inquiries," the man replied after a long beat, apparently satisfied.

"Thank you," Javier smiled his best *Navarre* grimace.

"Very well."

And then the Purser was gone, leaving Navarre and Hadiiye alone.

She was inspecting the edges of the roof with professional care, so she understood that they were going to be under some level of surveillance for as long as they were aboard.

Now the two of them just had to fool every single person aboard this ship.

Piece of cake.

PART TWO

THE SUITE where Javier found himself next was amazing. They might as well have just covered the walls with money, but that wouldn't have done it justice. Stewart Lace's cash was putting them up in a place that mixed the best elements of a hunting lodge, dark woods and earth tones; with the fragile elegance of a high-end brothel, the ones where they checked your credit score before even sending you an invitation.

Javier was pretty sure there was a name for such a joint, but he'd never been that rich, or that desperate, so he'd never given it much thought.

The main door let into a long hallway, with a kitchenette and bathroom on one side, and two small bedrooms on the other. Since Sykora was his bodyguard and not his lover, she would sleep there. Javier shuddered through his whole soul for a moment at the thought of sharing a bed with the Dragoon.

Black widow.

Beyond that, a salon on three levels, for no other reason than to have a sunken middle and a raised platform around one side. His own chamber, beyond that, had a bed big enough for a small orgy to be conducted safely, as well as a tub that could accommodate three friendly people at once. He was pretty sure his privacy was secured, though.

Given the nature of the guest list, Javier was willing to bet that the *Khatum* wasn't electronically monitoring the suites. Too much dealing and midnight assignations going on that nobody wanted recorded for posterity.

He and Sykora settled for doing a fast, hard search with a pair of handheld scanners he had rigged up for the occasion. Plus, he had brought Suvi along.

"What is that thing, really?" Sykora asked, pointing as Javier pulled out the smaller remote and bounced it in the air.

No weapons aboard meant that Suvi couldn't fly her larger, armed probe. It would have been nice, having a second bodyguard around, but the risk was too great.

She had bitched, but in the end was willing to return to her little grapefruit, once Javier had attached a small memory core to her charging ring, and filled it with enough books, music, and videos to keep even her entertained for a few months.

"Before you people killed my scout ship, I had to modify the Sentience's programming occasionally," Javier replied in a tight, angry voice. "I still know how. So I was able to make the probe more useful."

Suvi would be listening. And grumpy. But she understood the situation.

Javier watched his sidekick's fairy-ship hover in place, just below the ceiling, and paint the room with a laser and a sonic pulse he could feel in his ribs. Suvi moved on with great deliberation, scanning each of the other rooms as they watched, always moving with the care of a fragile, old man, rather than her normal scarf-in-the-wind flying.

"Just how intelligent is it?" Sykora probed.

"It's not," he fired back in a lie Sykora would never catch. "I got tired of having to do everything manually, so I started automating some of the functionality. Scanning. Perimeter security. That sort of thing. You and I are programmed in as friendly. It will normally sit in the cradle and pretend to be a piece of weird art, but we'll know if someone comes in while we're gone. I would have brought the armed version, but they would have never allowed it aboard. This will do for what I need."

"Okay," she said.

Sykora seemed to relax. A shade. As much as she ever did. Javier kept waiting for her to drop to parade rest or something.

Instead, she surprised him by stepping down into the central pit and stretching her long frame out in one of the comfie chairs, legs crossed at the ankles and smiling up at him.

"So now what?" she asked innocently.

Javier fought not to goggle at her behavior, so radically out of character.

Then he realized she was doing this deliberately, just to get a rise out of him.

Kids, riding in the back of the vehicle on a long trip, pushing each other to get the other one in trouble with the parents.

As close to a default setting as their relationship ever got.

He could work with this.

Javier decided to play along and took a spot at the far end of the big couch, nearly falling into the soft pillows as he settled. It left him almost exactly across the round area from her.

"We need to talk fashion," Javier smiled at her.

It was rewarding watching her fight against rolling her eyes at him. He wasn't sure she could actually resist the temptation, even in the privacy of their own suite.

"Fine," she finally said. "Fashion. Go ahead."

"The water in the lake is clean, because they keep a lot of it planted with a variety of species of tree and bush, both for the purpose of keeping the water pure, and to make it look pretty," he started. "People can swim, sail, tan, or play, and they don't need shoes or anything. Depending on the mores of your homeworld, clothing can run from a full bodysuit to nothing whatsoever."

"I have no tan lines," she fixed him with a challenging eye. "*Neu Berne* would either run to nearly full coverage, or *au naturel*, depending on the company."

"Everyone here will hopefully stay strangers," Javier replied. "Clothing, however, presents a challenge. We just can't afford it."

"What do you mean?" she asked, leaning forward enough to indicate she was listening.

"For no other reason than pique and money, many women here will be wearing one-piece suits, usually by elite fashion designers," he began.

"Okay."

"Hadiiye needs to understand that those suits start at around a thousand credits each and get really expensive from there."

"What?"

She didn't screech, but just barely

He had her attention now, so he just shrugged.

"You will either wear a simple cloth, loosely wrapped around your hips, like we talked about, or a pair of tight swim trunks, the kind that will cover your bum when you sit and keep sand out of sensitive areas. We are not here to compete with these people. Which any type of bathing suit would imply."

Sykora leaned back and eyed him speculatively. After a moment, she nodded.

"If we're not in their socio-economic class," Javier said, "then we're just poor relatives visiting the big city for the first time. I'm okay with being mistaken for a bumpkin on this job."

"Because they'll have no idea just how dangerous you really are," she replied, surprising him. "Or Navarre."

"Hopefully, none of them have heard of *Salekhard*," he replied. "So nobody will care who we are."

A knock at the outer door interrupted.

Javier took a deep breath and put on his game face.

This was when it was going to get interesting.

PART THREE

Djamila Sykora was not a natural actress.

She knew that. Appreciated that she could never make up for the amazing charisma and ease of self that Wilhelmina had brought to the role.

Or Aritza, but she was sure, after spending more than a year close to the man, that nobody had met the true Javier Aritza. Not in many years. Maybe never.

It was interesting, watching him walk, carrying that heavy case and following the same bureaucrat who had met them earlier.

Aritza looked like a pirate.

She still loathed the man, but could appreciate the professionalism he brought to the job when he wanted to.

Now, if she could only get him to act like that all the time, rather than when he wanted to. He might even turn into something useful.

She doubted it.

But she could play the role of a tall, intimidating woman. The kind willing to kick your ass if you got too close, or too fresh.

Or just because.

She had twenty-five years' experience with that, since she had first gotten taller than any man who wasn't a blood relative. They had all learned to take *no* for an answer, eventually.

Yes, she could do this.

Be this strange person, quiet and deadly. Stalk with fluid menace rather than marching in rigid rhythm. Walk like a great cat, rather than a warhorse.

Djamila looked out through what she imagined Wilhelmina had fashioned into Hadiiye's eyes. Threat assessment. Tactical maneuver. Bodyguarding.

But something else as well. Something new.

Barely-contained violence, but the kind tinged with mocking laughter. Wilhelmina had explained it to her once. How to use laughter as a knife on proud men. Especially from such a towering height.

Dr. Teague had done it by adding soles to her fighting boots, raising her from being merely the height of most men, to looking subtly down on them.

Djamila had always felt like an ogre with such incredible height. Teague had shown her how to be a goddess, instead.

The liberation was seductive. Perhaps addictive.

A whole new flavor of dangerous.

She came back to herself as they entered a larger chamber.

Djamila hadn't been day-dreaming, but she wasn't keyed to her normal level of twitchy paranoia in a dangerous situation here. They were on neutral ground, as Aritza had said, surrounded by people with no reason to view them as a threat. Still, time to pay attention.

The last door they had entered had felt something like the sort of airlock normally separating the engineering spaces from the rest of any well-made ship.

Now, she found herself in a lush lounge. Maybe the lobby of a very exclusive bank.

Soft benches and chairs in a rich maroon cloth. Wood paneling. Oil paintings on the wall and small statues on pedestals. Soft gray carpets everywhere.

A woman came out from a disguised side door. One of many such doors, carefully obscured by good interior design.

How many of them had guards hidden behind them?

Hadiiye took over now, assessing the new woman as Navarre's bodyguard.

Tall, for a woman, but lean, with long, bottle-blond hair. Extremely well-dressed in an understated way. Elegant, perhaps.

If the man who had brought them here was merely a bureaucrat, this new woman was a banker, the kind who dealt with women wearing thousand-credit-swimsuits. The thought nearly brought a smile to Hadiiye's lips.

Then she realized where she was, who she was, and grinned cat-like.

Something of it communicated to the stranger, who glanced up at her just long enough to ghost a smile back before turning her attention and charm to the pirate between them. The bureaucrat had not accompanied them into the chamber.

"I understand that your security is among the best there is," Navarre growled out in that buzzsaw rasp he used for a voice. He held up the box lightly in one strong hand. "Can you secure this?"

The woman was all smiles now. Soft but not passive. Accommodating a strong man and his desires in an unspoken, but no less sensual, way.

It was interesting, seeing the situation as Wilhelmina might have envisioned it.

Had she known that Djamila would need to play Hadiiye at some future point? Some of those observations, their conversations, didn't make any sense in other contexts, but did here.

Dr. Teague hadn't just been explaining how she had rescued Djamila, but also how she had become someone else, put on their skin, their eyes.

How to remember childhood stories about princesses and dragons.

"Well, Captain Navarre," the strange banker purred seductively. "I'll need to see what you have to offer, but I'm sure we can find a place to fit it."

Djamila blinked at the woman's tone, caught herself, remained in character.

Aritza was an impressive man, even playing a pirate. Attractive and charming when he wanted to be. Average height, but in extremely good shape. Not up to Djamila's standards, but what man was? Swarthy and a little too hairy, but intellectual and sharp.

She supposed some women would find that intriguing.

The way Aritza grinned ferally back at the woman didn't help.

"Do you have someplace private?" he asked. "I could show you."

Again, the woman glanced up at Hadiiye, questioning. Djamila was almost insulted by the implication, but then she realized the woman was subtly asking for permission.

What have you done to me, Doctor Teague? I wouldn't have even noticed that, six months ago.

Djamila shrugged with her eyes and her cheeks. A bodyguard didn't get physically or emotionally involved with her charge. In that way, it made this the perfect cover for her to be around Aritza.

"My bodyguard can wait here," Javier continued. "I'll presume we're safe."

The banker nodded.

"Can I get you something to drink while you wait?" she asked Djamila, all professional and courteous again, and no longer possibly infringing on another woman's claim.

"Tea would be lovely," Hadiiye replied with a long, low drawl. "Black and hot. With a little cream and two lumps, if possible."

Service with professionalism and a smile. The woman led her to a chair in a corner with a good view in all directions. It was the kind that was comfortable, but not too much so.

Perhaps just the place for bodyguards to wait while their principal conducted business close by. Another woman appeared nearly instantly to deliver tea in utter silence and vanish again.

Djamila settled and began a stretching routine that started with her toes individually and worked its way up her body, one isolation group at a time. Not quite meditation. Nor yoga.

Keep the body loose and the mind tight.

Eleven minutes passed.

Navarre and the banker emerged from the door on the far end of the chamber, presumably the one that led directly to a vault, or a room with small, individual lockers. The black box with Buday's helmet was no longer present.

Djamila joined them, interrogating the couple with her nose.

Aritza had the woman's perfume on him in ways that just being in the same room for that short of a time wouldn't convey. At the same time, neither of them had the sort of sweaty musk that would have suggested a quick romp in a side chamber. Nor had they stopped for a quick shower afterwards, not even a sonic pulse. That would have cleared her perfume as well.

So, at most, a quick grope and snog in a closet sort of thing. All part of the role.

She wasn't jealous of Aritza. In her duty as Dragoon, she had kept close tabs on his amorous escapades on the ship, mostly against security risk. Nothing about the man had suggested danger to any of the women he occasionally took to bed. And they were all adults.

No, she found her slightest hint of jealousy at the casual ease of it. Of

THE PLEASURE DOME

going into a private suite with a total stranger and flirting her up, to the point that her perfume ended up pervading your clothing.

Neu Berne didn't do things that way.

She doubted he was doing it to get under her skin. That was just the way Aritza was. Charming, confident, and receptive enough to let a woman worm her own way in, thinking it was her idea.

Again, Djamila nearly rolled her eyes. Hopefully, if the banker woman came to Javier's suite later, the walls would prove to be soundproofed enough that she could sleep.

She watched Navarre bow over the woman's hand and kiss the back of it in an old-fashioned, courtly manner.

The two of them twinkled with barely-suppressed lust before they separated. Djamila followed Aritza to the door and through it, concentrating on not puking at the gooiness of it all.

Seven minutes later, they were in their suite.

Djamila came to parade rest for a moment as the door locked behind her, and then threw caution to the wind and settled back in the chair she had claimed earlier.

Javier followed in her wake and ended up on the couch again. It was a lovely metaphor.

"We are early, ship's day," he began. "However late we are personal day. I think we need to go down and explore the beach, now that the box is secure."

Djamila processed his words and sneered at him briefly.

"You just want to get me nude," she said.

"Not *just*," he leered back, just a flash. "Call it a perk of the job."

She considered hitting him. She considered hating him. He knew *Neu Berne* culture too well.

This wasn't a scam on his part.

No, not *just*.

But she was in for a pound at this point.

Nothing this man did was going to break her will.

335

PART FOUR

She really had proved him wrong.

Javier could see that he was going to have to re-evaluate this dangerous woman. Again.

Djamila towered before him at parade rest, like a veteran waiting for the weekly inspection to end so she could get back to whatever it was she was doing before some idiot officer wandered along.

Like him, she wore only a light, thigh-length cloth, loosely wrapped around her hips. Hers was clipped on her right side, just in front of the point of the hip bone, concealing as much as it revealed when she walked.

Having no basis for prior comparison, Javier had no idea if the lack of hair on her legs was a new thing, or a standard of personal grooming, but her long, bronzed limbs were as smooth as glass, marred only by old scars: nicks and stitches and burns that just made her more impressive.

The hips weren't as soft as 'Mina's, nor the waist as waspish. But Teague had never had an eight-pack for a stomach in her life. Sykora's smallish breasts had the sort of pointed hardness that came from an excess of pushups every morning. Far less interesting than 'Mina's, but impressive nonetheless.

Javier knew the woman had body issues. Nobody else would understand, looking at her, except by the implication of how hard she worked, every day, to look like that. But she would also do nearly as good a job of distraction in this situation as Wilhelmina would have.

There just weren't that many women, nearly that impressive, anywhere in the galaxy.

Javier wore an identical cloth, clipped on his left. He generally worked out, and was in good shape for a spacer in his early forties, but nobody was in Sykora's league. Plus he was as hairy on legs and arms and chest as she was smooth.

At least none of it had started turning gray yet.

She studied him with a look of bored contempt that she must have learned from 'Mina, back when she was learning to walk sexy from the smaller woman. Javier grinned pure insolence up at her, and then nodded for her to precede him.

Out in the hallways, it was indeed early in the local day, probably set to *Altai*'s capital city. Locals were probably fast a-bed now, as the only people they saw while they walked wore the tan slacks and green shirts of staff, brightly different from the hard gray of technical crew.

They turned a corner after a few minutes, and passed through another over-scale airlock into something approximating a locker room, with restrooms, showers, and more helpful staff on hand.

Another, smaller airlock, beyond that, and Javier had warm sand in his toes, sun just rising in what was now officially east, and a morning breeze crossing from left to right. Waves, not ten meters away.

And not one, damned seagull to be found, anywhere.

"What's that?" a voice jarred him out of his happy spot.

Her voice. Sykora.

At least it was curiosity and not pique. At least as near as he could tell.

A giant tree branch suddenly stretched out over his shoulder and in front of him. It took a moment to identify her arm as such. She was pointing at the spot in the middle of the room.

A monumentally large room.

"Shangri-La," he replied. "Private island for by-invitation-only guests and very private parties. Not anyplace I want to go. You neither."

"Huh," she replied noncommittal. "It would be an easy swim."

"Sure," he said. "Six hundred meters from here. Less if you catch the short axis. I'm not that ambitious to get thrown off the ship that quickly."

"Okay, then now what?" she asked.

Javier ignored the woman and walked twenty or forty meters to one side, crossing a few dunes and some sedge grass until he found the right spot, not too far from the water, slightly private as dunes created a small amphitheater effect.

Perfect.

Javier unclipped his towel, stretched it out, and laid down to catch some of the early morning sun. He might be naturally much darker than Sykora, but his tan still needed work.

"Hey, what do I do?" she asked again as he closed his eyes.

Javier opened them again. From here, she was a kilometer tall.

"Bodyguard," he replied. "If you think a mermaid might get me. Tan, maybe. Nap? Or swim some. Up to you."

She glared prodigiously down at him, again Athena atop Olympus. For a moment, he thought the Dragoon might seriously go tactical on an empty beach, but she dropped her towel next to him, jutted a chin rudely in his direction, and raced out into the surf.

Aphrodite in reverse, disappearing under the waves.

"So," a new voice intruded on his consciousness after a few moments. "Should I read that as faith in the competence of my staff? Or insolence, on the part of yours?"

Javier's eyes snapped open to find a woman standing suddenly on his other side, grinning lightly at him.

Like Sykora, the stranger had worn only a wrap this morning. She wasn't as hardbody as the Dragoon, but that still left a lot of space for amazing, volume she filled like jasmine. Even 'Mina would have probably been a distant third.

Her skin wasn't as dark as Javier's, and it was a richer golden tone where his brownness tended towards ochre. Her hair was long and black, straight nearly down to her bottom. Pixyish green eyes.

Stunning. Utterly stunning.

And she knew it. Practiced it. Broadcast it on all channels.

"Both, Your Grace," Javier said evenly after a moment of appreciation.

He flipped a coin in his head and decided to remain horizontal, at least until she said something about it.

"You know who I am?" she inquired in a coquettish voice.

"I am staying in a guest room," he said. "Best to know who the host is."

"I see," she said.

She unhooked her wrap and laid it beside him, dropping down and folding herself into a perfect lotus, facing him from close enough he could feel the heat radiate off her knees, and smell the coconut oil she had rubbed on her legs in the last few hours.

"You are Navarre," she announced in a quiet, sure voice. "The pirate."

Javier knew a moment of pure panic.

That perhaps this beautiful woman had somehow been a friend of someone on Tamaz's crew. That he was a dead man, and had just found his executioner.

He studied her face sidelong, let his gaze drift and linger.

Black widow was another option.

Not necessarily the preferred outcome, but something about condemned men and last meals came to mind.

Navarre growled in his mind, so Javier let the man take over.

"And?" he rasped.

"Are you a killer, Navarre?" she asked. "Or merely a thief?"

"Or?" he asked back, rusty, jagged edges appearing in his voice.

He turned his head to face her more fully. She smiled wickedly.

"You left out gentleman, rogue, and card sharp," Javier said in a lighter tone, pushing the killer back into the shadows of his mind. "I also dance a pretty good Argentinian Tango."

"Do you now?" she pursued. "Tango? It can be hard around here, finding a man willing to force the rhythm, but comfortable letting a woman have the power to improvise. Who understands that there are lines that must be colored outside of, occasionally."

Javier smiled laconically and shrugged.

Black widow, indeed.

She leaned forward a bit. Not enough to block the pseudo-sun's light, but towering more over him now.

"Are you here to kill someone, Captain Navarre?" she purred.

Javier grinned up at her.

"No, actually," he confessed. "This is probably the one time where I get a vacation and nobody has to die."

"Has to?" she dripped verbal honey on his chest.

"There are always bad seeds, *Khatum*," he felt his smile grow harder. "Back home, we called it the *Texas* defense. As in: *Yer Honor, he needed killin'.*"

"Like Abraam Tamaz?" she asked.

Yup. A reputation could be a good thing, or a bad thing, but it was still a thing.

"There are few people more deserving," Javier said with a hard smile. "Somebody had to do it."

"So you are the kind of man who takes charge, when he sees

something that needs doing?" she asked lightly. "Grabs life by the hair and pulls?"

"Never without an invitation," he replied laconically.

Somehow, she was floating above him. Javier could only imagine the flexibility she must have, to remain in a full lotus and still be able to lean so far forward that they could start necking without him moving too much.

"I'll keep that in mind," she whispered.

Javier could smell the mouthwash she had gargled with this morning. Minty, but not overwhelming. His breath probably smelled like coffee, but that was the chance you took, hitting on strangers on a beach.

She glanced up suddenly and smiled at him with promise as she leaned back.

"Your bodyguard is getting nervous," she said, returning upright.

Javier watched her unhook her feet, wriggle a bit, and stand up in a single motion. Rather than hook the wrap about her hips, she tossed it over one forearm and began to walk away in such a direction that Javier had the best view of her bottom.

"We shall talk again, Captain Navarre," she called over one shoulder with a tinkling bell of a laugh as she disappeared over a dune.

"Sorry," Sykora observed from two meters away, without the least apology in her voice. "Didn't mean to interrupt the two of you rutting on the beach. Who was that?"

Javier turned his head the other direction, but not until the first woman was out of sight.

Sykora was dripping water into the sand. Cold water, from the tightness of her nipples, in spite of the warm breeze. Nude, just as the *Khatum* had been. Female, as well.

That was about where the comparisons ended.

No. Dangerous. Both of them.

Black widows. Just different kinds.

He hoped.

"The *Khatum of Altai*," he said. "Our host."

"Wow, you work quickly," she sneered down at him from her majestic perch.

"She generally doesn't discriminate," he fired back. "Feel free."

Sykora rewarded him with a silent snarl.

The first time he had said something like that to the Dragoon, she had bounced him off a bulkhead hard enough to give him a concussion. She was either relaxing as she grew up, or taking her role as his bodyguard more seriously.

Javier reached out and patted her towel with a serious look. The kind that said: *Don't argue.*

She thought about it anyway for a moment. That much was obvious, but she stretched out her towel and sat.

Two lovers enjoying the beach. As if.

"We need to move quickly," Javier said simply. "Our cover can't stand the kind of inspection that woman might bring to bear."

"Not going to play with your new friend?" Sykora asked sweetly.

"Hadiiye," he said in a quiet, serious tone. "She's likely to just shoot us in the back of the head if she thinks we're a threat. No trial. No excuses. Nothing. She knows who I'm supposed to be, so we need to get gone."

That got through.

Death-machine there drew a quiet breath that suggested the scale of risk was finally coming home.

"What did you find in the vault?" the Ballerina of Death asked quietly, pivoting with all the mental prowess she brought to combat.

She might have been commenting on the surf for all the emotion in her voice.

"A woman who likes to brag," Javier replied sourly. "Vanity and ego undo so many morons. But I never saw the vault itself. Handed over the box to a guard, got a receipt when it was delivered."

It was necessary to peek over his shoulder, like this was a bad holo, but he couldn't help himself.

Nobody was sneaking up on them. No arresting angels swooping in.

"Very few guests actually live here," he continued. "And those that do don't bring huge amounts of jewelry with them. There are way more interesting resorts at which to get dressed up and hit the casinos."

"So?"

Now Sykora had managed to sound bored. Obviously, another talent she was perfecting as she became an actor.

"So thirty-six boxes in one wall," he replied. "Different heights, escalating widths. Our helmet went into the fifth row, bottom spot, to give you an idea."

"And we know one of them holds our box?" she asked, ever so slightly interested now.

"We presume," he replied. "She had to brag that their security was good enough for visiting royalty. Present tense, not past. If I can get the probe in there through the air vents, we should be able to scan it and know how to get in."

"And then what?" Sykora asked.

Her voice was starting to edge into that place Javier liked to think of as High Priestess of the Goddess of Death. The amazing, lethal creature that had come to the fore when they were escaping *Salekhard*.

"Navarre was probably hired because someone wanted a mass casualty incident," Javier sneered at her. "Most of the ways to access that vault require a distraction of a scale that someone gets killed, even accidentally."

"So?"

"So I want a reputation as more than just a killer, Hadiiye," he retorted. "It opens us up to more opportunities, better jobs. That much faster I can pay you and Sokolov off and get on with my life."

"One of us probably still has to die first," she whispered fiercely.

"Maybe," he agreed. "But not today. Okay?"

Javier could see her weigh the alternatives. He probably looked like that around her, from time to time, because, yeah, one of them probably would have to die, but they could still be professionals about things until then.

She nodded, implicit with the sort of emotion and violence that drove Shakespeare to greatness.

"What's the immediate plan?"

"Back to the room in a while," he stated. "We'll have a good meal, and then beg off everything and everyone with a serious case of starship lag. I'll go to bed, as it were, to catch up on my sleep. You'll go seduce a crewmember."

"Seduce?" she snarled in a whisper. "Fornicate?"

"If that's what it takes, yes."

Javier felt his voice go cold and lethal.

"Anything less than that is also acceptable, as long as you get me the answers and gear we need to pull this off."

"Bastard," she hissed.

"Princess, you have no idea."

PART FIVE

Suvi took a moment to consider the right music for this sort of mission. In all the videos, the hero always flew into battle with some serious backbeat drums over a screaming string section, either an electric guitar or a full orchestra.

But she was really more of a cat burglar today, instead of potentially flying a hard strafing run in a tight canyon.

In the end, she settled for Rachmaninoff's Third Piano Concerto. Music for someone born without fear. Just for fun, she spun up a couple of jazz improvisation sub-routines for drums and bass, then let them duel elegantly with the piano as she moved.

The Dragoon had disappeared after the two of them had come back from dinner, leaving her and Javier alone to talk shop for several hours while he added a small electric screwdriver with a rotating multi-head to her outer shell.

Finally, *hands*. She was going to insist he add something at least as good to the big ship when they got home, plus a bigger waldo or something so she could manipulate things.

There was nothing as annoying as having to bonk your nose on a door chime to get it to ring.

And now, the thief in the night.

Someone had given a lot of thought to the architecture of this resort. The square air vent she was cruising down was forty centimeters tall and fifty wide. Too small for most humans, and too dusty for her to worry about running into a cleaning robot.

Not that she was really concerned about running into a drone, except that it might think she was a rodent or something. After all, what self-respecting AI would be happy as a maid-drone?

Nope. Flittering along, happily listening to one of the most dangerous men ever allowed to touch a piano. No annoying Red Baron. Nothing.

Just Suvi, dressed in a skin-tight, black, leather body suit. The kind without any seams at all, and nothing riding up uncomfortably as you moved.

You could do that when you were an AI.

She had kept the scanner pings down to nearly nothing, relying on Visual Flight Rules and passive sensors for now. There was enough light coming in from the regular vents that her optical sensors were fine.

A girl just had to peek and sneak past them, only committing a little voyeurism as she did.

Humans, for all their diversity, tended to be pretty predictable, but she wasn't really interested in expanding her horizons of experience today.

According to inertial guidance and some math, she should be getting close. Just around a corner and…

Yup. Paranoia.

Someone had hung a *something* there, right across the duct.

A human would have probably missed it, relying on eyes, but Suvi at least had been listening with all her extra senses. It was a field of some sort, but not a defensive grid.

She moved just close enough that an arcshield would have sparkled as a warning before it zapped her.

Nothing.

And she realized that everything beyond it was invisible on every wavelength except visual.

Huh. Somebody had a clue. Not a full one, but a clue.

Suvi hovered low enough to look at the emitters on top. She was pretty sure it was a simple electromagnetic shield, designed to prevent someone like Javier from flying a remote control drone in here, exactly like she was doing.

After all, who would pour a full AI into something so petite?

Okay, truth or dare time.

Suvi landed with a soft kiss, back about a meter. If this was really just a shield, she would lose most of her systems passing through, and have to reboot everything. A dumbbot could go autonomous on the other side, but that was exactly where you needed smarts.

She rolled herself forward like a marble, all the way through the field.

Oh, that tickles.

And darkness.

Suvi took a deep breath and climbed under her flight console to crack open the breaker box. Most of the switches had tripped, just as she expected.

She took a few seconds to rocker each one back on line, rather than just pushing the reset button.

Make it all good now, rather than miss something having issues later.

She peeked at the next air vent. It looked right. Big lobby with red sofas and stuff, just like Javier had described it.

And empty. Height of the party time. Everyone should be at the luau chomping down on fresh-cooked pig.

She took the next left and looked down from her parapet.

One guard. Headphones plugged in. Scanning a dozen monitors and a mixing board-worth of gauges.

And bored.

If he were panicking, he would have slammed shut the air vent, just in case, and be pushing buttons frantically. I'm just a mouse in the cupboard.

Suvi skittered past and found the room she wanted next. Empty.

The Vault. Long wall of cubicles you could shut, with curtains over there. Couple of comfy chairs. Seriously secured door. Wall of box-drawer-thingees full-o-stuff.

This was where it had gotten iffy. Javier had thought everything would work, but he wasn't four meters tall and couldn't just climb up here and make sure she could get the angle she needed.

It was going to be close.

Highest leftest. Maybe. Hung up on something. Oh, screw coming through the metal grate. Can't move it out of the way. Drop down, twist a little, bip back up. There.

Suvi took another deep breath, concentrating on her yoga sub-routines.

Oh, what the hell.

She cranked Sergei up loud enough she was pretty sure someone on the outside might see the shell physically vibrate.

She painted the room with a hard sensor pulse. A human might have actually felt that one, as the iron in their blood rotated for a microsecond.

Then she spent nearly ten seconds doing signal processing, washing out noise.

Talk about an eternity.

Let's see. Jewelry. Jewelry. Gun. Gold brick? Really? Hey, there's the helmet. Jewelry.

They had three potential targets when she was done. And four on the far right she had been unable to scan from here.

And seriously, who the hell used mechanical keys anymore? One kiss from a computer and you could open any of them.

Oh, right. Any of them. Yeah, no. Key actually made more sense. You could still pick it or masterkey it if you had to, but nobody could upload an AI into the system and just trigger all the doors and stuff.

Suvi backed out of her corner and began to backtrack, careful to peek at the one guard, but he was still sitting pretty and occasionally flipping a button.

Pretty sneaky, lady. I'll give you that. Ya went old school on me. Keys. But I can take you.

PART ELEVEN

BOOK ELEVEN: BLACK WIDOWS

PART ONE

Javier poured himself a highball glass of real Earth Scotch and added two cubes of ice, swirling the liquid just enough to start that magical, chemical reaction to turn paint thinner into caramelized smoke. He flipped on some modern dance pop synth and dialed it down to ambient noise.

Just enough.

He was just about to get stretched out and put his feet up when the door chime ran through the Westminster sequence politely.

Nothing good would come of it.

Sykora was off grinding her teeth and possibly shaking her ass. Probably in that order.

Suvi should be about a third of the way into the hoard of the dragon by now.

There was nobody else on this ship he wanted to talk to.

The chime rang again, insistent.

Javier sighed, already regretting.

"Room system," he said in a dreary voice. "Activate hall monitor."

The wall in front of him lit up with a slightly fish-eyed view of the corridor outside.

And a black widow.

She might be one of the most beautiful women he had ever met, but

Javier had no doubt that the *Khatum of Altai* wasn't here for intellectual stimulation.

No, he was most likely just the latest flavor of the week. Bored, rich aristocrats needed constant stimulation and degeneration.

Someone had once suggested that the alternative was actually turning their brains on and thinking, but too many would commit suicide, once they realized how dull and pointless their lives were. Usually, they just burned out on chemicals, ever-escalating the dosage, never addressing the underlying hollowness.

Javier had two ex-wives. And a former naval career. He understood that part.

At least he had gotten over himself, eventually.

"Room system, activate comm," he continued. "Good evening, madame. I will be right there."

Javier cut the audio and sipped a good hit of whiskey as he rose.

In for a penny, in for a pound.

The air vent cover was askew enough to let Suvi roam. Javier reached up and hung it back in place, pushing the screws into a handy drawer for now. Suvi had enough juice for weeks, and enough movies and books for at least one night.

He opened the door to his doom.

Whatever *it* was, she had it in spades.

Her smell embraced him as soon as the door opened. Light and sweet and flowery. The subtlest hint of just-blooming roses.

She wore black, possibly shrink-wrapped on, with panels cut out that just showed off the healthy glow of her golden skin and emphasized the curves and lines. He had already seen it all, but this just tantalized as a reminder that he had never touched.

Someone had braided her ebony hair up into a sort of mohawk, a blacktip shark's fin set to slice the water as she attacked. She was already tall for a woman. This put the top of her hair even with the top of his head.

Subtle, but effective.

Predator.

Black widow.

And she was alone.

"I wanted to make sure you were well," she murmured, stepping close enough to rest a palm on his chest. "They said you had an early dinner and then retired. And gave your Amazon the night off."

"Time synch issues," Javier lied blandly. "I was just having whiskey. Nightcap?"

Distracted women are less dangerous than thwarted ones. Bored girls like bad boys. Dilettantes didn't even notice science nerds.

"Please."

She smiled with perfect, gleaming teeth. Javier stepped back and to the side as she entered.

"So you're safe here?" she asked, walking over to the wetbar expectantly.

Javier took his cue and materialized a second glass from underneath. He let his back-brain work while he ogled the woman.

"I'm not expecting an assassin," he retorted wryly. "One is never sure about *safe*."

"Your Amazon is off enjoying herself," the woman purred.

"She only keeps me alive because she wants to kill me herself," Javier smiled.

It was the honest truth. Probably the only truth that would see the light of day on this mission.

He handed her the glass by stepping too close.

"You know how dangerous some women can get," he said.

He had to give her credit. The head tilt was perfect. The coy, coquettish giggle that escaped her lips could have won awards.

Her smell was desire itself.

"And Navarre isn't dangerous?" she whispered.

Javier leaned even closer. Not as a prelude to a kiss, but just to get almost nose to nose with this woman.

"Navarre will do absolutely *anything* to win."

Javier left just enough burr, just enough rusty razor blade in his tones, that the *Khatum*'s pupils dilated unconsciously.

Bored aristocrats. Even black widows.

Think they're tough. Have no clue what dangerous really looks like, cocooned warmly in the swaddling clothes of money.

His eyes sneered at her and her money. At her power. Even her perfection.

Navarre would kill her just as simply, just as easily, as he had Abraam Tamaz, if push truly came to shove.

"Anything?"

Her musk was palpable.

Javier rated himself about a nine for the performance. Some nights, the stars just aligned. He'd won a good chunk of the down-payment for *Mielikki* on *Merankorr*, on a night like that.

Javier leaned back a shade. His glass was still sitting on the end table, forlorn and forgotten.

"Everything."

Rough hands took her by the shoulders and turned her enough that his chest was suddenly pressed against her back, leaving his hands free to roam over the black silk, exploring the woman's perfection encased underneath.

He wasn't a priest, or a Speaker of the Word. Sin in his definition involved denying one's self the simple joys in life, like a beautiful woman demanding physical satisfaction.

There was nothing he could do about the ugliness that was her soul.

Maybe he'd have to send 'Mina here someday, to preach.

The *Khatum* leaned back heavily into him, purring, but otherwise still. He didn't figure that would last long, not with a woman like this. But he wasn't expecting either of the girls back anytime soon.

So he grabbed her by that lustrous, black hair, tugging it, just as bit, as he moved it to the side and nibbled on the woman's neck.

It would be in character, for a man like Navarre.

Just one of the sacrifices he was willing to make.

PART TWO

She knew she was in the right place by the lack of noise.

It wasn't one of the dance clubs that Djamila found herself in tonight. No, this had the feel of a neighborhood dive, that corner bar back home where most of the seats at the bar were specifically reserved by name and time, for the locals who would come in at the end of their day. That long, glass-mirrored, back bar, stacked with exotic bottles that would be refilled from industrial drums. The bald, heavy-set Publican in the stained apron, the kind with a gruff word and a scarred ear.

Djamila might have called it home.

Aritza had always been an officer. Had never served on the lower decks. Never answered beck and call. Might know places like this, but had never belonged to one for longer than his credit or his leave time.

The shifts on a ship in space would be constant. The clientele would turn over smoothly, without surging up and down as daylight came and went. Most of the people in here wore gray, although there were a few Staff in brighter colors. Those looked the surliest. Probably with reason.

Djamila pointed at the bar and then silently drew her hand to the left to indicate every stool. Most of them were empty, right now.

The Publican nodded in response, moving to one end of the bar and setting down an empty glass for her.

Djamila followed and climbed onto the stool.

She was supposed to be acting right now. Scouting. Seducing.

First, she needed a drink. Something that would provide a layer of insulation, demarcation, separation between who she was, and what she had to do tonight.

She already owed Aritza. Now she was keeping score.

The bartender held a bottle ready.

She nodded, digging out a couple of coins and a tip. He had already earned it, as far as she was concerned, just accepting her here. She was an outsider.

Always pay attention to the invisible people. They're the ones that make your life better or worse, regardless of your intent and actions.

The pour was blue. A subtle, bartender joke that actually brought a smile to her face, as hard and sour as it had been.

He grinned back, nodded that she knew what to ask for, and wandered to the other end of the bar, polishing a clean glass and surveying his bar like a bear roused mid-winter.

The liquor was potent enough that she could nearly taste the raw alcohol from here. She wondered if it was the man's own slash, a recipe distilled down from generations of barkeepers. Designed originally to strip grease off industrial equipment.

She sipped.

Potent. Almost undiluted acid as it went down.

It was right at home with Djamila tonight.

Another sip, and the heat began to fortify her. Perhaps power a transformation of a Dragoon into a bimbo secret agent.

That appeared to be Aritza's secret. Become someone else and everything you did left with them when you took the costume off.

If he could do it, she could. Would.

Anything you can do, asshole.

Djamila felt her shoulders come down. For a moment, she considered pressing the warm glass up against her forehead, to see if she could absorb the potency of the fluid that way. Then she realized that the role she was playing tonight allowed it.

She did.

It might have worked.

"That bad, huh?" a voice asked quietly.

Djamila's eyes snapped open, hands ready to lash out and shatter the glass into someone's face and then beat them to death.

Self-defense. The oldest law in the universe.

She had placed the man mentally when she sat down, but otherwise ignored him as a prop on her stage, occupying the middle of three stools on the short end of the bar, when she was on the last chair on the long axis. An empty stool separated them.

And light centuries.

Light skin, almost pale compared to her tan, or Aritza's natural brown. Short hair, dark enough under the dim quietness of the bar. The face looked forty. The eyes suggested four hundred.

If she radiated menace, he had all the emotional signature of a stone headland thrust into the face of the oncoming storm.

He wore gray. She remembered her mission. Even let a little truth out. Those make the best lies.

"I would really like to kill someone, right now," she drawled in a voice made up of all of her day.

"I could tell that," he replied easily. "But you aren't from around here."

"And *he* would never be caught dead in a place like this," she hissed. "Not money enough, unless he's slumming."

The stranger gave her an appraising look. Not sexual, but interested in her story.

Djamila had worn blue dungarees and a black tunic. It stood out against all the charcoal gray in here, but not much.

He was a bantam. That was the only word she could think of to describe the man. She had at least half a meter in height on the man, she guessed, and probably thirty kilos of mass.

She took another sip of angry courage and let the fire stoke her *transformation*.

"Bodyguard?" the man hazarded a guess.

Djamila shrugged.

"Lethal moll, at least," she growled.

It was easier playing a part when you weren't playing.

"Yeah, I got the lethal part," he agreed. "Long day with a moron boss who won't listen?"

Djamila nodded.

No. *Hadiiye*. This was a role. She was an actress. They were on stage.

Hadiiye fixed the man with a hard stare. Challenging his right to speak with her.

And then she softened it. Her purpose here required communication. She couldn't lose track of that part.

"Dumbass with more muscle than brains," she agreed. "Luck and timing are the only things that have kept him alive this long."

"There are always other jobs out there, you know," he replied in a quieter voice.

Whispering to a wild animal, perhaps.

Violence wasn't far from her surface right now.

But not against this man.

Navarre. Aritza. Whoever he was.

And Sokolov, for even suggesting to her that Sascha or Hajna could have handled this job better than she could.

Someone else to keep score against. To prove wrong.

"Violence seems to be the only thing people think I'm capable of," Hadiiye retorted.

"It has its place," the little man agreed. "Some of us even get paid well and treated respectably for it."

Her eyes narrowed and she studied the stranger closer.

Perfect stillness. Something learned, not a natural trait in anyone.

Calluses on his hands from striking things repeatedly in training. Like her own.

More dangerous than he had first seemed.

Or perhaps he had been masking that before. Actors, on a stage.

"Bouncer?" she guessed.

He shrugged with petite eloquence.

"They have a more polite title for it aboard ship," he said. "But you are essentially accurate."

"Gray?" she asked.

"Staff-side are the friendly ones in bright colors," he smiled. "Ship-side wear gray. Makes us invisible. Until we need to not be."

She considered the man. The implications. The danger.

The reward.

"Ever hire Amazons?" she hesitated. "Almost anything would be better than the asshole I'm working for right now."

A hard gleam appeared in his eyes.

"Stand up," he commanded in a light tone. "Turn around."

She did, channeling everything Dr. Teague had ever taught her about Hadiiye.

The man's eyes on her body were like fingers, exploring, probing.

Caressing her skin.

She faced him again.

"Can you contain the violence?" he asked.

Hadiiye felt a thrill spike her.

Aritza considered her nothing more than a gun-bunny. Point and shoot.

This stranger understood that violence was only half of the training. Controlling it was almost more effort than unleashing it. And more important.

"With my size, menace is almost more useful," Hadiiye replied. "Most of the time."

"How many people have you killed?" he asked. "Personally."

"When I was a soldier? Hundreds, perhaps thousands," she said. "Since then, dozens. Maybe scores. I don't really obsess or keep score."

"You might look good in gray," he hazarded.

"Ha. You haven't even got a uniform that would fit me," she spiked him with her eyes.

Challenge.

Not menace. Dare.

His eyes got cagey.

Challenge accepted.

"If you have an hour, we could try sneaking into the quartermaster section and stealing you something," he said, eyes lit with a mischievous fire.

She had learned the right way to arch an eyebrow from Dr. Teague. Compelling disbelief conveyed, without sarcasm or sound.

"Sounds like an excuse to get me someplace private and take advantage of me," Hadiiye purred.

Not quite an invitation. Maybe.

The mission.

Again, his eyes roamed. Scales in his head weighed options.

"Maybe," he said. "A little."

He held out a hand.

"Farouz," he introduced himself.

"Hadiiye," she took his hand. "I don't normally let strangers seduce me in bars, you know."

"That's because you intimidate the hell out of most people," he replied.

"Most?"

"Most," he grinned, sliding off the stool.

She joined him.

One hundred sixty-five centimeters tall. Maybe. Wiry and hard.
His eyes were about on a level with her nipples.
Probably a good thing that dancing wasn't on the menu.
Presently.
She joined him, a tree next to a rosebush.
"Lead on," she said.
This was when it was going to get interesting.

PART THREE

Javier felt like ten kilometers of bad, gravel road.

Heaven forbid that if he ever decided to take up running marathons, he would probably feel like this for the first six months. Which would be the point he gave up and went back to less strenuous pursuits.

The *Khatum* didn't snore, but she was purring, fast asleep on a cream, silk-covered bed that looked like a mugging. The chair by the door was in worse shape, with all their clothes thrown at it as they went by. Destructive whirlwind kind of night.

For a woman with four grown children, a topic he had researched before arriving, she still looked and acted like she was thirty-two standard. And possibly a nymphomaniac at that.

Or just bored with all the fashion-model aristocrats and boy-toys around here. Not much had changed.

If he was planning to stay long, she'd probably work him to death.

But that wasn't going to be a problem. The only risk was dying if she caught his lies, or decided to send ninjas after him later.

At least the bed was big enough he could stretch out on his side and leave three quarters of it for her. He pulled a couple of pillows up and leaned back, sipping a glass of water from the table. It wouldn't do to fall asleep with this woman here. Not with the other two women due back at some point.

At the same time, he couldn't go anywhere.

Javier could just see Suvi's flitter returning, and him pulling the grate open for her, right as the *Khatum* staggered from the bedroom looking for him.

Talk about lethally awkward.

Sykora wouldn't be as bad, but there was always a chance her mission would end up requiring her to bring a guy back here. He really didn't want to end up being her dad, tonight.

The purring stopped.

She stretched in place for a moment, athletic beauty a distraction all by itself, and then rolled over to look at him.

"That could be addicting," she murmured. "It's a good thing you're only passing through."

Navarre's cold mask studied the woman before it relented into something like a smile.

"Oh?" he asked.

"Some people are obsessed with wealth and power," she said, pulling the silk sheets up to make a little cocoon fortress around herself. "They sniff around and try to worm their way in. Those I've already defeated."

"Did you now?" he asked in a soft, lyrical tone. "How?"

"When I became the heir, I changed the rules," she said. "Any man wanting me was required to make a set of deposits in a sperm bank ahead of time. I left them there for five years and let the men make their case."

"And how did that turn out?" Javier asked.

This was certainly a novel way to handle men, and probably a pretty effective method.

"When I was ready, I used those samples to impregnate myself," she smiled cruelly. "None of the men was told who, and they all looked close enough alike. I ended up with boy/girl fraternal twins on the second round, and now I have four children, with twelve fathers. One of the children will become the heir, and the other three will be married off well."

"And did it succeed?" Javier asked, rolling a little onto his side to focus more of his attention on her. She felt vulnerable right now.

It might be an act. It might be a trap. It might be an opportunity. And maybe she was hungry for a second round or a second dinner.

Javier's only mission right now was distraction. And she made that such a chore. Honest.

"Boring," the woman sulked a bit. "Beautiful songbird. Golden cage. A story as old as time and money."

She shrugged with her whole body, stretching the semi-translucent silk tight to distract him. It worked.

"And I'm just another bad boy?" Javier teased.

"Worse," she replied. "A consummate professional with a goal. I just happen to be a pleasant diversion. If I hadn't come along, you might have listened to opera all night instead, wouldn't you?"

"*Cyranean* Pulse," Javier replied. "But yes, you are essentially correct, *Khatum of Altai*."

"I have a name," she snapped.

"And we have not been formally introduced, madam," Navarre's voice whip-cracked back at her.

He waved at the remains of the bed.

"Though this hardly qualifies as a formal salon against which we could explore the social geometries of Kierkegaard," he continued in a cruel voice.

She shifted herself around, almost angrily, until she was also upright, with a pillow behind her and those distracting golden-brown breasts resting on a sea of ecru silk. Her eyes were fire.

And then they sparkled.

"No, I suppose not," she said with a sudden, bright giggle, also waving at the destroyed bedding. "But our activities here would either constitute a concrete refutation of existentialism, or its logical conclusion. Two strangers seeking meaningless pleasure in one another. I suppose one's take on the balance between Deism and Romanticism would determine which side of the coin landed upright, wouldn't you agree? And you may call me Behnam, at least in private."

For a moment, Javier knew pure lust.

All that, and brains, plus an amazingly rare level of education. Certainly not the sort of woman to take home to meet his parents, but *wow*.

"My mother named me Eutrupio," Javier said.

And it wasn't even a lie.

Javier Eutrupio Aritza. Or Eutrupio Navarre, he supposed, if one wanted to be philosophical.

Navarre would never admit to softer emotions or philosophical permutations, but he was a boring shit. Too linear.

"If the Creator actually cares," Javier opined, waving a hand at the room, "then we're probably all going to hell. Perhaps we did and just haven't been judged wanting. At least not yet."

"Who are you, Navarre-the-killer?" she asked, leaning towards him.

"A man making his way best he can," Javier replied with a shrug. "There are amazing distractions, if one stops to smell the roses."

"And you'll be here an entire month?" she asked breathlessly. "On someone else's credit?"

"That's the current plan," he lied breezily. "It will depend on the buyer's ability to get here."

She rolled away from him and stood up on her side of the bed.

"In that case," she said, sashaying towards the pile of clothing. "Next time, I might let you scrub my back. But we should save some things. Wouldn't want to show you everything all at once."

Javier let himself stare lustfully at the woman. It was rude, and she seemed to thrill in it, stretching the black fabric around her in ways that made her body even more interesting than it was nude. There was nothing to do about the remains of her mohawk braid, except pull it all back and strut home.

Oh, the hard life of a space pirate.

"Will you be recovered enough to join us for an event tonight?" Behnam, the *Khatum of Altai*, asked lightly. "Or should we give you another day?"

Javier shrugged. Navarre was a bad-ass who would admit no fear, no exhaustion. Nothing.

And boring as shit.

"I'm still star-lagged," he replied. "Someone interrupted what would have been a solid night of meditation and sleep, so I would vote for another day of rest, if I need to show up all the locals."

She grinned back at him and subtly transformed back out of that vulnerable girl she had been and into the hard-ass businesswoman who was one of the richest people in the sector, and one of the most dangerous.

"Then you will most definitely need your rest, Navarre," she smiled cruelly. "There are many who will want to take your measure."

Without another word, she turned and left.

Javier let her go. There was nothing to be gained by trying to get in a last word, not now.

Because there was no way in hell he was going to be here in two days to say it.

PART FOUR

Djamila watched Farouz peek out the door one last time and then close it in silence. She found herself leaned back against a shelving unit taller than she was. The whole room was an oversized closet, maybe four meters by six, with clothing neatly folded and stacked by size. All of it gray.

He turned back and smiled up at her.

"So far, so good," he said in a voice barely above a whisper.

They had stealthily made their way back down a series of otherwise hidden hallways, accessible from the main part of the ship in many places, but separate from the world of wealth and dissipation outside.

"Why mechanical locks everywhere?" she asked, more curious than anything. "And where did you learn to pick them?"

He shrugged and stepped away from the door. Not close, but closer.

"We get a number of really smart people here," he said. "Bankers and finance people. Good with computers. Got to be too much hassle to keep them from damaging systems trying to override them. Mechanical locks are so old-school that you have to study them in order to get by. And develop a very soft touch."

"Soft?" she asked.

Farouz took another partial step closer.

"Just so," he agreed. "Light enough to find the right spot. Firm enough to tease it into position. Strong enough to hold it perfectly still, while everything else moves for you."

"We're still talking about locks?" she teased.

"Everything is secured," Farouz grinned. "Getting it open so you can access something takes time and patience."

He was suddenly close. Arm's reach for him with shorter arms. His eyes had a gleam in them Djamila wasn't sure she'd ever seen before.

Desire.

Not lust. Not power. Not control.

Want.

It was alien to the Ballerina of Death, but not necessarily unwelcome.

"So did you bring me here to seduce me?" she whispered. "Or show off your lock-picking skills?"

"There's a difference?" he whispered back, staring up at her from breathing range.

"Yes," she said. "You still haven't shown me anything in gray that would convince me this is the kind of place I might fit."

"Fit is important," he agreed. "We should find you something that fits just right. Fills that burning need."

Djamila suddenly felt fifteen again, on the verge of losing her virginity to a fellow student. It hadn't been that great, nor had others, but the edge of excitement and danger was there.

She smiled. Considered kissing the man. And not kissing him. Danced wickedly outside of herself.

Farouz took a step back and studied her in slow detail. His hands flexed like he wanted to use his fingers to measure her and not just his eyes.

"It helps that you are proportioned more like a man," he said. "I can only imagine the impossibility of finding pants if you were all leg."

He turned to his left and studied the shelves.

Djamila let out a silent breath. So close. And so strange.

When was the last time she had felt desire?

Farouz kneeled down and pulled a bundle from a bottom shelf, unfurling it and holding it up to her hip.

"Perhaps a single roll at the hem, until you sew it under," he said with a leering smile. "Jacket will be easier."

A moment or two later, he handed her a shirt and a jacket from another shelf.

"Try this on," he said, moving to the door and turning his back on her.

Djamila started to strip immediately, but Hadiiye stopped her.

"You aren't going to watch?" Hadiiye asked slowly.

"It might be considered rude," he said back over a shoulder. "Seeing things I wasn't supposed to."

"Supposed to?" she inquired with a saucy edge so unlike herself she nearly gasped. "I think you should see how everything fits. You brought me here, you know. You have some responsibilities for the fashion."

She watched him turn slowly back, facing her while leaning back on the door. She was expecting a leer, but got a warm smile instead.

Slippers off first, she pulled the tunic over her head. It was a thick fabric, and they were shipboard, so she had nothing under it but tan.

The slacks went next. Again, nothing but skin.

She lingered over the new t-shirt, putting it to one side after a few beats so she could pick up the pants and slide them over her long, bronze legs, watching his eyes every step of the way.

He stared right back at her, eyes locked as she moved.

Farouz's eyes drifted when she pulled the shirt over her head and tucked it down tight against her skin.

She told herself it was cold in here.

The jacket was last, and then she stood before him transformed.

"How long is your moron boss going to be aboard?" Farouz asked in a breathless voice.

"We're scheduled for several weeks," Hadiiye purred back. "I'll have a lot of personal time available."

He stepped closer. Again, close enough to breathe on, but not touching her at all.

Pointedly so.

"I have to go on shift in an hour or so, and pull a double because Derek is on medlist," Farouz replied. "I would like to take you out to dinner in forty-eight hours, and then properly seduce you."

"And not now?" Djamila asked, breathless all of a sudden.

One of his hands went around her hip and pulled her close. She leaned down so they could kiss, but it was over almost immediately.

Djamila lurched, but only in her head.

"Cheap flings are just that," he murmured. "I'd rather show you a better side of the world."

He stepped back.

"Thank you for that, though," he said. "I could never have imagined something so amazing."

She let the thrill fill her. And relaxed.

"What about this?" she asked, starting to unbutton the jacket.

"Keep it," he said. "A crew this big will never notice, and if you wore it in two days, we could go nearly anywhere aboard ship and nobody would ask."

She smiled.

"It's a date."

PART TWELVE
BOOK TWELVE: GRAY

PART ONE

JAVIER WAS TYPING into Suvi's communication keyboard rather than talking out loud, because he couldn't be sure how late Sykora would be out. The rest of the board didn't really do anything important, except play music, and make cute, little, furry animals dance across her dashboard. She did all the flying.

But it also irritated her to have to wait for him to type.

Javier suspected she was reading various books while she waited for him to use such a slow method of chatting. He considered flipping to an ancient Morse code keyboard to really slow things down, but she was already tart in her responses.

Not worth pushing it.

She was a good kid. With way more than she should. If not for him, she'd still be the monotonously-boring AI system that had come with his ship. Before he'd turned her into someone fun.

The outer door chimed once, and then opened.

Javier was in the main room. He wasn't sure if Sykora was alone, or if he'd even see her tonight. Creator knew she was furious with him for assigning her that mission.

Her fault. Either of the pathfinder babes could have handled the job easier. Her professional pride would get her killed one of these days.

If this wasn't already such a dicey situation, he would have arranged for it to be sooner, rather than later.

And he had expected her to stomp into the room.

Instead, she entered like an ice skater, gliding effortlessly to a halt beside him.

Javier triple-taked and then nearly jumped out of the chair.

She was dressed in gray, holding a small bag of what he presumed were the clothes she had gone out in.

And she had a goofy grin on her face.

Man, this was probably worse than *Homicidal Amazon*.

She sniffed. Pointedly.

"Wow, you really do work fast," she announced in disbelief. "She's already been here, rolled you once, and left?"

"Sit," he commanded sourly. "We have to be done with this mission in twenty-six hours, then steal the cargo lighter and escape."

"Why?" she pushed back. "What's the rush?"

"You got a date or something?" Javier turned and looked up at her. Inspecting those little details.

Pupils dilated. Breathing shallow. Skin flushing suddenly. Jaw dropping open in shock.

Shit. She really did have a date. Her? Here? What the hell had she been up to, the last six hours?

Javier pointed at the sofa.

"Down," he commanded a second time. "If it's that important, we can always kidnap him at gunpoint later and take him with us."

Wow. Blush all the way down to her collar now. Like she was seriously considering it.

He watched her stumble to the sofa and collapse onto it.

"And I've never come home in someone else's clothes sober," Javier sneered at her. "So I'll assume you were successful. Spill."

Even more blush? How was that possible? And was she going to pass out shortly from all the blood flowing into her face?

It took a few seconds for her breath to get normal. And her usual anger to resurface.

The Ballerina of Death returned, took possession of the Dragoon. Good.

She was more predictable now. More professional. Possibly less dangerous.

"I made contact with a member of the security crew," she finally said, tones clipped sharp enough to shave on. "Allowed him to seduce me. Arranged a date for forty-six hours from now."

The blush returned, but nowhere near as bright.

"I was able to locate and acquire a uniform for myself," she gestured to those endless legs. "I can get you to the same location."

"Portal security?" he asked.

She was tactical now. He just needed to prod her in the right direction and duck, like pointing a cannon.

"There is a secondary set of corridors for Operations crew only," she responded. "Access is via a physical key turning counter-clockwise in a mechanical cylinder lock."

Damn, that was new. Or old, depending. And useful.

"How many keys did the man have?" Javier asked.

"Farouz only used one, that I saw," Sykora said, blushing some more.

Farouz, huh? Probably an ogre even taller than her. Must be a monster.

"How frequently were the corridors airlocked off?" he asked.

"Infrequent," she said. "And open, once we got into them. The only other time he needed to key a door was to get into the uniform closet."

Javier leaned back and thought. Suvi was listening, and could fill in all sorts of details later. From what he had already seen in the vault, getting into the boxes was also a mechanical process.

Everything was mechanical.

That was a maneuver so devious he could have never predicted it, but he had spent two hours in close contact with the mastermind behind it all. Nothing the *Khatum* did would surprise him.

Hopefully.

And hopefully, she wouldn't be terminally pissed at him when this was done.

He leaned forward and started typing into Suvi's keyboard.

Now was not the time to ask her to look something up for him. At least, not out loud.

The encyclopedia he had uploaded into her system was heavy on biology and applied sciences. It took up a tiny fraction of the space she had dedicated to books and movies.

Javier felt like a barbarian, working with stone knives and bear skins, to quote the ancient wisdom.

One article led to a second, a third, a fourth.

Ah. There you are.

The Science of Lock-picking. And the ancient tools of the trade. Something called a snap gun.

Insert a bar into the key slot. Turn the mechanism enough to just rub the pins inside and hold them tight. Tab them all upward simultaneously with a hinged pivot. Feel all the upper half of the pins come clear and release the lock. Turn the cylinder the rest of the way.

Billiards you played with small metal pins, using the same physics as an opening break.

Devious. Not a single i/o portal anywhere that he could plug Suvi into and let her tickle a computerized lock open, or beat the controlling software to death.

And he knew she had been so looking forward to it.

"I'll need access to a machine shop, or something similar," he said finally. "Twenty or thirty minutes and the right tools."

Sykora had been watching him, hawk-like.

He spun the display around for her to see.

"That's so ancient that I'm nearly offended," he continued. "But it's also genius. And easy enough for a competent systems tech to keep repaired. I had been planning to use software uploaded into the probe to defeat the door systems."

"And now?" she asked, breathless. "Are we blocked?"

The tone brought Javier's head up.

Was she looking for an excuse to get physical enough with this Farouz-fellow to lift his key? Sykora? The Ballerina of Death?

Officially weird. And yucky.

"No," Javier countered. "We sleep. We eat. We get ready. In about twenty-two hours we sneak out, do this thing, and then commit an act of piracy on the cargo lighter that will be docked and unloading. Those come in every twelve hours, so we should be good, if we can do everything else on time and get clear."

"And if not?" she asked.

"I'm sure the *Khatum* can find a yardarm to hang us from."

PART TWO

Suvi had dialed the music down. Because now was most definitely not the time to get distracted by ten-finger, seventy-key piano solos.

A little Tchaikovsky for the booms, but mostly petite, chamber orchestras or octets. It fit with the gray uniform that Javier had stolen from the linen closet, itself a match with the one the Dragoon had apparently seduced her way into.

Ew.

Javier was carrying her right now in a fabric bag that barely blocked her visual sensors, to say nothing of everything else she had cranked up. Listening on just about every wavelength and pitch imaginable.

And he hadn't even had to let her hack into anything to steal the secret plans to this mammoth starship. Some fool had just left them on the entertainment system for the traveling engineer who was bored and wanted to see how the ship worked.

Suvi just knew that most people would never bother. Security by obscurity, after all, was as old as things to steal.

And even her digital scan of the locks in the vault wasn't going to be all that helpful. Boss was going to go and invent himself an icepick, or a lockpick, or a stungun for lock systems.

Something.

She was too pissed at the whole situation to be rational at a time like this.

At least they had done a good job sneaking this far. But what fool put a simple air vent next to a secured door and expected everyone to miss it? Granted, Javier had, until she had highlighted it on the map and exploded it up as a full schematic with a small piano fanfare.

I mean, hello?

And Javier had finally stopped arguing with her and had let her hack the thing when they got there.

Was that the right term? What do you call it when you fly up to a wall and unscrew the four bolts holding the damned screen in?

Stupid and amateur, that's what. Bad design engineering by a guy who really should have known better.

And then back into the damned bag.

<grumblegrumblegrumble />

Suvi pinged an A-flat below middle C. Not too loud. Just enough to get Javier's attention.

And the psycho, paranoid floozy.

"What was that?" Sykora whispered in a tone shot through with adrenaline.

And craziness.

"Audio warning that we're approaching the machine shop," Javier murmured back in a tone right up there with soothing rabid Chihuahuas. "Remember, I programmed the probe to be much more autonomous than it used to be."

Or something like that.

Whatever lies ya gotta tell these nutjob pirates until we can escape, boss.

Javier's big mitt was warm as he reached into the bag, wrapping around her nude body like King Kong on a cold, Gotham night.

"Probe. Access Command Mode," Javier said formally, the phrase they had agreed to so she could pretend to be smarter than the waffle-maker. "Initiate security perimeter surveillance."

And then she was flying.

Free.

Well, stuck in a hallway that was dim by human standards and probably smelled weird, from the olfactory bio-readings she was tracking.

Good enough.

Suvi peeked once at the passive readings, and then booped the hallway with an ultrasonic pulse. Bats would be annoyed and bitchy right now, but nothing she had seen so far indicated sensors capable of detecting her call.

They were busy looking for radar and other silliness.

Nothing in the hallway either direction for a damned good distance. It was the middle of the night.

Next, she blasted the door with something kinda like X-rays, but not that far down the scale. Still let her see through walls.

Or would have.

Stupid bulkhead was apparently twice as thick as EVERY OTHER BULKHEAD ON THIS DAMNED SHIP.

Fine.

Suvi imagined big-girl panties she could pull up a notch, and then cranked the bass on her dashboard up to eleven.

<BONG />

Oh, yeah. That's more like it.

Apparently, nobody needed to secure the machine shop from vandals. And nobody was home.

She played a quick E-sharp/D trill. It sounded pleasant in her ears. A quick spotlight nailed the door handle rather than the lock mechanism.

Javier grinned at her and nodded to the crazy woman.

He put a hand on the knob and twisted it open silently.

Inside was a paradise to make a girl engineer all tingly in the right places. Lathes, presses, laser beds. There was even a gas-flame welding bottle, for those times when you had to get all steel-welding and stuffff.

When using your own hands to do the job was going to be so much more satisfying than relying on mechanical assistance.

Suvi drifted into the room and took a deep sniff of heaven, the two humans trailing in her wake like amateur remorae.

Javier turned right immediately after closing and locking the door. Really thin bar stock was in a pigeonhole system, waiting for him like a poisoned princess.

Suvi was really pissed that the Dragoon was along.

There was no way in hell that Javier'd let her drive all these awesome machines, just like the girl back on *Storm Gauntlet* had gotten to make the helmet because there was no way to explain Javier programming the CNC machines to that level of pure awesomeness.

Still, he had promised her that the Dragoon was going to meet an unfortunate accident one of these days.

Suvi could wait.

PART THREE

It was one of the joys of a competent machine shop, Javier decided. And a well-organized one, as well. Everything was right where it was supposed to be.

The device he had thrown together was ugly. Rough. Crap, really, but it should do the trick. According to Suvi, they used a six-pin system here, with four heights programmable, or whatever the term was. Paranoid, compared to what was in the file, but not impossible.

Ninety-nine-point-something percent of the people that would pass through here would be stumped by all this. Of course, they hadn't been studying piracy with monomaniacal devotion for the last year, either. Javier did not appreciate what Sokolov and the Dragoon had turned him into, but he'd be utterly damned if he was going to do a half-assed job of it.

And now it was done. There was no locksmith shop in here for him to test against, but there were other ways.

"Get the door," he told Sykora as he moved that way.

She had been standing around, politely keeping her mouth shut for the fifteen minutes this took.

The woman just glowered at him.

"Please," Javier added.

Navarre never said please. Too much of him around lately. Even with Sykora.

"Probe. Access Command Mode," Javier called. "Scan the hallway when the door opens."

He waited.

The door opened on silent hinges, and nobody was standing there with a gun, waiting patiently.

So far. So good.

Suvi floated out, did her magic, and played him a happy trill.

Now the hard part.

Javier slid the thin metal bar into the lock awkwardly. Maybe some spray lubricant when they left? Something.

The theory was sound, but there'd been nothing to experiment on, and he knew it was all touch from what the files said.

Lock the latch from the back. Doorknob won't turn.

Damned barbarians and their lack of electronic keycards. At least the guest suites were civilized.

Jam it all the way in. Extra tap to be sure. Turn the metal until it stops moving. Hold firm.

Spin the little snapper thingee that was supposed to pop up all the pins at once.

Nothing.

Snap it again.

Hey, that was motion. Maybe half the pins?

"It's not working," Sykora said in a voice that somehow combined boredom with technical superiority.

"You don't get to use a crowbar to pry them open," Javier snarled quietly back. "And that would take a powered ram anyway. No way they wouldn't notice."

He turned back to the lock.

Snap it a third time, turning a little harder and the lock turned in his grip.

Stupid barbarians.

Okay, we can open locks. Painfully slow. Stupidly primitive. Brilliantly secure.

Bastards.

PART FOUR

DJAMILA FELT HER HANDS TWITCH, fingers itching for a firearm. Something lethal to hold.

She had considered grabbing a piece of bar stock to carry, but that would be out of character for the crew. Ditto grinding an edge onto a piece of flat steel.

Besides, there was nothing here that would make her any more dangerous than her bare hands and feet, anyway.

Aritza's poisonous apple floated out ahead, high and up in the left-hand corner of the ceiling as they went. Humans tended to look up and left when they walked, so it might be invisible on their right.

Subtle things, but at least Aritza had programmed the device with some level of professional sense. Even if he never seemed to exhibit his own.

He had the controls now, but they were in his bag, and he was controlling the device with quiet, verbal commands. Again, an improvement. He could watch where he walked.

Djamila was torn on whether or not she missed the armed version that he had used to break her out of captivity. Any gun handy would make her feel better. Even in his hands.

At least the hallway was empty.

She knew they were close, having memorized a variety of entry and exit paths.

The probe stopped over a closed door, dropped half a meter, and spun three-hundred-sixty degrees before bouncing back up to the ceiling.

She had been trailing Aritza. He glanced back at her and nodded.

The hallway was probably monitored by the man inside, if he was awake. The probe had carefully maneuvered to stay out of sight of the camera.

Djamila put on her acting persona and broadcast bored as she walked up and kind of stood next to the man.

Suspicious people act suspicious. She had just been called to duty to do something inane, when she could be out dancing. Djamila affected a slouch that wrapped her like a python, while maintaining a complete tactical perception field in three directions.

Child's play.

Aritza held a can of spray lubricant in one hand, and his lock-pick device in the other. A quick hiss, nearly inaudible, and then the whine of metal on metal.

Thrum-click.

Thrum-click.

Right about now, she came to know regret that she hadn't secreted a pry bar by her side as she walked. Something a meter and a half long, forged of hull metal, with a point on one end, and a wedge tip on the other.

Dumb-ass and his toy were going to fail. And the guard inside would wake up, panic, and trigger the alarm.

Djamila doubted they would hang.

The woman on the beach had looked like the kind to walk them out an airlock with a view portal, and make a party of it, with champagne and finger food, while a string quartet played.

The kind of people who had made Djamila an outsider her entire life.

One might not choose to be a pirate, but one can make the most of it.

Thrum-click.

Third time apparently was lucky.

The handle turned.

The door opened inward.

Djamila already knew there was nobody in range, reinforced by the floating apple, so she stepped up and kicked the door with one, oversized, right foot.

It moved about fifty centimeters and bounced. Not enough to stop her mass. That was why she had used a foot and not a shoulder. More *oomph* behind it.

Someone inside had heard the noise and stood up to investigate. Djamila had just knocked him on his butt.

Another dumb-ass. He should have signaled an alarm of some sort first.

Maybe he had, and it just didn't sound in the hallway. Not her job, right now.

Djamila landed on the guy like a sack of potatoes as he struggled to get up.

Quick fist to the nose. Not enough to kill him. Just a stinger to blind and stun. An old fashioned crowd-control technique.

Open right palm to the cheekbone, backed by all her upper body. Again, not lethal. Just enough to rattle the brain around inside the skull. Mild concussion when done right.

Left hand, open palm. Snap him back the other direction.

Good night.

Djamila could almost feel the man's eyes roll back. He went limp under her.

She rolled him over onto his face, so he wouldn't choke on his tongue or anything, and checked over her shoulder.

Net time, less than two seconds.

Aritza and the probe were already inside the room, door closed and locked.

What idiot forgot to put a simple bar on this side, to keep people from doing exactly what they just had?

Oh, the arrogance of wealth.

Aritza pulled some ties from his bag, but Djamila had already found the cuffs the man kept in a pouch. She pulled both hands back, made sure everything was good, and snapped them into place.

She climbed off the poor man and moved around to check his pupils. Stunned and out cold, but nothing that a few hours of rest and some aspirin wouldn't cure.

A professional job.

She stood up.

The poor man even had a pistol in a holster he had never drawn. It was hers now. She attached it to her belt and drew the weapon.

Standard stun model. Short range. Good to take down nearly anyone, but not kill them, unless they suffered a stress-induced heart attack in the struggle. At which point, why the hell were they here instead of at a hospital getting that fixed up?

Aritza was already investigating the board with fingertips that never quite touched. He hummed quietly to himself as he did.

"Probe. Access Command Mode," he said, pulling a retractable cord from the console. "Standard i/o interlink available. Log in and review security systems."

The device dropped down and turned into a gray balloon floating above the console.

"Doesn't look like he sounded any alarms," Aritza continued, turning to her. "Did you check him for keys?"

Djamila blinked at him.

"Didn't think so," Javier said, kneeling down and grabbing a spool from the man's belt.

"This gets us halfway," he said as she continued to stare.

Djamila felt a blush come on. But she deserved this one. She had been unprofessional. Sure, take the man down rapid and silent. But she had gotten wrapped up in the gun and forgotten to check him for anything else.

She did now, but he had no radio tucked into a pocket, nor a knife. Nothing but pocket change.

Djamila stood, chastened.

And pissed.

Aritza kept making her look junior varsity, when she was the professional pirate.

She needed to up her game again. It was an arms race, now and forever.

"Halfway?" she asked.

"Every box has two keys," he said. "Guest has one. House has one. His. Now I only have to pick one lock each time."

Djamila nodded, looking down at the poor sap on the floor.

She had hoped otherwise, but her date with Farouz was definitely gone at this point.

Something else she owed Aritza.

PART FIVE

OUT OF THE SECURITY BOOTH, down a short hall, and into the main vault Javier went, trailed by the two most important women in his life. Only one of them fell on the good side, but even the Amazon killer was important.

At least for now. Maybe she would suffer an accident at some point.

The risks of the profession.

The Vault hadn't changed in the last thirty-six hours.

On his right, a bank of cubby-holes for people to rest a box and sift through it behind a privacy curtain, as he had done before handing over the box and getting a key back. Several overstuffed chairs and a bench.

And paradise.

Six columns of lock-boxes. Six rows tall.

Farthest left were the narrowest at twenty centimeters wide. The top one was ten centimeters tall, and each of the five beneath it was five centimeters bigger as it went.

They got five centimeters wider with each column to the right.

Javier touched the bottom box on the fifth row, just for luck.

"This one is us," he said to the air.

Sykora just grunted back at him and moved to a spot where she could probably shoot anybody coming through either door into the place. She was like that.

Javier had already had a long conversation with Suvi, but he brought up the handheld anyway to be sure. Three distinct maybes. Four outside her scan range. Or had been, from the overhead air vent.

Not now.

"Probe. Access Command Mode," he called to her. "Hard scan the sixth column while I work."

He stuck the guard's master key into the lock. Or, tried to.

Wrong lock. Too wound up.

Deep breath. Calm. Professional.

Put it into the RIGHT lock and turn. Yes. There. Better.

Javier felt his whole being blip for a moment.

What the hell?

Oh. Right. Hard scan. And that was just the back-scatter on her electromagnetic pulse? I wonder if we could turn it up and make a short-range weapon out of it, one of these days.

Remember to ask her. Or have her make a note to remind you.

Something.

Javier sprayed the magic liquid into the first three locks Suvi had identified, and then put the bottle away for now.

Give it a moment to go to work.

Breathe.

He stuck the pick bar into One-Two and snapped the spinner. His own key to Five-Six only showed four teeth, so maybe this would be easier.

The lock turned. Either he was getting better at this, or he'd gotten lucky.

And I'd rather be lucky than good.

The outer face hinged open, revealing a fire-proof metal box.

He pulled it out, sat it on the floor and flipped it open.

Papers.

Deeds. Will. Identity papers from five different planets, in five different names, all with the same picture.

Stack of bearer bonds. Walk into any civilized bank and turn into money. Lots of money.

How many zeroes?

The evil conscience on his left shoulder giggled madly and then fell over dead as the good conscience on the right quick-drew a six gun and shot him.

"You don't even need to listen to that fool," the good angel said.

Javier agreed. None of this was what he wanted.

And if he took it, wouldn't that make him just another pirate? Like the crazy bitch behind him?

No. Not going there. Not for you, lady. Not for anyone.

He carefully restored it, closed the box, and stuffed it back into place.

The second box was harder to access. Five tries on the spinner before it bit.

Javier chalked that one up to nerves and adrenaline.

Inside was what appeared to be a manuscript. A big one. Printed on real paper. Hundreds of pages of what looked like some sort of lurid, historical romance, set in the Gas-Sailors Era of Old Earth, just before starflight.

Weird.

Javier had half a mind to find the owner and ask why it had never been published. But then he remembered where he was. These people had so much money that it became oxygen, only noticeable by a sudden absence. And few of them had the courage to face the sort of intellectual rejection that publishing your inner secrets carried.

Javier wondered how many Hemingways might be hiding out behind all the booze and complex pharmaceuticals in this place.

Four-Two and…there it was.

Oh, crap.

A small block carved from a white stone lit through with red threads. No bigger than two of his fingers.

A *Baiwen* seal. With a small woman's compact he just knew was filled with silk seal paste in a red so bright as to be impossible.

Talk about ancient.

Javier wondered how many millennia old that stone was. Had it originated on Earth?

He popped the cover open to quick scan the face. It was *Traditional Chinese*, the ancient'est tongue.

These people were serious.

He must have muttered something. Or stopped breathing.

Sykora was suddenly lurking over him.

"Is that it?" she asked in a near-whisper. "How does it work?"

"Give me your hand," Javier nearly giggled, pulling out the compact and twisting it open.

He dabbed the face of the *Baiwen* into the paste, just enough, and looked up expectantly.

She glowered down at him for a moment, but then curiosity apparently got the better of her. The left hand came down.

Javier grabbed it, turned it over, and pressed the chop onto the inner portion of her forearm, right where he usually got nightclub stamps after paying the cover.

"Technically, this might make you his property," Javier said.

She tried to jerk her arm back, but he was prepared and had all his weight into the grip. She barely moved.

"Bastard," she hissed.

Javier shrugged with an evil grin. Not like she didn't have it coming.

He put the stone away with all the care of a holy relic, wrapping it back up and stowing it and the paste compact into his bag.

The next document was a birth certificate in a leather satchel, two and a half centuries old, annotated with dates and subsequent births to the eighth generation, a boy who would be about thirty now. It was sealed with each addition.

Legally binding. And probably the kid's death sentence, were it found. Were he found.

Javier wondered about the people paying to destroy the evidence. At least they were willing to let the kid be.

Unless this was all some machination to have the guy killed or kidnapped later, when he was just a commoner, and no longer the true Emperor of *Changzhuo*, hiding from the people who held the planet and the government now.

Or someone had hired Navarre and expected an entirely different outcome from this.

This is not my circus. These are not my monkeys.

Javier took about half the papers with him. All the legal stuff. The boring identification went back into the box. He left the bank statements alone, and the bonds, and the jewelry. The kid would need them, tomorrow.

Carefully, he stowed the box back into the wall and locked it up.

"Okay," he said. "Let's go."

"You're leaving the helmet?" she asked, incredulous.

"That's right," he said. "Hopefully, she'll see it as a peace offering when she reviews the tapes and realizes how much damage we could have done."

"You're insane, Navarre," Hadiiye muttered at him.

How much of it was roleplay, he had no idea. They were long past that point.

Now they just had to get out of here alive.

PART SIX

Djamila found it educational, watching Aritza work. She could appreciate the rare moments when the man exhibited professional care and sensibilities. She just wished he would act more like a grown-up, more of the time.

She might even be able to respect him, if he did that. However long those odds might be.

He opened the boxes with ease. Never a wasted movement.

And left behind, literally, a king's ransom in the first of two boxes.

From the third box, only the stone stamp, the crimson ink, and a handful of official-looking papers.

Nothing more.

"Okay," he said. "Let's go."

"You're leaving the helmet?" she was shocked.

All that effort to find the metal, craft it. Everything. And just leave it here. What was the value, even if it wasn't a priceless antique?

"That's right," the man replied brusquely. "Hopefully, she'll see it as a peace offering, when she reviews the tapes and realizes how much damage we could have done."

"You're insane, Navarre," Djamila growled at him.

But she couldn't really blame him.

Javier Aritza operated by his own code. Navarre had inherited the tendencies, if not the patterns.

Djamila blinked at herself, happy that Aritza was already to the door and leaving. He hadn't seen her face.

Was it possible to understand that code, and respect the man for it?

Wilhelmina Teague had suggested that just because not everyone approached life with the same focused ferocity she did, didn't mean there wasn't value in what they did.

For anybody but Aritza, Djamila was willing to understand.

He needed to get his shit together. Grow up.

Act like management.

She shook her head and followed him through the door with one last look around. But for the video of their adventures, and the faintest hint of machine oil, nobody would know they had been in here.

Out past the security trussed-up security guard, into the main hall. Just another two crew members coming off their shift, although she was trailing Aritza by about four meters.

Javier stopped cold, hands in the air.

"What are you doing now?" she hissed.

Djamila was on top of Aritza before she saw the other figure step out from a doorway.

Armed. Competent. Aimed.

Angry.

Farouz.

One strong hand held a pistol identical to the one on her hip. It had been centered on Aritza. Now it was aimed at her heart.

They were a simple model. Pump a great deal of energy into the target at something less than ten meters, watch them fall over.

It wasn't even a beam like a laser. More like a shotgun, impacting a target just under half a meter across at ten meters.

Nothing she could easily avoid, even with her reflexes.

"Thief in the night, Captain Navarre?" he asked in a quiet, deep voice.

"You don't know the half of it, pal," Javier growled back.

How had Farouz managed to evade the probe?

She remembered the elegant way the man had walked. How he had stalked her in the clothing closet.

Precise. Controlled. Compact.

Something like she had done. Did. Was.

Special Operations.

Not *Neu Berne*, but something similar. Someplace that required the efforts of a dangerous few when the applications of mass would not work.

Diamond cutter.

A killer.

"What have you done, Navarre?" Farouz continued.

"Removed a player from the board," Navarra sneered.

"Who have you assassinated, now?"

Djamila could see Farouz growing angry.

Angrier.

Short of temper.

"Nobody, Farouz," she interjected, careful not to move.

He might fire on movement. The blade was that finely balanced.

"Nobody?" the bantam sneered. "Captain Navarre and his lethal moll Hadiiye? Nobody?"

"One guard with a mild concussion," she said evenly. "The rest are papers to be destroyed."

"Papers?" Farouz asked.

She could see confusion begin in his eyes. Eyes previously a warm brown gone coldly lethal with anger.

He was not undressing her with those eyes now, appreciating her for her muscles where other men were disappointed by the lack of ponderous breasts.

No, he was measuring her for a coffin.

"Legal papers," Aritza said.

Javier's voice was less Navarre, now.

Less killer. More Science Officer.

"I do not understand."

"Birth certificates," Javier continued. "Proof of identity. Genetics registry. The works. So yeah, maybe an assassination, depending on how you want to measure it. Tomorrow, he has to become the person he's been pretending to be, all these years."

"Why?"

Djamila could measure the confusion in those eyes. She had seen her soul reflected in them before.

They were turbid.

"Because I'm more than just a mass casualty incident waiting to happen, pal," Javier growled. "Sometimes, it's possible to split a diamond with a single tap, and not a bucket of nitroglycerin."

"And you, Hadiiye?" Farouz asked. "All that to get access to the system?"

The gun never wavered from the spot exactly between her breasts.

Farouz might consider Navarre dangerous, but he was taking no chances with her.

She was angry. Torn.

Not insulted at the implications. That was the cost of being in this business.

The lies that went with it.

No, this anger was for that look. That touch, standing in the tiny closet, considering kissing this man when he asked politely, rather than all the other the men who had demanded it as some right.

The loss.

She could lie now.

The emotional break would be better.

Cleaner.

Final.

And wrong.

"That had been my mission, Farouz," she replied simply. "We went well beyond mission parameters, you and I."

"And had we gone to bed?" he snarled.

She nodded.

"That would have been of the body, Farouz," she said. "Nothing else. Nothing *more*."

He stood there, perfectly still.

Seconds passed.

She wanted to say something. Anything.

There was nothing else that needed saying.

Farouz realized that as well. Doubt disappeared from his eyes. Sadness crept in to replace it.

He nodded.

"Yes," he agreed. "You are correct."

Djamila let a small sigh escape her soul.

"So now we've got a problem, buddy," Javier said sharply. "You're not taking us in."

Djamila watched Aritza lower his hands slowly, peacefully.

"No?" Farouz asked. "And why would that be, Captain Navarre?"

"Because your boss will kill us for this," the man known as Navarre declared. "I'm not interested in that outcome."

"I'm sorry, Captain Navarre," Farouz said in a polite tone. "You no longer have a choice in the matter."

"I have lots of options, punk," Navarre rasped.

Djamila watched him take a small step to his left. Not charging directly at Farouz. Not even really threatening him.

Just moving.

She held perfectly still.

Navarre took a second step, this one closer towards Farouz.

"And you don't get to stop me," Navarre continued.

Farouz turned to point the pistol at Navarre.

Perhaps it was a threat. Perhaps a statement. Perhaps he forgot his foe.

Later, perhaps, she considered that perhaps it hadn't been an accident.

Djamila drew, aimed, and fired at a nerve speed that nobody she had ever met, and only the most expensive training robots, could match.

The Ballerina of Death.

Aritza had told crew members of *Storm Gauntlet* that she actively worshipped the Goddess of Destruction.

But he had no clue what made a woman like Djamila Sykora tick.

Farouz's eyes flickered back to track her faster than the pistol could follow.

It wouldn't have mattered.

No human could have reversed course and gotten off a shot.

Even Farouz only came close.

This model of pistol was nearly silent, save for the faintest pop in the air, mostly static electricity bleeding off the target as every nerve overloaded and everything inside went to white noise.

It didn't even have the physical kick of a small chuck of lead slamming into someone at the speed of sound. Nothing to knock a man back. Nothing to indicate success.

Farouz just crumpled silently to the ground.

Only his pistol made a sound, clattering loudly as it tumbled into a corner from nerveless hands.

Djamila ranted in several languages in her head.

Nothing showed on the outside.

Neu Berne.

Navarre turned a cold eye on her.

No, not Navarre.

Aritza.

"I will say this exactly once," he said in a quiet voice. "If asked later, I will deny everything. Do we need to kidnap this man and take him with us?"

391

Djamila stared daggers at the man. Wished she could strangle him with her bare hands.

He had seen weakness. Identified it. Could exploit it later.

And yet...

He was offering to do something *for* her, rather than to her.

Farouz might never forgive her. Either way. And the chances of them ever meeting again were pitifully low, unless one sought out the other.

And she did not dare.

For that way lay weakness. Fallible flesh.

Wilhelmina Teague appeared in her vision for a split second. Perhaps her memory.

"No, Djamila," Dr. Teague replied calmly. "We call that humanity."

Djamila growled. Mostly under her breath.

Took a deep breath. Held it.

Let it go.

"No," she finally said, after an eternal heartbeat. "He will understand."

She grabbed the tiny man and lifted him carefully, almost lovingly.

The door to the security room was closed. Locked.

"Open it," she commanded Aritza, trailing in her wake.

He did and stepped quickly aside as she entered.

Farouz would be out for a while. Long enough.

They could still make their escape.

Most of her would.

A small part of her soul, she knew she would leave on this deck.

PART SEVEN

The Land Leviathan had not changed, except to roll perhaps a thousand miles forward in time and space.

Javier found the desert air dry and nasty. It fit his mood.

Two months had passed. Four since he had first landed on the big iron whale. Sokolov and *Storm Gauntlet* had been up to minor jobs, but nothing particularly profitable.

Keeping the lights on and the crew in socks and cream.

It was the same limo flying them in, with the same blemish in the right armrest. Zakhar had napped again.

They landed on the same last platform and disembarked to the same hard man in the nice suit. The two killers were different, but they were the same.

Javier wore the same Navarre outfit from before. Boots, britches, doublet, headband.

The only difference was the satchel he held in one hand. An old, leather and canvas job he had found in *Storm Gauntlet*'s Lost and Found, left over from some Barrister that had been through.

And the belt with the sword and the pulse pistol.

Unlike last time, it was charged.

The hard man held out a hand, expecting Javier to hand over his weapons.

"No," Navarre snarled back.

The man blinked, reconsidered, and survived the day.

Javier paid more attention as he walked. They were aboard the fourth car, having crossed from each on a catwalk to the next.

She was there. Like before.

Stewart Lace. Banker to pirates. Fixer for people needing things fixed.

Still well dressed. Still proper. Still fadingly beautiful.

Tea. Cheese and garlic scones. Antipasti plate.

Civilized.

Javier sat between her and Captain Sokolov.

Pinkies were out.

Javier decided he had played enough. He sat down his tea mug and saucer and reached for the satchel. Inside, a smaller leather carryall that Kianoush had whipped up to transport the priceless artifacts.

That came out. Madame Lace quickly rested her tea in order to take the prize from him.

She shared a secret smile with him as their fingers touched.

"My backer was surprised at the outcome, Captain Navarre," she purred.

"That's because you work for a moron," Javier barked back at her.

It had taken nearly a month to get Navarre to finally shut up. This woman had the potential to mess with his *wa*.

Unacceptable.

"Were you expecting a marine assault?" he sneered. "Perhaps a full ambush with pulse cannons and ship-killing missiles? Abraam Tamaz?"

"I believe that was more in keeping with their expectations, yes," she said, a trifle on defense.

Obviously, she hadn't been immune to that line of logic, either.

Fool.

"Fine," Javier said diplomatically. "Understand that this will be the last job for that patron. Ever. Next time, tell them to hire a psychopath."

"Instead of a professional?" she teased.

"You wanted a job done, Lace," Sokolov said. "If you wanted more, the price would have probably been too high, even for them."

"I see," she replied, opening the case.

Nothing had changed. Chop in a nice little felt bag. Cerise inker. Eight pieces of paper rolled up carefully.

She looked up, fixed Javier with a hard eye.

"Ask now, Madame Lace," Javier growled. "This topic is off-limits tomorrow."

"How did you manage everything?" she finally inquired. "I had been told the job would have been impossible without significant casualties. And yet you managed."

"No," Javier went cold. "Trade secrets. End of discussion."

"I can appreciate that," Lace said with a discreet nod.

She turned and pulled a small messenger bag of her own out from behind a pillow.

In the blink of an eye, Javier had nearly shot her. Well, Navarre had.

Close enough.

She opened the small bag with a great deal more care than she had grabbed for it. Maybe she realized how close she had been to dying, just now.

Kianoush's bag went in. Two small envelopes came out.

The first went to Zakhar.

"Captain Sokolov," she nodded gravely. "Receipt of a payment wired into your account, as contracted. With a small bonus."

Zakhar accepted in utter silence.

"Captain Navarre," Stewart Lace said in a most reserved voice. "This second envelope was delivered to me by way of several layers of intermediaries. It has not been opened, but it has been scanned for danger. We have not read the message, but are confident that it is safe."

Javier grunted.

Even from here, he could smell the perfume she had infused into the paper. It was better than a signature.

The writing on the front was calligraphic, but legible. Perfect. Like she was.

E. Navarre.

Another clue. As if he needed one.

Javier took it from the woman's hand and stuffed it into his unbuttoned doublet.

There was no way in hell he was opening it here.

"Thank you," he said.

Nothing more.

Nothing needed.

Javier took her by surprise by rising.

"Madame Lace," he bowed formally. "Perhaps we will meet again. In less uncertain circumstances."

She rose and took his hand. Firm. Strong.

Ever so slightly damp.

Flop sweat was a bitch.

And then he left, leaving Sokolov to trail in his wake. Hard man and the two killers waited outside the room, escorted them silently back to the VTOL, remained behind when they took off.

Zakhar started to say something, but thought better of it. He closed his eyes and leaned back instead.

It was as much privacy as Javier would get, at least until he got back to the ship.

The envelope was lavender paper. The ink was probably real vermillion, the expensive kind and not just the product of a good chemistry lab. She was like that.

The seal was wax, melted and pressed with a signet ring, leaving a unique imprint of *Shangdu*.

The paper was a heavy, handmade stock randomly multi-colored from the source material.

Her handwriting was simply exquisite.

E,

It is obvious that you can get into places you were never intended. And do so with care and style, not damaging things without a purpose. Thank you. Farouz has recovered from his anger, as well.

I am keeping the helmet. As you said, a peace offering. And it fits marvelously.

It is my wish that you not necessarily be a stranger, and we not be enemies. Perhaps I might even be able to put your unique skills to occasional use. There is great potential.

B

p.s. And please enjoy the enclosed and think of me occasionally.

JAVIER REACHED BACK into the envelope. There was a smaller envelope inside, like a matryoska doll. And inside that envelope was a picture printed on paper, like an antique, ten centimeters by twenty.

The face was obscured, shadowed, by masterful use of lighting and the way the Helm of Athena's cheek pieces came down. Only her smile was clear.

And she had pulled her long, black hair down and around her, just enough to make the picture cheesecake and not porn, but it was obvious that she wasn't wearing anything but the helmet as she kneeled on what had been his bed.

The picture hanging from the wall in the background gave that away.

She was still utterly exquisite, but you had to have seen the *Khatum of Altai* that way previously, completely nude, to recognize her now.

The galaxy's most beautiful black widow spider. Possibly the deadliest, as well.

Javier found himself as frightened of seeing her again as he was aroused at the prospect.

If he walked back into her web, would he ever escape? Did he want to?

Javier smiled and laughed under his breath.

"What did she say?" Zakhar asked, never opening his eyes.

"You knew?" Javier replied.

"I've read your report," Sokolov said. "And I know you well enough to read between the lines. Two plus two still equals four when you're around."

Javier laughed a second time.

"So maybe everything will turn out okay, after all," Javier said.

"I could have told you that, Mr. Science Officer," Sokolov said. "You just never want to listen."

Javier had to give the man that. They shared that much heritage.

Dancing with a black widow had gotten him so much closer to paying off his debt to the man.

Maybe he needed spin his own webs.

After all, he still had to kill Sykora, one of these days.

READ MORE!

Be sure to pick up the other books in the Science Officer series! The last four books make up what is known as the mini-series, "War of the Pirate Clans".

The Doomsday Vault

Three more to come! Current working titles are:

The Last Flagship
The Hammerfield Gambit
The Hammerfield Payoff

ABOUT THE AUTHOR

Blaze Ward writes science fiction in the Alexandria Station universe: The Jessica Keller Chronicles, The Science Officer series, The Doyle Iwakuma Stories, and others. He also writes about The Collective as well as The Fairchild Stories and Modern Gods superhero myths. You can find out more at his website www.blazeward.com, as well as Facebook, Goodreads, and other places.

Blaze's works are available as ebooks, paper, and audio, and can be found at a variety of online vendors (Kobo, Amazon, iBooks, and others). His newsletter comes out quarterly, and you can also follow his blog on his website. He really enjoys interacting with fans, and looks forward to any and all questions-even ones about his books!

Never miss a release!

If you'd like to be notified of new releases, sign up for my newsletter.

I only send out newsletters once a quarter, will never spam you, or use your email for nefarious purposes. You can also unsubscribe at any time. http://www.blazeward.com/newsletter/

ABOUT KNOTTED ROAD PRESS

Knotted Road Press fiction specializes in dynamic writing set in mysterious, exotic locations.

Knotted Road Press non-fiction publishes autobiographies, business books, cookbooks, and how-to books with unique voices.

Knotted Road Press creates DRM-free ebooks as well as high-quality print books for readers around the world.

With authors in a variety of genres including literary, poetry, mystery, fantasy, and science fiction, Knotted Road Press has something for everyone.

Knotted Road Press
www.KnottedRoadPress.com

Made in the USA
Las Vegas, NV
13 December 2022

62408133R00227